Earl John Russell

The Life and Times of Charles James Fox

Volume 1

Earl John Russell

The Life and Times of Charles James Fox
Volume 1

ISBN/EAN: 9783337094478

Printed in Europe, USA, Canada, Australia, Japan

Cover: Foto ©Raphael Reischuk / pixelio.de

More available books at **www.hansebooks.com**

THE

LIFE AND 

OF

~~HARLES JAMES FOX~~

BY

EARL RUSSELL

VOLUME I.

"Et vitam impendere vero."

LONDON:

~~RIC~~HARD BENTLEY, NEW BURLINGTON STREET,

Publisher in Ordinary to Her Majesty.

1866.

[The Author reserves the right of Translation.]

PREFACE.

————

IN the fourth volume of the "Correspondence of Charles James Fox" I have said : "I shall endeavour, in a separate form, to place in a connected narrative the relation of Mr. Fox's political career and an account of his Times. In that manner the great events of his life will be prominently set forth, and his public policy fully discussed."

I have found it impossible to perform this task without entering very fully into the Parliamentary History of the Times. A great leader, who took a prominent part in the main discussions of the House of Commons from 1775 to 1806, is identified with that which is the life of England— her free debate in Parliament.

Lord Holland had intended to give a description of Mr. Fox's domestic life, and such fragments of his conversation as the memory of his friends could supply. In these respects my work must be very deficient. On the other hand, many volumes published of late years, such as the "Memoirs of the Marquis of Rockingham," "The Court and Cabinets of George III.," and other lives and memoirs, have furnished materials for history of which Lord Holland was not possessed.

I have, therefore, attempted rather to follow the political career than to portray the private life of Mr. Fox.

Such mighty events as the American War, the French Revolution, and the French Revolutionary Wars, deserve to be studied in all their different aspects. They are the great elevations from which the streams of modern history must flow towards the ocean of time.

I have ventured to give many extracts from the speeches of Mr. Fox. I am aware how imperfectly these reported speeches, uncorrected by the great orator, represent his fire, his force, his language. But the following pages, from Lord Erskine's letter to the Editor of his collected Speeches, give a measure of the value of the treasure which is lost, while they show a just appreciation of the grandeur of the remains which we possess.

" This extraordinary person, then," says Lord Erskine, " in rising generally to speak, had evidently no more premeditated the particular language he should employ, nor frequently the illustrations and images by which he should discuss or enforce his subject, than he had contemplated the hour he was to die; and his exalted merit as a debater in Parliament did not, therefore, consist in the length, variety, or roundness of his periods; but in the truth and vigour of his conceptions; in the depth and extent of his information; in the retentive powers of his memory, which enabled him to keep in constant view, not only all he had formerly read and reflected on, but everything said at the moment, and even at other times, by the various persons whose arguments he was to answer; in the faculty of spreading out his matter so clearly to the grasp of his own mind, as to render it impossible he should ever fail in the utmost clearness and distinctness to others; in the exuberant fertility of his invention, which spontaneously brought forth his ideas at the moment, in every possible shape by which the understanding might sit in the most accurate judgment upon them; whilst, instead of seeking afterwards to enforce them by cold, premeditated illustrations, or by episodes, which, however beautiful, only distract attention, he was accustomed to repass his subject, not *methodically*, but in the most *unforeseen* and fascinating review, enlightening every part of it, and binding even his adversaries in a kind of spell for the moment of involuntary assent.

"The reader must certainly not expect to be so carried away by the sketches now before me. Short-hand alone, secured too at the moment, against the numerous imperfections inseparable from following the career of so rapid and vehement an elocution, could have perpetuated their lustre and effect; but still the correct, and often the animated, substance remains, which preserves from oblivion more that is worthy of preservation, than by such means would apply to almost any other speaker in the world. Eloquence which consists more in the dexterous structure of periods, and in the powers and harmony of delivery, than in the extraordinary vigour of the understanding, may be compared to a human body, not so much surpassing the dimensions of ordinary nature as remarkable for the symmetry and beauty of its parts. If the short-hand writer, like the statuary or painter, has made no memorial of *such* an orator, little is left to distinguish him; but in the most imperfect relics of Fox's speeches THE BONES OF A GIANT ARE TO BE DISCOVERED.

"This will be found more particularly to apply to his speeches upon sudden and unforeseen occasions, when certainly nothing could be more interesting nor extraordinary than to witness, as I have often done, the mighty and unprepared efforts of his mind, when he had to encounter with the arguments of some profound reasoner, who had deeply considered his subject, and arranged it with all possible art, to preserve its parts unbroken. To hear him *begin* on such occasions, without method, without any kind of exertion, without the smallest impulse from the desire of distinction or triumph, and animated only by the honest sense of duty, an audience *who knew him not,* would have expected but little success from the conflict; as little as a traveller in the East, whilst trembling at a buffalo in the wild vigour of his well-protected strength, would have looked to his immediate destruction when he saw the boa moving slowly and inertly towards him on the grass. But Fox, unlike the serpent in everything but his strength, always taking his station in some fixed, invulnerable principle, soon surrounded and entangled his adversary, disjointing every member of his discourse, and strangling him in the irresistible folds of truth.

"This intellectual superiority, by which my illustrious friend was so eminently distinguished, might nevertheless have existed in all its strength without raising him to the exalted station he held as a public speaker. The powers of the understanding are not *of themselves* sufficient for this high purpose. Intellect *alone*, however exalted, without strong feelings, without even irritable sensibility, would be only like an immense magazine of gunpowder, if there were no such element as fire in the natural world. It is the *heart* which is the spring and fountain of eloquence. A cold-blooded, learned man might, for anything I know, compose in his closet an eloquent book; but in public discourse, arising out of sudden occasions, could by no possibility be eloquent.

"To carry on my ideas of oratory, by continuing to identify it with Fox, he possessed, above all men I ever knew, the most gentle and yet the most ardent spirit—a rare and happy combination! He had nourished in his mind all the manly and generous sentiments which are the true supports of the social world ; he was tremblingly alive to every kind of private wrong or suffering ; and from the habitual and fervent contemplation of the just principles of government, he had the most bitter and unextinguishable contempt for the low arts of political intrigue, and an indignant abhorrence of every species of tyranny, oppression, and injustice."*

Horace Walpole says: "Fox had not the ungraceful hesitation of his father, yet scarce equalled him in subtlety and acuteness. But no man ever excelled him in the closeness of argument, which flowed from him in a torrent of vehemence, as declamation sometimes does from those who want argument." Burke has called him "the greatest debater the world ever saw;" Mackintosh "the most Demosthenean speaker since Demosthenes." We must be content with these testimonies. Of eloquence it has been eloquently said: "Eloquentia sicut flamma, materie alitur, motu excitatur, urendo clarescit." Mr. Pitt thus happily rendered the passage: "It is of eloquence as of a flame: it requires matter to feed it, motion to excite it, and it brightens as it burns." But it also wastes like a flame. The bright stars of poetry shine to us in the heavens as they shone to our fathers three thousand years ago; the flames of oratory have, in too many cases, blazed like earthly fires, scorching and consuming in the hour of their fierceness;

* "Fox's Speeches," vol. i. Letter of Lord Erskine.

pale and glimmering when that hour is past and their work is done. But in the work itself orators have their true fame. Those who, like Pym and Hampden, have withstood a despotic Court—who, like Somers, have restored the liberties of their country—who, like Chatham, have exalted its reputation—or who, like Fox, have placed on a height their beacon to save the wandering friends of freedom from destruction,—may be content to let their speeches moulder in the dust of libraries, while their names are hallowed in the temples they have founded, adorned, and preserved.

CONTENTS.

CONTENTS.

CHAPTER VII.

CHAPTER VIII.

CHAPTER IX.

CHAPTER X.

CHAPTER XI.

CHAPTER XII.

CHAPTER XIII.

CONTENTS.

CHAPTER XIV.

CHAPTER XV.

CHAPTER XVI.

CHAPTER XVII.

THE LIFE AND TIMES

OF

CHARLES JAMES FOX.

CHAPTER I.

FROM THE BIRTH OF CHARLES JAMES FOX, 1749, TO HIS ENTRANCE INTO THE HOUSE OF COMMONS, 1769.

SIR STEPHEN Fox, the father of the first Lord Holland, and the grandfather of Charles James Fox, held several subordinate offices in the reigns of Charles II. and William III. He was of humble origin, owed his introduction at Court to Lord Percy, his promotion to Lord Clarendon, his favour with Charles II. to his punctuality in business, and his rise in the world under different sovereigns to his diligence and integrity. He married a second time at the advanced age of seventy-seven; and by his second marriage had two sons, who were made peers by the titles of Ilchester and Holland. He was by principle a Tory, and by affection a Jacobite.

Henry Fox, the first Lord Holland, was a man of great parts, loose morals, more fond of money than of power, warm in his domestic attachments, jovial in his manners, an able debater, a corrupt politician. Devoted to the party of Sir Robert Walpole, he was, by the favour of the Duke of Newcastle, made Secretary of State, with the lead of the House of Commons. But he was not entrusted with the patronage, and he thought himself unequal to the double task of managing the House of Commons and conducting public affairs in a difficult time.   He therefore withdrew to the less conspicuous but lucrative office of Paymaster of the Forces, which in time of war yielded thirty, forty, and even fifty thousand pounds in one year to its fortunate possessor.   He married, against the will of her father, Lady Caroline Lennox, the daughter of the Duke of Richmond.   The Duke's repugnance to this connexion has been attributed to family pride, but other reasons may have weighed with him.   For Henry Fox had not only been embarrassed in his circumstances, but by his notorious want of principle, as well as of fortune, must have alarmed the parents of a young lady who was among the noblest and fairest of the land.

After following Mr. Pitt for some years as Paymaster, Mr. Fox was fixed upon by Lord Bute as the ablest leader he could find to defend the peace of Paris.   In order to do this he deserted the Duke of Cumberland, with whom he was then connected, and again became Secretary of State. He has been accused of an extent of corruption and intimidation with a view to obtain a majority for the peace unequalled in the history of the House of Commons.   But this is probably an exaggeration.   He stipulated for a peerage with the rank of earl as the reward of his success ; a barony was given him, but the earldom was withheld. When Lord Bute, being reproached by Mr. Fox with this breach of faith, said, " It was only a pious fraud," Lord Holland quickly replied, " I perceive the fraud, my Lord, but not the piety."   Lord Holland was forced by the Grenville ministry to resign the pay office ; the rest of his life was passed in some favour with the Court, but in no ostensible position in office, or in the House of Lords. A singular remark is quoted of his dying hours, which at least shows composure and good humour: "If Mr. Selwyn calls again," he said to his servant, "let him in; if I am alive, I shall be very glad to see him, and if I am dead, he will be very glad to see me."

Charles James Fox, the third son of Lord Holland, was born in Conduit-street, on the 24th of January, 1749 (N.S.). He became very early the favourite child of his father, who was accused of spoiling him by indulgence.

"There's a clever little boy for you," writes Lord Holland when he was little more than two years and a half old, and had made one of those intelligent remarks with which lively children at that age are so apt to delight their parents. When he was little more than three, his father writes, "I never saw Charles so well as he is now; I grow immoderately fond of him."

His father seems to have thought it no part of his duty to rebuke his faults, or correct his temper. "Charles is dreadfully passionate, what shall we do with him?" said Lady Caroline to Mr. Fox. "Oh, never mind," replied Mr. Fox, "he is a very sensible little fellow, and will learn to curb himself." It happened very fortunately that this conversation was overheard by his son Charles, who, repeating it long afterwards, added, "I will not deny that I was a very sensible little boy, a very clever little boy, and what I heard made an impression on me, and was of use to me afterwards." But his overhearing this conversation was mere accident. It would have been of still more use to him if his mother had been encouraged to check the passionate temper she deplored.

When he was seven years old, Lord Holland writes to

his mother, " I found Charles very well, very pert, and very argumentative." When he was eight years old he was sent to a private school kept by a M. Pampelonne, at Wandsworth. When he was between nine and ten, in the autumn of 1758, he was placed at Eton, and remained there, or rather belonged to the school, till the summer of 1764.

There can be no doubt that at Eton he laid the foundations of that grammatical knowledge, and that classical taste which pervaded so agreeably his great speeches, and which gave him so much delight in his retirement from public affairs. Six years of reading, even occasionally interrupted, to a boy of Charles Fox's quickness of parts and excellent memory must have been invaluable.

He was assisted in his studies by Mr. Francis, the translator of Horace. Mr. Francis was much connected with Lord Holland; and those who believe his son, Sir Philip Francis, to have been Junius, attribute to this connexion the comparative mercy with which Lord Holland is treated.

Charles was not allowed to pursue his studies without interruption. Before he was fourteen he was taken by his father to Paris and Spa, where he was introduced to the gaming table, the fatal source of much subsequent vice and misery.

He appears to have been at Paris likewise in the following spring. According to family traditions he was indulged in all his youthful passions, and when he showed any signs of boyish modesty and shame, was ridiculed for his bashfulness by his injudicious and culpable father.

In his correspondence with Gilbert Wakefield, Mr. Fox mentions that his reading at school was principally confined to the Eton books of Extracts. In the collection called "Musæ Etonenses" there are two very elegant elegiac exercises by Charles Fox, of which one was written in the fifth form; the other in the sixth. This seems, on first consideration, a very small contribution to the classical poetry of Eton; but the fact is accounted for by the rules and usages then prevalent in the school. These rules and usages are explained in a letter to me from the learned and accomplished Provost of Eton,* of which the following is an extract: "Mr. Fox left school very shortly, I believe a month or two, after he reached the sixth form. Now the verses of this collection were, as a general rule, selected from what are called 'play exercises;' that is, the exercises of sixth-form boys, which were sent to the Provost on the Tuesday of 'regular weeks,' in order to give a claim for 'play,' or no school after twelve o'clock on the following Thursday.

"'Regular weeks' used to be, owing to saints' days and other occasional interruptions of the usual course, in fact rather the exception than the rule; and consequently, a very clever boy who did not remain at school long after he reached the sixth form, might leave Eton without ever having received this distinction.

"Fifth-form exercises were 'sent up for good,' that is, sent as a distinction, to the Head Master whenever they might deserve it, without any reference to the accidents of the week."

On his return to Eton from Spa, after having been a member of a brilliant and dissipated society, he was laughed at by the boys and soon after flogged by the master. At this time Lord Holland wrote to Mr. Campbell of Cawdor (the first Lord Cawdor) in the following terms: "My son Charles really deserves all that can be said of his parts, as

* Dr. Hawtrey.

I will convince you when I see you at Holland House; but he has what I value much more—good sense, good nature, and as many good and amiable qualities as ever met in any one's composition. I have two sons here: the eldest bids fair for being as universally and as much beloved as ever I was hated. Thus happy in private life, am I not in the right to leave the public?" &c.

It is said that at the trial of Lord Ferrers, in 1760, Lord Mansfield being asked the name of a young gentleman present, replied, "That is Fox's son Charles, with twice his parts and half his sagacity."* Considering that Charles Fox was then only eleven years old, it may be doubted whether the date of this remarkable instance of sound judgment and foresight has been rightly placed.

In the autumn of 1764, Charles Fox, being then between fifteen and sixteen years of age, went to Oxford, and was placed at Hertford College under the care of Dr. Newcome. Dr. Newcome, who was made a bishop in Ireland during Lord Rockingham's administration, and afterwards promoted to the Primacy during the short Lieutenancy of Lord Fitzwilliam, was an able, pious, and charitable divine. Charles, in spite of his father's indulgence, seems to have studied hard at Oxford. In a letter to Sir George Macartney, written in December, 1764, and consequently a very short time after his admission to the University, he says, "I like Oxford well enough; I read there a great deal, and am very fond of mathematics." In the following February he writes to the same person: "I read here much, and like vastly (what I know you think useless) mathematics; I believe they are useful, and I am sure they are entertaining, which is alone enough to recommend them to

* "Memoirs of the Whig Party."

me. I did not expect my life would be so pleasant as I find it; but I really think, to a man who reads a great deal, there cannot be a more agreeable place." The word "entertaining" applied to mathematics appeared to his nephew, Lord Holland, a whimsical epithet. But to a young student of vigorous powers of understanding, the study of the elements of geometry may fairly be called entertaining. That he had not gone beyond the elements of geometry when he wrote this letter may be gathered from a letter of Dr. Newcome's of the following spring, when he was again carried to Paris by his father. "Application like yours," says Dr. Newcome, "requires some intermission, and you are the only person with whom I have ever had connexion, to whom I could say this. I expect that you will return with much keenness for Greek and for lines and angles. As to trigonometry, it is a matter of entire indifference to the other geometricians of the college (who will probably continue some time here) whether they proceed to the other branches of mathematics immediately, or wait a term or two longer. You need not, therefore, interrupt your amusements by severe studies; for it is wholly unnecessary to take a step onwards without you, and therefore we shall stop until we have the pleasure of your company."*

In a letter from Kingsgate, dated July 25th, 1765, his father says: "Charles has been here, but is now at Oxford studying very hard, after two months at Paris, which he relished as much as ever. Such a mixture in education was never seen, but, extraordinary as it is, it seems likely to do well."

That this education enabled Mr. Fox to read the Greek and Latin poets with facility, to make himself familiar with

* "Correspondence," vol. i. p. 22.

French and Italian literature, and to become very early a man of the world, cannot be disputed. But, on the other hand, it led to desultory habits of study, and, what was much worse, to a fondness for the pleasures of unbridled youth, which in his after life marred the effect of his brilliant talents, and prevented his acquiring the entire confidence of the moral and sober part of the nation.

It must have been in 1767 that his mother paid a visit to Lady Chatham, of which she gave the following account to her husband : "I have been, this morning, with Lady Hester Pitt, and there is little William Pitt, now eight years old, and really the cleverest child I ever saw, and brought up so strictly and so proper in his behaviour, that, mark my words, that little boy will be a thorn in Charles's side as long as he lives." A very singular prediction, showing not only the early cleverness of the two boys, but the cherished ambition of their parents, the wise strictness of Lord and Lady Chatham, and the sagacity of Lady Holland.

Charles left Oxford in the spring of 1766, and in the autumn of that year went abroad with Lord and Lady Holland. He was absent from England, with short intervals, from September, 1766, to the autumn of 1768. In the course of this time he spent a winter with his father at Naples : he was for some time at Florence; he saw Voltaire at Ferney, and became thoroughly initiated into the gay society of Paris.

His life during this period was thoughtless, idle, and licentious ; his letters treat of private theatricals, of low amours, and of the distinctions and promotions of his friends. To serious politics he seems hardly to have given a thought.

Yet, in the midst of this indulgence and dissipation he

did not neglect the study of poetry, which, as it was one of the earliest, was likewise one of the most enduring of his pursuits. In a letter to Sir George Macartney, dated Florence, 6th of August, 1767, he says : " At present I read nothing but Italian, which I am immoderately fond of, particularly of the poetry. You, who understand Italian so well yourself, will not at all wonder at this. As to French, I am far from being so thorough a master of it as I could wish, but I have so much of it that I could perfect myself in it at any time with very little trouble, especially if I pass three or four months in France. . . . . I want such an example as yours to make me conquer my natural idleness, of which Lady Holland will tell you wonders. Indeed, I am afraid it will in the end get the better of what little ambition I have, and that I shall never be anything but a lounging fellow."* Six weeks afterwards, in a letter, dated Florence, September the 22nd, 1767, he writes to Richard Fitz Patrick : " For God's sake learn Italian as fast as you can, if it be only to read Ariosto. There is more good poetry in Italian than in all other languages that I understand put together : in prose, too, it is a very fine language."†

Stephen Fox, the eldest brother of Charles, married, in 1772, Lady Mary Fitz Patrick, the sister of the Earl of Upper Ossory and of Richard Fitz Patrick.

Richard Fitz Patrick remained through life the most intimate private and political friend of Mr. Fox. His wit was exquisite, his judgment excellent, his manners courteous, his taste refined. There was no man whose opinion was so highly valued by Mr. Fox. He seldom spoke in Parliament, and wrote but little. His epigrams, his verses

* " Correspondence," vol. i. p. 42.   † Ibid. p. 44.

in the "Rolliad," and pieces of light poetry, are well known, and generally admired.

Charles Fox was returned for Midhurst in May, 1769, when he was only nineteen years and four months old. He took his seat in the following November. He, therefore, sat in Parliament when he was under twenty years old.

Before we enter on his Parliamentary career, it may be well to give a sketch of the drama upon which he appeared as an actor.

CHAPTER II.

STATE OF PARTIES IN GREAT BRITAIN—FAMILY OR GEORGE II.—
COMMENCEMENT OF THE REIGN OF GEORGE III.

THE reign of the first Prince of the House of Hanover was not marked by any of those dissensions between the Sovereign and his subjects which had so violently disturbed the rule of the Stuarts. Born and bred in Germany, a stranger to our laws and our manners, he had accepted as his Ministers the chiefs of the Whig party, and for the last seven years of his reign submitted himself quietly to the guidance of Sir Robert Walpole. That eminent statesman obtained an equal ascendency over his son and successor.

When Queen Caroline died, she recommended her helpless husband to the experienced statesman; a fact of which, with singular humility and good humour, the King frequently reminded his faithful and able Minister.

When Sir Robert Walpole was forced by cabal and clamour to quit the helm, the King attempted to indulge his Hanoverian partialities, and to bring the resources of Great Britain in aid of his German politics. Lord Granville, a man of classical knowledge and ready wit, became the organ of the Court policy; but the nation distrusted the King, was jealous of Continental connexion, and overthrew the aspiring favourite.

The rule of the Pelhams was easy, constitutional, and pacific; but when Henry Pelham died, and the Seven Years' War was approaching, a strong administration was required. The Duke of Newcastle, by a skilful management of boroughs and a large command of patronage, had secured a majority of votes in the House of Commons. But Henry Fox, whom he made Secretary of State, had none of the genius which befitted the conductor of a great war.

On the other hand, the Duke of Devonshire, who attempted, with Mr. Pitt, ·to form a Government, was thwarted by the secret opposition of the Duke of Newcastle and forced to retire from office. At length a coalition was formed between the Duke of Newcastle, the dispenser of patronage, and William Pitt, the orator and the statesman.

From this time the House of Commons was submissive and the nation satisfied. The King, who had at first been shocked at the notion of having a Secretary of State who had not read Wicquefort, became reconciled to the arrangement. The Duke of Newcastle was content to enjoy his office, distribute his patronage, pocket his perquisites, and marshal his majority. "The Duke of Newcastle lent me his majority to carry on the government," was the phrase which, in speaking of this time, Mr. Pitt afterwards used. Thus relieved from all trouble in the House of Commons, he sent Wolfe to Canada, furnished liberal subsidies to the Great Frederick, and covered his country with glory. This happy state of things was destined not to survive the Prince upon the throne. The greatest anxieties of George II. had arisen in the bosom of his own family. Lord Hervey in his "Memoirs" has lifted the curtain which concealed, in part at least, the painful animosities between

George II. and Frederick Prince of Wales.*   Queen Caroline had no affection for her son.   The Prince of Wales had no passion so strong as a desire to vex and harass his parents.

Frederick Prince of Wales, with some liveliness of parts, had a mean understanding, and a meaner heart.   His boyhood was not promising.   Horace Walpole says: "The following anecdote was told me by Mr. Fox, who said the King himself told it him, and that the late Lord Hervey had told him the same particular from the Queen.   One day, when the Prince was but a boy, his governor was complaining of him; the Queen, whose way (as the King said) was to excuse him, exclaimed: '*Ah! je m'imagine que ces sont des tours de page.*'   The governor replied: '*Plût à Dieu, madame, que ces fussent des tours de page! ces sont des tours de laquais et de coquins.*' "†   His father, recollecting his own opposition to George I., and apprehensive of a similar conduct from his son, kept him at Hanover until he was twenty-one; but he did not thereby avoid embarrassments.   The Prince was desirous of marrying his cousin, the Princess of Prussia; and when his father, from dislike of the King of Prussia, forbade the match, the Prince of Wales wrote to the Queen of Prussia, her mother, and proposed a secret marriage.   The Queen of Prussia, although she favoured the project, imprudently confided the secret to the English Minister, who lost no time in informing his own Court.   George II. suddenly commanded his son to England, and thereby defeated the scheme.   But the troubles he had wished to prevent by

* Yet much of his narrative has been suppressed by the prudence or delicacy of his descendants. See preface to Lord Hervey's "Memoirs," by Mr. Croker.

† "Memoirs of George II." vol. i. p. 66, 4to.

keeping his son in ignorance of the country he was born to govern, now sprung up in abundance.

Frederick, thwarted in his design, consented indeed to marry the Princess of Saxe-Gotha; but he connected himself with the leaders of the Opposition. Chesterfield, Cobham, Pulteney, among the discontented Whigs; Pitt and Lyttelton, chiefs of the young patriots, together with some leading Tories, frequented his house and enlivened his society: there, too, Pope, received as a representative of poetry and wit, could boast of the friendship of the Heir-apparent.

> " And if still higher the proud list should end,
> Still let me boast no flatt'rer but a friend."

Bolingbroke, the spirit of all mischief, inspired the councils of the Prince. Thus supported, he did not fear to incur the utmost displeasure of the King his father. He appealed to the House of Commons for an increase of income, and put his case in the hands of the Opposition. He gave still more offence by bringing away the Princess from Hampton Court, at the commencement of her labour, to be confined in London.

This offence was never pardoned—the King would not be reconciled, and Queen Caroline, even on her death-bed, refused to see or to forgive her son. Pope says, sarcastically,—

> " Waft Carolina to the realms of rest,
> All parts perform'd, and all her children blest."

The Prince was not dismayed: he relied on his own youth and the age and ill-health of his father as a means of attracting adherents. One day, having closeted Lord Harrington and Lord Chesterfield to no purpose, he at last said: " My Lord, remember the King is sixty-one and I am thirty-seven."* In this spirit of presumption the

* " Marchmont Diary."

Prince distributed the patronage as if he were really king. He promised to Dr. Lee the office of Chancellor of the Exchequer, and desired Doddington to kiss his hand as Secretary of State, with a peerage. Other places and peerages were scattered with profusion among his little Court.

There was, however, a source of weakness to the expectant monarch which often marred the efforts of his followers. They were not held together by any common principle: their personal jealousies led to perpetual squabbles; and the Prince, by his insincerity and want of truth, only widened these breaches. For instance, when Doddington entered the Prince's service, he was assailed in a pamphlet which evidently came from within the circle of Leicester House. Doddington, with proper spirit, called the Prince's servants together, and denounced the pamphlet. The Prince expressed his wonder that any one should have been guilty of writing so malignant a libel; yet it was written by his own Attorney-General, and had been submitted to the Prince before it went to press.*

Thus surrounded and thus counselled, the Prince confidently reckoned on his father's speedy decease. But, alas for human calculations! The presumptuous schemes and private cabals of Frederick Prince of Wales were abruptly terminated, in 1756, by his sudden death of an abscess.

His widow, with good sense and good feeling, placed herself with all submission in the hands of the King. The King, on his side, though he acted with decency, must have been relieved by the event, and was disposed kindly

---

* From a note in MS. by Horace Walpole, in a copy of "Doddington's Diary," at Holland House.

to welcome as his heir a quiet boy of sixteen years old, under the care of a discreet and prudent mother.

The Duke of Cumberland, with less feeling or less propriety, said, "It is a great loss, but I hope the country will recover it."

The following account is given by Doddington of a conversation he had with the Princess in 1752: "I then took the liberty to ask her what she thought the real disposition of the Prince to be? She said that I knew him almost as well as she did; that he was very honest, but that she wished he was a little more forward and less childish at his age; that she hoped his preceptors would improve him. After some talk about the preceptors, the Princess continued, that she did not observe the Prince to take very particularly to anybody about him but his brother Edward, and she was very glad of it, for the young people of quality were so ill-educated and so very vicious, that they frightened her. I told her I thought it a great happiness that he showed no disposition to any great excesses, and begged to know what were his affections and passions. She repeated that he was a very honest boy, and that his chief passion seemed to be for Edward."*

To this account may be added the observations of Lord Waldegrave, a sensible and impartial man, who succeeded Lord Harcourt in the post of governor:—

"The Princess of Wales was reputed a woman of excellent sense by those who knew her very imperfectly; but in fact was one of those moderate geniuses who, with much natural dissimulation, a civil address, an assenting conversation, and few ideas of her own, can act with tolerable propriety, as long as they are conducted by wise and prudent counsellors."

* Doddington's "Diary," p. 172.

Next for the Prince, then entering on his twenty-first year :—

"His parts, though not excellent, will be found very tolerable, if ever they are properly exercised. He is strictly honest, but wants that frank and open behaviour which makes honesty appear amiable. His religion is free from all hypocrisy, but is not of the amiable sort—he has rather too much attention to the sins of his neighbour; he has spirit, but not of the active kind; and does not want resolution, but [it] is mixed with too much obstinacy. He has great command of his passions, and will seldom do wrong, except when he mistakes wrong for right; but as often as this shall happen, it will be difficult to undeceive him, because he is uncommonly indolent, and has strong prejudices.

.   .   .   .

"He has a kind of unhappiness in his temper, which, if it be not conquered before it has taken too deep a root, will be the source of frequent anxiety. Whenever he is displeased, his anger does not break out with heat and violence, but he becomes sullen and silent, and retires to his closet, not to compose his mind by study and contemplation, but merely to indulge the melancholy enjoyment of his own ill-humour. Even when the fit is ended, unfavourable symptoms too frequently return, which indicate that on certain occasions his Royal Highness has too correct a memory."*

In another place he says: "I found his Royal Highness uncommonly full of princely prejudices contracted in the nursery and improved by the society of bedchamber-women and pages of the back-stairs."† Again: "During the

* Waldegrave's "Memoirs," p. 9.   † Ibid. p. 63.

course of the last year there has been indeed some alteration; the authority of the nursery has gradually declined, and the Earl of Bute, by the assistance of the mother, has now the entire confidence."* It is to be observed that at the time of the Prince's death, Walpole speaks of "the quiet, inoffensive good sense of the Princess, who had never said a foolish thing nor done a disobliging one, since her arrival in this country."† Nor is there any reason to think that she much departed from this course, at a time when she was accused of inordinate ambition. But partiality, affection, or weakness of judgment led her to distinguish with too conspicuous favour a nobleman who by that favour attained a height for which no other qualities fitted him. Distrustful of the interested politicians who surrounded her, she gave him a confidence so absolute and intimate as to cause scandal in the Court and clamour in the country.

Lord Bute, even before George II.'s death, seems to have been alarmed at the waves of the tempestuous sea on which he was about to embark. In a letter to Baron Mure, dated January 14th, 1759, he says, " What strange things have passed since you left this! *O quando licebit procul negotiis,* &c. Why am I doomed to climb ambition's steep and rocky height, who early in life had the meanest opinion of politicians—opinions that mature age and dear-bought experience too well confirm."‡

The Earl of Bute was owner of an estate somewhat dilapidated, possessed warm affections, had generous purposes, some taste for literature, and some knowledge of architecture and painting. But his whole acquaintance

* Waldegrave's "Memoirs," p. 10.

† "Mem. of George II." Walpole speaks of her differently in the "Memoirs of George III."

‡ "Caldwell Papers," vol. i. pp. 2, 119; privately printed.

with the political world was confined to the inheritance of
certain Tory maxims suitable to his name, and a pompous
delivery of commonplaces. So that Frederick Prince of
Wales used to say of him that he would be a good
minister at a small German court where there was no
business. The Prince, in his gathering of forces against
his father, attached Lord Bute to his household; and the
Princess, his widow, gave him a position which excited envy
and made enemies. He was the Cardinal Mazarin of the
Princess Dowager; and her son, like Louis XIV., was
somewhat impatient of the yoke, though in no hurry to
throw it off.

Prince George, with a mind more ready to imbibe prejudice than to assimilate learning, seems not to have acquired
from any of his preceptors a knowledge of classical or even
English literature. He never understood or appreciated
Shakespeare,* and few English gentlemen wrote in a style
so inelegant and so ungrammatical. But if he attained no
proficiency either in the lofty lessons of history or the
delightful study of poetry, he seems to have learnt very
early the habit of secrecy and dissimulation, so natural to a
court. A characteristic instance of these qualities was observed by those near him when he first heard of the death
of George II. He was out riding when the intelligence
reached him: he said aloud, without betraying any emo-
tion, that his horse had fallen lame, and turned towards
home. When he dismounted, he said quietly to the groom,
"I have said this horse is lame, I forbid you to say the
contrary."†

His first beginnings were in keeping with this prudent
reserve. But the scene gradually unfolded, and displayed

* See "Memoirs of Madame d'Arblay."   † "Mem. of George III."

a Sovereign who did not indeed resemble the Stuarts in their arbitrary assumptions, or in their pedantic pretensions, but who bent his whole mind to the ambition of ruling absolutely, according to his own will, through the forms of a free constitution.

The Earl of Bute had imbibed himself, and instilled into his pupil, the Tory doctrine that the king ought not to govern by connexions, or, in other words, by party. The notion struck deep root into his mind. Lord Bute himself affected an indifference to power, and a fondness for arts and letters. But while he thus nursed in secret his infant greatness, the confidence placed in him by the Princess, the docility with which the young Prince listened to his instructions, and the new aspirations of the Tory party, tempted him forward. The more ambitious of that party were content to graft their old Stuart principles on a Hanoverian stock. Hence the cohesion of politicians, in itself loose and slight, became the sport of interested cabal, of sudden resentment, and discordant tempers.

Had the character of Mr. Pitt been more conciliatory, his great qualities might have rallied around him a national party. It is melancholy to notice the defects which prevented a union of able and honest men, equally desirable for his own fame and the public welfare. We shall see in the present volume fatal instances of his unbending ambition and sullen discontent, the bright flashes of genius, and the darkening cloud of infirmity. Neither did there exist any large atmosphere of public opinion in which politicians moved. In the confined space, from which air was excluded, the guinea and the feather were of equal weight.

Upon the accession of George III. the nation expected,

but did not desire, a marked change in the policy of the State. The influence of the Princess Dowager over the young King, and the Tory predilections of Lord Bute, made the world, and especially the curious part of it, watch with interest the beginnings of the new reign. But the young Sovereign was not enterprising or precipitate, and Lord Bute hesitated on the threshold of power. The first day of the new reign was significant, though not decisive; Mr. Pitt, the Secretary of State, was kept two hours waiting before the King admitted him to his presence. The Duke of Newcastle, who came from Claremont on a hasty summons, was immediately received, and graciously informed that he might retain his office of First Lord of the Treasury. Mr. Pitt had afterwards an interview with Lord Bute. The favourite endeavoured to renew his former connexion with Mr. Pitt, and offered him, with certain reserves, the support of the King. Mr. Pitt, on his side guarded and resentful, intimated, amidst many professions of loyalty, that less than the entire direction of the war would not satisfy him. They both spoke in measured terms, and separated without cordiality.*

Lord Bute appears to have thought that he could govern a constitutional monarchy as a favourite courtier might govern a despotic state, solely by the will of the Prince. He wished to glide upon the scene without ostentation, and unfold gradually his pretensions and his powers. But the execution of such a scheme was dangerous, and might prove fatal to his creeping ambition. He entertained a design of becoming Secretary of State by making Lord Holderness pretend to quarrel with his colleagues and resign in apparent anger. But this indirect and cowardly expedient was not

* From a memorandum of Sir Gilbert Elliot, MS. at Minto.

relished even by Bubb Doddington, the most intriguing statesman of the age, and only served to show how unequal his mind was to his fortune.*

The Duke of Newcastle therefore remained First Lord of the Treasury, thwarted, indeed, by the underhand cunning of the favourite, but in the apparent possession of his former supremacy. "There is nothing new under the sun," said Horace Walpole. " Nor under the grandson," replied George Selwyn.

Notwithstanding these outward signs, the Earl of Bute had conceived, and was ready to prompt, a new scheme of foreign and domestic policy. In regard to the former, while he was averse to a sudden abandonment of our Continental allies and a relaxation of our maritime exertions, he wished to calm down the warlike fervour of the nation, and to secure the repose of Europe by an honourable peace.

In respect to domestic affairs, he aimed at no less than the dissolution of party connexions, and the ascendency of the King over the Parliament. " *Mettre le Roy hors de page*," says Mr. Burke, "became a sort of watchword. And it was constantly in the mouths of all the runners of the Court that nothing could preserve the balance of the constitution from being overturned by the rabble, or by a faction of the nobility, but to free the Sovereign effectually from ministerial tyranny, under which the royal dignity had been oppressed in the person of his Majesty's grandfather."†

Some extracts from the evidence of witnesses of opposite opinions will show the progress and success of the

* Lord Melcombe's " Diary."
† " Thoughts on the Causes of the Present Discontents."

new policy. The first extract I shall give is from the
"History" of Mr. Adolphus, who speaks the language of
the Court :—

"At the dissolution of the first Parliament called by
George III. the aspect of affairs presented no consolatory
views to his mind. The King, from the beginning of his
reign, had manifestly sought the advantage and honour of
his people; yet such were the effects of a constant and
acrimonious opposition, that not only the prudence of his
measures, but the purity of his intentions, was doubted. At
his accession he found a large portion of his subjects, conspicuous both for property and talent, excluded from all
share in the Government, and by an affected stigma rendered
incapable of enjoying confidence or rendering service to
the Crown. He relieved them from this proscription, and
sought, by abolishing party and national distinction, to
reign, indeed, king and protector of all his people. This
measure, so just and wise in itself, was productive of endless
feuds and jealousies. Every introduction of a new servant
or family occasioned dissatisfaction and disgust; the disappointed formed new parties, avowed new principles, and
sought by every device to distress and impede the operations of Government. Thus, so many successive ministries
who assumed the direction of public affairs were all feeble
and inefficient, while no single opposition was in itself
strong or respectable. Every leader of a party commanded
his share of influence, which, joined to the influence resulting from ministerial situation, was sufficient to procure
a majority. But the Parliament itself, delivered to so
many opposite leaders, making laws in one session, repealing them in the next, affirming a principle at one
period, and retracting it at another, lost much of the respect

and confidence which ought to flow from the people to their representatives."*

Let us now hear Mr. Burke, speaking of the same period, but in the sense of the Whigs and the Rockingham Opposition :—

" Nobody, I believe, will consider it merely as the language of spleen or disappointment, if I say that there is something particularly alarming in the present conjunction. There is hardly a man in or out of power who holds any other language. That Government is at once dreaded and contemned; that the laws are despoiled of all their respected and salutary terror; that their inaction is a subject of ridicule, and their exertion of abhorrence; that rank, and office, and title, and all the solemn plausibilities of the world, have lost reverence and effect; that our foreign politics are as much damaged as our domestic economy; that our dependencies are slackened in their affection, and loosened from their obedience; that we know neither how to yield nor how to enforce; that hardly anything above or below, abroad or at home, is sound and entire; but that disconnexion and confusion, in offices, in parties, in families, in Parliament, in the nation, prevail beyond the disorders of any former time. These are facts universally admitted and lamented."†

So far the political philosopher scarcely differs, except in the vigour of his style, from the courtly writer. Let us now consult Horace Walpole, Earl of Orford, who hated the Court and the Rockingham party, and had his own somewhat peculiar predilections and violent aversions. He begins with a description of Lord Mansfield as " by principle

---

* Adolphus's " History of the Reign of George III." vol. i. p. 360.
Burke's " Works," vol. i. p. 493, 4to.

a tyrant;" Lord Holland as "cruel, revengeful, daring, subtle;" Grenville, though "in principle a republican," as "bold, proud, dictatorial, and so self-willed that he would have expected Liberty herself should have been his first slave." Next, "the Bedford faction," except the Duke himself, as "devoid of honour, honesty, or virtue;" and the Scotch as lending their mischievous abilities towards the ruin of the constitution. After thus disposing of most of the principal leaders and parties in the State, he comes to the Court. "All those individuals or factions, I do not doubt, accepted and fomented the disposition they found predominant in the Cabinet (the King's Cabinet), as they had severally access to it; and the contradictions which the King suffered in his ill-advised measures riveted in him a thirst of delivering himself from control, and to be above control he must be absolute. Thus, on the innate desire of unbounded power in all princes, was engrafted a hate to the freedom of the subject; and therefore, whether the King set out with a plan of extending his prerogative, or adopted it, his subsequent measures, as often as he had an opportunity of directing them himself, tended to the sole object of acting by his own will. Frequent convulsions did that pursuit occasion, and heavy mortifications on himself. On the nation it heaped disgrace, and brought it to the brink of ruin; and should the event be consonant to the King's wishes, of establishing the royal authority at home, it is most sure that the country will be so lowered, that the Sovereign will become as subject to the mandates of France as any little potentate in Europe."*

Admitting the truth of this testimony, I will add a few remarks on the character of the Sovereign who governed

* " Memoirs of George III." vol. i. p. 127.

this great country from 1760 to 1810; a period of half a century in length, but far more remarkable for the birth of the American republic and the vicissitudes of the French Revolution.

George III. was animated by a conscientious principle and a ruling passion. The conscientious principle was an honest desire to perform his duty; and the ruling passion was a strong determination to make the conclusions of his narrow intellect and ill-furnished mind prevail over the opinions of the wisest, and the combinations of the most powerful, of his subjects.

For the space of fifty years these two traits of his character had a mighty influence on the fortunes of Great Britain and of Europe. His domestic life, the virtuous example which he gave in his own Court, his sincere piety, contributed much to the firmness with which the nation resisted the example of the French Revolution, and gave solid support to the throne on which he sate. But his political prejudices prolonged the contest with America; his religious intolerance alienated the affections of Ireland; his national pride, and his hatred of democracy promoted the wars against France, whether monarchical or Jacobin.

On the other hand, it was the task of Mr. Fox to vindicate, with partial success, but with brilliant ability, the cause of freedom and the interests of mankind. He resisted the mad perseverance of Lord North in the project of subduing America. He opposed the war undertaken by Mr. Pitt against France, as unnecessary and unjust. He proved himself at all times the friend of religious liberty, and endeavoured to free both the Protestant and Roman Catholic dissenter from disabilities on account of their religious faith. He denounced the slave trade. He supported at all times a reform of the House of Commons.

These views and sentiments made him through life obnoxious to the King. We shall see the results of this antagonism, which was throughout, on both sides, not only political, but also in some degree personal. Thus, for a great part of his life, he appears as a kind of rival to the Sovereign upon the throne. We shall see that in 1784 this opposition of character produced a contest which is one of the most memorable in the history of our Parliamentary struggles.

CHAPTER III.

MR. FOX'S CONDUCT IN PARLIAMENT TILL HIS FINAL RUPTURE WITH
LORD NORTH IN 1774.

MR. Fox made his first speech in the House of Commons on the 9th of March, 1769, when he was little more than twenty years of age. It seems to have been on a point of order, a singular topic for so young a man.

At this time the only popular and effective opposition to the Court came from a tainted source. John Wilkes, one of the most unprincipled of men, had become notorious for the profligacy of his private life. In public he had affected a patriotism which he was far from feeling—indeed, he rather made a boast of his insincerity. Standing on the hustings at Brentford, his opponent said to him, "I will take the sense of the meeting."—"And I will take the nonsense," replied Wilkes, "and we shall see who has the best of it." Some years after, when his popularity had declined, the King, receiving him at his levee, asked him after his friend Sergeant Glyn. "Sir," said Wilkes, "he is not a friend of mine; he was a Wilkite, which I never was." Yet this man, by pandering to the national prejudice against the Scotch, and a certain low talent for invective, raised a popular storm, was saluted with the cry of "Wilkes and Liberty!" and was compared by his friend Churchill to the most illustrious patriots of antiquity.

The contest on general warrants, the denunciation of Wilkes's "Essay on Woman" by the Earl of Sandwich, one of his boon companions, the expulsion of Wilkes by the House of Commons, and his re-election for Middlesex, hardly require notice from a biographer of Mr. Fox; yet these occurrences all served to illustrate the disordered state of public affairs, the violent and illegal conduct of the Ministry, the intemperance and faction of the leaders of the multitude. In this state of affairs constitutional statesmen found some difficulty in resisting the undue pretensions of authority without abetting the encroachments of an unprincipled demagogue.

On the 14th of April Charles Fox spoke in favour of the expulsion of Wilkes. On this occasion Horace Walpole says: " Stephen Fox indecently and indiscreetly said Wilkes had been chosen by the scum of the earth; an expression after retorted on his family, his grandfather's birth being of the lowest obscurity. . . . Charles Fox, with infinite superiority in parts, was not inferior to his brother in insolence."

On the 8th of May Mr. Fox spoke against the petition of the electors of Middlesex in favour of their right of electing Wilkes. Of this speech Horace Walpole observes: " Charles Fox, not yet twenty-one, answered Burke with great quickness and parts, but with confidence equally premature."* Sir Richard Heron, in a letter to Sir Charles Bunbury, says: " Mr. Charles Fox, who I suppose was your schoolfellow, and who is but twenty, made a great figure last night upon the petition of the Middlesex freeholders. He spoke with great spirit, in very Parliamentary language, and entered very deeply into the question on constitutional principle."

* " Memoirs of the Reign of George III." by Lord Orford.

Lord Holland, proud of his favourite boy, writes thus to his friend Mr. Campbell of Cawdor: "I delayed thanking you for your kind letter of April 27th, till the Parliament should be up; which it was on Tuesday, after a debate of Monday till two o'clock on Tuesday morning, in which I am told (and willingly believe it) Charles Fox spoke extremely well. It was all off-hand, all argumentative, in reply to Mr. Burke and Mr. Wedderburne; and excessively well indeed. I hear it spoke of by everybody as a most extraordinary thing, and I am, you see, not a little pleased with it. My son Ste. spoke too (as they say he always does), very short and to the purpose. *They neither of them aim at oratory*, make apologies, or speak of themselves, but go directly to the purpose, so I do not doubt they will continue speakers; but *I am told Charles can never make a better speech than he did on Monday.*"*

Although these early speeches of Charles Fox displayed quickness, and were the more promising, as his father, an old debater, remarks, because they were " all off-hand," his doctrines at this time of his life were neither favourable to popular liberty nor agreeable to the practice of the constitution. Mr. George Grenville, provoked by an observation of Mr. Onslow, that Alderman Beckford was not at liberty to speak against a resolution of the House of Commons, exclaimed, with great animation of manner—" Sir, he who will contend that a resolution of the House of Commons is the law of the land is a violent enemy of his country, be he who or what he will. The law of the land and the usage of Parliament is to be the guide of every man in the kingdom. No power—not an order of the House of Commons—can set that aside, can change, diminish, or augment it."

* " Memoirs and Correspondence of C. J. Fox," vol. i. p. 54.

Immediately after this speech Mr. Grenville was seized with a spitting of blood. He died in November, 1770. This contest was, on the part of the Court and the House of Commons, unconstitutional, violent, and imprudent. Happily, the resolutions in Wilkes's case were afterwards expunged from the Journals; and it seems to be now a settled doctrine that, although the House of Commons may expel a member for conduct they deem criminal or disgraceful, no permanent disqualification can take place unless it is founded on the law of the land as either contained in Acts of Parliament or sanctioned by clear and unquestioned usage.

Such was the course followed in the case of Lord Cochrane, who was expelled after a conviction in a court of law, and immediately afterwards returned again for Westminster. Thus, while the House of Commons preserves its power of expulsion, the rights of the electors can only be restricted by the general operation of law.

In the following October Charles Fox went, with Lord and Lady Holland, to Paris, where he suffered great losses at play. He returned at the beginning of the year 1770, and spoke both on the 9th and 25th of January. On the 25th of January the House of Commons went into a Committee of the whole House on the State of the Nation, when Dowdeswell moved, " That the House of Commons is bound to follow the laws of the land and the usage of Parliament, which is part thereof." Lord North said, as he supposed the motion alluded to the case of Wilkes, he would add the words, " And had been so followed in the late election for the county of Middlesex."

Wedderburne went into the law part of the question; and his position that there had been no question exactly in point made great impression on the House, no member being a more acute or more accurate speaker. "Young Charles Fox, of age but the day before, started up and entirely confuted Wedderburne, producing a case decided in the courts below but the last year, and exactly similar to that of Wilkes. The Court, he said, had no precedent, but had gone by analogy. The House roared with applause."* Lord North's amendment was carried by 224 to 180, a formidable minority. On the first day of the session the majority of the ministers had been 116.

On the 29th of January the Duke of Grafton resigned. His resignation had been preceded by the removal of Lord Camden, and was followed by the retirement of General Conway from the Cabinet. The way being thus cleared, Lord North was on the 30th of January appointed First Lord of the Treasury. His chief colleagues were Lord Sandwich, Lord Gower, Lord Hillsborough, and Lord Stormont.

In less than a month from this time Mr. Fox accepted office as one of the junior Lords of the Admiralty. Such a beginning of official life was very far indeed from auspicious, still less did it give any promise of that strenuous contest for freedom, and that hostility to unjust war, to which he afterwards devoted his eloquence and his life.

Indeed, it may more truly be said that his early parliamentary career seemed to indicate a perverse desire to gain the favour of the Court, and a wayward indifference to public opinion. Thus, in 1771, on a clause of the *Nullum Tempus* Act, which Sir William Meredith sought to repeal, Walpole says: "Charles Fox, the phenomenon of the age, undertook the patronage of it, and gave as much satis-

* "Memoirs of George III." vol. iv. p. 63.

faction to the party as disgust to the Opposition, by the great talents he exerted on the occasion."

So also, upon the quarrel of the House of Commons with the City of London, on the motion for committing the Lord Mayor, "Charles Fox, as if impatient to inherit his father's unpopularity, abused the City as his father had used to do, but Ministers were moderate."

In January, 1772, Mr. Fox gave notice of a motion to repeal the Marriage Act; thus reviving the old dispute in which his father had taken so conspicuous a part. On the 20th of February he resigned his seat at the Board of Admiralty; his own account of his motive for this step is given in a letter to Lord Ossory: "I should not have resigned at this moment merely on account of my complaints against Lord North, if I had not determined to vote against this Royal Marriage Bill, which, in place, I should be ashamed of doing."

The occasion of the proposed measure was the marriage of two of the King's brothers with subjects; that of the Duke of Cumberland with Mrs. Horton, and that of the Duke of Gloucester with Lady Waldegrave. The purport of the Act was to restrain such marriages by requiring the King's consent, except in certain special cases, to all marriages of the descendants of George II.: the policy was to prevent entangling connexions of the Princes and Princesses, members of the Royal Family. Webs of intrigue, like those which were spun in the reigns of Edward IV. and Edward VI., might, it was supposed, gather in the halls of royalty and involve the Sovereign in the disputes of contending houses: nor can it be denied that such families, if powerful, might embarrass the action, if obscure, might dim the lustre of the crown. It may be doubted, however, whether these reasons, though of much weight, should be allowed to prevail against the natural right of persons of mature age to contract the bonds of marriage with the objects of their affection. It is assuredly a restriction unfavourable to morals, and which nothing but manifest necessity can justify.

It must be noted that, in resisting the Royal Marriage Bill, Mr. Fox disclaimed all intention of going into opposition. He writes to Lord Ossory, when announcing his resignation: "Upon the whole I am convinced I did right, and I think myself very safe from going into opposition, which is the only danger." So in his first speech on the subject, he said: "That it gave him much pain to be obliged to differ from a Minister whose general conduct he so much approved, and whose *political principles he admired;* a Minister who, with unexampled resolution, had stood forth in the most critical and dangerous moment to free his country from that anarchy and confusion into which it was about to be plunged by factious and ill-designing men." To this compliment Lord North, in a similar strain, re-rejoined: "That he should always lament when a gentleman of whose abilities and integrity he had so high an opinion differed from him, and that the manly, open, and spirited manner in which that gentleman had from the first communicated to him his objections to the bill, and his intention of opposing it, had increased instead of lessening the esteem in which he held him."*

The following remarks from Lord Orford's "Memoirs of the Reign of George III." are worth reading, as those of a shrewd observer who had heard Walpole, Pulteney, and Pitt.

* "Parliamentary History," vol. xvii.

April 7th. " Though I had never been in the House of Commons since I had quitted Parliament, the fame of Charles Fox raised my curiosity, and I went this day to hear him. He made his motion for leave to bring in a bill to correct the old Marriage Bill, and he introduced it with ease, grace and clearness, and without the prepared or elegant formality of a young speaker. He did not shine particularly, but his sense and facility showed that he could shine. He said the two great points of the former bill were to fix the notoriety of marriages, and to prevent improper marriages by establishing a nullity. He approved the first; he highly condemned the second. To encourage marriage by facilities was the business of a republican kind of government; but the late bill had been the work of a proud aristocracy, and he believed had hurt propagation, though he was not ready with proofs that it had. Colonel Burgoyne, a pompous man, whose speeches were studied, and yet not striking, seconded him. Lord North, who had declared he would not oppose the introduction of the new bill, now unhandsomely opposed it, to please the Yorkes and the peers, and spoke well. He said formerly the bill had been matter of speculation. It was no longer so; twenty years had shown its utility. It ought not to be laid aside unless proofs could be brought that it had done hurt. T. Townshend supported the motion. Ellis, who owned he had been strongly against the old bill, said he had been converted to it on many points by Lord North's supporting it, but should not oppose considering how to amend it. Ongley and Cornwall were, the first for the old, the second for the new bill. Cornwall, a comely, sensible man, decent in his manner and matter, but of no vivacity. Burke made a long and fine oration against the motion.

Burke was certainly in his principles no moderate man, and when his party did not interfere, generally leaned towards the more arbitrary side, as had appeared in the late debates on the Church, in which he had declared for the clergy. He laid his chief stress on the impropriety of allowing men to have children till they were of an age by strength and prudence to maintain them. He spoke with a choice and variety of language, a profusion of metaphors, and yet with a correction of diction, that were surprising. His fault was copiousness above measure; and he dealt abundantly, too much, in establishing general positions. Two-thirds of this oration resembled the beginning of a book on speculative doctrines, and yet argument was not the *forte* of it. Charles Fox, who had been running about the house talking to different persons and scarce listening to Burke, rose with amazing spirit and memory, answered both Lord North and Burke, ridiculed the arguments of the former and confuted those of the latter with a shrewdness that, from its multiplicity of reasons, as much exceeded his father in embracing all the arguments of his antagonists, as he did in his manner and delivery.* Lord Holland was always confused before he could clear up the point, fluttered and hesitated, and wanted diction, and laboured only one forcible conclusion. Charles Fox had great facility of delivery; his words flowed rapidly; but he had nothing of Burke's variety of language or correctness, nor his method,

---

* "He (Charles Fox) said ingeniously that the clandestine marriages made in Scotland had prevented some of the bad effects of the bill, and yet that he disliked those marriages, because by preventing those mischiefs they had prevented the repeal of the bill. He maintained what Burke denied, that it was an aristocratic bill: and he asked if it was the mildness of the aristocracy that had saved the bill when a repeal of it had twice passed the House of Commons."—H. W.

yet his arguments were far more shrewd. He was many years younger. Burke was indefatigable, learned, and versed in every branch of eloquence; Fox was dissolute, dissipated, idle beyond measure. He was that very morning returned from Newmarket, where he had lost some thousand pounds the preceding day; he had stopped at Hocherel, where he found company, had sat up all night drinking, and had not been in bed when he came to move his bill, which he had not even drawn up. This was genius, was almost inspiration. Being so very young, he appeared in that light a greater prodigy than the famous Charles Townshend. Townshend's speeches, for four or five years, gave little indication of his amazing parts; they were studied, pedantic, and like the dissertations of Burke, with less brilliancy. Charles Fox approached to Charles Townshend only in argument. Charles Townshend grew idle; he had taken pains : both could illuminate themselves from the slightest hints. But Townshend's wit exceeded even Burke's, and he could shine in every science, in every profession, with a quarter of Burke's application. All three were vain, and kept down by no modesty. Townshend knew his superiority over all men, and talked of it; Fox showed that he thought as well of himself; Burke endeavoured to make everybody think so of him. Burke had most ambition and little judgment; Townshend no judgment and most vanity; Fox most judgment in his speeches, and none of Townshend's want of courage and truth. If Fox once reflects, and abandons his vices, in which he is as proud of shining as by his parts, he will excel Burke; for, of all the politicians of talents that I ever knew, Burke has the least political art. None of the three were well calculated to command adherents. No man could trust or believe Townshend; and though he would flatter grossly, he would the next moment turn the same men into ridicule. Fox was too confident and overbearing; Burke had no address or insinuation. Men of less talents are more capable of succeeding by art, observation, and assiduity. The House dividing, Lord North was beaten by 62 to 61, a disgraceful event for a Prime Minister. Since he would oppose Fox's motion contrary to his declaration, he ought to have taken care to have his members about him; but he daily showed that he was only a subservient Minister. The Scotch cabal and the Tories could sway him as they pleased, and his negligence demonstrated that he followed their dictates, not his own objects. In fact *he disliked his post*, and retained it only from hopes of securing some considerable emolument for his family. He was indolent, good humoured, void of affectation of dignity, void of art, and his parts and the goodness of his character would have raised him much higher in the opinion of mankind if he had cared either for power or applause."*

At the end of 1772 a new disposition of offices was made expressly to open a place for Charles Fox, who was named one of the Commissioners of the Treasury.

But it was soon found that a subordinate situation in office was not suited to his talents, his activity, or, we must say, his daring temper. Within little more than a year of his acceptance of office, on a question of committing Woodfall the printer to the custody of the Sergeant-at-Arms, Mr. Fox burst out against the Press and the City, and moved that Woodfall be committed to Newgate. Lord North promised his support, tried to retract, owned himself bound to vote with Fox if he persisted, and finally was dragged off

* "Corr. of C. J. Fox," p. 83.

by his junior Lord of the Treasury in a minority of 68 to
152.　The King noticed the transaction in the following
terms :—

"I am greatly *incensed* at the presumption of Charles
Fox in forcing you to vote with him last night; but approve
much of your making your friends vote in the majority.
Indeed, that young man has so thoroughly cast off every
principle of common honour and honesty, that he must
become as contemptible as he is odious.　I hope you will let
him know that you are not insensible of his conduct towards
you."*

On the 24th of February Charles Fox was dismissed
from the Board of Treasury.　It is said that on this occasion
Lord North wrote him the following laconic note: " His
Majesty has thought proper to order a new Commission of
Treasury to be made out, in which I do not see your name.
—North."

Horace Walpole says, speaking of Lord North: " With
his usual hurry after indolence, he turn'd out Charles Fox,
as a threat to those who might incline to desert, but without
effect."†

It is to be lamented that during this period of his life
Mr. Fox entered deeply—almost madly—into the pursuit
of gaming.　Lord Egremont afterwards suspected that he
was the dupe of foul play.　Be that as it might, he borrowed to such an extent, that the purchase of the annuities
he had granted cost his fond and indulgent father no less a
sum than 140,000*l.*

Dr. Parr has truly said, in his somewhat pompous Latin:—

" Erupisse in eo fatebor illum impetum ardoremque, qui,
sive ad literas humaniores, sive ad prudentiam civilem,

* " Corr." vol. i. p. 99.　　　　† " Corr." vol. i. p. 101.

sive ad luxuriam amoresque inclinaret, id unum ageret, id toto pectore arriperet, id universum hauriret."*

Horace Walpole, in less stately phrase, tells us: "As the gaming and extravagance of young men of quality had arrived now at a pitch never heard of, it is worth while to give some account of it. They had a club at Almack's, in Pall Mall, where they played only for rouleaus of 50*l.* each, and generally there was 10,000*l.* in specie on the table. Lord Holland had paid above 20,000*l.* for his two sons. Nor were the manners of the gamesters, or even their dresses for play, undeserving notice. They began by pulling off their embroidered clothes, and put on frieze greatcoats, or turned their coats inside outwards for luck. They put on pieces of leather (such as are worn by footmen when they clean the knives) to save their laced ruffles; and to guard their eyes from the light and to prevent tumbling their hair, wore high-crowned straw hats with broad brims and adorned with flowers and ribbons; masks to conceal their emotions when they played at quinze. Each gamester had a small neat stand by him, to hold their tea, or a wooden bowl with an edge of ormolu to hold their rouleaus. They borrowed great sums of Jews at exorbitant premiums. Charles Fox called his outward room, where those Jews waited till he rose, his Jerusalem Chamber."

* Dr. Parr's Preface to " Bellendenus," &c.

CHAPTER IV.

ORIGIN OF THE AMERICAN WAR.

THE adoption of the plans of Columbus by Ferdinand and Isabella led to the acquisition of immense possessions by those Sovereigns. The valour of the Mexicans, the gentleness of the Peruvians, were unable to cope with the bold genius of Cortes, or to resist even for a time the merciless ferocity of Pizarro. From Florida to Lima a vast territory was swayed by the sceptre of Charles V., or obeyed his successors on the throne of Spain. The other powers of Europe appeared to rest satisfied with the leavings of the Spaniard. Portugal ruled over Brazil. In the middle of the seventeenth century, France possessed the mouths of the Mississippi and of the St. Lawrence, and stretching to the West from each point, embraced the valley of the Ohio, thus connecting the lakes of Canada with the great rivers which poured their waters into the Gulf of Mexico. England had sent her emigrants to Virginia in the south, to Boston and New Plymouth on the north, but between these settlements the Dutch and the Swedes held the intervening provinces. In this century the power of Great Britain in America was greatly increased by conquest and by treaty. Cromwell failing Hispaniola, conquered Jamaica; Charles II. obtained by arms and by the treaty of Breda the territory which, on being granted to his brother, was called New York. A century afterwards, the peace of Paris secured and extended this new empire. France, by that treaty, so glorious to Great Britain, ceded Canada and a part of the shores of the Mississippi. Spain gave up Florida in return for Havannah.

Thus, instead of being hemmed in by a rival and hostile race, the Anglo-Saxon colonists found themselves in a vast country neither tempted to indolence by the abundance of gold and silver, nor enervated by the heat of a sultry and burning climate. Like the Athenians of old, their difficulties were their means.

The warriors and statesmen of France — Montcalm, Choiseul, and Vergennes—amid all their losses, derived consolation from the thought that British America, no longer fearing the neighbourhood of the French, and no longer needing the aid of the English, would aim at independence.

This calculation was so just, and the prospect so alarming to Great Britain, that it obviously behoved her rulers to endeavour by every means to confute the prophecy and avert the calamity. England and her American subjects had fought together in a glorious struggle; it would have been politic to encourage the feelings of common sympathy and national pride. The British Americans, nearly three millions in number, would naturally seek to enlarge their commerce and increase their wealth; it would have been wise to relax restriction and encourage exertion. The emigrants who had left Europe for America had been partly Puritans, of stout hearts and sturdy faith, who were resolved to break loose from the fetters of Laud; and partly English gentlemen, who preferred seeking adventures in the wilderness to a mere competency in the old country.

It would be dangerous to tamper with the rights, or to narrow the liberties of either class. In a word, the treatment of British America, extended, enriched, animated with the love of freedom of the Roundheads, and the spirit of chivalry of the Cavaliers, required the most cautious forbearance, the largest indulgence, and the most liberal policy.

There was another circumstance which would have afforded matter of reflection to prudent rulers. The Americans were fond of the study and the practice of law. Of Blackstone's "Commentaries" nearly as many copies were sold in America as in England. Burke well observed, in his great speech on conciliation, " that when great honours and great emoluments do not win over this knowledge to the service of the State, it is a formidable adversary to government. If the spirit be not tamed and broken by these happy methods, it is stubborn and litigious. *Abeunt studia in mores.* This study renders men acute, inquisitive, dexterous, prompt in attack, ready in defence, full of resources. In other countries the people, more simple, and of a less mercurial cast, judge of an ill principle in government only by an actual grievance; here they anticipate the evil and judge of the pressure of the grievance by the badness of the principle. They augur misgovernment at a distance, and snuff the approach of tyranny in every tainted breeze."*

A wise government, dealing with three millions of subjects of such a spirit, and at so great a distance, would have been peculiarly cautious and forbearing; they would have remembered the temper in which the parent country herself had resented the encroachments of her kings, and

* Burke's "Works," vol. iii. p. 56.

if any trifling quarrel had disturbed their concord, would
have said, like Brutus to his friend :—

" And henceforth,
If you are over-earnest with your Brutus,
He'll think your mother chides, and leave you so."

Instead of such a course, no sooner was the Peace of Paris
signed than the Government of George III. began to carry
into effect a plan to harass the trade, to violate the privileges, and to offend the pride of the Americans. With
incredible imprudence they provoked a contest on the
principle which New England had derived from the great
patriots of the age of Charles I., that taxation and representation should go together.

A plan thus unwisely conceived was not likely to be
successful. But the changes and vacillations of the
English Government, the obstinacy of the Monarch, and
the weakness of his Ministers, made the task utterly
hopeless.

The field of quarrel was a wide one. The Navigation Act,
and the policy of what Adam Smith calls the mercantile
system, restricted the Americans to the use of British
manufactures, and confined their trade to Great Britain and
her colonies. But distance from the metropolis, a wide extent
of coast, and the industry of a free people had relaxed in
practice what was grievous in law. Americans imported to
some extent foreign productions, and above all, they carried
on an illicit trade with the Spanish possessions, from which
they received gold and silver, and to which they sent the
manufactures of the mother country. This illicit commerce had been noticed with indulgence and favour by Sir
Robert Walpole. When, during the clamour on the excise
plan, he was urged to adopt some absurd scheme of

restriction on the American trade, he exclaimed, " What! I have Old England against me; do you want me to have New England against me too?" But in the eyes of George Grenville and Lord Halifax any infringement of the laws of monopoly was a serious crime.

For the purpose, therefore, of carrying the revenue laws into strict execution, cruisers were stationed not only on the coasts of Great Britain and Ireland, but also on those of North America and the West Indies. Naval officers in command of these vessels were entrusted with the powers, and ordered to discharge the duties of revenue officers. It may again be noticed that the American trade, interrupted and harassed by these regulations, was of the most beneficial nature. The middle and northern colonies exported pro-visions and lumber to the West Indies, and obtained thence the precious metals and tropical productions which were the fruits of the smuggling trade between the West Indies and the Spanish coast. This chain of illicit trade supplying wants, promoting industry, and fraught with all the benefits of friendly intercourse between nations, was rudely snapt by the new measures. Discontent, irritation, complaints of the conduct of the British officers, law-suits in the courts, invectives in the American press, were the crop which grew in abundance from these poisonous plants. In addition to these measures of administration, a Bill was brought into Parliament for imposing duties on certain kinds of merchandize, when imported into the colonies, requiring the payment of such duties to be made in gold and silver, and ordering them to be paid into the exchequer, where, with the produce of all former parliamentary duties, they were to be set apart as a separate fund, to be applied, under the disposition of parliament, *"for defraying the future charges of protecting, defending, and securing the colonies."* This Act received the royal assent on the 5th of April, 1764. Mr. Grenville had not, however, exhausted his budget; another arrow remained in his quiver to be aimed at the very heart of American prosperity. He brought forward in the House of Commons fifty-five resolutions, one of which (of the 10th of March) was to the following purport: "That towards further defraying the expenses of protecting and securing the colonies, it may be proper to charge certain stamp duties in the colonies." But he did not propose to carry this project into execution till the following year.

These resolutions appear not to have excited much attention. The House was thin, the opposition languid. But the Minister had "sown the dragon's teeth, which were to come up in armed men."

These measures accomplished or proposed, Mr. George Grenville did not omit to extol his own great feats in the royal speech at the prorogation of Parliament.

"The wise regulations," thus ran the speech, "which have been established to augment the public resources, to unite the interests of the most distant possessions of my Crown, and to encourage and secure their commerce with Great Britain, call for my hearty approbation."* King and Parliament were satisfied with their work. In America the temper was very different. The vexations of the British cruisers were sensibly felt by trade, the threatened stamp duties were protested against by the New England States, and petitions were sent to England, praying they might not be imposed. Notwithstanding these signs of repugnance, the plan was carried on to completion.

* "Parliamentary History."

In February, 1765, fifty resolutions were adopted in the Committee of Ways and Means; a Bill founded on these resolutions was carried after a short debate. In the only division which took place in the House of Commons, the minority were only forty, and in the House of Lords there was neither division nor debate.

Far different was the temper in which this measure was received on the other side of the Atlantic.

In America the Stamp Act produced the greatest excitement. It was reprinted, with a death's-head prefixed instead of the royal arms, and a name was given to it not inappropriate: ". England's folly and America's bane." At Boston the flags of the shipping were hoisted half-mast high, the church bells were muffled and tolled a funeral knell. More deliberate resistance followed : proceedings in the courts of justice were suspended, that stamps might not be required; merchants refused to pay debts incurred for English importations; associations were formed for the exclusive use of colonial manufactures; the collectors sent over to distribute the stamps were maltreated, and resigned in a panic. Finally, public offices and private houses were pillaged by a disorderly mob.

These riots took place in August, 1765. When the intelligence reached England, a new Ministry was in power. Lord Rockingham was at the head of that Ministry; General Conway was their leader in the House of Commons, and Mr. Burke, although then little known, was the private secretary and confidential adviser of the head of the Government.

The situation was perilous and perplexing. It was impossible to pass unnoticed the flagrant disobedience of America. It was folly to persist in executing an unjust and unwise law.

Parliament met on the 14th of January, 1766. On the address to the Crown occurred that famous debate on the right of Great Britain to tax the colonies, which, in fact, decided the question.

Amid breathless silence Mr. Pitt rose to address the House of Commons. After speaking of the large proportion of property held by the Commons of England, compared with the Crown, the Lords, and the Church, he concluded his argument by saying: "When, therefore, in this House we give and grant, we give and grant what is our own; but in an American tax, what do we do? We, your Majesty's Commons of Great Britain, give and grant to your Majesty—what? Our own property? No! We give and grant to your Majesty the property of your Majesty's Commons of America. It is an absurdity in terms."

Mr. Grenville made a laboured reply, and quoted the precedents of Chester and of Durham.

Mr. Pitt rose again. There was some doubt whether he was in order; but, as only part of the address had been read, and the desire of the House to hear him was great, he was allowed to proceed.

He treated Mr. Grenville with scorn and sarcasm. He proclaimed aloud his sympathy with America: "The gentleman tells us America is obstinate—America is almost in open rebellion. I rejoice that America has resisted! Three millions of people so dead to all feelings of liberty as voluntarily to submit to be slaves, would have been fit instruments to make slaves of the rest. I come not here armed at all points with law cases and acts of Parliament, with the statute-books doubled down in dogsears, to defend the cause of liberty; if I had, I myself would have cited the two cases of Chester and of Durham."

He concluded with this advice: "Upon the whole, I will beg leave to tell the House what is precisely my opinion. It is that the Stamp Act be repealed, absolutely, totally, and immediately. That the reason for the repeal be assigned, that it was founded on an erroneous principle. At the same time, let the sovereign authority of this country over the colonies be asserted in as strong terms as can be devised, and made to extend to every kind of legislation whatsoever. That we may bind· their trade, confine their manufactures, and exercise every power whatsoever, except only that of taking their money from their pockets without their own consent."

Unhappily, the opponents of the policy of Mr. Grenville regarding America were divided. Mr. Pitt maintained that the British Parliament had no right whatever to impose taxes on the colonies. But he asserted loudly an unlimited power to fetter their trade, and declared, on behalf of the manufacturers, that he would not allow the Americans to make a horseshoe nail in their own country.

On the other hand, Lord Rockingham and Mr. Burke, while they condemned the policy of the Stamp Act, maintained the right of Parliament to legislate for America even in cases of taxation. When required to define this right, Mr. Burke alluded to the extreme case of the necessities of the mother country, when all ordinary rules must yield to the safety of the empire. But Mr. Burke held liberal doctrines respecting trade, and was quite willing to relax restrictions which impeded the commerce of the colonies with foreign countries. Mr. Pitt would not listen to these notions, subversive, as he thought, of colonial dependency.

These differences amongst wise and good men were subsequently the cause of much evil. Lord Rockingham, as we have seen, was first Lord of the Treasury, and was at the head of affairs when the account of the disturbances at Boston reached England. After long deliberation, he determined to propose to Parliament the total repeal of the Stamp Act, and at the same time a declaratory bill, asserting the right of Great Britain to legislate for the colonies in all cases whatsoever. An attempt of the King to undermine the Minister by private intrigue was defeated by the firmness of Lord Rockingham; and both these measures received the sanction of Parliament. In examining the positions taken by Mr. Pitt and Lord Rockingham, neither of them appears impregnable, though either might be tenable for a time. If Mr. Pitt had prevailed, questions of manufactures and trade must soon have arisen; upon which the Americans would as little bear to be fettered as upon taxation itself. Indeed, it was the fear of being crippled in their foreign trade and domestic manufacture, by the jealousy and monopoly of the mother country, which induced the Americans, when the quarrel once began, to refuse terms of accommodation apparently liberal. Nor could it be supposed that the infant giant would allow himself to be strangled in his cradle by the coils and folds of commercial restriction.

On the other hand, although the supreme right to govern, to bind, and even to tax America, might be abstractedly true, there seemed little wisdom in asserting a power, of which nothing but the last necessity could justify the exercise. It would have been better, probably, to have been silent on the powers asserted by the Declaratory Act, and to have left an extreme case for the time when an extreme case should arise. Mr. Fox, however, probably spoke the truth when he said, many years afterwards, that not the 'inclination of Lord Rockingham, but the necessity of his situation, was the cause of the Declaratory Act.*

It was unfortunate that this difference of opinion kept aloof from each other Lord Rockingham and Mr. Pitt, who, with their respective followers, were the only men and the only parties who could have withstood the personal policy of the King, and have reconciled the thirteen colonies to the parent State. Had Lord Rockingham yielded on the question of taxation, and Mr. Pitt on that of commerce—had Mr. Pitt combined with Lord Rockingham, instead of sneering at his weakness—rivers of blood would have been spared, and England would have been saved the ignominy of defeat in an unjust cause. The narrative of what happened will show with how little wisdom affairs were actually conducted.

The Ministry of Lord Rockingham was not strong in the talent of speaking : Lord Rockingham himself spoke very seldom, General Conway was somewhat feeble, Dowdeswell was awkward, and Burke was not in a position to take a leading part. Thus we find that Mr. Fox, writing to Sir George Macartney, observes :† " The Ministry goes on just as it did, everybody laughing at them and holding them cheap, but, according to the fashionable phrase, doing justice to their good intentions."

Mr. Pitt, in more pompous phrase, addressing them in public, said: " Pardon me, gentlemen, confidence is a plant of slow growth in an aged bosom." Their own Chancellor, Lord Northington, told the King that the Ministry was too weak to last.

* Debate on Mr. Wilkes' motion, "Parliamentary History," vol. xix. p. 563, Dec. 10th, 1777.

† "Correspondence," vol. i. p. 66.

In later times it has been the practice for the Sovereign to wait till the Prime Minister himself declares his inability to go on. This course relieves the Crown from much em-. barrassment, and lays upon the Ministers a responsibility which justly belongs to them.

In the present case the King sent for Mr. Pitt, who, taking the Privy Seal and an earldom for himself, formed that curious piece of mosaic, "unsound to touch and utterly unsafe to stand upon," which Burke has so well described.

Among those who had occurred to Lord Chatham's colleagues as useful acquisitions to Government, Mr. Burke had been mentioned by the Duke of Grafton. Lord Chatham thus repels the suggestion: "The gentleman your Grace points out as a necessary recruit I think a man of parts and an ingenious speaker. As to his notions and maxims of trade, they can never be mine. Nothing can be more unsound or more repugnant to every first principle of manufacture and commerce than the rendering so noble a branch as the cottons dependent for the first materials upon the produce of French and Danish islands, instead of British. My engagement to Lord Lisburne for the next opening at the Board of Trade is known to your Grace. Nor is it a thing possible to have for Mr. Burke."* Thus narrow were the notions of this great man. We might perhaps ask, who was the Lord Lisburne for whom the man of genius was set aside? At all events, Mr. Burke was not excluded by the jealousy of the great Whig families, to whom Lord Chatham at this time seems to have conceived so much aversion.†

* Lord Mahon, vol. v. appendix.

† Lord Mahon, fair and candid as he is disposed to be, shares fully in this prejudice against the Whigs.

The consequences of supplanting Lord Rockingham by the appointment of Lord Chatham were, as regarded America, singular and unexpected. If there was one principle more than another which Mr. Pitt had proclaimed in the House of Commons, it was that the British Government had no right to tax America. Such being his conviction, it might naturally have been supposed that he would have been careful to select a Chancellor of the Exchequer imbued with his own views. But either in confidence of his own power of dictation, or from ignorance of men, or from regard for a relation, the person he fixed upon to manage the finances was Charles Townshend; a man utterly without principle, whose brilliant talents only made more prominent his want of truth, honour, and consistency. Townshend himself knew little of Lord Chatham, and was desirous of retaining his office of Paymaster, which yielded him 7000*l.* a year, instead of accepting that of Chancellor of the Exchequer, with a salary of 2500*l.* But Pitt was anxious to obtain the office of Paymaster for James Grenville, his brother-in-law, and forced Charles Townshend to accept the less lucrative but more important office.

Charles Townshend was not long in showing his own difference from Lord Chatham. "In regard to America," writes Lord Shelburne to Lord Chatham on the 1st February, 1767, "the enclosed minute from the House of Commons will show your Lordship Mr. Grenville's question. Mr. Townshend answered him, but agreed as to the principle of the Stamp Act and the duty itself, only the heats which prevailed made it an improper time to press it, and in treating the distinction between external and internal as ridiculous in everybody's opinion except the American's, and, in short, *pledged himself* to the House to find a revenue if not adequate (which Lord George Sackville pressed him with, with a view to pin him down as much as possible), yet nearly sufficient to answer the expense when properly reduced. What he means I cannot conceive."*

Melancholy consequences followed. The Rockingham party and George Grenville acted together in opposition, and by an unwise and unpatriotic vote, took off a shilling of the land-tax. Charles Townshend, finding the notion of an American revenue agreeable to the Court and not unpalatable to the House of Commons, proposed in 1767 duties payable on importation into the colonies on glass, paper, white and red lead, painters' colours, and tea. These duties were to be paid to commissioners appointed in this country, though sent to reside in America; thus marking the British origin and British purpose of the new taxes.

It might be supposed that there were two men in the Ministry who would have opposed the revival of Mr. Grenville's plan of raising a revenue from America.

These two men were Lord Chatham, the nominal head of the Ministry, and General Conway, the nominal leader in the House of Commons. But Lord Chatham was unfortunately ill, and neither the Duke of Grafton nor Lord Shelburne, who professed themselves his followers, urged the Cabinet to refrain from a scheme so contrary to his whole policy.

As for General Conway, he had, unfortunately for his character, consented to remain in office on condition that he should not be bound to vote for the measures of the Ministry of which he was the organ, and accordingly he seems to have given some kind of faint and futile. opposi-

* "Chatham Correspondence," vol. iii. p. 184.

tion to Charles Townshend's plan. The Chancellor of the Exchequer was thus successful.

The lamentable weakness of General Conway's conduct was thus commented on many years afterwards by Mr. Fox: " Were we to look back to the series of events and causes that had progressively brought this country to its present state, he should name the political liberality of the Right Honourable gentleman as the cause of almost all the misfortunes that had been brought upon the country; so that, if he were to be asked who was the person who of all others had most contributed to the misfortune of the American War, he should be tempted so say, the Right Honourable General; and if, again, he should be asked who was the man with the most upright intentions, and who had pursued measures with the most disinterested integrity, he should say with much pleasure, the Right Honourable General." Nothing appears more paradoxical, yet nothing is nearer the truth than this judgment.*

It might have been pretended that duties on commodities came under the head of regulations of trade. But no such excuse can be given for the duties in question; they were taxes on British manufactures, and as such in contradiction to all the prevailing notions on trade.

In September, 1767, Charles Townshend, the author of these unhappy measures, died; and on the 1st of December Frederick Lord North became Chancellor of the Exchequer. The new Minister had at least no parental fondness for the absurd taxes lately imposed. Accordingly the very next year the Cabinet determined to consider of the repeal of these duties as contrary to the principles of commerce. On the 1st

* Fox's " Speeches," vol. ii. p. 80.

of May, 1768, the Duke of Grafton's Cabinet met for this purpose.

It was readily agreed that the duties on glass, paper, painters' colours, and lead should be repealed. But there remained the duty on tea, yielding about 16,000l. a year. It is hardly to be believed that, for the sake of obtaining a nominal revenue and preserving a nominal power over the taxation of America, this paltry tax was retained. What makes the matter still more extraordinary is that there was a division in the Cabinet; that the tea duty was maintained by a majority of one; and that the Prime Minister and the leader of the House of Commons were in the minority.

To make the course of repealing the duties the more ungracious, it was resolved to conceal the decision till the next year.

In 1769 all these duties except the tea duty were repealed.

In 1770, however, a new device was imagined. Lord North, now Chancellor of the Exchequer, proposed that the duty on tea exported to the colonies should be entirely remitted, leaving only the duty to be paid in America. The East India Company, at the same time, instead of selling at the India House to the exporting merchants, who would have sent the tea in mixed cargoes in proportion to the demand, undertook to export the tea themselves to certain consignees in America, who were to pay the duties. The tea ships, consigned to known and unpopular persons, were the red flag at the sight of which the American bull was inflamed to fury. Whether Lord North intended this provocation, that he might rouse and subdue resistance, or whether this measure, like the rest, was merely a piece of folly, cannot certainly be known : the latter is the most probable solution. Let it be noted and remembered, however, that for 100,000*l.* a year of revenue, George Grenville provoked America, and that for 16,000*l.* a year of revenue Lord North lost America.

When men are roused to suspicion, and put into ill-humour, every little circumstance augments their suspicions and embitters their temper. It so happened that in Mr. Grenville's time an alteration had been made in the Mutiny Act, by which the Provincial Assemblies were ordered to provide vinegar and salt to the soldiers of the King's army. In ordinary times this enactment might have passed as an undoubted exercise of the supreme authority; and it was obvious that, as no money was to go to the Exchequer, no tax was intended. The saving, if saving there were, must have been trifling. But, in the existing state of irritation, the colonies resisted this new enactment on the part of the Parliament of Great Britain.

Lord Shelburne, in a letter to Lord Chatham, says of this Act : "It was first suggested by the military, and intended to give a power of billeting in private houses, as was done in the war. It was altered by the merchants' agents, who substituted empty houses, provincial barracks, and barns in their room, undertaking that the Assembly should supply them with the additional necessaries; and it passed, I believe, without that superintendence or attentive examination on the part of Government which is so wanting in all cases where necessity requires something different from the general principles of the constitution."* Lord Chatham had said most truly, in a letter of an earlier

* "Chatham Correspondence," vol. iii. p. 208.

date: "It is a literal truth to say, that the Stamp Act, of most unhappy memory, has frighted those irritable and umbrageous people quite out of their senses."*

British America was in this manner thrown into a fever of discontent, almost amounting to disaffection; yet some men, of whom George Washington was the most eminent, still looked to a redress of grievances, and preserved their loyalty to Great Britain. Others, of whom Benjamin Franklin was the most able, favoured every step which might lead to separation. The great mass felt themselves aggrieved, but were convinced of their inability to cope with a power which had so recently stripped France of her colonies, and sustained Frederick of Prussia on his throne. Thus the allegiance of America might still have been retained. The illness of Lord Chatham, the fickleness and want of principle of Charles Townshend, the weakness of the Duke of Grafton, the vacillation of General Conway, and, lastly, the folly of Lord North, were the immediate causes of the American War. But before the contest actually commenced, the changes which had taken place in the British Councils had entirely altered their complexion, and restored to the Tory party a predominance which they had lost since the death of Queen Anne.

In the autumn of 1768 Lord Shelburne was dismissed, and Lord Chatham resigned. At the end of 1769 the Bedford party had made their peace with the Duke of Grafton; Lord Gower became Lord President of the Council; Lord Weymouth Secretary of State. This party had been always strongly opposed to the American pretensions, and the substitution of Weymouth for Conway was unfavourable to the prospects of peace.

* "Chatham Correspondence," vol. iii. p. 193.

A few months afterwards, at the beginning of the Session of 1770, Lord Camden, who disagreed with the Duke of Grafton on the subject of Wilkes's expulsion, was deprived of the Great Seal.

On the 29th of January, 1770, the Duke of Grafton himself resigned, and was succeeded on the 30th by Lord North.

Frederick, Lord North, the eldest son of the Earl of Guildford, inherited the Tory politics which, in the days of Charles II., had placed his ancestor in the highest ranks of the law and of the State. It was his boast in the House of Commons, that since he had had a seat there he had voted against all popular, and in favour of all unpopular measures. His person was awkward, but his mind full of readiness and resource. His wit was ever at command, his temper never ruffled; since the death of Charles Townshend he had held the seals of Chancellor of the Exchequer, and had acquired a considerable knowledge of finance. His eloquence, wit, good humour, and quickness made him an admirable leader of the House of Commons, and enabled him to preserve the affections and confidence of the majority amid the violent tempest of the State, against Lord Chatham, Burke, and Fox, in spite of the grossest errors of policy, and notwithstanding the overwhelming calamities of a disastrous war.

His good humour and readiness were of admirable service to him when the invectives of his opponents would have discomfited a more serious Minister. He often indulged in a real or seeming slumber; an opponent in the midst of an invective exclaimed, "Even now, in the midst of these perils, the noble Lord is asleep."—"I wish to God I was," rejoined Lord North. Alderman Sawbridge, having accompanied the presentation of a petition from Billingsgate with accusations of more than ordinary virulence, Lord North began his reply in the following words: "I cannot deny that the Hon. Alderman speaks not only the sentiments, but the very language of his constituents."

Lord North, as a minister, had the weakness of being always ready to surrender his own judgment to that of others. The King, whose will was much stronger than that of Lord North, though his understanding was very inferior, reaped the benefit of this defect, and always made his Minister yield to his own narrow views of national policy.

Such was the state of American and domestic politics when Mr. Fox first took an active and independent part in the House of Commons.

CHAPTER V.

THE coming of the tea-ships was preceded by the most ominous portents. In Philadelphia handbills were circulated warning the people against the attempt of the British Government to poison them, and advising the pilots to make the river Delaware unsafe for those who should approach the port. At New York the people were called upon by public notice to resist the attempt to impose fetters upon them. The tea was landed only by means of a guard of soldiers, and shut up in a warehouse, from which no one was allowed to take it out.

The proceedings at Boston were more serious. The consignees were threatened with violence, and the tea-ships were ordered by a popular meeting to leave the port. As this was not permitted, either by the consignees or the governor, a number of men, disguised as Mohawks, boarded the ships in the harbour, and without doing violence to the crews, or any person on board, threw the tea-chests into the sea.

This outrage was committed at the end of December, 1773; the news reached England in March, 1774. A message was immediately sent to the two Houses of Parliament, and both Houses readily promised to assist the

Crown in providing for the due execution of the laws, and securing the dependence of the colonies upon the Crown and Parliament of Great Britain.

The Minister then proceeded to introduce his measures. One was a bill for levying a fine on the town of Boston, by way of compensation for the tea destroyed, and taking away the privileges of the port till the Crown should be pleased to restore them. Another bill suspended free government in the province of Massachusetts Bay, and gave to the Crown the power of appointing a legislative council and judges during pleasure. This was, in fact, a bill for abrogating the charter of Charles II., which had been confirmed and regranted by William III. A measure more subversive of freedom, more contrary to all constitutional principles, and more likely to excite America against imperial authority, could not well be framed.

On the Boston Port Bill Mr. Fox spoke only once, and that upon the clause giving the Crown the power of restoring the privileges of the port. But some members of the House of Commons, who had allowed the Boston Port Bill to pass without a division, thought it would be right to accompany coercion with conciliation. Mr. Rose Fuller, in compliance with their wish, proposed the repeal of the tea duty. On this occasion Mr. Burke made his famous speech on American taxation. In the same debate Mr. Fox, speaking for the first time on behalf of freedom, is said to have expressed himself to the following effect :—

" Let us consider, sir, what is the state of America with regard to this country ; the Americans will become useful subjects, if you use them with that temper and lenity which you ought to do. When the Stamp Act was repealed, murmurs ceased, and quiet succeeded. Taxes have produced a contrary behaviour; quiet has been succeeded by riots and disturbances. Here is an absolute dereliction of the authority of this country. It has been said that America is not represented in this House, but the Americans are fully as virtually taxed, as virtually represented. A tax can only be laid for three purposes; the first for a commercial regulation, the second for a revenue, and the third for asserting your right. As to the two first, it has clearly been denied that it is for either; as to the latter, it is only done with a view to irritate and declare war against the Americans, which, if you persist in, I am clearly of opinion you will effect, or force them into open rebellion." *

Mr. Rigby having expressed an opinion that when tranquillity was restored, the Americans might be taxed, Mr. Fox said :—

"Sir, I am glad to hear from the right honourable gentleman who spoke last, that now is not the time to tax America; that the only time for doing that is, when all these disturbances are quelled, and the people are returned to their duty; so, I find, that taxes are to be the reward of obedience; and the Americans, who are considered to have been in open rebellion, are to be rewarded by acquiescing in their measures. When will be the time that America ought to have heavy taxes laid upon her? The right honourable gentleman tells you that that time is when the Americans are returned to peace and quietness. The right honourable gentleman tells us also, that we have a right to tax Ireland; however I may agree with him in regard to the principle, sure I am that it would not be policy to exercise it. I believe we have no more right to tax the one than the other. I believe America is wrong in resisting this

* Fox's "Speeches," vol. i. p. 28.

country, with regard to its legislative authority. It was an old opinion, and I believe a very true one, that there was a dispensing power in the Crown ; but whenever that dispensing power was pretended to be exercised, it was always rejected and opposed to the utmost, because it operated on the subject, to the detriment of his property and liberty. But, sir, there has been a constant line of conduct practised in this country towards America, consisting of violence and weakness. I wish such measures to be discontinued; nor can I think that the Stamp Act would have been submitted to without resistance, if the administration had not been changed. The bill before you is not what you want; it will irritate the minds of the people, but does not correct the deficiencies of the government of Massachusetts Bay."*

Let us now see what effect these violent proceedings had in America. The people of Boston held a town meeting, at which they agreed to call upon the inhabitants of the colonies of North America to suspend all commercial intercourse with Great Britain either by exports or imports. In Virginia some of the more active men assembled, and considered what they could do to rouse the people to a sense of their danger, and kindle among them a spirit of resistance. They looked over a copy of Rushworth, and imitating the old Puritan precedents, ordered a general fast.†

The Boston Port Act was to come into operation on the 1st of June; the House of Burgesses of Virginia set apart the 1st of June "as a day of fasting, humiliation, and prayer, to implore the Divine interposition for averting the heavy calamity which threatened destruction to their civil rights and the evils of civil war, and to give them one heart

* Fox's "Speeches," vol. i. p. 29.   † "Memoirs of Jefferson."

and mind firmly to oppose, by all just and proper means, every injury to American rights." The Governor dissolved the Assembly.

On the next morning, however, the members of Assembly, nowise terrified, met at a tavern, to the number of eighty-nine, and resolved to establish committees to correspond with all the American colonies, with a view of appointing deputies to meet in a general Congress. This was the first resolution for that purpose.

Among those who went to church and fasted on the 1st of June, was George Washington. As he soon became the hero of the American revolution; as among the great men of modern times, his fame, if not the most splendid, shines with the purest light; we may here pause to consider his origin, his past career, and his present object.

The family of Washington held, from the year 1538, the Manor of Sulgrave, in Northamptonshire.* Two brothers, of the name of John and Lawrence Washington, emigrated to Virginia about the year 1657. One of the family, Sir Henry Washington, was renowned for defending Worcester against the Parliamentary forces. Sir William Washington, the elder brother of John and Lawrence, married a half-sister of George Villiers, Duke of Buckingham. We may conclude from these facts that the Washingtons belonged to that class of country gentlemen from which sprang John Hampden and Francis Pym, and in a later age, Robert Walpole, Earl of Orford, and William Pitt, Earl of Chatham. We may conclude, also, that the Washingtons, who went, in 1657, to the aristocratic colony of Virginia, were Royalists, vanquished by the Parliamentary forces, but dissatisfied with the rule of Cromwell. The grandson of

* Sparks's " Life of Washington."

John Washington, Augustine by name, married twice. By his first wife he had one son, who survived him. His second wife, Mary Bull, was the mother of George, born on the 22nd of February, 1732. Augustine died on the 22nd of April, 1743, at the age of forty-nine, when George was eleven years old.

George Washington was brought up in a manner rather hardy and vigorous, than literary and scientific. He went to a common school, where he was famous for running, jumping, tossing the bar, and being the leader in mimic fights and boyish sports. He never learnt Latin and Greek, and it was only during the War of Independence that he acquired so much of French as enabled him to read, but not to write or speak that language.

When he grew up, he found himself the owner of a small estate, which was soon increased by the death of his half-brother. He commanded a company of Militia, devoted himself to farming, and was much esteemed for his good sense, integrity, and public spirit. The hostilities which broke out in 1756, between England and France, gave him an apprenticeship in the art of war. In the capacity of aide-de-camp to General Braddock, he was present at the disastrous action of Monongahela, and almost alone of that detachment showed presence of mind and intrepidity. The Indians, seeing him unhurt amid their balls, thought he bore a charmed life. In the following year he contributed much to the capture of Fort Duquesne, the name of which was changed to Fort Pitt. He afterwards retired to his country house, which had been called Mount Vernon in honour of the admiral of that name, married, and led the quiet life of a farmer.

The passing of the Stamp Act roused, as its repeal

soothed, his indignation. But when the duty on tea revived that dormant quarrel, he took a decided part in the cause of his country.

On the 5th of September, 1774, the first Congress of America, consisting of delegates from the different colonies, met at Philadelphia. On the part of Virginia, the members named were Randolph, Lee, Washington, Patrick Henry, Bland, Harrison, and Pendleton.

This Congress framed and promulgated a petition to the King, an address to the people of Great Britain, an address to the inhabitants of Quebec, and a memorial to the inhabitants of the British colonies.

In the petition to the King, the colonists affirmed, " that a necessity has been alleged of taking our property from us without our consent, to defray the charge of the administration of justice, the support of civil government, and the defence, protection, and security of the colonies. But we beg leave to inform your Majesty," they went on to say, " that such provision has been, and will be, made for defraying the two first articles, as has been, and shall be judged by the legislatures of the several colonies, just and suitable to their respective circumstances; and for the defence, protection, and security of the colonies, their militias, if properly regulated, as they earnestly desire may be immediately done, would be fully sufficient, at least in times of peace; and in case of war, your faithful colonists will be ready and willing, as they ever have been, when constitutionally required, to demonstrate their loyalty to your Majesty, by exerting their most strenuous efforts in granting supplies and raising forces. . . . . We ask but for peace, liberty, and safety. We wish not a diminution of the prerogative; nor do we solicit the grant of any new right in our favour; your royal authority over us, and our connexion with Great Britain we shall always carefully and zealously endeavour to support and maintain."

This address, drawn up by Dickinson, was agreeable to the feelings of the moderate party in the Assembly, whose support the rest were most anxious to obtain. It did not, therefore, fully represent the sentiments, although it conveyed the general sense of the Assembly. When the reading of it was finished, Mr. Dickinson said: "Mr. President, there is but one word in that address which I do not like, and that is the word 'Congress.'" Mr. Benjamin Harrison immediately rose and said: "Mr. President, there is but one word in that address which I like, and that is the word 'Congress.'"*

In the address to the people of Great Britain, the Congress said: "You restrained our trade in every way that could conduce to your emolument; you exercised unbounded sovereignty over the sea; you named the ports and nations to which alone our merchandize should be carried, and with whom alone we should trade; and though some of these restrictions were grievous, we nevertheless did not complain; we looked up to you as our parent state, to which we were bound by the strongest ties, and were happy in being instrumental to your prosperity and your grandeur."

In the address to the people of Great Britain was this remarkable statement: "You are told that we are seditious, impatient of government, desirous of independency. Be assured that these are not facts, but calumnies."

In a declaration made at the same time, the Congress promulgated their determination not to import any goods from Great Britain, not to purchase any slave, not to be con-

* "Life of Jefferson."

cerned themselves, or sell their commodities to any who were concerned in the slave trade.

Washington, in a private letter to Captain Mackenzie, an officer of the British army, then stationed at Boston, says: "Although you are taught to believe that the people of Massachusetts are rebellious, setting up for independency and what not, give me leave, my good friend, to tell you that you are abused, grossly abused. This I advance with a degree of confidence and boldness which may claim your belief, having better opportunities of knowing the real sentiments of the people you are among, from the leaders of them, in opposition to the present measures of the administration, than you have from those whose business it is, not to disclose truths, but to misrepresent facts, in order to justify to the world as much as possible their conduct. Give me leave to add (and I think I can announce it as a fact) that it is not the wish or interest of that government, or any other upon this continent, separately or collectively, to set up for independence; but this you may at the same time rely on, that none of them will ever submit to the loss of those valuable rights and privileges which are essential to the happiness of every free state, and without which, life, liberty, and property are rendered wholly insecure. These, sir, being certain consequences which must naturally result from the late acts of Parliament relative to America in general and the government of Massachusetts Bay in particular, is it to be wondered at, I repeat, that men who wish to avert the impending blow should attempt to oppose it in its progress, or prepare for their defence if it cannot be averted? Surely I may be allowed to answer in the negative? And, again, give me leave to add, as my opinion, that more blood will be spilled on this occasion, if the Ministry are determined to push matters to extremity, than history has ever yet furnished instances of in the annals of North America, and such a vital wound will be given to the peace of this great country as time itself cannot cure or eradicate the remembrance of."*

This seems to have been a fair opportunity for effecting a reconciliation with America. Had the obnoxious acts been repealed—had the troops been withdrawn from Boston—had the right of taxation for imperial purposes been renounced at the commencement of 1775, as was afterwards done at Lord North's own suggestion, in 1778—had the judges been appointed during good behaviour, and the Courts of Admiralty been re-modelled,—there can be little doubt that the majority of the colonists would have been reconciled to British supremacy. It is even doubtful whether it would have been necessary to repeal the Declaratory Act. But the moment was lost, never to return. The King and his counsellers were equally infatuated, blinded by wilful pride and the high maxims of Tory prerogative.

Instead, therefore, of endeavouring to heal the wounds of the colonies, the King's Ministers, intent only on their own power, proceeded to dissolve the Parliament. The reasons for this measure, which was afterwards arraigned by Lord Chatham, are thus explained and justified by Lord Suffolk, then Secretary of State: "As to the first (the measure of dissolving Parliament), he avowed himself to be one of the principal advisers, as he foresaw from the beginning that all the steps taken by the Americans, in Congress and elsewhere, would be to influence the general election, by creating jealousies, fears, and prejudices among the mercantile and trading part of the nation ; that he was happy the ideas he

* Sparks's Washington," pp. 130, 131.

had expressed had prevailed, by which means those sinister designs were prevented from taking effect," &c.   In other words, the Ministers were afraid of the effect which might be produced by the knowledge of facts relating to America among the mercantile and trading parts of the community, and the opposition which might thence arise to the Ministerial plan of coercion.   Lord Suffolk's foresight was fully justified; the abrupt dissolution prevented any influence being exercised by American affairs on the temper of the elections, and a Parliament was returned prepared to enter with alacrity the dreadful portal of civil war.

CHAPTER VI.

NEW PARLIAMENT—PUBLIC AFFAIRS, 1774-5—COMMENCEMENT
OF CIVIL WAR IN AMERICA.

THE new Parliament met for the first time on the 29th of November, 1774. The King declared in his speech his firm resolution to withstand every attempt to weaken or impair the supreme authority of the Legislature over all the dominions of the Crown. The Duke of Richmond moved an amendment in the House of Lords, which was rejected by 63 to 13. Lord John Cavendish moved a similar amendment in the House of Commons, requesting information, and promising serious consideration and advice. This amendment was rejected by 264 to 73. Thus the nation had the satisfaction of finding that it had a strong Government. But a strong Government which overleaps wisdom and violates justice is one of the worst evils that can befal a country. Parliament adjourned before Christmas to the 19th of January. On the 20th of that month Lord Chatham moved an address to the Crown. He began his speech by stating the purport of his motion. It was to pray that "it may graciously please His Majesty that immediate orders be despatched to General Gage for removing His Majesty's forces from the town of Boston as soon as the rigour of the season, and other circumstances indispensable to the safety and accommodation of the said troops, may render the same practicable."

In advising this step he said :—

"When I urge this measure of recalling the troops from Boston, I urge it on this pressing principle, that it is necessarily preparatory to the restoration of peace and the establishment of your prosperity. It will then appear that you are disposed to treat amicably and equitably, and to consider, revise, and repeal, if it should be found necessary, as I affirm it will, those violent acts and declarations which have disseminated confusion throughout your empire.

"Resistance to your acts was necessary, as it was just; and your vain declarations of the omnipotence of Parliament, and your imperious doctrines of the necessity of submission, will be found equally impotent to convince or to enslave your fellow subjects in America, who feel that tyranny, whether *ambitioned* by an individual part of the legislature, or the bodies who compose it, is equally intolerable to British subjects.

"I remember, some years ago, when the repeal of the Stamp Act was in agitation, conversing in a friendly confidence with a person of undoubted respect and authenticity on that subject; and he assured me, with a certainty which his judgment and opportunity gave him, that these were the prevalent and steady principles of America; that you might destroy their towns, and cut them off from the superfluities, perhaps the conveniences, of life, but that they were prepared to despise your power, and would not lament their loss whilst they have—what, my Lord?—their *woods* and their *liberty*. The name of my authority, if I am called upon, will authenticate the opinion irrefragably.*

* It was Dr. Franklin.

" If illegal violences have been, as is said, committed in America, prepare the way, open the door of possibility, for acknowledgment and satisfaction; but proceed not to such coercion, such proscription; cease your indiscriminate inflictions; amerce not thirty thousand; oppress not three millions for the fault of forty or fifty individuals. Such severity of injustice must for ever render incurable the wounds you have already given your colonies; you irritate them to unappeasable rancour. What though you march from town to town, and from province to province; though you should be able to enforce a temporary and local submission, which I only suppose, not admit, how will you be able to secure the obedience of the country you leave behind you in your progress to grasp the dominion of eighteen hundred miles of continent, populous in numbers, possessing valour, liberty, and resistance?

"This resistance to your arbitrary system of taxation might have been foreseen: it was obvious from the nature of things and of mankind; above all, from the Whiggish spirit flourishing in that country. The spirit which now resists your taxation in America is the same which formerly opposed loans, benevolences, and ship-money in England; the same spirit which called all England *on its legs*, and by the Bill of Rights vindicated the English Constitution; the same spirit which established the great fundamental, essential maxim of your liberties, *that no subject of England shall be taxed but by his own consent.*

" This glorious spirit of Whiggism animates three millions in America, who prefer poverty with liberty to gilded chains and sordid affluence, and who will die in defence of their rights as men—as freemen. What shall oppose this spirit, aided by the congenial flame glowing in the breasts of every Whig in England, to the amount, I hope, of double the American numbers? Ireland they have to a man. In that country, joined as it is with the cause of the colonies, and placed at their head, the distinction I contend for is and must be observed. This country superintends and controls their trade and navigation; but they *tax themselves*. And this distinction between external and internal control is sacred and insurmountable; it is involved in the abstract nature of things. Property is private, individual, absolute. Trade is an extended and complicated consideration; it reaches as far as ships can sail or winds can blow; it is a great and various machine. To regulate the numberless movements of its several parts, and combine them into effect, for the good of the whole, requires the superintending wisdom and energy of the supreme power in the empire. But this supreme power has no effect towards internal taxation; for it does not exist in that relation; there is no such thing, *no such idea in this Constitution, as a supreme power operating upon property*. Let this distinction, then, remain for ever ascertained—taxation is theirs, commercial regulation is ours. As an American I would recognise to England her supreme right of regulating commerce and navigation; as an Englishman by birth and principle I recognise to the Americans their supreme unalienable right in their property—a right which they are justified in the defence of to the last extremity. To maintain this principle is the common cause of the Whigs on the other side of the Atlantic and on this. ' 'Tis liberty to liberty engaged,' that they will defend themselves, their families, and their country. In this great cause they are immovably allied; it is the alliance of God and nature—immutable, eternal—fixed as the firmament of heaven.

"To such united force, what force shall be opposed?—What, my lords? A few regiments in America, and seventeen or eighteen thousand men at home!—The idea is too ridiculous to take up a moment of your lordships' time. Nor can such a national union be resisted by the tricks of office or ministerial manœuvre. Laying of papers on your table, or counting numbers on a division, will not avert or postpone the hour of danger; it must arrive, my lords, unless these fatal acts are done away; it must arrive in all its horrors; and then these boastful Ministers, spite of all their confidence and all their manœuvres, will be forced to hide their heads. They will be forced to a disgraceful abandonment of their present measures and principles, which they avow but cannot defend; measures which they presume to attempt, but cannot hope to effectuate. They cannot, my lords, they cannot stir a step; they have not a *move* left; they are *check-mated*.

"But it is not repealing this act of Parliament, it is not repealing a *piece of parchment*, that can restore America to our bosom; you must repeal her fears and her resentments; and you may then hope for her love and gratitude. But now, insulted with an armed force posted at Boston, irritated with a hostile array before her eyes, her concessions, if you could force them, would be suspicious and insecure; they will be *irato animo;* they will not be the sound honourable passions of freemen, they will be the dictates of fear and extortions of force. But it is more than evident that you cannot force them, united as they are, to your unworthy terms of submission : it is impossible; and when I hear General Gage censured for inactivity, I must retort with indignation on those whose intemperate measures and improvident councils have betrayed him into his present situation. His situation reminds me, my lords, of the answer of a French general in the civil wars of France. Monsieur Condé was opposed to Monsieur Turenne; he was asked how it happened that he did not take his adversary prisoner, as he was often very near him : 'J'ai peur,' replied Condé, very honestly, 'j'ai peur qu'il ne me prenne'—'I'm afraid he'll take me.'

"When your lordships look at the papers transmitted us from America—when you consider their decency, firmness, and wisdom,—you cannot but respect their cause, and wish to make it your own. For myself I must declare and avow that, in all my reading and observation—and history has been my favourite study—I have read Thucydides, and have studied and admired the master states of the world— that for solidity of reasoning, force of sagacity, and wisdom of conclusion, under such a complication of difficult cir- cumstances, no nation or body of men can stand in pre- ference to the general Congress at Philadelphia. I trust it is obvious to your lordships that all attempts to impose servitude upon such men, to establish despotism over such a mighty continental *nation*, must be vain, must be fatal. We shall be *forced ultimately to retract ;* let us retract while we can, not when we must. I say we must necessarily undo these violent, oppressive acts; *they must be repealed —you will repeal them ; I pledge myself for it, that you will in the end repeal them ; I stake my reputation on it, I will consent to be taken for an idiot if they are not finally repealed.* Avoid, then, this humiliating, disgraceful necessity. With a dignity becoming your exalted situation, make the first advances to concord, to peace, and happiness; for *that* is your true dignity, to act with prudence and justice. That *you* should first concede is obvious, from sound and rational policy. Concession comes with better grace and more salutary effect from superior power; it reconciles superiority of power with the feelings of men, and establishes solid confidence on the foundations of affection and gratitude. So thought a wise poet and a wise man in political sagacity —the friend of Mæcenas, and the eulogist of Augustus. To him, the adopted son and successor of the first Cæsar, to him, the master of the world, he wisely urged this conduct of prudence and dignity: 'Tuque prior, tu parce, projice tela manu.'

"Every motive, therefore, of justice and of policy, of dignity and of prudence, urges you to allay the ferment in America by a removal of your troops from Boston, by a repeal of your acts of Parliament, and by a demonstration of amicable dispositions towards your colonies. On the other hand, every danger and every hazard impend to deter you from perseverance in your present ruinous measures. Foreign war hanging over your heads by a slight and brittle thread. France and Spain watching your conduct, and waiting for the maturity of your errors; with a vigilant eye to America, and the temper of your colonies, more than to our own concerns, be they what they may."*

Besides a report of this magnificent speech from Mr. Hugh Boyd, we have two accounts of it—one from a very young, and one from a very old observer, Mr. William Pitt and Dr. Franklin. Mr. Pitt says: "Nothing prevented his speech from being the most forcible that can be imagined, and administration fully felt it. The matter and manner both were striking, far beyond what I can express. . . . Lord Suffolk I cannot say answer'd him, but spoke after him. He was a contemptible orator indeed,

* "Corr. of Lord Chatham," vol. iv. p. 378. "Parl. Hist."

with paltry matter, and a whining delivery. Lord Shelburne spoke well, and supported the motion warmly. Lord Camden was *supreme*, with only *one* exception, and as zealous as possible. Lord Rockingham spoke shortly, but sensibly; and the Duke of Richmond well, and with much candour as to the Declaratory Act. Upon the whole it was a noble debate. The Ministry were violent beyond expectation, almost to madness. Instead of recalling the troops now there, they talked of sending more,"* &c.

Dr. Franklin, in a letter to Lord Stanhope, says: " Dr. Franklin is filled with admiration of that truly great man ! He has seen, in the course of life, sometimes eloquence without wisdom, and often wisdom without eloquence; in the present instance he sees both united, and both, as he thinks, in the highest degree possible."†

The Lords rejected the motion by 68 to 18.‡ A petition from the merchants of London having been presented to the House of Commons, was referred by Ministers to a separate committee instead of the Committee on American Affairs. The merchants complained, or rather Mr. Burke complained in their name, of being sent to this "committee of oblivion." Mr. Fox spoke warmly on this occasion. He arraigned, in the severest terms, the acts of the last Parliament, as framed on false information, conceived in weakness and ignorance, and

* "Correspondence of Lord Chatham," vol. iv. p. 376.   † Ibid. p. 386.
‡ The names of the minority are worth preserving. They were :—
 Dukes—Cumberland, Richmond, Portland, Manchester.
 Marquis—Rockingham.
 Earls—Abingdon, Chatham, Fitzwilliam, Spencer, Stanhope, Tankerville, Thanet.
 Bishop—Exeter.
 Barons—Camden, Grosvenor, Ponsonby, Sondes, Wycombe (Lord Shelburne).

executed with negligence. "We were promised that, on the very appearance of troops, all was to be tranquillity at Boston; yet, so far from subduing the spirit of that people, these troops were, by the neglect of those who sent them, reduced to the most shameful situation, and dishonourably intrenched within the lines of circumvallation, which a necessary precaution for their own safety obliged them to form. He said that the contrary effect of what the Minister had promised was foretold; but that the Minister, forsooth, in his usual negligence, avowed that, when he was pursuing a measure of the last degree of importance, he thought it would be blameable in him so much as to inquire what were to be the effects of his measures. He believed it was the first time any minister dared to avow that he thought it his duty not to inquire into the effects of his measures! But it was suitable to the whole of the conduct of the noble lord, who had no system or plan, no knowledge of business. He had often declared his unfitness for his station, and he agreed that his conduct justified his declaration, and that the country was incensed and on the point of being involved in a civil war by his incapacity. He pledged himself to join Mr. Burke in pursuing the noble lord, and bringing him to answer for the mischiefs occasioned by his negligence, his inconsistency, and his incapacity; he said not this from resentment, but from a conviction of the destructive proceedings of a bad minister."

Afterwards, in reply to Lord North, he said : "That my private resentments have not influenced my public conduct will be readily believed when I assert that I might long since have justly charged the noble Lord with the most unexampled treachery and falsehood." Here Mr. Fox was called to order, and the House grew clamorous. He sat down twice or thrice, and on rising each time repeated the same words; but at length, assuring the House he would abstain from everything personal, he was permitted to proceed. He then repeated his former charges of negligence, incapacity, and inconsistency, and added that, though he at one time approved of part of the noble lord's conduct, he never approved of the whole. Lord North, in the course of his speech, observed that Mr. Burke and Mr. Fox constantly made a point, not only of attacking but even of threatening him. As to general charges, he could only answer them in general terms; and when that black, bitter, trying day should come, which had been prophecied by one of those gentlemen, and he should bring any particular charge against him, he trusted he should be able to give it a particular answer. As to the other gentleman, who found so many causes of censure, and who disclaimed all resentment, he was sure, though the honourable gentleman now discovered in him so much incapacity and negligence, there was a time when he approved of, at least, some part of his conduct.

On the 2nd of February the whole question, in its breadth and extent, was debated.

On this day Lord North moved an address, which ended with these words: " We consider it as our indispensable duty humbly to beseech his Majesty that his Majesty will take the most effectual measures to enforce due obedience to the laws of the supreme legislature; and that we beg leave, in the most solemn manner, to assure his Majesty that it is our fixed resolution, at the hazard of our lives and properties, to stand by his Majesty against all rebellious attempts in the maintenance of the just rights of his Majesty and the two Houses of Parliament." Some vague promises of attending to real grievances preceded this wager of battle.

Mr. Fox, upon this, moved to leave out nearly the whole address, and to substitute the following words : " But deploring that the information which the papers have afforded, serves only to convince this House that the measures taken by his Majesty's servants tend rather to widen than to heal the unhappy differences which have so long subsisted between Great Britain and America, and praying a speedy alteration of the same." This amendment led to two nights of debate. Of Mr. Fox's speech we have no other record than a short notice in the " Parliamentary History," and the following sentence in a letter of Mr. Gibbon : " The principal men, both days, were Fox and Wedderburne on the opposite sides : the latter displayed his usual talents ; the former, taking the vast compass of the question before us, discovered powers for regular debate which neither his friends hoped nor his enemies dreaded."*

The numbers were,—

For Lord North 304

For Mr. Fox 105

Majority 199

It would be very desirable to ascertain how far this great majority represented the opinion of the country. We have not many indications to guide us. The general election of the previous year was conducted in a state of ignorance and apathy upon this subject, hardly conceivable at the present day. Wilkes and the Middlesex election absorbed nearly all the popular sympathy in the country. Even Lord Chatham, in 1767, had thought more of India than of

* " Miscellaneous Works," vol. i. p. 489.

America. The leading statesmen, if statesmen they could be called, who belonged to the Ministry, had a foolish contempt for the Americans, and openly taunted them for cowardice.

Lord Sandwich, in the debate of March 16th, 1775, said: "The noble Lord (Lord Camden) mentions the impracticability of conquering America; I cannot think the noble lord can be serious on this matter. Suppose the colonies do abound in men, what does that signify? They are raw, undisciplined, cowardly men. I wish, instead of 40,000 or 50,000 of these brave fellows, they would produce, in the field at least 200,000; the more the better, the easier would be the conquest," &c. He continued, after relating an anecdote of Sir Peter Warren: "Believe me, my lords, the very sound of a cannon would carry them off, in his (Sir Peter's words), as fast as their feet would carry them." Such was the language of a chief counsellor of the Crown!

Yet suspicion began to arise in some quarters that our quarrel was not only unjust, but likely to be unprofitable. Lord Camden, writing to Lord Chatham in February, 1775, says: "I am grieved to observe that the landed interest is almost altogether anti-American, though the common people hold the war in abhorrence, and the merchants and tradesmen, for obvious reasons, are altogether, against it. Nevertheless, my opinion of the justice and the success of it is precisely the same, and does not yield to the majority within doors, or the powerful assent without."*

Thus, parties were divided nearly as they had been at the end of the reign of Queen Anne: the Court and the landed

* Chatham's "Correspondence," vol. iv. p. 401.

gentry, with a majority in the House of Commons, were with the Tories; the trading interest and the popular feeling with the Whigs.

On the 1st of February Lord Chatham, after making an eloquent speech, laid on the table a bill which he called a Provisional bill for settling the troubles in America. : By this bill he proposed to repeal all the acts of Parliament regarding America, passed since 1764, and explicitly to renounce, on the part of Great Britain, any right of taxation; declaring and enacting that no tax, or tallage, or other charge for the revenue, should be levied from any body of British freemen in America without the consent of its own Representative Assembly. The powers of the Admiralty and Vice-Admiralty Courts were to be restrained within their ancient limits; judges in America, as in England, were thenceforth to hold their offices during good behaviour. On the other hand, the dependency of the colonies upon the British Crown, and their subordination to the British Parliament in all matters touching the general weal of the whole empire, and especially in the regulation of trade, was explicitly declared. A Congress was to be convoked for the 9th of May, for the purposes of supplying the expenses of civil government, and of making a perpetual free grant to the King, to be applied to diminish the charge of the National Debt.

Lord Dartmouth was disposed to allow Parliament time for consideration, but Lord Sandwich and Lord Gower declared for the immediate rejection of the bill. Lord Dartmouth, with some embarrassment, retracted his candour. Lord Chatham, in his reply, said, with severity and with truth : " Such are your well-known characters and abilities, that sure I am, that any plan of reconciliation, however moderate, wise, and feasible, must fail in your hands. Who, then, can wonder that you should put a negative on any measure which must annihilate your power, deprive you of your emoluments, and at once reduce you to that state of insignificance for which God and Nature designed you?"

The bill was rejected by 61 to 32.

On the 10th of February, 1775, Lord North brought in a bill to restrain the trade of the thirteen Colonies, therein named, with Great Britain and the West Indies, and restraining their fishery in Newfoundland and other places. Some objections having been taken to this bill, on the ground that it would produce a famine, Mr. Dundas, Solicitor-General for Scotland, expressed his fears that it would not have that effect. At this moment, while the system of terror seemed to be the deliberate choice of the Government, Lord North, who was perpetually oscillating between tyranny and weakness, produced his so-called conciliatory propositions. They were to the effect that, when the governor, council, and assembly of any colony shall make provision, "according to the condition, circumstances, and situation of such province or colony for contributing their proportion to the common defence," and shall provide for the civil government and administration of justice in each colony, then, "if such proposal shall be approved by his Majesty and the two Houses of Parliament," the taxes imposed by Parliament, except such as it might be expedient to levy for the regulation of commerce, should be repealed. Although nothing could be more futile and more delusive than this proposal, the very notion of conciliation raised a storm among the adherents of Government. Gibbon writes to Mr. Holroyd: "We go on with America, if we can be said to go on, for on Monday a conciliatory motion of allowing the colonies to tax themselves, was introduced by Lord North, in the midst of lives and fortunes, war and famine. We went into the House in confusion, every moment expecting that the Bedfords would fly into rebellion against those measures. Lord North rose six times to appease them, but all in vain, till at length Sir Gilbert declared for administration, and the troops rallied under their proper standard."

Lord North was, as Horace Walpole calls him, the "ostensible Minister." The real Minister was the King, and Sir Gilbert Elliot, the organ of the King's party, was obeyed, as conveying the King's wishes. The Bedfords consisted of Lord Gower, Lord Sandwich, Rigby, and others, who after the Duke of Bedford's death still retained his name. They were more eager for the American War than Lord North, the nominal head of the Government.

On the proposal itself Mr. Burke said with truth: "I contend that it is a far more oppressive mode of taxing than that hitherto used, for here no determinate demand is made. The colonies are to be held in durance by fleets and armies until singly and separately they shall do— what? Until they shall offer to contribute to a service which they cannot know, in a proportion which they cannot guess, on a standard which they are so far from being able to ascertain, that the Parliament which is to hold it has not ventured to hint what it is they expect. They are to be held prisoners of war, unless they consent to a ransom, by bidding at an auction against each other and against themselves, until the King and Parliament shall strike down the hammer, and say, ' Enough.' "*

Mr. Fox said: " Besides the opposition which the noble

* " Parliamentary History."

Lord found obstructing his way, he felt that even his friends and allies began to grow slack towards the rigour of his measures; he was therefore forced to look out for some propositions that might still induce them to go on with him, and that might, if possible, persuade the Americans to trust their rights to his candour and justice. What he has now proposed to you does accordingly carry two faces on its very first appearance. To the Americans and to those who are unwilling to proceed in the extremes of violence against them, he holds out negotiation and reconciliation. To those who have engaged with him on condition that he will support the supremacy of this country unimpaired, the proposition holds out a persuasion that he never will relax on that point; but, sir, his friends perceive that he is relaxing, and the Committee sees that they are all ready to withdraw from under his standard. No one in this country who is sincerely for peace will trust the speciousness of his expressions, and the Americans will reject them with disdain."

On the 22nd of March Mr. Burke brought forward his resolutions for conciliating America, and made a speech which, combining profound knowledge of the vast subject on which he spoke, wisdom in devising remedies for pressing evils, eloquence in expounding his views, beauty of language and fertility of fancy, has no superior in the records of Parliamentary discussion. Other occasions may have produced a close phalanx of argument, or a splendour of diction, or a quickness of reply which have won equal or more admiration at the moment; but as a work of human genius and a lesson of statesmanship, this speech will ever command the veneration of the student of English history and English eloquence.

In touching on the disputed question of right, Mr.

Burke declined to enter on the abstract merits of the dispute—

> "That great Serbonian bog,
> Betwixt Damiata and Mount Casius old,
> Where armies whole have sunk."

But he wholly gave up the exercise of this supposed right, and thereby laid the ground for an amicable settlement.

Mr. Burke ended his speech with the following magnificent peroration :—

" I, for one, protest against compounding our demands : I declare against compounding, for a poor limited sum, the immense, overgrowing, eternal debt which is due to generous government from protected freedom; and so may I speed in the great object I propose to you, as I think it would not only be an act of injustice, but would be the worst economy in the world, to compel the colonies to a sum certain, either in the way of ransom or in the way of compulsory compact.

" But, to clear up my ideas on this subject, a revenue from America, transmitted hither—do not delude yourselves —you never can receive it. No, not a shilling. We have experience that from remote countries it is not to be expected. If, when you attempted to extract revenue from Bengal, you were obliged to return in loan what you had taken in imposition, what can you expect from North America ? for certainly, if ever there was a country qualified to produce wealth, it is India; or an institution fit for the transmission, it is the East India Company. America has none of these aptitudes. If America gives you taxable objects, on which you lay your duties here, and gives you, at the same time, a surplus by a foreign sale of her commodities, to pay the duties on these objects which you tax at home, she has performed her part to the British revenue. But with regard to her own internal establishments, she may—I doubt not she will—contribute in moderation. I say in moderation, for she ought not to be permitted to exhaust herself. She ought to be reserved to a war, the weight of which, with the enemies that we are most likely to have, must be considerable in her quarter of the globe. There she may serve you, and serve you essentially.

"For that service—for all service, whether of revenue, trade, or empire, my trust is in her interest in the British constitution. My hold of the colonies is in the close affection which grows from common names, from kindred blood, from similar privileges, and equal protection. These are ties which, though light as air, are as strong as links of iron. Let the colonies always keep the idea of their civil rights associated with your government; they will cling and grapple to you, and no force under heaven will be of power to tear them from their allegiance. But let it be once understood that your government may be one thing and their privileges another—that these two things may exist without any mutual relation—the cement is gone, the cohesion is loosened, and everything hastens to decay and dissolution. As long as you have the wisdom to keep the sovereign authority of this country as the sanctuary of liberty, the sacred temple consecrated to our common faith, wherever the chosen race and sons of England worship freedom, they will turn their faces towards you. The more they multiply, the more friends you will have; the more ardently they love liberty, the more perfect will be their obedience. Slavery they can have anywhere. It is a weed that grows in every soil. They may have it from Spain they may have it from Prussia; but until you become lost to all feeling of your true interest and your natural dignity, freedom they can have from none but you. This is the commodity of price, of which you have the monopoly. This is the true Act of Navigation, which binds to you the commerce of the colonies, and through them secures to you the wealth of the world. Deny them this participation of freedom, and you break that sole bond which originally made and must preserve the unity of the empire. Do not entertain so weak an imagination as that your registers and your bonds, your affidavits and your sufferances, your cockets and your clearances, are what form the great securities of your commerce. Do not dream that your letters of office, and your instructions, and your suspending clauses, are the things that hold together the great contexture of this mysterious whole. These things do not make your Government. Dead instruments, passive tools as they are, it is the spirit of the English communion that gives all their life and efficacy to them. It is the spirit of the English constitution which, infused through the mighty mass, pervades, feeds, unites, invigorates, vivifies every part of the empire, even down to the minutest member. Is it not the same virtue which does everything for us here in England? Do you imagine, then, that it is the Land-tax Act which raises your revenue, that it is the annual vote in the Committee of Supply which gives you your army, or that it is the Mutiny Bill which inspires it with bravery and discipline? No!— surely no! It is the love of the people, it is their attachment to their Government, from the sense of the deep stake they have in such a glorious institution, which gives you your army and your navy, and infuses into both that liberal obedience, without which your army would be a base rabble, and your navy nothing but rotten timber. All this, I know well enough, will sound wild and chimerical to the profane herd of those vulgar and mechanical politicians who have no place among us—a sort of people who think that nothing exists but what is gross and material, and who therefore, far from being qualified to be directors of the great movement of empire, are not fit to turn a wheel in the machine. But to men truly initiated and rightly taught, these ruling and master principles, which, in the opinion of such men as I have mentioned, have no substantial existence, are in truth everything, and all in all. Magnanimity in politics is not seldom the truest wisdom, and a great empire and little minds go ill together. If we are conscious of our situation, and glow with zeal to fill our places as becomes our station and ourselves, we ought to auspicate all our public proceedings in America with the old warning of the Church—*Sursum corda!* We ought to elevate our minds to the greatness of that trust to which the order of Providence has called us. By adverting to the dignity of this high calling our ancestors have turned a savage wilderness into a glorious empire, and have made the most extensive and the only honourable conquests—not by destroying, but by promoting the wealth, the number, the happiness of the human race. Let us get an American revenue as we have got an American empire. English privileges have made it all that it is; English privileges alone will make it all it can be."

Mr. Burke's resolutions differed but little from the bill of Lord Chatham.

Mr. Fox spoke, and it is said with great spirit and ability, in support of Mr. Burke. Lord John Cavendish, Mr. Hotham, Mr. Tufnell, and Mr. Sawbridge also supported him. He was opposed by Thurlow, Attorney-General, by Mr. Jenkinson, and others. It was absurdly argued that the Bill of Rights assumed the power of taxation to rest solely in the Parliament of Great Britain.

On a division there were,—

For Mr. Burke 78

Against 270

———

Majority 192

On the 15th of May Mr. Burke presented a remonstrance from the General Assembly of the province of New York, and moved,—

"That the representation and remonstrance of the General Assembly of the Colony of New York be brought up." Lord North, objecting to the tenor of this document, moved to add the words, "in which the said Assembly claim to themselves rights derogatory to, and inconsistent with, the legislative authority of Parliament."

Mr. Fox said: "The right of Parliament to tax America was not, as a simple assertion, denied in the remonstrance, but only as coupled with the exercise of it. The exercise was the thing complained of, not the right itself. When the Declaratory Act was passed, asserting the right in the fullest extent, there were no tumults in America, no opposition to Government in any part of that country; but when the right came to be exercised in the manner we have seen, the whole country was alarmed, and there was a unanimous determination to oppose it. The right simply is not regarded—it is the exercise of it that is the object of opposition. It is this exercise that has irritated, and made almost desperate several of the colonies; but the noble lord [North] chooses to be consistent; he is determined to make them all mad alike. The only province that was moderate [New York], and in which

England had some friends, he now treats with contempt. What will be the consequence when the people. of this. moderate province are informed of this treatment? That representation which the cool and candid of this moderate province had framed with deliberation and caution is rejected, is not suffered to be presented, no, not even to be read by the clerk. When they hear this they will be inflamed, and hereafter be as distinguished by their violence as they have hitherto been by their moderation. It is the only method they can take to regain the esteem and confidence of their brethren in the other colonies, who have been offended at their moderation. Those who refused to send deputies to the Congress, and trusted to Parliament, will appear ridiculous in the eyes of all America; it will be proved that those who distrusted and defied Parliament had made a right judgment; and those who relied upon its moderation and clemency had been mistaken and duped. The consequence of this must be, that every friend the Ministers have in America must either abandon them, or lose all credit, and every means of serving them in future."

The House divided on Lord North's amendment, yeas 186, noes 67. Upon American questions the numbers in a full House were usually about 260 to less than 90.

Some other attempts were made in the course of the session to reverse the policy of the Minister. The measure of employing German troops against our American fellow-subjects was marked with grave reprobation. Lord Camden endeavoured to repeal the Quebec Act; General Conway to obtain the instructions given to General Howe and to Lord Howe. But all was in vain. On the 26th of May the King closed the session with a temperate speech from the throne. The efforts of the Opposition to awaken the King and the country to the dangers of the position had been fruitless.

In the meantime Lord Chatham, perhaps exhausted by the violence of his efforts, had sunk into one of those periods of nervous depression which attended his attacks of gout. So great was his prostration, that a letter from General Carleton, with whom Lord Pitt was serving as aide-de-camp in America, was concealed from him by Lady Chatham. She said the names of his son and America together would be too much for him. He trembled at the mention of political exertion, and might have exclaimed, like the Hebrew king represented by Alfieri :—

> " Che piu ? chi 'l crederia ? spavento
> M' è la tromba di guerra, alto spavento
> È la tromba a Saul."

The mighty warrior was hid from sight; his spear hanging on the wall, and his mind lost in melancholy dejection.

We must now turn to America, and observe the rapid progress of alienation, soon to be inflamed into open hostility.

General Gage having been appointed governor and commander-in-chief of the forces, arrived in May, 1774, at Boston. It was not long before it became obvious that he would have to maintain himself there by force. He therefore fortified the neck of land which connected Boston with the main land, and sent for more troops. Towards the end of the year a proclamation, which had been issued in England, forbidding the exportation of warlike stores to the colonies, arrived in America. The people in Rhode Island immediately seized forty pieces of cannon, which had been mounted for the defence of the harbour, and removed them to the interior of the country. In the province of New

Hampshire a number of armed men surprised and took a small fort called the William and Mary, garrisoned by a British officer and five soldiers, removing the guns, ammunition, and stores. General Gage, on his side, sent a field officer to Salem to take possession of some brass cannon and field-pieces; but the officer found they had been conveyed away on the morning of his arrival. These operations on both sides, however significant of hostilities, had taken place without bloodshed. But the day was at hand when this fatal war between men of the same race, both born free, both descended from the nation which had resisted the tyranny of the Stuarts, was to dye with blood the fields of America. Happy, indeed, would it have been had the principles which the patriots of Great Britain and New England professed in common been of virtue sufficient to maintain amicable union or lead to amicable separation! But it was not to be so! General Gage received intelligence that a quantity of military stores had been collected and deposited at Concord, a place about twenty miles from Boston. He determined to send there Colonel Smith with the Grenadiers and light infantry of his army. Colonel Smith was to march in the night of the 18th of April, and to be supported the following morning by the movement of sixteen companies of foot and a body of marines under Earl Percy. This plan was executed in the manner intended, but the design appears to have been made known to the Americans.* The first detachment reached Lexington, distant fifteen miles from Boston, about five in the morning of the nineteenth. Upon approaching the place a body of armed militia was perceived drawn up on a green near the road : the King's officers ordered them to break their

* Stedman's " History of the American War."

ranks and disperse. They did not obey, and the object was not effected without some firing on both sides; one man was wounded on the side of the royal troops, some of the militia were killed, and the rest were scattered. Lord Percy, with the second detachment, followed the march of Colonel Smith. On his way an officer observed to him that apparently there would be little opposition, as the houses on the road were deserted, and the windows shut. "So much the worse," replied Lord Percy, "for on our return we shall be fired at from those very houses."

The united force now march on to Concord, where they destroyed the military stores, not, however, without sharp firing and the loss of some men. The return to Boston was difficult and disastrous. The whole country was roused; the militia and volunteers, or minute men,* fired on the troops from the rear and from the flank; every house contained a rifle, and every rifle was aimed at the retreating force. About sunset the British troops reached Boston, having lost 65 killed, 136 wounded, and 49 missing; a total loss of 251 men out of 1800.†

General Gage has been blamed by an American writer for sending his troops on a mission of plunder and bloodshed.‡ But as the guns and stores at Concord were obviously intended for the destruction of his troops, he surely deserved no censure on that score. In other respects his expedition was rash and unfortunate. He exposed his troops to a retreat before a militia whose want of discipline unfitted them for manoeuvres in the field, but whose habits and skill as marksmen qualified them admi-

---

* The minute men were volunteers who engaged to be ready at a minute's warning.

† Stedman's "History of the American War." "American Archives."

‡ Sparks's "Life of Washington."

rably for an irregular fight. They only required a skirmish of this kind to give them confidence and hope. Accordingly the whole continent of North America rang with the fame of this first trial of the prowess of the insurgents—an operation successful in its object became a real defeat in its effects.

A more serious action was at hand. Boston is situated on a peninsula; opposite the town, upon a similar peninsula, was another town called Charlestown. The heights which rose above Charlestown, called Breed's Hill and Bunker's Hill, commanded the harbour of Boston. The Americans, by a well-contrived surprise, took possession of these heights in the night of the 18th of June. Early in the morning of the 19th the firing of the British frigate Lively revealed the fact.

General Gage, hastening to atone for his supineness, directed General Pigot to land on the peninsula and drive away the insurgents. General Pigot landed about noon; but finding the enemy strongly posted, and increasing in numbers, he sent for reinforcements. When these arrived, the British troops amounted to 2000 men. With this force an immediate attack was made on the American position. The resistance was obstinate, and the British troops were twice repulsed; but General Clinton coming up, rallied the broken forces, and the whole line advancing with signal courage, carried the heights. The Americans were not pursued, and were allowed to retire from the peninsula. In the action Charlestown was set on fire. This victory was dearly purchased. The number of killed and wounded on the side of the British was one thousand and fifty-four, more than half of the whole force engaged.

The military conduct of General Gage was severely

blamed. It was said, in the first place, that he ought not to have left so commanding a position unfortified and unoccupied. In the next place it was observed that, if he had attacked the left of the American line, defended only by a slight breastwork, he might have turned their whole position. And lastly, the general was censured for sending the soldiers to mount a steep hill on a hot day in June, laden with heavy knapsacks and three days' provisions.*

Civilians, who did not enter into these military criticisms, remarked, with concern and alarm, that the raw levies of America, raised in haste, and chiefly from a single colony, had advanced unperceived, occupied their post with skill, resisted regular troops with courage, and inflicted a heavier loss on the renowned infantry of Great Britain than they themselves had sustained.

The flame which had been kindled at Boston now spread to other parts of the North American continent. Lord Dunmore, the Governor of Virginia, was forced to retire on board a ship; from which safe port he carried on an inglorious warfare against towns on the coast, but had not even the triumph of a dishonest victory. Mr. Martin, the Governor of North Carolina, was in a similar manner compelled to fly.

In the meantime the Americans proceeded in the work of organization, civil, political, and military. The Congress met for the second time, in Philadelphia, in May, 1775. The most important question for the Assembly was the organization of their army and the appointment of a commander-in-chief. Washington had been noted by his colleagues of the first Congress for the sagacity he manifested on every subject in discussion. When Patrick Henry returned home, he was asked who he thought the greatest

* Stedman's " History of the American War."

man in Congress; he replied, " If you speak of eloquence,
Mr. Rutledge, of South Carolina, is by far the greatest
orator; but if you speak of solid information and sound
judgment, Colonel Washington is unquestionably the
greatest man on that floor."

Washington had acquired much of that information, and
ripened his naturally sound judgment in his service with
the British troops during the Seven Years' War. At that
time he felt as a loyal and ardent subject of the Crown.
" Will, then, our injured country," he wrote on the subject
of military mismanagement, " pass by such abuses? I
hope not. Rather let a full representation go to his Majesty.
Let him know how grossly his glory and interest and the
public money are prostituted."*

How much folly and injustice were required before such
a man could be driven to arms against his sovereign !

Washington took the command in the month of July.
He found a large numerical force of militia, but provided
with ammunition for only three days, and divided into
as many commands as there were colonies. It was his
first business to organize this force, to reform their discipline, and obtain an influence over their minds.

Among the first military enterprises of the American
Congress was an attempt upon Canada. A person of the
name of Eathan Allen, with a body of fifty men, obtained
by stratagem possession of Ticonderoga and Crown Point.
Arnold led his militia forces on another side to the siege of
Quebec. After an ineffectual movement he was joined by
General Montgomery, who already enjoyed a high reputa-
tion as a soldier. An assault was resolved upon. The
Americans advanced bravely in two columns; but both

* Sparks's " Life of Washington," vol. i.

were repulsed with loss, and Montgomery, who led one of them, was killed.

After this, General Burgoyne arrived in the St. Lawrence with reinforcements, and the Americans retired from Canada unsuccessful, but unmolested.

Such was the commencement of the American War.

The Court of Great Britain was arrogant and confident; the Parliament indifferent, ignorant, and submissive; the Americans far from unanimous, but generally determined to be free subjects or a free commonwealth. The more moderate thought liberty might be preserved without separation; the more able and ambitious looked to separation as the opening of a higher destiny, the triumph of democracy at home, and the assertion of an equal place among the greatest nations of the globe.

CHAPTER VII.

MEETING OF PARLIAMENT—DEBATES—DECLARATION OF INDEPENDENCE—CAMPAIGN IN AMERICA—BATTLE OF BROOKLYN—CONQUEST AND EVACUATION OF NEW JERSEY.

1775 — 1776.

PARLIAMENT met on the 26th of October, 1775. The King again urged in his royal speech the necessity of reducing the Americans to obedience. He informed his Parliament that, in testimony of his affection for his people, he had sent his Electoral troops to Gibraltar and Port Mahon, with a view of employing a greater portion of his regular forces in America.

Although the language of conciliation was sometimes used, it now took the shape rather of clemency to rebels, when they should be at the mercy of the Crown, than of any compliance with the wishes of the colonists. The argument for coercion, as the only course possible, was put in a more plausible shape by Lord Mansfield, in the House of Lords, than by any of the Ministers. He regretted, he said, the Stamp Act of 1763, and the attempt to obtain a revenue from America; he blamed still more strongly the renewal of that attempt in 1767. But, he argued, that was not now the question to be decided. Congress had not only denied the right of Parliament to tax the colonies, but they had also blamed the appointments of judges, the Admiralty courts, the post office and other parts of the administration. So that, in fact, pretension was advanced so far as to leave the King with only a barren sceptre in his hand, and the attempt was made to assert a real if not a declared independence. The condition of Scotland before the Union was the model at which the Americans aimed. Unless Parliament were prepared to concede this claim, there was no course open but an appeal to arms. Lord Mansfield's view of the objects of even the more temperate of the American patriots was hardly an exaggeration. They disliked the struggle, but when forced into it, they entered the field with large views and projects. The course taken by Lord Rockingham, in 1765, could no longer be reconciled with American claims, and would not at this time have led to a final settlement. The Americans looked to be what Scotland was before the Union, what Canada is in 1858. But in accordance with the commercial doctrines of that age, they were willing to grant to Great Britain many preferences for her trade and manufactures ; or, if England should be willing to renounce her interference with trade, there were some who would be willing to grant her a fixed revenue voted by their assemblies. Had the genius of Chatham presided over the councils of the State, there is every reason to believe that the right of taxation being expressly renounced, and other grievances fairly redressed, America might, even at this time, have been reconciled to Great Britain. With the King urgent for total submission, with Ministers the subservient organs of his will, with a House of Commons obedient to the Crown, and the country blinded by false representations, there was no hope of such a reconciliation.

One more attempt to preserve peace had, however, been lately made by Congress. At the suggestion of Dickinson, as we have seen, the Congress had adopted a petition to the King, conveying in general terms their desire to renew their old relations of protection and allegiance with Great Britain. On the 1st of September Richard Penn had delivered to Lord Dartmouth, for presentation to the King, this conciliatory petition, known in America by the name of "The Olive Branch." Lord Dartmouth received the petition in silence, and three days afterwards informed Penn by letter that no answer would be given. Civil war, that terrible evil to which, according to Cicero, the worst peace is to be preferred, was thus the deliberate choice of George III. and his Minister.

The next question which arises is, supposing the Ministers right in requiring unconditional submission—did Lord North and his colleagues take the measures best fitted to that end? To this question the answer must be, that the means prepared were totally inadequate to the end proposed.

In December, 1774, such was the short-sighted policy of the Government, the Navy Estimates for the year showed a reduction of 4000 men. This force was augmented by 2000 in the following February, but the whole naval force voted for the year 1775 amounted only to 18,000 men. The land forces voted for North America and the West Indies did not exceed 34,000 men. Such were the armies and navies by which a great continent and three millions of the British race were to be subdued! The spirit of resistance was rife over a great continent; the merchants gave up trade, the farmers forsook their tillage to take up arms against Great Britain. Washington and Franklin, Adams and Jefferson, spoke only of war. The British troops were cooped up in Boston, blockaded by an American army. Every other seaport was in the hands of the insurgents. It would have required 60,000 or 80,000 of the best troops of Britain to hold only the most important points of the vast territory from Massachusetts to Virginia, and a fleet of ten sail of the line to overawe New York and Charleston. In this emergency the means to which the British Ministry had recourse increased their unpopularity in America much more than it added to the effective force of Great Britain. The King made treaties with Hesse, and with Brunswick, by which 12,000 Hessians and 5000 other German troops were engaged to fight in North America for British pay. In Germany, Frederick of Prussia made these troops pay the toll on the passage of cattle, saying, " they had been sold as such." In America these hired foreigners were represented as engaging in a quarrel in which they had no other interest than the pay they were to receive. The cause of British supremacy might, it was argued, engage the sympathy of the royal troops, however mistaken their feelings might be. But the attempt to establish despotism by the hands of foreign mercenaries, was an act which would justify the severance of all ties between the colonies and the mother country. We now return to the proceedings in Parliament.

While Lord Mansfield defended the policy of the American War in the debate on the Address, Lord John Cavendish moved the following amendment in the House of Commons: "That we behold with the utmost concern the disorders and discontents in the British colonies, rather increased than diminished by the means which have been used to suppress and allay them—a circumstance alone sufficient to give this House just reason to fear that those means were not originally well considered, or properly adapted to answer the ends to which they were directed.

.We are satisfied by experience that this misfortune has, in a great measure, arisen from the want of free and proper information being laid before Parliament of the true state and condition of the colonies, by reason of which measures have been carried into execution injudicious and inefficacious, from whence no salutary end was reasonably to be expected, tending to tarnish the lustre of the British arms, to bring discredit on the wisdom of his Majesty's councils, and to nourish, without hope of end, a most unhappy civil war. Deeply impressed with a sense of this melancholy state of the public concerns, we shall, on the fullest information we can obtain, and with the most mature deliberation we can employ, review the whole of the late proceedings, that we may be enabled to discover, as we shall be most willing to apply, the most effectual means for restoring order to the distracted affairs of the British Empire, confidence to his Majesty's Government, obedience, by a prudent and temperate use of its powers, to the authority of Parliament, and satisfaction and happiness to all his people. By these means, we trust, we shall avoid any occasion for having recourse to the alarming and dangerous expedient of calling in foreign forces to the support of his Majesty's authority within his own dominions, and the still more dreadful calamity of shedding British blood by British hands."

Mr. Fox on this occasion spoke warmly in favour of the amendment, and described Lord North as the blundering pilot who had brought the nation into its present difficulties. "Administration," he said, "exult at having brought us into this dilemma. They have reason to triumph. Lord Chatham, the King of Prussia, nay, Alexander the Great, never gained more in one campaign than the noble lord has lost — he has lost a whole continent. Although he thought the Americans had gone too far, and were not justifiable in all that they had done, yet they were more justifiable for resisting than they would have been had they submitted to the tyrannical acts of a British Parliament; for, when the question was whether a people was to submit to slavery or to aim at freedom by a spirited resistance, the alternative which must strike every Englishman was, the choice of freedom. He combated the argument in the King's speech, which inferred that America aimed at independency, and by a chain of reasoning showed that, to be popular in America, it was necessary to talk of dependence on Great Britain, and to hold that out as the object in pursuit. He rallied Lord North on the rapid progress he had made in misfortune, having laid out nearly as large a sum to acquire national disgrace as that most able minister Lord Chatham had expended in gaining that glorious lustre with which he had encircled the British name. He did not approve of everything that had been done by Lord Chatham, but all must confess his great and surprising talents as a minister. He declared opposition to be cordially united in every part. He retorted on administration for their having last year roused the younger part of the House by their appeals to the spirit of Englishmen to enforce vigorous measures, and asked whether that spirit was discernible in the pitiful party of the military sent to Boston, or in the vigorous measures of that party; declaring that, if the spirit the Ministry had appealed to was still in existence, it would not be possible for them to keep their places. After severely rebuking them for endeavouring to shift the blame from themselves to General Gage, he concluded with advising Administration to place

America where she stood in 1763, and to repeal every act passed since that period which affected either her freedom or her commerce." His father having been attacked, and his own conduct in the previous session arraigned, he protested that he had been deceived by the Minister; he had been taught to believe that Government had so many friends in America that the appearance of a few regiments there would secure an obedience to our laws, and ensure peace; that upon this principle he voted for sending over the forces last session; peace was his object in that measure; but now that the Minister declared himself for war, he could not but oppose his proceedings. " He could not consent to the bloody consequences of so silly a contest about so silly an object, conducted in the silliest manner that history or observation had ever furnished an instance of, and from which we were likely to derive nothing but poverty, disgrace, defeat, and ruin."

Horace Walpole gives the following account of Fox's speech on this occasion: " The Solicitor-General (Wedderburne) having argued well from ill success, as the late war had begun ill and ended gloriously, Burke took this up to ridicule; 'but Charles Fox took it up better and said, ' The late war had not turned to success till the Ministry had been changed' (forgetting Lord Chatham had come in and his own father been of the former Administration; but with his usual quickness he soon recovered that slip and said), ' Lord Hardwicke had been a great lawyer, but a wretched politician, and when he gave place to Lord Chatham all had prospered. But,' continued he, rising in energy, ' not Lord Chatham, not the Duke of Marlborough, no, not Alexander, nor Cæsar, had ever conquered so much territory as Lord North had lost in one campaign.' "

These are but faint reflections of the eloquence of Mr. Fox. Mr. Grattan being asked which were the best speeches he ever heard, answered, without hesitation, " Fox's, during the American War." Certain it is that this struggle first called forth his energies, and revealed to the world his surprising abilities. Mr. Gibbon has described in his "Memoirs" the effect produced upon his mind by the parliamentary eloquence of this period, and he reserves Mr. Fox for the climax of his enumeration. "I assisted," he says, "at the debates of a free assembly; I listened to the attack and defence of eloquence and reason ; I had a near prospect of the characters, views, and passions of the first men of the age. The cause of Government was ably vindicated by Lord North—a statesman of spotless integrity—a consummate master of debate, who could wield with equal dexterity the arms of reason and of ridicule. He was seated on the Treasury bench, between his Attorney and Solicitor-General, the two pillars of law and State, *magis pares quam similes*, and the Minister might indulge in a short slumber while he was upholden on either hand by the majestic sense of Thurlow and the skilful eloquence of Wedderburne. From the adverse side of the House an ardent and powerful Opposition was supported by the lively declamation of Barré, the legal acuteness of Dunning, the profuse and philosophic fancy of Burke, and the argumentative vehemence of Fox, who in the conduct of a party approved himself equal to the conduct of an empire."*

In the House of Lords, Lord Rockingham, prompted by Burke, and guided by his own good sense and judgment, led the Duke of Richmond and the Whig Peers in many a

* Gibbon's " Miscellaneous Works."

manly protest. Lord Chatham, in the decay of his bodily vigour, yet in whom—

> "Old experience did attain
> To somewhat of prophetic strain,"—

Uttered from time to time sublime invectives and gloomy vaticinations. Lord Gower and Lord Sandwich defended feebly the cause of the Ministry. Yet, while the conduct of the Government tended evidently to the separation of the American colonies, the Opposition, strong as they were in abilities, were internally divided and desponding. Lord Chatham was alternately active without concert or absent from infirmity; the Duke of Richmond was steady to his principles, but disinclined to attendance; Sir George Saville did not like to be unpopular in the cause of the people.

The Duke of Richmond wrote on one occasion to Lord Rockingham, who had invited him to a conference: "And as to my opinions in consultations, you know already so entirely my thoughts, that I am sure my being present would serve only for repetition; and as to getting various persons to give way, and agree to one opinion, that is your *forte*, and very far from mine."* On the 20th of November, Lord North moved to bring in a bill to prohibit all trade and intercourse with the thirteen colonies of North America, with the exception of parts of Delaware, and to repeal three acts passed in former sessions. Mr. Fox said: "As the noble lord had now proposed the repeal of three oppressive acts, he begged to ask him, as a man of honour and a gentleman, whether he did not wish that he had adopted the opinion of the noble duke [of Grafton], who was First Lord of the Treasury, when the repeal of the

---

* "Rockingham Correspondence."

tea duty was moved? He repeated that there were differences of opinions amongst persons high in office at that time; and he asked the noble lord whether he did not now wish he had been of opinion with those who were for repealing that duty, because they saw, and therefore wished to avoid, that chain of misfortunes which the continuance of it had drawn after it? This proposition of peace, he said, like that of last year, was meant to lead on this country under a delusion of flattering hopes of peace, and to endeavour to deceive, which it would not do, the Americans into a belief, that this country wished for a peace of the description which the noble lord held out, or was unanimously determined to prosecute the war, if such peace could not be effected. The whole was insidious, and therefore could have no other effect upon the Americans than to destroy their confidence in Government, if any such yet remained. If the Americans should believe the spirit of this country to be unanimous against their rights, they had nothing to do but prepare immediately for war, as their only defence against a system of despotism. This proposition, therefore, was a declaration of perpetual war; and were he to give his vote for it, he should consider himself as giving his vote for a declaration of war. However, as he had always said that he would support any measure of reconciliation, he should go so far with the noble lord as the repeal of the three acts he had mentioned. He, therefore, moved an amendment to leave out all the words except those of ' for repealing' the acts mentioned." The amendment was rejected by 192 to 64. On the report of the Bill, Mr Fox· said : " I have always given it as my opinion that the war now carrying on against the Americans is unjust; but, admitting it to be a just war, admitting that it is practicable, I insist that the means made use of are not such as will obtain the end. I shall confine myself singly to this ground, and show that this bill, like every other measure, proves the want of policy, the folly and madness of the present Ministers. I was in great hopes that they had seen their error, and had given over coercion and the idea of carrying on war against America by means of acts of Parliament. In order to induce the Americans to submit to your legislature, you pass laws against them cruel and tyrannical in the extreme. If they complain of one law, your answer to their complaint is to pass another more rigorous than the former. But they are in rebellion, you say; if so, treat them as rebels are wont to be treated. Send out your fleets and armies against them and subdue them, but let them have no reason to complain of your laws. Show them that your laws are mild, just, and equitable; that they therefore are in the wrong, and deserve the punishment they meet with. The very contrary of this has been your wretched policy. I have ever understood it as a first principle, that in rebellion you punish the individuals, but spare the country; but in a war against the enemy, it is your policy to spare the individuals and lay waste the country. This last has been invariably your conduct against America; I suggested this to you when the Boston Port Bill passed; I advised you to find out the offending persons, and to punish them; but what did you do instead of this? You laid the whole town of Boston under terrible contribution, punishing the innocent with the guilty. You answer, that you could not come at the guilty. This very answer shows how unfit, how unable you are, to govern America. If you are forced to punish the innocent to come at the guilty, your government there is, and ought to be, at an end. But, by the bill now before us you not only punish those innocent persons who are unfortunately mixed with the guilty in North America, but you punish and starve whole islands of unoffending people, unconnected with, and separated from them. Hitherto the Americans have separated the right of taxation from your legislative authority ; although they have denied the former, they have acknowledged the latter. This bill will make them deny the one as well as the other. 'What signifies,' say they, 'your giving up the right of taxation, if you are to enforce your legislative authority in the manner you do ? This legislative authority so enforced will at any time coerce taxation, and take from us whatever you think fit to demand.' The present is a bill which should be entitled, a Bill for Carrying more effectually into Execution the Resolves of the Congress." * The question being put on Lord North's motion, the House divided: Yeas 143, Noes 38. Mr. Fox moved, "That it be referred to a committee to inquire into the causes of the ill success of his Majesty's arms in North America, as also into the causes of the disaffection of the people of the province of Quebec." On this occasion I find the following outline of Mr. Fox's speech, which shows the line of argument he followed. After granting, for argument sake, that Ministers had been right in adopting a plan of coercion, " he then entered into an historical detail of the means employed to carry this plan of coercion into effect, in which he painted in the strongest colours, and held to view in the most striking lights, such a scene of folly in the Cabinet, of servile acquiescence in Parliament, and of misconduct and ignorance in office and in the field, as had

* Fox's " Speeches."

never before disgraced this nation, or, indeed, any other. He added, that our Ministers wanted both wisdom and integrity; our Parliaments, public spirit and discernment; and that our commanders, by sea and land, were either deficient in abilities, or, which was the most probable, had acted under orders that prevented them from executing the great objects of their command. No man could say but there had been mismanagement and misconduct somewhere. It was the chief object of his intended motion to gain that species of information which might be the means of discovering the true causes of both. Public justice demanded such an inquiry. The individuals on whom the obloquy rested were entitled to be heard in their own defence. To withhold the information necessary to their justification would be an insult to the nation, as well as an act of private injustice. None but the guilty could wish to evade it. No man as a soldier or sailor, be his rank ever so high, was sure of his honour a single minute if he was to be buried under public disgrace, in order to protect or palliate the blunders and incapacity of others. If the Ministers had planned with wisdom, and had proportioned the force to the service—if the great officers in the several efficient departments had done all that depended on them ably and faithfully, then it was plain that the whole of the miscarriages that had happened might be deservedly imputed to our naval and military commanders. If, on the other hand, the latter had acquitted themselves according to their instructions, and had carried on their operations in proportion to the force given them, it was no less plain that the cause of all the disgraces the British arms had suffered arose from ignorance in those who planned, and incapacity

and want of integrity in those to whom the carrying them
into execution was in the first instance entrusted."

The previous question being moved, there were, on a
division,—

For 104

Against 240

____

Majority 136

Such was the triumphant majority by which the Minister
was supported at the commencement of this fatal war.
There are two circumstances worth noting, as they show
the signification attached to the terms Whig and Tory,
both in Old and in New England. Mr. Fox having called the
Ministry a Tory administration, Lord North thought proper
to vindicate himself from the charge, and remarked that the
Americans might with more justice be called Tories, as they
appealed to the King's prerogative, while the British
Ministry upheld the authority of Parliament. The other
circumstance is, that the colonists who took the part of
the mother country were uniformly called Tories by the
Americans. The fact is that the old ground of the Tory
party had been, from the accession of George III., abandoned,
and the Whig doctrines of the Constitution, as they had been
professed in the reigns of William III. and George I., were
adopted by the leading statesmen of all parties, however
they might differ as to the immediate questions of
foreign or domestic policy. As to the remark of Lord
North, it had no doubt some foundation, but the fact to
which he alludes will bear a very different interpretation.
The Americans could not object to the Houses of Parliament as advisers of the Crown, but when the House of
Commons voted taxes to be levied in America, they natu-

rally deprecated the interference of Parliament in a matter which properly belonged to themselves, and appealed to the Crown on the ground of their charter. Lord North soon again returned to his favourite policy of vain and foolish appearances of conciliation. The name of Howe was popular in America. Admiral Lord Howe was sent to join his brother, General Howe, and a joint commission was given them to treat for pacification. But as their instructions merely empowered them to receive submissions and remedy grievances, after the convention, committee, or association of any province, "which have usurped powers," should have been dissolved, these overtures were rather endeavours to divide the people of America, than to give them real satisfaction. They were, in fact, so considered.

We must now attend to the proceedings in America. In the beginning of 1776 General Howe, who had succeeded Gage, evacuated Boston, and retired to Halifax, where he remained till June. In the beginning of that month he embarked his troops for New York. He was there joined by Lord Howe with his conciliatory proposals. But by the time Lord Howe arrived, the Americans had not only drawn the sword, but had thrown away the scabbard. The Congress met for the second time in May, 1776. On June 7th the delegates from Virginia moved, in obedience to instructions from a convention of that colony, that the Congress should declare, in the name of the colonies there represented, that these united colonies are, and of right ought to be, free and independent states; that they are absolved from all allegiance to the British Crown; that all political connexions between them and the State of Great Britain is and ought to be totally dissolved; that measures should be immediately taken for procuring the assistance of foreign powers;

and that a confederation be formed to bind the colonies more closely together. On the following day (June 8th) this proposal was taken into consideration. It was opposed by Robert R. Livingston, E. Rutledge, Dickinson, and Wilson, and was supported by J. Adams, Lee, Wythe, Jefferson, and others. Against the resolution it was argued that the people of the middle colonies—Maryland, Delaware, Pennsylvania, the Jerseys, and New York—were not yet ripe for dissolving the connexion with Great Britain, and that the ferment excited by the resolution of Congress to suppress the exercise of all powers derived from the Crown, proved that the colonists had not yet accommodated their minds to a separation from the mother country; but that they were fast ripening, and in a short time would join the general voice of America, and declare for independence. That if any of the colonies were unwilling so to declare, other colonies could not declare it for them; that a rupture among the colonies themselves would weaken them more than any assistance from foreign powers could give them strength. That France and Spain had reason to be jealous of a rising state which would certainly one day strip them of all their foreign possessions. That at all events no long time would elapse before the disposition of the French Court would be ascertained from the American agent sent to Paris for that purpose. These reasons, directed against the time and not the right or the policy of a separation from Great Britain, prevailed so far, that it was resolved to postpone the final decision till the 1st of July. But in the meantime a committee, consisting of Thomas Jefferson, Dr. Franklin, John Adams, Robert R. Livingston, and Roger Sherman, was appointed to prepare a Declaration of Independence.* The

* "Memoirs of Thomas Jefferson," London, 1829.

Declaration, drawn up by Jefferson, was laid on the table on the 28th of June. On the 1st of July the resolution of the delegates of Virginia was again proposed, and carried by nine colonies against two. Pennsylvania and South Carolina were the two which voted against it; Delaware was divided: the delegates from New York were for it themselves, but their instructions being a twelvemonth old, they did not think themselves authorized to concur in the vote. As this document is one of extreme importance, I copy from the " Memoirs of Thomas Jefferson" the original draft of the Declaration, as reported by the committee, with the amendments made by Congress :*—

A Declaration by the Representatives of the United States of America in General Congress assembled.

" When in the course of human events it becomes necessary for one people to dissolve the political bands which have connected them with another, and to assume among the powers of the earth the separate and equal station to which the laws of Nature and of Nature's God entitle them, a decent respect to the opinions of mankind requires that they should declare the causes which impel them to the separation.

" We hold these truths to be self-evident ; that all men are created equal ; that they are endowed by their Creator with (*inherent and*) inalienable rights ; that among these certain are life, liberty, and the pursuit of happiness ; that, to secure these rights, governments are instituted among men,

* The parts struck out by Congress are printed in *italics*, and enclosed in parentheses ; those inserted by them are placed in the margin or in a concurrent column.

deriving their just powers from the consent of the governed; that, when any form of government becomes destructive of these ends, it is the right of the people to alter or to abolish it, and to institute new government, laying its foundation on such principles, and organizing its powers in such form, as to them shall seem most likely to effect their safety and happiness. Prudence, indeed, will dictate that governments long established should not be changed for light and transient causes ; and accordingly all experience hath shown that mankind are more disposed to suffer while evils are sufferable, than to right themselves by abolishing the forms to which they are accustomed. But when a long train of abuses and usurpations (*begun at a distinguished period, and*) pursuing invariably the same object, evinces a design to reduce them under an absolute despotism, it is their right, it is their duty, to throw off such government, and to provide new guards for their future security. Such has been the patient sufferance of these colonies, and such is now the necessity which con-

alter

strains them to (*expunge*) their former systems of government. The history of the present King of Great Britain

repeated

all having

is a history of (*unremitting*) injuries and usurpations (*among which appears no solitary fact to contradict the uniform tenor of the rest, but all have*) in direct object the establishment of an absolute tyranny over these States. To prove this, let facts be submitted to a candid world (*for the truth of which we pledge a faith yet unsullied by falsehood*).

" He has refused his assent to laws the most wholesome and necessary for the public good.

" He has forbidden his governors to pass laws of immediate and pressing importance, unless suspended in their operation till his assent should be obtained ; and, when so suspended, he has utterly neglected to attend to them. He has refused to pass other laws for the accommodation of large districts of people, unless those people would relinquish the right of representation in the legislature—a right inestimable to them, and formidable to tyrants only. He has called together legislative bodies at places unusual, uncomfortable, and distant from the depository of their public records, for the sole purpose of fatiguing them into compliance with his measures.

" He has dissolved representative houses repeatedly (*and continually*) for opposing with manly firmness his invasions on the rights of the people.

" He has refused for a long time after such dissolutions to cause others to be elected, whereby the legislative powers, incapable of annihilation, have returned to the people at large for their exercise, the State remaining, in the mean time, exposed to all the dangers of invasion without and convulsions within.

" He has endeavoured to prevent the population of these States ; for that purpose obstructing the laws for naturalization of foreigners, refusing to pass others to encourage their migrations hither, and raising the conditions of new appropriations of lands.

" He has (*suffered*) the administration of justice (*totally* obstructed *to cease in some of these States*), refusing his assent to laws by for establishing judiciary powers.

" He has made (*our*) judges dependent on his will alone for the tenure of their offices, and the amount and payment of their salaries.

" He has erected a multitude of new offices (*by a self-assumed power*), and sent hither swarms of new officers to harass our people and eat out their substance.

" He has kept among us in times of peace standing armies (*and ships of war*), without the consent of our legislatures.

" He has affected to render the military independent of, and superior to, the civil power.

"He has combined with others to subject us to a jurisdiction foreign to our constitutions, and unacknowledged by our laws, giving his assent to their acts of pretended legislation for quartering large bodies of armed troops among us; for protecting them by a mock trial from punishment for any murders which they should commit on the inhabitants of these States; for cutting off our trade with all parts of the world; for imposing taxes on us without our consent; for depriving us (*in many cases*) of the benefits of trial by jury; for transporting us beyond seas to be tried for pretended offences; for abolishing the free system of English laws in a neighbouring province, establishing therein an arbitrary government, and enlarging its boundaries, so as to render it at once an example and fit instrument for introducing the same absolute rule into these (*States*); for taking away our charters, abolishing our most valuable laws, and altering fundamentally the forms of our governments; for suspending our own legislatures, and declaring themselves invested with power to legislate for us in all cases whatsoever. He has abdicated government here (*withdrawing his governors and declaring us out of his allegiance and protection*).

"He has plundered our seas, ravaged our coasts, burnt our towns, and destroyed the lives of our people.

"He is at this time transporting large armies of foreign mercenaries to complete the works of death, desolation, and . . . . already begun with circumstances of cruelty and . . . . ( ) unworthy the head of a civilized nation.

"He has constrained our fellow citizens taken captive on the high seas to bear arms against their country, to become the executioners of their friends and brethren, or to fall themselves by their hands.

"He has ( ) endeavoured to bring on the inhabitants of our frontiers the merciless Indian savages, whose known rule of warfare is an undistinguished destruction of all ages, sexes, and conditions (*of existence*).

"(*He has incited . . . . . insurrections of our fellow-citizens, with the allurements of forfeiture and confiscation of our property.*

"(*He has waged cruel war against human nature itself, violating its most sacred rights of life and liberty in the persons of a distant people who never offended him, captivating and carrying them into slavery in another hemisphere, or to incur miserable death in their transportation thither. This piratical warfare, the opprobrium of* INFIDEL *powers, is the warfare of the* CHRISTIAN . . . . *of Great Britain. Determined to keep open a market where* MEN *should be bought and sold, he has prostituted his negative for suppressing every legislative attempt to prohibit or to restrain this execrable commerce. And that this assemblage of horrors might want no fact of distinguished dye, he is now exciting those very people to rise in arms among us, and to purchase that liberty of which he has deprived them by . . . . the people on whom he also obtruded them : thus paying off former . . . . committed against the* LIBERTIES *of one people, with . . . which he urges them to commit against the* LIVES *of another*).

" In every stage of these oppressions we have petitioned for redress in the most humble terms; our repeated petitions have been answered only by repeated injuries.

"A prince whose character is thus marked by every act which may define a . . . . is unfit to be the ruler of a (   ) people (*who mean to be free. Future ages will* free *scarcely believe that the hardiness of one man adventured, within the short compass of twelve years only, to lay a foundation so broad and so undisguised for . . . . over a people fostered and fixed in principles of freedom*).

" Nor have we been wanting in attentions to our British brethren. We have warned them from time to time of attempts by their legislature to extend (*a*) jurisdiction over (*these our States*). We have reminded them of the circumstances of our emigration and settlement here (*no one of which would warrant so strange a pretension ; that these were effected at the expense of our own blood and treasure, unassisted by the wealth or the strength of Great Britain ; that in constituting, indeed, our several forms of government, we had adopted one common King, thereby laying a foundation for perpetual league and amity with them ; but that submission to their Parliament was no part of our constitution, nor ever in idea, if history may be credited : and*) we (　　　) appealed to their native justice and magnanimity (*as well as to*) the ties of our common kindred, to disavow these usurpations, which (*were likely to*) interrupt our connexion and correspondence. They, too, have been deaf to the voice of justice and of consanguinity (*and when occasions have been given them, by the regular course of their laws, of removing from their councils the disturbers of our harmony, they have, by their free election, re-established them in power. At this very time, too, they are permitting their chief magistrate to send over not only soldiers of our common blood, but Scotch and foreign mercenaries to invade and destroy us.*

" (*These facts have given the last stab to agonizing affection, and manly spirit bids us to renounce for ever these unfeeling brethren. We must endeavour to forget our former love for them, and hold them, as we hold the rest of mankind, enemies in war, in peace friends. We might have been a free and a great people together, but a communication of grandeur and of freedom, it seems, is below their dignity. Be it so, since they will have it. The road to happiness and to glory is open to us too. We will tread it apart from them, and*) acquiesce in the necessity which denounces our (*eternal*) separation (　　　).

Marginal notes (left margin):

have

and we have conjured them by

would inevitably

We must, therefore,

and hold them as we hold the rest of mankind, enemies in war, in peace friends.

"We, therefore, the representatives of the United States of America, in general Congress assembled, do, in the name and by the authority of the good people of these (*States, reject and renounce all allegiance and subjection to the Kings of Great Britain, and all others who may hereafter claim by, through, or under them; we utterly dissolve all political connexion which may heretofore have subsisted between us and the people or Parliament of Great Britain; and, finally, we do assert and declare these colonies to be free and independent States*), and that, as free and independent States, they have full power to levy war, conclude peace, contract alliances, establish commerce, and to do all other acts and things which independent states may of a right do. And for the support of this declaration we mutually pledge to each other our lives, our fortunes, and our sacred honour."

———

"We, therefore, the representatives of the United States of America, in general Congress assembled, appealing to the Supreme Judge of the world for the rectitude of our intentions, do, in the name, and by the authority, of the good people of these colonies, solemnly publish and declare that these United Colonies are, and of right ought to be, free and independent States; that they are absolved from all allegiance to the British Crown, and that all political connexion between them and the State of Great Britain is, and ought to be, totally dissolved; and that, as free and independent States, they have free power to levy war, conclude peace, contract alliances, establish commerce, and to do all other acts and things which independent States may of right do.

And for the support of this declaration, with a firm reliance on the protection of Divine Providence, we mutually pledge to each other our lives, our fortunes, and our sacred honour."

It appears singular that in a contest arising so entirely from practical grievances and the violation of chartered rights, the Congress should have thought it necessary to refer to the abstract doctrines "that all men are created equal," "that they are endowed by nature with certain inalienable rights," and that "among these are life, liberty, and the pursuit of happiness." These doctrines, however true in the abstract, are not very consistent with the state of society anywhere. The equality of a young man to his father cannot be said to exist even among the rudest savages; the equality of a slave to his master did not exist in the ancient republics, in the despotisms of Asia, or in these very colonies of North America. That the principle of equality in the eye of the law has been established, is the utmost that could be affirmed of the most advanced nations of Europe. Or we might say, with Mr. Fox, that men have equal rights to unequal things. As a statement of practical grievances justifying insurrection and separation, the Declaration is remarkable for the slight stress which is laid upon the right of taxation claimed by Great Britain. Was it that its authors found that this grievance might be redressed, and the colonists might be called upon, the cause being removed, to forego the effects? Was it that this grievance had been less felt than complained of? Was it that the Congress was resolved, at all events, upon separation, and wished to multiply grounds of justification? All these reasons, perhaps, influenced the able men who now determined to cut the towing-rope and steer a course for themselves over the world's ocean. The great moral and political question remains: Were the Americans justified in dissolving the connexion between themselves and Great Britain? In order to solve this question, let us examine their position in order to arrive at a fair judgment. The only terms upon which the most moderate of the colonists of North America would have been content to remain in subjection to Great Britain were, that their legislatures should be perfectly free; that no money should be exacted from them without their own consent; and that their judges should hold office during good behaviour. Recent suspicions had made Franklin and other Americans add to these terms a condition that no British trrops should be quartered in the colonies without the consent of the provincial legislatures. These terms were surely, in the then posture of affairs, reasonable and fair. Had not the troops been employed to bend America to submission, a restriction of the prerogative in this branch could not properly have been demanded. But circumstances had rendered such a condition necessary. It was clear, however, that no such terms would be granted by the King of Great Britain. Every overture for conciliation, even the petition to the King drawn up by Dickinson, and which Mr. Penn was charged to present, had been contumeliously rejected. An entire and absolute submission was required in return for some vague promise of not taxing the colonies, provided the colonies taxed themselves for imperial purposes, according to a rate to be fixed by the British Minister. As such a submission would have been intolerable, as the freedom of America would have been thenceforth dependent on the absolute will of the King, or the narrow policy of his Ministers, the Declaration of Independence became justifiable, because necessary for the liberty and welfare of the colonies. The sentiments of Washington on this subject are manly and noble: "With respect to myself," he writes to a friend, "I have never entertained an idea of an accommodation since I heard of the measures which were adopted in consequence of the Bunker's Hill fight. The King's speech has confirmed the sentiments I entertained upon the news of that affair; and if every man was of my mind, the Ministers of Great Britain should know in a few words upon what issue the cause should be put. I would not be deceived by artful declarations nor specious pretences; nor would I be amused by unmeaning propositions; but in open, undisguised, and manly terms, proclaim our wrongs, and our resolution to be redressed. I would tell them that we had borne much; that we had long and ardently sought for reconciliation, upon honourable terms; that it had been denied us; that all our attempts after peace had proved abortive, and had been grossly misrepresented; that we had done everything which could be expected from the best of subjects; that the spirit of freedom rises too high in us to submit to slavery. This I would tell them, not under covert, but in words as clear as the sun in its meridian brightness."

It must, I think, be granted that the Declaration of Independence flowed naturally from the love of free and equal laws, which the English race had carried with them to the West. It was a corollary of the Bill of Rights.

While such was the resolution displayed by Congress on the question of independence, neither they nor the people they represented made military preparations at all adequate to the occasion. Washington in vain endeavoured to pro-cure a law for enlisting men for the whole period of the war. His troops were generally under engagements for only one year; their numbers sometimes rose to thirty thou-sand, but more frequently sunk to fifteen, and at one time to eight, thousand. The soldiers chose their own officers;

they exacted a promise that the officers' pay should be thrown
into the same purse with the pay of the private soldiers.
The troops were scantily supplied with ammunition, and
often marched barefoot for weeks and months together.
The fortitude, resolution, gallant spirit, and calm sense of
Washington, never failed; but he sometimes exposed himself and his army to great hazard from his want of military
experience. In the month of August, 1776, his men
were posted in Long Island, with no retreat except by sea.
Sir William Howe at the same time had thirty thousand
good troops under his command. The campaign was
opened on the 22nd of August; on the 26th the battle of
Brooklyn was fought. The British attacked; the Americans
retired in confusion. They were not pursued, and on the
29th they made good their retreat to New York. The
passage of the river, or rather arm of the sea, was effected
in thirteen hours. Within this time nine thousand men
passed over in boats, besides field artillery, ammunition,
provisions, cattle, horses, and carts.

A British historian of the war thus describes the operation: "The circumstances of this retreat were particularly
glorious to the Americans. They had been driven to the
corner of an island, where they were hemmed in within the
narrow space of two square miles. In their front was an
encampment of near twenty thousand men; in their rear
an arm of the sea a mile wide, which they could not cross
but in several embarkations. Notwithstanding these difficulties, they secured a retreat without the loss of a man."*
The position of the American army, however, was not
tenable. New York was therefore evacuated by Washington;
and Fort Washington, having been retained against his

* Stedman's "American War," vol. i. p. 197.

opinion, surrendered to the British with a garrison of 2800 men. The Americans then abandoned New Jersey, and retired beyond the Delaware. It was generally said that the British general had now an opportunity of striking a great blow. He commanded 30,000 well-armed and disciplined troops against 5000 or 6000 men ill-armed and worse equipped.

On advancing into New Jersey, the British were received with open arms, and the province hastened to make its submission. The conquest of at least the whole coast seemed inevitable. At this critical moment the opposite characters of Howe and Washington turned the fortune of war. Howe allowed his Hessian troops to plunder loyalists and insurgents alike : having thus lost the returning affections of the colonists, he scattered his fine army in detached posts over eighty miles of country, with the Hessian troops in advance on the frontier. Washington, with great sagacity, marked the opportunity. On the night of Christmas he crossed the Delaware, surprised Trenton, and took 1000 prisoners. Alarmed at this success, General Howe sent for Lord Cornwallis, and ordered him at once to advance against Washington. Lord Cornwallis soon found himself at the head of 7000 or 8000 men, divided from the American army only by the Assanpink. Sir W. Erskine advised him to attack Washington at once, but he declined, saying, " he would be sure to bag the fox in the morning." In the night, however, Washington, by a bold movement, got in the rear of his enemy, and surprised three British regiments, the 17th, 40th, and 55th, at Princeton. By a rapid advance these regiments were separated from each other ; the 17th, with heavy loss, marched on to Trenton ; the 55th retired by a by-road to Brunswick ; a great part of the 40th surrendered. The loss of the

British was 100 killed and 300 prisoners. When Lord Cornwallis came up, Washington had disappeared. While the American general raised the spirits of his troops by these military exploits, he at the same time issued a proclamation requiring the inhabitants of the province to pay allegiance to Congress. Soon after, General Howe abandoned New Jersey, thus losing without a battle the only fruits of his former success, and of his great numerical superiority. Washington, on the other hand, animated his army by his resources in difficulties, and his determination never to submit. He justly earned the name of "the American Fabius." But no Hannibal appeared on the side of the British.

CHAPTER VIII.

DESPONDENCY OF THE WHIGS—SECESSION—CAMPAIGN IN AMERICA—
BATTLE OF BRANDYWINE—CAPITULATION OF SARATOGA.

1776 — 1777.

WHEN the news of the landing of the King's troops, under
Lord Howe, in Long Island, and of their success at
Brooklyn, reached England, the nation appears to have been
transported with the prospect of the speedy submission of
America.   Charles Fox, in writing to Lord Rockingham,
after advising against secession, goes on to say : " Above
all, my dear lord, I hope that it will be a point of honour
among us all to support the American pretensions in adversity as much as we did in their prosperity, and that we
shall never desert those who have acted unsuccessfully upon
Whig principles, while we continue to profess our admiration of those who succeeded on the same principles in the
year 1688. . . . . Believe me, my dear lord, the expectation of your lordship and all your friends, must in a great
measure depend on the part you act at this critical juncture.
I am sure you are a person whom we need not advise to
take a *firm* one ; but I am so clear that firmness in Whig
principles is at present become so much more necessary
than ever, that I cannot help conjuring you over and over
again to consider the importance of the crisis.   In regard
to myself, I dare hope that professions are unnecessary,
and I will therefore trouble your lordship no further than

to assure you that I am resolved in the present situation of affairs to adhere still more, if possible, than I have done, to those principles of government which we have always recommended with respect to America, and to maintain that, if America should be at our feet (which God forbid!), we ought to give them as good terms at least as those offered in Burke's propositions."*

Sir George Savile, writing in the beginning of 1777, in a less cheerful tone, says: "We are not only patriots out of place, but patriots out of the opinion of the public. The reported successes, hollow, as I think them, and the more ruinous if they are real, have fixed or converted ninety-nine in one hundred. The cause itself wears away by degrees from a question of right and wrong between subjects to a war between us and a foreign nation, in which justice is never heard, because love of one's country, which is a more favourite virtue, is on the other side. I see marks of this everywhere, and in all ranks; I am, I think, sure of it. . . . We have been used to this consolation at the bottom of our cup, that we had the public opinion. It is hard to give it up. We have it not most certainly. A proper, temperate, and steady behaviour may replace us in a long time; trying at it, never: unless we can submit to even this disgrace on a yet larger scale, we have no virtue."†

While such was the despondency of the leading Whigs and the unfavourable state of public opinion, it is strange to learn that Lord North despaired of the success of his own policy. In November, 1779, three years after this period, Lord Gower, in retiring from the King's Cabinet

* "Correspondence of the Marquis of Rockingham," vol. ii. p. 298.

† Sir George Savile to Lord Rockingham, Jan. 15th, 1777: "Correspondence of the Marquis of Rockingham."

Council, said to Lord North, "I cannot think it the duty of a faithful servant to endeavour to preserve a system which must end in ruin to his Majesty and to the country." Lord North endeavoured to dissuade him, but in reporting the result to the King, he adds: "In the argument, Lord North had certainly one disadvantage, which is, that he holds in his heart, and has held for three years past, the same opinion with Lord Gower."* Thus it appears that Lord North, so early as the year 1776, was of opinion that the system he was pursuing would end in ruin to the King and to the country. He continued, however, to obey the commands of his sovereign, and to pursue a policy which he foresaw must terminate in *ruin*. That his conduct was the result rather of weakness of character, and misplaced devotion to the personal wishes of the sovereign, than of any corrupt love of office or conscious dishonesty, may be admitted; but such extreme weakness and such slavish devotion are surely inconsistent with the constitution of a free country, and fatal to the welfare of any state.

Parliament met on the 31st of October, 1776. The speech from the throne declared that, "No people ever enjoyed more happiness, or lived under a milder government than the revolted provinces; a fact proved by their progress in the arts, their numbers, their wealth, and strength by sea and land, which inspired an over-weening confidence. He was desirous to restore to them the blessings of law and liberty, equally enjoyed by every British subject, which they had fatally and desperately exchanged for the calamities of war and the arbitrary tyranny of their chiefs." Lord Rockingham opposed the address. In speaking of the Ministry, he said: "I will put the whole of their defence

* Correspondence of Lord North: in Fox's "Correspondence."

on this short issue. I ask them, in the course of their experience, whether they ever heard, or can now be persuaded
to think, that a whole people, so numerous, and living
under so many different forms of government, though
members of the same political body, ever unanimously con-
federated to join in a revolt under a mild, wise, and equitable administration of public affairs?" Lord Rockingham
then moved an amendment, of which, on account of the
importance of the declaration of principles, and the description of policy which it contains, I shall insert the greater
part. The amendment proposed to assure his Majesty that,
" animated with the most earnest and sincere zeal for his true
interest, and the real glory of his reign, we behold with in-
expressible concern the minds of a very large and lately
loyal and affectionate part of his people entirely alienated
from his government. Nor can we conceive that such an
event as the disaffection and revolt of a whole people could
have taken place without some considerable errors in the
conduct observed towards them. . . . These erroneous measures, we conceive, are to be imputed to a want of sufficient
information being laid before Parliament, and to too large
a degree of confidence being reposed in those Ministers,
who from their duty were obliged, and from their official
situation were best enabled to know the temper and disposition of his Majesty's American subjects, and were therefore
presumed most capable of pointing out such measures as
might produce the most salutary effect. Hence the schemes
which were formed for the reduction and chastisement of a
supposed inconsiderable party of factious men have driven
thirteen large provinces to despair. Every act which has
been proposed as a means of procuring peace and submission has become a new cause of war and revolt; and we now

find ourselves almost inextricably involved in a bloody and expensive civil war, which, besides exhausting at present the strength of all his Majesty's dominions, exposing our allies to the designs of their and our enemies, and leaving this kingdom in a most perilous situation, threatens in its issue the most deplorable calamities to the whole British race.

" We cannot avoid lamenting that, in consequence of the credit afforded to the representations of Ministers, no hearing has been given to the reiterated complaints and petitions of the colonies; neither has any ground been laid for removing the original cause of these unhappy differ-ences, which took their rise from questions relative to par-liamentary proceeding, and can be settled only by parlia-mentary authority. By this fatal omission the commis-sioners nominated for the apparent purpose of making peace were furnished with no legal powers but those of giving or withholding pardons at their pleasure, and of relaxing the severities of a single penal act of Parliament, leaving the whole foundation of this unhappy controversy just as it stood at the beginning.

" To represent to his Majesty that, in addition to this neglect, when, in the beginning of the last session, his Majesty, in his gracious speech to both Houses of Parlia-ment, had declared his resolution of sending out commis-sioners for the purposes therein expressed as speedily as possible, no such commissioners were sent until near seven months afterwards, and until the nation was alarmed by the evacuation of the only town then held for his Majesty in the thirteen united colonies. By this delay acts of the most critical nature, the effect of which must as much depend on the power of immediately relaxing them on sub-

mission, as in enforcing them upon disobedience, had only
an operation to inflame and exasperate. But if any colony,
town, or place had been induced to submit by the operation
of the terrors of these acts, there were none in the place of
power to restore the people so submitting to the common
rights of subjection. The inhabitants of the colonies,
apprised that they were put out of the protection of Government, and seeing no means provided for their entering into
it, were furnished . with reasons but too colourable for
breaking off their dependency on the Crown of this
kingdom. . . .. .

"We should look with the utmost shame and horror on
any events, of what nature soever, that should tend to break
the spirit of any large part of the British nation, to bow
them to an abject, unconditional submission to any power
whatsoever, to annihilate their liberties, and to subdue them
to servile principles and passive habits by the mere force
of foreign mercenary arms; because, amidst the excesses
and abuses which have happened, we must respect the
spirit and principles operating in these commotions. Our
wish is to regulate, not to destroy them; for, though
differing in some circumstances, those very principles evidently bear so exact an analogy with those which support
the most valuable part of our own Constitution, that it is
impossible, with any appearance of justice, to think of
wholly extirpating them by the sword, in any part of his
Majesty's dominions, without admitting consequences and
establishing precedents the most dangerous to the liberties
of this kingdom."

Lord John Cavendish moved a similar amendment in the
House of Commons. On this occasion Mr. Fox delivered
a speech, a part of which has been thus reported:—

"We have been told that it is not for the interest of Spain and France to have America independent. Sir, I deny it. Is not the division of the enemy's power advantageous? Is not a free country engaged in trade less formidable than the ambition of an old corrupted government, their only formidable rival in Europe? The noble lord who moved the amendment said that we were in the dilemma of conquering or abandoning America. If we are reduced to that, I am for abandoning America. What have been the advantages of America to this kingdom? Extent of trade, increase of commercial advantages, and a numerous people growing up in the same ideas and sentiments as ourselves. Now, sir, would these advantages accrue to us if America was conquered? Not one of them. Such a possession of America must be secured by a standing army, and that, let me observe, must be a very considerable army. Consider, sir, that that army must be cut off from the intercourse of social liberty here, and accustomed in every instance to bow down and break the spirits of men, to trample on the rights and to live on the spoils cruelly wrung from the sweat and labour of their fellow-subjects. Such an army, employed for such purposes and paid by such means, for supporting such principles, would be a very proper instrument to effect points of a greater or at least more favourite importance nearer home—points, perhaps, very unfavourable to the liberties of this country."

Lord Chatham, Mr. Burke, and Mr. Fox constantly dwelt on the dangers which might accrue to the liberties of their own country if America were conquered by force of arms. Such men, said Lord Chatham, would be fit instruments to make slaves of the rest. Had the Americans been entirely subdued, this reasoning seems to be logically correct. But it is not easy to conceive three millions of Englishmen so degraded as to live contentedly deprived of the rights of the British Constitution; disturbance would have succeeded to disturbance, insurrection to insurrection; the three millions would in no long time have become six, and ere many years could elapse America would have armed and fought again, not again to be subdued. The amendment was negatived in the House of Lords by 91 to 26, and in the House of Commons by 242 to 87.

On the 6th of November Lord John Cavendish moved: "That this House will resolve itself into a Committee to consider of the revisal of all Acts of Parliament by which his Majesty's subjects in America think themselves aggrieved." Mr. Burke seconded this motion, and it was supported in a speech of his usual ability by Mr. Fox. On a division 109 voted for the Minister and only 47 for the Opposition. From this time many of the minority began systematically to absent themselves upon all questions relating to America. Indeed several of them attended only to the private business of the House in which their constituents had some interest, and as soon as a public question was introduced made their bow to the Speaker, and formally withdrew. Lord Mahon says, after quoting the words of the "Annual Register," "that the Opposition appeared in their places only upon such matters of private bills in which they had some particular concern or interest:" "In other words they neglected the public business, and but applied themselves to their personal affairs; and such conduct was called patriotism."* This is a strange remark from a person of so much parliamentary experience as Lord

* "History of England," vol. vi. pp. 209, 210.

Mahon. What are called private bills often affect the welfare of a community in a sensible degree. The watching and lighting, the supply of water for a town, the making of roads, streets, docks, and many other public matters which are the subjects of private bills have nothing to do with personal affairs. It must be owned, however, that the general question of parliamentary secession is one of considerable importance and no slight difficulty. It is sanctioned by the precedents of Pulteney in the time of Sir Robert Walpole, of Burke in the period of which we are treating, and of Fox and Grey during the French Revolutionary War. The principle of secession, indeed, is not easily defended; for to what end are men chosen representatives of the people if they refrain from voting on the interests of the people, irrespective of the views of other representatives? Is a majority in Parliament a quantity so fixed and unchangeable that it may not be shaken by argument, or persuaded by eloquence, or even converted by the still more convincing logic of adverse circumstances?

On the other hand, it must be admitted that practically a minister gains strength from the repetition of fruitless attempts to overthrow his policy. Resistance consolidates his party: constant victory animates and binds together his supporters. The publicity of debate gives appearance of fairness to the contest, and the country is apt to rest satisfied with a verdict pronounced after argument heard, evidence weighed, and authority examined. It may, therefore, be practically expedient to retire for a season from opposition to a policy which is deliberately approved, though in error, by the Crown, the Parliament, and the nation. Reflection may produce that conviction which argument has failed to attain. But, however advisable a total secession may be, there could be no greater mistake than a partial, fitful, and capricious withdrawal from public business. It has the air of a loss of temper rather than the silent reserve of dignity or the calm patience of wisdom. This was, however, the course which the Rockingham Whigs pursued. The suspension of the Habeas Corpus Act being announced, Lord Rockingham held a meeting to consider whether the Whigs should return to oppose it. Lord Rockingham himself, Burke, and the Cavendishes adhered to secession, but Charles Fox would not agree; and he accordingly, on the second reading, attended to oppose the suspension.

The Duke of Richmond, writing on this subject to Lord Rockingham, says: "I am much obliged to you for the trouble you have taken in writing me so particular an account of the difficulties you have been under with your friends about non-attendance. I confess that the inconveniences which presented themselves to every plan, when we discussed them so fully at your house, made me think it of no great consequence which was followed; and the worst I see has happened—that is, the plan that was adopted has not been steadily pursued. This indeed was foreseen, and was a part of the difficulty."*

It was after the Christmas recess that Lord North brought in his bill to suspend the Habeas Corpus Act in respect to all persons suspected of high treason in America or on the high seas. Mr. Fox, in conformity with his declared intention, opposed this bill. The debates became long, animated, and highly interesting, yet the numbers of the Opposition on the second reading were but forty-three, and in the third reading only thirty-three. It was on the third reading

* Feb. 19, 1777: "Rockingham Correspondence," vol. ii. p. 308.

that Mr. Fox made the following remarkable statement :
" He affirmed, from his own knowledge, that we were on the
eve of a war with France, immediately preceding the meeting of the present session, in the month of October. He
was of opinion that Administration were extremely negligent in respect of home security and national defence,
particularly in not calling out and embodying the militia,
when it was well known what a defenceless state we were
in at the time, and still, he was sorry to say, continued to
be. At present the disposition of France, he allowed, was
much changed. The Courts of Versailles and Madrid,
whatever their latent or remote intention might be, took
care carefully to conceal the one, or had prudently post-
poned the other, till they were sufficiently prepared to
strike a decisive, perhaps a fatal, blow, which was certainly
not the case at present. Their peaceable demeanour, their
promises and appearances, were most assuredly the consequence of necessity, not choice. The disposition of the
French nation in general, and the sentiments of such as
turned their thoughts to foreign politics, respecting the
civil war in America, bore testimony how much they considered that war as a matter that promised to be extremely
favourable to their interests in the final event. He had
other proof, which confirmed the conclusion now made in
a much clearer manner—that was, the disposition of the
French cabinet, which daily manifested itself in a variety of
circumstances. He did not mean to enter into details; but
the facts he was about to mention were important, and
such, too, as would not leave a doubt of their tendency.
He alluded to the conduct of the French Ministry to two
of the members of the American Congress, now resident at
Paris, Dr. Franklin and Mr. Silas Deane. He was war-

ranted in affirming, from his own knowledge, that they both appeared publicly at Paris and Versailles; they were known to hold conferences with the King's Ministers, to treat and negotiate with them, and to be received by them substantially on the same footing as the representatives of any independent power in Christendom. The correspondence held between them was of the same nature with that usually carried on between two powers, where one of them seeks for assistance, and the other, from motives of policy, listens, deliberates, and determines upon the propriety or impropriety of adopting the schemes, or entering into the measures of the power which thus applies for succour. Sometimes Franklin and Deane received greater encouragement, at other times less, according to the tone of the Court and the prevailing sentiments and opinions at the time; but, however these might vary, one important truth might be gathered from the whole—that France was secretly hostile to Great Britain; that she publicly and privately received, treated, and negotiated with the members of the American Congress, or with persons authorized and deputed for them."

The remainder of the session presented nothing worthy of remark. But if the session of Parliament was barren of interest, the campaign in America was full of events, and those events almost decisive of the struggle. At the commencement of the year the British forces greatly over-matched the regular troops of the colonies. Sir William Howe had upwards of 20,000 well-disciplined soldiers in New York and Rhode Island. The British army in Canada was strong enough to detach 7000 men in aid of their countrymen. On the other side, General Washington, with only 11,000 men, and those ill-armed and clothed, was obliged

to confine himself to a defensive position on the Delaware.
He was further weakened by the necessity of detaching
a force, under General Gates, to watch the Canadian frontier.
The whole of the American forces, including recruits, did
not amount to 25,000 men, while the British had 32,000
regular troops.   In these circumstances it was obvious that
the operations of the two British armies should have been
governed upon one plan.   Either General Burgoyne, who
was to command the army in Canada, should have combined his movements with those of Sir W. Howe in such a
manner as to separate the New England States from the
other revolted colonies, or the Canadian detachment should
have been sent to New York, and Sir W. Howe should
have fallen with all his forces upon Washington.   Neither
of these plans was pursued, nor does there seem to have
been any concert between the British generals.   In June
Sir W. Howe advanced to the Delaware, but, finding
Washington strongly posted, soon retired.   After this loss
of time, a part of the army under Lord Cornwallis was
embarked, and landed at Cape Elk.   On the 13th of September General Howe defeated Washington on the Brandywine, with considerable loss.   His victory might have been
fruitful of great consequences.   Washington, finding himself outnumbered and defeated, abandoned Philadelphia,
and the British took possession of that city.   Franklin, at
Paris, said, however, "It is not General Howe who has
taken Philadelphia; Philadelphia has taken General Howe."
His remark was a true one.   Philadelphia had no strategical
importance.   Its celebrity was owing to its being the temporary seat of the Congress; but to mistake the capital of
an insurgent Congress for a permanent seat of government,
like Paris, Vienna, or Berlin, was at once a military fault and

a political blunder. The Congress retired, and General Howe was caught in his own trap.

While Howe was exhausting his energy, and fatiguing his troops by a vain triumph, Burgoyne was conducting his own unconnected movement from Canada. Towards the end of the month of June he marched with 7000 European troops and 1000 Indians to Ticonderoga. Pursuing his course, he arrived in July at Fort Edward, and, constructing a bridge of boats over the Hudson, sent General Fraser to take possession of the heights of Saratoga. An American magazine was placed at Bennington. Thither Burgoyne sent Colonel Baum with 500 Germans, followed by Colonel Breyman with another German detachment. But Baum was defeated, wounded, and taken prisoner; Breyman was scarcely able, after suffering severely, to secure his retreat. The loss of the Germans and British was 200 killed, 700 wounded and taken prisoners. By this time the spirit of New England was up; militiamen flocked to the American standard; the barbarities committed by our Indian allies excited a strong desire for revenge, and the whole country bristled with men armed to assert the security of their home, and the independence of their country. General Burgoyne, in a private letter to the Secretary of State, thus describes his situation : " Wherever the King's forces point, militia to the amount of three or four thousand assemble in twenty-four hours ; they bring with them their subsistence, and the alarm over, they return to their farms. The Hampshire grants, in particular, a country unpeopled, and almost unknown during the last war, now abounds in the most active and rebellious race of the Continent, and hangs like a gathering storm upon my left. In all parts the industry and management in driving cattle and removing corn are indefatigable and certain; and it becomes impracticable to move without portable magazines.   Another most embarrassing circumstance is the want of communication with Sir William Howe; of the messengers I have sent, I know of two being hanged, and am ignorant whether any of the rest arrived."*   In spite of these adverse circumstances, General Burgoyne, instead of making good his retreat, waited a month to collect provisions, and then crossed the Hudson, abandoning his communications with Canada. He must have done this at a time when less than 5000 effective soldiers were with the colours. The rest of the story is soon told.

On the 19th of September Burgoyne attacked General Gates's army, which was strongly posted on Behmus Heights; after four hours' severe fighting, the British remained masters of the ground. On the 7th of October he again attacked the American army, but was repulsed with loss; and General Arnold, following up his success, penetrated the British position in the part held by the German auxiliaries. Burgoyne the next day retreated to Saratoga, where he was so closely surrounded that there was not a single spot in his camp which was not exposed to cannon or rifle shot. On the 23rd of October he assembled a council of war, which was unanimous for treating, provided honourable terms could be obtained. On the 24th it was agreed by capitulation that the British army should march out of the camp with the honours of war; should pile their arms at the river-side, and should be embarked for Great Britain, on condition of not serving again during the war. The force which capitulated under

* Private Letter to Lord G. Germaine, Aug. 20th, 1777 : Lord Mahon's
" History of England."

Burgoyne consisted of 3500 effective men. The return of
General Gates's army gave as present, fit for duty, 13,216;
on command, 3875. The British army had but six days'
provisions, and the number of their enemies increased every
day. Their surrender, therefore, was a matter of necessity.
One is tempted to ask, however, how it happened that a
British general found himself with 3500 men without
relief, support, or communications, in the midst of a hostile
country, and surrounded by an enemy vastly superior in
numbers? The answer to this question must be that the
whole plan of campaign had no combination, connexion, or
common sense. Six weeks after General Burgoyne arrived
on the Hudson, General Clinton undertook an expedition
up that river with 3000 men, and had captured three forts
when he heard of the capitulation of Burgoyne's army. He
had waited for the arrival of 1700 men from England, who
ought to have been sent early in the spring. It may be
said that General Howe ought to have lent a hand to
General Burgoyne; that General Clinton ought to have
marched sooner to his assistance; that Burgoyne himself
ought never to have given up his communications. These
criticisms and many more on the details of the campaign
are just. But the main failure was at home; Lord
George Germaine, who had incurred the censure of his
country by his conduct in the field, ruined its prospects of
success by his mistakes in the Cabinet; Lord North, without earnestness or vigour, confined his warfare to the debate
of the day; and the King, who inspired the war, contributed nothing but obstinacy and prejudice to a cause
which had no foundation in justice, and no support from
wisdom. Thus, in the course of two years from the time
when Lord Sandwich had pronounced the Americans to be

cowards, they had recovered Boston, had displayed the utmost gallantry in the field, and had compelled a British division, in spite of the aid of their Hessian troops, and of their Indian savage auxiliaries, to lay down their arms. From this time France and Spain were encouraged to espouse the rising cause; and the loyalists of America shrank from openly assisting by arms that ancient monarchy to which in their hearts they still fondly clung. Yet the British arms were not without a gleam of success, and the American prospects were not without clouds of discouragement.

General Howe had gained a victory at Brandywine; but the British general could not derive fruit from success, nor the American be depressed by disaster. Neither good nor ill-fortune disturbed the calm and resolute mind of Washington. Beset by enemies, undermined by cabals, his troops suffering from nakedness and famine, his conduct and his language, during this critical period, bear the stamp of a great and good man. When his soldiers were ill-supplied with provisions, he thus quietly explained his reasons for refraining from peremptory requisitions :—

"I confess I have felt myself greatly embarrassed with respect to a vigorous exercise of military power. An ill-placed humanity, perhaps, and a reluctance to give distress, may have restrained me too far; but these were not all. I have been well aware of the prevalent jealousy of military power, and that this has been considered an evil much to be apprehended, even by the best and most sensible among us. . . . The people at large are governed much by custom; to acts of legislation or civil authority they have ever been taught to yield a willing obedience, without reasoning about their propriety; on those of military power, whether immediate, or derived originally from another source, they have ever looked with a jealous or suspicious eye."* In another place he says: " It will never answer to procure supplies of clothing or provisions by coercive measures. The small seizure made of the former a few days ago, in consequence of the most pressing and absolute necessity, when that or to dissolve was the alternative, excited the greatest alarm and uneasiness, even among our best and warmest friends. Such procedures may give a momentary relief, but, if repeated, will prove of the most pernicious consequence. Besides spreading disaffection, jealousy, and fear among the people, they never fail, even in the most veteran troops under the most rigid and exact discipline, to raise in the soldiery a disposition to licentiousness, to plunder and robbery, difficult to suppress afterwards, and which has proved not only ruinous to the inhabitants, but in many instances to armies themselves. I regret the occasion that compelled us to the measure the other day, and shall consider it among the greatest of our misfortunes if we should be under the necessity of practising it again."†

Washington at this time became the object and might have been the victim of an infamous intrigue, in which a person of the name of Conway took a prominent part, and to which General Gates was not a stranger. Although his sagacity enabled him to detect the signs of this conspiracy, his high and manly spirit would not allow him to adopt any means to counteract it. Conway afterwards repented, and confessed the villany to which he had been a party. Among other means of injuring Washington, anonymous accusations were freely employed. A letter of this kind

---

* Sparks's " Life of Washington," vol. i. p. 263.   † Ibid.

having been sent him by President Laurens, he replied, with the candour of conscious worth :—

"As I have no other view than to promote the public good, and am unambitious of honours not founded in the approbation of my country, I would not desire in the least degree to suppress a free spirit of inquiry into any part of my conduct that even faction itself may deem reprehensible. The anonymous paper handed to you exhibits many serious charges, and it is my wish that it should be submitted to Congress. This I am the more inclined to, as the suppression or concealment may possibly involve you in embarrassments hereafter, since it is uncertain how many or who may be privy to the contents. My enemies take an ungenerous advantage of me: they know the delicacy of my situation, and that motives of policy deprive me of the defence I might otherwise make against their insidious attacks. They know I cannot combat their insinuations, however injurious, without disclosing secrets which it is of the utmost moment to conceal. But why should I expect to be exempt from censure, the unfailing lot of an elevated station? Merit and talents, with which I can have no pretensions of rivalship, have ever been subject to it. My heart tells me that it has been my unremitting aim to do the best that circumstances would permit, yet I may have been very often mistaken in my judgment of the means, and may in many instances deserve the imputation of error."* Washington had discouraged the exercise of military authority in order to compel civilians to furnish supplies to his army, but was no less ready to defend the army when attempts were made to mark the military as objects of jealousy, suspicion, and distrust to the

* Sparks's " Life of Washington."

people.   He thus writes, in a letter to a member of Congress :—

"If we would pursue a right system of policy, in my opinion, there should be none of these distinctions.   We should all, Congress and army, be considered as one people, embarked in one cause, in one interest, acting on the same principle and to the same end.   The distinction, the jealousies set up, or perhaps only incautiously let out, can answer not a single good purpose.   They are impolitic in the extreme.   Among individuals, the most certain way to make a man your enemy is to tell him you esteem him such.   So with public bodies, and the very jealousy which the narrow politics of some may affect to entertain of the army, in order to a due subordination to the supreme civil authority, is a likely means to produce a contrary effect, to incline it to the pursuit of those measures which they may wish it to avoid.   It is unjust, because no order of men in the thirteen States has paid a more sacred regard to the proceedings of Congress than the army, for without arrogance or the smallest deviation from truth, it may be said that no history now extant can furnish an instance of an army's suffering such uncommon hardships as ours has done, and bearing them with the same patience and fortitude.   To see men without clothes to cover their nakedness, without blankets to lie on, without shoes (for the want of which their marches might be traced by the blood from their feet), and almost as often without provisions as with them, marching through the frost and snow, and at Christmas taking up their winter quarters within a day's march of the enemy, without a house or hut to cover them, till they could be built, and submitting without a murmur, is a proof of patience and obedience which in my opinion can scarce be paralleled."*

The sufferings of the army in the winter quarters of Valley Forge were indeed excessive. "For some days past," writes Washington, "there has been little less than a famine in camp. A part of the army have been a week without any kind of flesh, and the rest three or four days." Nor were the wants of clothing less grievous. Many were so ill-clad, that they could not leave the huts. The scarcity of blankets was such, that, in order to guard against the cold, the soldiers in numerous instances sat up all night by the fires.†

In this extremity of the fortunes of the revolted colonies, it may be affirmed that the character of Washington alone preserved the liberties and achieved the independence of his country. Had he been disposed to encourage the licence of his troops, the freedom of the people would have been subverted. Had he not magnanimously persevered in the command in spite of calumny and conspiracy, it is probable that a more ambitious chief would have risen on his ruin, perhaps a Cæsar or a Cromwell would have acquired despotic power in the State as a reward for services in the field, and would have crushed the liberty of his country as the price of asserting her independence.

* Sparks's "Life of Washington." In regard to all these extracts quoted from Mr. Sparks, it should be noted that Lord Mahon has intimated an opinion, formed on no light grounds, "that Mr. Sparks has printed no part of the correspondence precisely as Washington wrote it." See also Mr. Sparks's reply.

† Ibid.

CHAPTER IX.

LETTER OF MR. BURKE—MEETING OF PARLIAMENT—DECLARATIONS OF LORD
CHATHAM AND MR. FOX ON THE INDEPENDENCE OF AMERICA.

1777 — 1778.

THE state of the Whig Opposition at this period will be
best understood by the perusal of the following letter from
Mr. Burke to Mr. Fox. It should be borne in mind that
Mr. Fox was not yet accounted a regular member of the
Rockingham party, and that his ardent nature bore very
ill the cautious and hesitating policy of the elder and more
timid Whigs.

In the summer of 1777 Mr. Fox made a journey to
Ireland, in company with Mr. (afterwards Lord) John
Townshend. It was a mere party of pleasure, settled
between them when riding out at Chatsworth. They took
their horses over, and accompanied Mr. and Lady Louisa
Conolly on an excursion to the Lakes of Killarney. Mr.
Fox on this occasion contracted a sincere friendship for
Mr. Grattan, whom he met at Lord Charlemont's. Irish
local politics were little discussed, and had not at that
time much attraction. While at Dublin the two strangers
were much caressed, and were constantly invited to dinners,
where there was usually much lively conversation, and a
prodigious quantity of wine. A wild and hazardous freak
of the two friends made a great noise, and, what seems
strange, raised their reputations in Ireland, where every-

thing that is rash is considered as a proof of spirit. They bathed in the Devil's Punch Bowl, near Killarney, and fortunately escaped the consequences to be apprehended from its extreme coldness. It was during this journey that the letter now inserted was written.

MR. BURKE TO MR. FOX.

"Beaconsfield, Oct. 8th, 1777.

" MY DEAR CHARLES,—I am, on many accounts, exceeding pleased with your journey to Ireland; I do not think it was possible to dispose better of the interval between this and the meeting of Parliament; I told you as much, in the same general terms, by the post. My opinion of the infidelity of that conveyance hindered me from being particular. I now sit down with malice prepense to kill you with a very long letter, and must take my chance for some safe method of conveying the dose. Before I say anything to you of the place you are in, or the business of it, on which, by the way, a great deal might be said, I will turn myself to the concluding part of your letter from Chatsworth. You are sensible that I do not differ from you in many things, and most certainly I do not dissent from the main of your doctrine concerning the heresy of depending upon contingencies. You must recollect how uniform my sentiments have been on that subject. I have ever wished a settled plan of our own, founded in the very essence of the American business, wholly unconnected with the events of the war, and framed in such a manner as to keep up our credit and to maintain our system at home, in spite of anything which may happen abroad. I am now convinced, by a long and somewhat vexatious experience, that such a plan is absolutely impracticable. I think with you, that some faults in the constitution of those whom we most love and trust are among the causes of this impracticability: they are faults, too, that one can hardly wish them perfectly cured of, as I am afraid they are intimately connected with honest disinterested intentions, plentiful fortunes, assured rank, and quiet homes. A great deal of activity and enterprise can scarcely ever be expected from such men, unless some horrible calamity is just over their heads, or unless they suffer some gross personal insults from power, the resentment of which may be as unquiet and stimulating a principle in their minds as ambition is in those of a different complexion. To say the truth, I cannot greatly blame them ; we live at a time when men are not repaid in fame for what they sacrifice in interest or repose.

"On the whole, when I consider of what discordant, and particularly of what fleeting, materials the Opposition has been all along composed, and at the same time review what Lord Rockingham has done, with that and with his own shattered constitution, for these last twelve years, I confess I am rather surprised that he has done so much, and persevered so long, than that he has felt now and then some cold fits, and that he grows somewhat languid and desponding at last. I know that he and those who are much prevalent with him, though they are not thought so much devoted to popularity as others, do very much look to the people, and more than I think is wise in them, who do so little to guide and direct the public opinion. Without this they act, indeed, but they act as it were from compulsion, and because it is impossible, in their situation, to avoid taking some part. All this it is impossible to change, and to no purpose to complain of. As to that popular humour, which is the medium we float·in, if I can discern anything at all of its present state, it is far worse than I have ever known or could ever imagine it. The faults of the people are not popular vices, at least they are not such as grow out of what we used to take to be the English temper and character. The greatest number have a sort of a heavy, lumpish acquiescence in Government, without much respect or esteem for those that compose it. I really cannot avoid making some very unpleasant prognostics from this disposition of the people. I think many of the symptoms must have struck you; I will mention one or two that are to me very remarkable. You must know that at Bristol we grow, as an election interest, and even as a party interest, rather stronger than we were when I was chosen. We have just now a majority in the corporation. In this state of matters, what, think you, have they done? They have voted their freedom to Lord Sandwich and Lord Suffolk; and the first at the very moment when the American privateers were domineering in the Irish Sea, and taking the Bristol traders in the Bristol Channel; to the latter, when his remonstrances on the subject of captures were the jest of Paris and of Europe. This fine step was taken, it seems, in honour of the zeal of these two profound statesmen in the prosecution of John the Painter, so totally negligent are they of everything essential, and so long and so deeply affected with trash the most low and contemptible; just as if they thought the merit of Sir John Fielding was the most shining point in the character of great ministers, in the most critical of all times, and, of all others, the most deeply interesting to the commercial world. My best friends in the corporation had no other doubts on the occasion, than whether it did not belong to me, by right of my representative capacity, to be the bearer of this auspicious compliment. In addition to this, if it could receive any addition, they now employ me to solicit, as a favour of no small magnitude, that, after the example of Newcastle, they may be suffered to arm vessels for their own defence in the Channel. Their memorial, under the seal of Merchants' Hall, is now lying on the table before me.

"Not a soul has the least sensibility on finding themselves, now for the first time, obliged to act as if the community was dissolved, and, after enormous payments towards the common protection, each part was to defend itself, as if it were a separate state. I don't mention Bristol as if that were the part furthest gone in this mortification. Far from it; I know that there is rather a little more life in us than in any other place. In Liverpool they are literally almost ruined by this American War; but they love it as they suffer from it. In short, from whatever I see, and from whatever quarter I hear, I am convinced that everything that is not absolute stagnation is evidently a party spirit, very adverse to our politics, and to the principles from whence they arise. There are manifest marks of the resurrection of the Tory party. They no longer criticise, as all disengaged people in the world always will, on the acts of Government; but they are silent under every evil, and hide and cover up every ministerial blunder and misfortune, with the officious zeal of men who think they have a party of their own to support in power. The Tories do universally think their power and consequence involved in the success of this American business. The clergy are astonishingly warm in it, and what the Tories are when embodied and united with their natural head the Crown, and animated by their clergy, no man knows better than yourself. As to the Whigs, I think them far from extinct. They are, what they always were (except by the able use of opportunities), by far the weakest party in this country. They have not yet learned the application of their principles to the present state of things; and as to the Dissenters, the main effective part of the Whig strength, they are, to use a favourite expression of our American campaign style, ' not all in force.' They will do very little; and, as far as I can discern, are rather intimidated than provoked at the denunciations of the Court in the Archbishop of York's sermon.* I thought that sermon rather imprudent when I first saw it, but it seems to have done its business.

"In this temper of the people I do not wholly wonder that our Northern friends look a little towards events; in war, particularly, I am afraid it must be so. There is something so weighty and decisive in the events of war, something that so completely overpowers the imagination of the vulgar, that all counsels must, in a great degree, be subordinate to, and attendant on them. I am sure it was so in the last war very eminently. So that, on the whole, what with the temper of the people, the temper of our own friends, and the domineering necessities of war, we must quietly give up all ideas of any settled, preconcerted plan. We shall be lucky enough if, keeping ourselves attentive and alert, we can contrive to profit of the occasions as they arise; though I am sensible that those who are best provided with a general scheme, are fittest to take advantage of all contingencies. However, to act with any people with the best degree of comfort, I believe we must contrive a little to assimilate to their character. We must gravitate towards them if we would keep in the same system, or ex-

---

* Archbishop Markham. His sermon was political.

pect that they should approach towards us. They are, indeed, worthy of much concession and management; I am quite convinced that they are the honestest public men that ever appeared in this country, and I am sure that they are the wisest by far of those who appear in it at present. None of those who are continually complaining of them but are themselves just as chargeable with all their faults, and·have a decent stock of their own into the bargain. They (our friends) are, as you truly represent them, but indifferently qualified for storming a citadel. After all, God knows whether this citadel is to be stormed by them or by anybody else, by the means they use or by any means. I know that, as they are, abstractedly speaking, to blame, so there are those who cry out against them for it, not with a friendly complaint, as we do, but with the bitterness of enemies. But I know, too, that those who blame them for want of enterprise, have shown no activity at all against the common enemy; all their skill and all their spirit have been shown only in weakening, dividing, and, indeed, destroying their allies. What they are, and what we are, is now pretty evidently experienced; and it is certain that, partly by our common faults, but much more by the difficulties of our situation and circumstances of unavoidable misfortune, we are in little better than a sort of *cul-de-sac*. For my part, I do all I can to give ease to my mind in this strange position. I remember, some years ago, when I was pressing some points with great eagerness and anxiety, and complaining with great vexation to the Duke of Richmond of the little progress I made, he told me kindly, and I believe very truly, that, though he was far from thinking so himself, other people would not be persuaded I had not some latent private interest in pushing these matters, which I urged with an earnestness so extreme, and so much approaching to passion. He was certainly in the right. I am thoroughly resolved to give, both to myself and my friends, less vexation on these subjects than hitherto I have done; much less indeed. If *you* should grow too earnest, you will be still more inexcusable than I was; your having entered into affairs so much younger, ought to make them too familiar to you to be the cause of much agitation; and you have much more before you for your work. Do not be in haste. Lay your foundations deep in public opinion. Though (as you are sensible) I have never given you the least hint of advice about joining yourself in a declared connexion with our party, nor do I now; yet, as I love that party very well, and am clear that you are better able to serve them than any man I know, I wish that things should be so kept as to leave you mutually very open to one another, as I am anxious that you should be always in all changes and contingencies; and wish this the rather, because (presuming that you are disposed to make a good use of power) you will certainly want some better support than merely that of the Crown. For I much doubt whether, with all your parts, you are the man formed for acquiring real interior favour in this Court or in any; I therefore wish you a firm ground in the country, and I do not know so firm and so sound a bottom to build on as our party."*

The rest of the letter relates to Ireland.

The session of Parliament was opened by the King on the 18th of November, 1777. At the conclusion of his royal speech the King said he should consider, as the

* Burke's "Works," 8vo, vol. ix. pp. 148–156.

greatest happiness of his life, and the greatest glory of his reign, the restoration of peace, order, and confidence to his American colonies.

Lord Chatham on this occasion made one of his greatest speeches. He urged a change of councils, and a repeal of the obnoxious acts. Yet he strongly protested against the acknowledgment of the independence of America: "The independent views of America," he said, "have been stated and asserted as the foundation of this address. My lords, no man wishes for the due dependence of America on this country more than I do. To preserve it, and not confirm that state of independence to which your measures hitherto have driven them, is the object which we ought to unite in attaining. The Americans,. contending for their rights against arbitrary exactions, I love and admire; it is the struggle of free and virtuous patriots, but, contending for independency and total disconnexion from England, I cannot wish them success; for in a due constitutional dependency, including the ancient supremacy of this country in regulating their commerce and navigation, consists the mutual happiness and prosperity both of England and America." Again: "I would participate to them every enjoyment which the colonizing subjects of a free state can possess, or wish to possess; and I do not see why they should not enjoy every fundamental right in their property, and every original substantial liberty which Devonshire, or Surrey, or the county I live in, or any other county in England, can claim; reserving always, as the sacred right of the mother country, the due constitutional dependency of the colonies. The inherent supremacy of the State in regulating and protecting the navigation and commerce of all her subjects is necessary for the mutual benefit and preservation of every part, to constitute and preserve the prosperous arrangement of the whole empire."*

The Duke of Richmond spoke a different language; at the close of a long and able speech, he said: "In regard to the amendment proposed, my only objection to it is, that it seems to convey to the world an idea that we are still in time to recover those invaluable provinces to Great Britain. I much fear it is elapsed. I do not say that it is impossible to re-unite America with England in some shape or other, or that it should not be attempted; but I would not have the people of this country raised to an expectation in which I fear they would be deceived. I will not despair, because I am convinced that an equitable and fair union would be most advantageous to the inhabitants of both countries; but, after the exasperated state to which things have been driven between the army and the Americans, I doubt they will never be reconciled to hold any dependence on a nation from which they have received such unpardonable injuries. A Secretary of State has said, that he was glad to hear the noble earl who moved the amendment declare that he was still for the dependency of America, and that he understood all who supported the noble lord agreed in the same sentiment. I know not from what premises such a conclusion is drawn; but, lest silence should be deemed acquiescence, I must for once declare that, although I much wish to see the Americans return of their own accord to a reasonable degree of dependency on this country, yet I will not say that any alliance with them as free states ought to be rejected. If we can obtain the benefits of their commerce in return for our protection, it is all that is essential;

* "Parliamentary History," vol. xix. p. 364: Mr. Boyd's report.

still less might be beneficial.   I would treat, and get what I could with their consent, but I would sooner give up every claim to America than continue an unjust and cruel civil war."*

The amendment was rejected by 97 to 28.

We see in this debate the elements of a fresh difference between Lord Chatham and the Rockingham Whigs.   It was further manifested by the declarations made at a later period by Lord Shelburne on the one side and by Mr. Fox on the other.   On the 5th of March, 1778, Lord Shelburne declared that "he would never consent that America should be independent.   The idea he ever entertained of the connexion between the two countries was that they should have one friend, one enemy, one purse, and one sword, and that Great Britain should superintend the interests of the whole, as the great controlling power.   That the two countries should have but one will, though the means of expressing that will might be different, distinct, and varied. It was once optional, and still possible, and he would never adopt any scheme which would go to dissever our colonies from us."   To make his meaning free from all obscurity, he declared emphatically, "the sun of Great Britain is set, and we shall no longer be a powerful or respectable people the moment that the independency of America is agreed to by our Government."†

On the 10th of April, 1778, on Mr. Powys's motion, "That the powers of the commissioners appointed to treat with America be enlarged, and that they be authorized to declare the Americans absolutely and for ever independent," Mr. Fox said, "He had formed a decided opinion upon the present question, and if he should happen to differ

* "Parliamentary History," vol. xix.   † Ibid. p. 850.

in his sentiments from a venerable character whom he honoured and revered (Lord Chatham), the committee would give him credit that no early prejudice, no childish pique, directed his judgment or influenced his mind. He had considered this matter abstracted from every other object, and his judgment was formed upon logical as well as natural reasoning and deduction. The dependency of America he thought it impossible, from our situation, as well as from the nature of the object, for us to regain. She had joined with France in an amicable and commercial treaty. The latter had recognised her independency, and both were bound in gratitude to defend one another against our resentment on the one hand, or our attempt to break the alliance on the other. If by concession or coercion we should attempt to recover the dependency of America, we should have the powers of France and America, and perhaps Spain, to encounter. If we should attempt to punish France for recognising the independency of America, America would join her, and we should have, in either case, two, if not three powers to combat. It was probable that the greatest part of Europe would join in the recognition. Gratitude on the one hand, and obligation on the other, would unite them in one bond, and we should experience the joint efforts of all, if we attacked one. If, on the contrary, the committee agreed to the motion, and thereby recognised the independency of America, we should be no longer bound to punish the European powers, who had already, or who might do the same; *and we should probably secure a larger share of the commerce of the Americans by a perpetual alliance on a federal foundation, than by a nominal dependence.*"*

Whatever may have been the expediency of Lord Chat-

* "Parliamentary History," vol. xix. p. 1082.

ham's original proposition, that taxes for revenue should be given up, and duties for regulation of trade retained, it was clear that at this time peace was not to be obtained by compromise. Not even the veneration in which the name of Chatham was justly held, could have made such an arrangement possible. The Americans had made up their minds to independence, and would not have agreed to submission on any terms. When Lord North proposed the conciliatory bills, Washington wrote thus to a member of Congress: "Nothing short of independence, it appears to me, can possibly do. A peace on any other terms would, if I may be allowed the expression, be a peace of war. The injuries we have received from the British nation were so unprovoked, and have been so great and so many, that they can never be forgotten. Besides the feuds, the jealousies, the animosities that would ever attend a union with them, besides the importance, the advantages which we should derive from an unrestricted commerce, our fidelity as a people, our gratitude, our character as men, are opposed to a coalition with them as subjects; but, in case of the last extremity, were we easily to accede to terms of dependence, no nation, upon future occasions, let the oppressions of Britain be ever so flagrant and unjust, would interfere for our relief, or at most they would do it with a cautious reluctance, and upon conditions most probably that would be hard, if not dishonourable to us."*

In this division of opinion there can be little doubt that the Duke of Richmond and Mr. Fox were in the right. The march of General Burgoyne showed the general enthusiasm of New England in the cause of independence; the little progress made by General Howe in the south proved

* Sparks's "Life of Washington," vol. i. p. 287.

that Washington might be driven back, but could not be destroyed. Lord Chatham and Lord Shelburne were mistaken in thinking that with the loss of America the sun of England would set for ever. Seven years of unavailing contest, and seventy-five years of the greatness of the British empire after separation, have proved the wisdom of the advice which the Rockingham Whigs gave to their country. Mr. Fox said truly, that commerce with America on friendly terms would serve us better than a nominal dependence. Experience has proved the truth of his assertion. The trade between Great Britain and America has increased at least fivefold since the separation. Not all the jealousy of the mercantile system, not all the prohibitions to which Lord Chatham adhered, nor all the taxes which the financial genius of Mr. Grenville could have devised, could have furnished to Great Britain any advantages to be compared with the profits of unrestricted intercourse founded on the sense of mutual benefits, and the amity of two great independent States.

CHAPTER X.

PROCEEDINGS IN PARLIAMENT—WAR WITH FRANCE—PROGRESS OF AFFAIRS IN AMERICA—NEGOTIATIONS—DEATH OF CHATHAM.

1778.

SOON after the meeting of Parliament, Colonel Luttrell, complaining that in a certain morning paper he had been grossly misrepresented, informed the House that for his future safety and protection he was determined to move that the Standing Order of the House for excluding strangers from the gallery should be strictly enforced.

Mr. Fox laid down the true doctrine of publicity on this occasion. He said : " That he was convinced the true and only method of preventing misrepresentation was by throwing open the gallery, and making the debates and decisions of the House as public as possible. There was less danger of misrepresentation in a full company than in a thin one, as there would be a greater number of persons to give evidence against the misrepresentation. The shutting of the gallery could not prevent the proceedings of the House from finding their way to public view; for, during a certain period, when the gallery was kept empty, the debates were printed, let the manner of obtaining them be what it might, and, in fact, the public had a right to know what passed in Parliament."

On the 2nd of February Mr. Fox, in a committee on the

state of the nation, moved, " That no more of the old corps should be sent out of the kingdom." Public expectation having been raised by Mr. Fox's notice, the lobbies were crowded, and the doors being closed, strangers forced their way, in spite of the doorkeepers, into the gallery. Nearly sixty ladies, including the Duchess of Devonshire, were also present. But the House, resenting the forcible entrance of strangers, ordered the gallery to be cleared, and on the suggestion of Governor Johnstone, the ladies were likewise excluded. The following extracts are taken from the report of Mr. Fox's speech :—

" Sir, I shall not now enter into any more of the proceedings relative to America than are necessary to show the immediate steps which have brought us into our present situation. Without discussing the various questions which have been for many years agitated in Parliament, I shall take up the measures relative to America in the year 1774, when the riots at Boston first called for the attention of this House; papers were, indeed, called for and granted, but there were some things that tended that year to shut the eyes of Ministers to the true state of that country, and the true interest of this; which was to prevent, rather than stimulate and increase the general discontents in the colonies. Every one must allow that the agreement with the East India Company was a most unfortunate one, and the immediate source of all the troubles that have since followed. Here began a capital mistake of the Ministry; they mistook the single province of Massachusetts Bay for the American empire. Virginia, a colony no less jealous of its rights, nor less warm in its assertion of them, was entirely forgotten; it was not thought possible that any other colony should unite with Massachusetts; now, who-

ever fights against ten men, and thinks he is contending only with one, will meet with more difficulties than
if he was aware of the force brought against him; for I
believe I may lay it down as an undoubted maxim in
politics, that every attempt to crush an insurrection with
means inadequate to the end, foments instead of suppressing
it. The case here was, you took a great object for a small
one, you took thirteen provinces for one; and not only that,
you imagined the other twelve were with you, when the
very act you were then doing made those twelve equally
hostile. Sir, another mistake at this time was the taking
a violent step against the town of Boston. If America was
not before sufficiently united in a determined resistance to
the claims of this country, this measure made all America
combined; they were all from that moment united with the
town of Boston, which might have been before the object
of the jealousy of the rest. Another mistake was the altering the government of the province of Massachusetts
Bay; whereas the acts of all the other colonies as well as
this, plainly showed it was not the form of government in
that province which occasioned the commotions there, because other provinces which depended more on the Crown,
and which have the appellation of royal governments, were
not less early or less vigorous in their opposition and resistance. Now, sir, if the form of this government was
not itself the cause of the troubles in that country, then the
alarm given by the alteration of that government was certainly a most capital mistake; because it gave the whole
continent reason to fear that they had no security in the
permanency of their government, but that it was liable to
be altered or subverted at our pleasure, on any cause of
complaint, whether real or supposed. Thus their natural

jealousies were awakened, for by the same reasoning on which your acts were grounded, the governments of the other colonies, though much more dependent on the Crown, might be rendered entirely despotic; and they were all thence taught to consider the town of Boston as suffering in the common cause, and that they themselves might very soon stand in need of that assistance which they were now lending to that unfortunate town."

After adverting to the coercive measures of 1775, Mr. Fox proceeded :—

" But, as if all this was not enough to exasperate, and to prove they had no resource left but in resistance, we rejected, before the end of the session of 1775, the petition from New York, drawn up in the most affectionate and respectful terms that could be, considering the state of the contest. This was the last effort of the moderate party, your own friends, who were told, on the news going back to America, ' You see what dependence is to be put in Great Britain ; how will she treat us when she has thus treated you?' Sir, a few weeks before the arrival of the reinforcements the civil war began. Then followed the battle of Bunker's Hill. This ought at least to have been a lesson to the Ministry that America was unanimous, and determined to put everything at stake. Sir, there is one circumstance I omitted to mention in its place, and that is the conciliatory proposition of the noble lord [North]. It has been often considered, and I will only say, what everybody must allow, that this House was left to judge of the *quantum*, which was one of the very principal objections urged by the Americans, that they did not know how far this claim of ours might extend ; it was in fact not only asserting the right, but establishing it in practice. I beg leave to stop here for a moment, and ask this question, Does any man seriously think it better to give up America altogether, unless we can exercise the right of taxation in the uncontrolled and unlimited manner in which we claim it?"

The Ministers made no reply, and the question being called for, the committee divided :—

For Mr. Fox 165
Against 259

Majority 94

The feelings and views of Mr. Fox at this time are described, with the frankness and candour which were habitual to him, in a letter to Richard Fitzpatrick, then serving in America, written on the day following this debate :—

"I think you are the best describer of military operations I ever knew, for I perfectly understand them by your letters, which I scarce ever do from those of others. What a scene of folly it has been! But it has not yet had all the effect here that you at a distance imagine it would have. I think you are too violent in some of your ideas; but as this letter may possibly be read by others as well as you, I cannot now tell you my mind upon those subjects. What the Ministers intend doing, besides keeping their places, upon which they are very decided, I cannot even guess. They know as little how to make peace as war. In short, they are as completely at a *non plus* as people can be; but they still keep a great majority, though we begin to increase considerably. We divided last night (2nd of February) on a motion for the state of the nation, 165 to 259; which is certainly a very good division compared with the last, but a very bad one in my mind, considering the circumstances of the country. I made the motion in a very long speech, in which I went over the whole of the American business, and I really thought the House went a good deal with me in most of it. I purposely avoided all topics that related to the justice of the war, and confined myself merely to the absurdity of it in all its parts, and the absolute madness of continuing it. The resolution moved was, that none of the old corps now in Europe should be spared for the American War. We had several Tories with us; and I really think it was a great day for us. The Ministry, not by concert, I believe, but by accident, did not say one word; which scandalized even their own friends a good deal, as I had opened the affair so very fully, for I spoke two hours and forty minutes. They now pretend to say that Ellis and Wedderburne were up (I did not see them), and while they were complimenting one another the question was put. The fact is, that it is such a cause as no man can defend well, and therefore nobody likes to attempt it. We shall soon go into an inquiry upon the Canada expedition, in which how Lord G—— [George Germaine] will defend himself is much above my comprehension. They mean to be hard upon Burgoyne, which is a baseness beyond what even you or I could have expected from them. The inquiry is also in my hands, so that I have business enough, indeed more than I can well manage; for though I like the House of Commons itself, I hate the preparatory business of looking at accounts, drawing motions, &c., as much as you could do. *I am convinced we shall so far succeed as to get great divisions* in the House of Commons, and to convince all the world that the Ministers deserve all possible contempt. *But when we have done that, I think we shall have done all we can do, and that the Ministers, though despised*

*everywhere, and by everybody, will still continue Ministers.
I am thoroughly persuaded of this,* but the general opinion is
otherwise. There is a report of Lord Chatham being to
come in immediately, but I have good reasons for totally
disbelieving it. I think I have given you enough of
politics, considering I have nothing but reports and con-
jectures to give you. With respect to my own share, I can
only say that people flatter me that I continue to gain
rather than lose my credit as an orator; *and I am so convinced that this is all I ever shall gain (unless I choose to
become the meanest of men), that I never think of any other
object of ambition.*

"*I am certainly ambitious by nature,* but I really have, or
think I have, totally subdued that passion. I have still as
much vanity as ever, which is a happier passion by far,
because great reputation I may acquire and *keep,* great
situation I *never* can acquire, nor, if acquired, *keep without
making sacrifices that I never will make.* If I am wrong,
and more sanguine people right, *tant mieux,* and I shall be
as happy as they can be; but if I am right, I am sure I
shall be the happier for having made up my mind to my
situation.

"I need not say how happy I am at the thoughts of
your coming; I should be so at all times, but I really want
you at present to a great degree. I have other friends
whom I love, and who I believe love me, but I foresee
possible cases where I am determined to act against all the
advice they are likely to give me. I know they will not
shake me, for nothing ever shall; but yet it would be a great
satisfaction to have you here, who I know would be of my
opinion. You guess, I dare say, the sort of cases I mean.
I shall be told by prudent friends that I am under no sort

of engagements to any set of men. *I certainly am not;* but there are many cases where there is no engagement, and yet it is dishonourable not to act as if there was one. But even suppose it were quite honourable, is it possible to be happy in acting with people of whom one has the worst opinions, and being on a cold footing (which must be the case) with all those whom one loves best, and with whom one passes his life? I have talked to you a great deal about myself, but I know it will interest you, and I have really little else to tell you, as I know Ossory has written to you."*

Mr. Fox, according to Lord Holland, had told Lord John Townshend at Chatsworth in the preceding summer, that he meant to connect himself formally with the Rockingham Whigs. For three years before he had acted in concert with them, and from this time he must be considered a member of that party.

The Rockingham Whigs must be esteemed as a revival of that party which had obtained for the country the Revolution of 1688, and had established the House of Hanover on the throne. The virtue of the Whigs had greatly declined under Newcastle; but Rockingham, Burke, and Fox, combined with good men in a great and just cause, had rekindled the sacred flame, and under the old title had formed a new band of patriotic statesmen. Such was the beginning of the new Whig party, which put an end to the American War, abolished the Slave Trade, obtained religious liberty for the Roman Catholics, and carried Parliamentary Reform.

On the 19th of February, 1778, Lord North rose in the House of Commons to move a fresh conciliatory budget. He

* "Correspondence and Memoirs of Fox," vol. i. p. 167.

proposed: 1. To repeal the tea duty absolutely. 2. To renounce by act of Parliament all right of taxing the colonies for revenue, and to provide that the produce of any duties imposed for the regulation of trade should be paid over to the colonies. 3. To appoint commissioners who should have the power to treat with Congress as such to put a stop to the war, and to suspend all laws of which the Americans might complain, and which the commissioners should be willing to revoke. A dull, melancholy silence succeeded the delivery of Lord North's speech. Astonishment, dejection, and fear overloaded the whole assembly. No mark of approbation appeared from any part of the House.* Nor was this to be wondered at. Members who had supported the war must have seen the fabric of empire, which Lord North had hitherto displayed before their eyes, vanish into air, with feelings of consternation. Others of a different stamp, who had warned the Ministry not to repeat the experiment of the stamp duty, must have reflected with sorrow that ten years earlier the concession now made might have saved millions of treasure, rivers of blood, and the affections of three millions of people. Mr. Fox spoke immediately after Lord North. The following was the substance of his speech: " He said that he could not refuse his assent to the propositions made by the noble lord, that he was very glad to find that they were, in the main, so ample and satisfactory, and that he believed they would be supported by all those with whom he had the honour to act. That they did not materially differ from those which had been made by an honourable friend of his [Mr. Burke] about three years ago; that the very same arguments which had been used by the minority, and very

* "Annual Register," 1778.

nearly in the same words, were used by the noble lord upon this occasion. He was glad to find that the noble lord had wholly relinquished the right of taxation, as this was a fundamental point : he was glad, also, that he had declared his intention of giving the commissioners power to restore the charter of Massachusetts Bay ; for giving the satisfaction which the noble lord proposed, it would be necessary for Parliament to give the same security with regard to charters which it had given with regard to taxation ; that the Americans were fully as jealous of the rights of their assemblies as of taxation, and their chief objection to the latter was its tendency to affect the former.

" He wished that this concession had been made earlier and upon principles more respectful to Parliament. To tell them that, if they were deceived, they had deceived themselves, was neither kind nor civil to an assembly which for so many years had relied upon the noble lord with such unreserved confidence. All public bodies of the nature of the House of Commons must give a large confidence to persons in office ; and their only method of preventing the abuse of that confidence was to punish those who had misinformed them concerning the true state of their affairs, or conducted them with negligence, ignorance, or incapacity. The noble lord's arguments upon this subject might be all collected into one point, his excuses all reduced into one apology— his total ignorance. The noble lord hoped, and was disappointed. He expected a great deal, and found little to answer his expectations. He thought America would have submitted to his laws, and they resisted them ; he thought they would have submitted to his armies, and his armies were beaten by inferior numbers ; he made conciliatory propositions, and he thought they would succeed, but they were rejected; he appointed commissioners to make peace, and he thought they had powers, but he found they could not make peace, and nobody believed that they had any powers. He had said many such things on his conciliatory proposition; he thought it a proper mode of quieting the Americans upon the affair of taxation. If any gentleman would give himself the trouble of reading that proposition, he would find not one word of it correspondent to the representation made of it by its framer. The short account of it was, that the noble lord in that proposition assured the colonies that, when Parliament had taxed them as much as they thought proper, they would tax them no more. He would vote for the present proposition, because it was much more clear and satisfactory, for necessity had forced the noble lord to speak plain. But if the concession should be found ample enough, but should be found to come too late, what punishment would be sufficient for those who adjourned Parliament in order to make a proposition of concession, and then had neglected to do it until France had concluded a treaty with the independent States of America? He said he could answer with certainty for the truth of his information: it was no light matter, and came from no contemptible authority; he therefore wished that the Ministry would give the House satisfaction on this interesting point, whether they knew anything of this treaty, and whether they had not been informed previously to the making of their proposition of a treaty which would make that proposition as useless to the peace as it was humiliating to the dignity of Great Britain?"

The allusion in this speech to a treaty between France and America is thus explained by Horace Walpole: " My cousin Thomas Walpole had acquainted me that the treaty with France was signed. We agreed to inform Charles Fox; but, as we both distrusted Burke, and feared the childish fluctuations of Lord Rockingham, we determined that Fox should know nothing of the secret till an hour or two before the House met. Accordingly, Thomas Walpole communicated the notice of the treaty to the Duke of Grafton on the 16th, and engaged him to acquaint Charles Fox but just before the House should meet next day. This was done most exactly, and Burke knew nothing of the matter till he came into the House. As soon as Lord North had opened his two bills, Charles Fox rose, and, after pluming himself on having sat there till he had brought the noble lord to concur in sentiments with him and his friends, he astonished Lord North by asking him whether a commercial treaty with France had not been signed by the American agents at Paris within the last ten days? 'If so,' said he, 'the Administration is beaten by ten days—a situation so threatening that, in such a time of danger, the House must concur with the propositions, though probably now they would have no effect.' Lord North was thunderstruck, and would not rise. Burke maintained that Lord North had taken precisely the plan that he (Burke) had offered two years before, and he called on him to answer to the fact of the treaty. Still the Minister was silent till Sir G. Savile rose and told him that it would be criminal and a matter of impeachment to withhold an answer, and ended by crying, 'An answer! an answer! an answer!' Lord North, thus forced up, owned he had heard a report of the treaty, but desired to give no answer to the House at that moment; he had no official intelligence on the subject. The report might be vague. Some time ago the ministers of France had denied it. Such evasive answers convinced everybody of the truth of the report."*

On the 5th of March, when the Conciliatory Bills were in the House of Lords, the Duke of Grafton repeated the question put by Mr. Fox. He said that his kinsman had in the other House of Parliament put the question to the Minister, who had given an evasive answer; but the matter was of too important a nature, and at that time too immediately critical, to be passed over in silence. " If the information was true, it was absurd to insult Parliament with the appearance of reconciliation that was no longer practicable. If Ministers should reply in the affirmative, they were culpable in the highest degree in concealing intelligence of so important a nature from Parliament, and, under the cover of that concealment, leading it into measures of futility and public dishonour. If they should reply in the negative, their conduct was, if possible, still more reprehensible; their incapacity more glaring in being entirely wanting in that species of information which it was the duty of their stations to procure." He desired the House of Lords to bear in mind that it was on the 5th of March he put this question.†

Lord Weymouth, after some preface, assured the House, in the plainest and most precise manner, that he knew not of any such treaty having been entered into, " and he desired the House to recollect that it was on the 5th of March that he gave this answer." Notwithstanding this denial, a Treaty of Amity and Commerce had been signed on the 6th of February between the Court of France and the Congress of the United States. By a Treaty of

---

* " Memorials and Correspondence," vol. i.
† " Parliamentary History," vol. xix. pp. 834, 835.

Alliance, concluded at the same time, it was stipulated that if France should become involved in war with Great Britain, America and France were to co-operate; if any conquests should be made on the continent of North America, they were to belong to the Congress; if any of the West India Islands should be taken, they were to belong to France. Lord Weymouth was fully aware of this fact when he made the denial which has been quoted. On the 6th of February Lord Stormont wrote to him, "I think I am now able to speak to your lordship with some precision with regard to the treaty between this Court and the rebels. My informer assured me it is actually signed; but Dr. Franklin, not thinking himself authorized to grant all the demands made by France, has signed *sub spe rati.*" Again, on the 18th he writes: "Both these treaties were, I am assured, actually signed on Friday, the 6th inst., by M. Gérard."* Thus, Ministers were guilty of concealment, and of leading Parliament, as the Duke of Grafton had said, to "measures of futility and public dishonour." Indeed, the disposition of France to join in the war had been made known to the Ministers by Lord Stormont some time before. On the 6th of February Burke made a speech of nearly three hours and a half in moving for papers relating to the military employment of Indians on the continent of America in the present civil war. His speech seems to have been one of wonderful eloquence. Walpole says: "His wit made North, Rigby, and Ministers laugh; his pathos drew tears down Barré's cheeks." The "Annual Register" tells us that, while one member wished to have the speech posted on the church doors, "a member of great distinction congratulated the Ministers upon admitting no

* Lord Mahon's "History of England," vol. v. appendix.

strangers on that day into the gallery, as the indignation of the people might have been excited against them to a degree that would have endangered their safety."* Mr. Burke seems on this occasion to have anticipated the eloquence, if not the glory, of one of his great orations against Hastings.

An abortive negotiation between the Court and some of the Opposition took place in the month of March of this year. It is remarkable as showing the determination of the King to have no other Minister than Lord North. Thus he writes to Lord North, in answer evidently to a letter expressing the Minister's wish to retire: " On a subject, which has for many months engrossed my thoughts, I cannot have the smallest difficulty instantly to answer the letter I have just received from you. My sole wish is to keep you at the head of the Treasury, and as my confidential Minister. That end obtained, I am willing, through your channel, to accept any description of persons that will come avowedly to the support of your administration, and as such I do not object to Lord Shelburne and Mr. Barré, who personally, perhaps, I dislike as much as Alderman Wilkes, and I cannot give you a stronger proof of my desire to forward your wishes than taking the unpleasant step. . . . But I declare in the strongest and most solemn manner that, though I do not object to your addressing yourself to Lord Chatham, yet that you must acquaint him that I shall never address myself to him but through you, and on a clear explanation that he is to step forth to support an administration wherein you are First Lord of the Treasury, and that I cannot consent to have any conversation with him till the Ministry is formed;

* " Annual Register," 1778. The member was Governor Johnstone.

that if he comes into this, I will, as he supports you, receive him with open arms. I leave the whole arrangement to you, provided Lord Suffolk, Lord Weymouth, and my two able lawyers are satisfied as to their situations; but choose Ellis for Secretary at War in preference to Barré, who in that event will get a more lucrative employment, but will not be so near my person. Having said this, I will only add—to put before your eyes my most inward thoughts—that no advantage to this country, nor personal danger to myself, can ever make me address myself to Lord Chatham, or any other branch of Opposition. Honestly, I would rather lose the Crown I now wear than bear the ignominy of possessing it under their shackles. I might write volumes, if I would state the feelings of my mind, and what I will never depart from. Should Lord Chatham wish to see me before he gives his answer, I shall most certainly refuse it; I have had enough of personal negotiations, and neither my dignity nor my feelings will ever let me again submit to it. Men of less principle and honesty than I pretend to may look on public measures as a game. I always act from conviction, but I am shocked at the base arts all these men have used—therefore cannot go towards them; if they come to your assistance I will accept them. You have now full powers to act, but I do not expect Lord Chatham and his crew will come to your assistance; but if they do not, I trust the rest of the arrangement will greatly strengthen, as it will give efficiency to, the Administration. Thurlow as Chancellor, Yorke as Secretary of State, will be efficient men. Numbers we have already. Lord Dartmouth as Steward, and Lord Weymouth Privy Seal, will please them both I am certain. Lord W——'s conduct, on your last vacancy of the seals, gives him a right to this change, if agreeable to him."

Mr. Eden, who was authorized to see Lord Shelburne, gives the following account of his conversation with him: "At a quarter past seven I called on Dr. Priestley, who introduced Lord Shelburne to me and left us. We sat together till half-past ten, though he told me at first that he was appointed at eight o'clock to attend an Opposition meeting (at the Duke of Richmond's). I confided to him my copy of the French Ambassador's declaration (which I knew, however, that he was already in possession of). He read it aloud, as a paper quite new to him, but commented on it very frankly, and said that it was impossible to consider it otherwise than as a declaration of war; that we must act accordingly; that New York should be strongly armed; the frontiers of Canada secured; Florida strengthened; Pennsylvania evacuated; the fisheries defended; the West India Islands and all other possessions secured; the proposed commission desisted from, as now become nugatory, but all the American acts to be repealed; measures of force against France to be adopted. In talking of himself, he said that he abhorred intrigue; that his temper and feelings led him to the utmost unreserve and frankness; that his disposition was best suited to private life; that he was naturally indolent, &c. &c.; that he abhorred all parties; that when gentlemen of Opposition came to him, he always advised them to prefer Lord Rockingham; that when anything was said to him tending to a connexion with Government, he could say nothing but that ' Lord Chatham must be the dictator.' When I asked him what Lord Chatham would dictate, he said that I must have heard, both through the Duke of Northumberland and *through another channel,* that when his Majesty last parted with Lord Chatham, his Majesty was pleased to say he foresaw he should, on future occasions, want his advice and assistance, and that the occasion was now come. He knew, he said, that Lord Chatham thought any change insufficient which did not comprehend and annihilate every party in the kingdom; that the Duke of Grafton and Lord Rockingham must be included; that a great law arrangement would, in Lord Chatham's opinion, be material; and that Lord Mansfield ought to be removed. He was liberal in solemn assurances to me that no one syllable of our conversation should ever transpire; was sorry, he said, to collect nothing from me that tended to produce a general reformation in Government. He professed no disregard to Lord Suffolk and Lord North (possibly through politeness), but dwelt with some asperity on Lord Gower's principles of government, and on Lord George's insufficiency (in which he made some allusions to General Carleton). He intimated that Lord Chatham would not wish, perhaps, to give the Treasury to Lord Rockingham, but would, perhaps, offer to make him Lord Chamberlain. It was agreed, in the close of our conversation, that we should mutually act as if we had never met, but that I should call again on Tuesday evening at a quarter past eight."

The King, when this account is submitted to him, thus breaks forth in indignation against his powerful subject: " You can want no further explanation of the language held to Mr. Eden the last evening. It is so totally contrary to the only ground on which I could have accepted the services of *that perfidious man,* that I need not enter on it. Lord Chatham, as dictator—as planning a new Administration—I appeal to my letter of yesterday, if I did not clearly speak out upon. If Lord Chatham agrees to support your Administration (or, if you like better), the fundamentals of the present Administration—viz., Lord N—— at the head of the Treasury; Lords Suffolk, Gower, and Weymouth in great offices to their own inclinations; Lord Sandwich at the Admiralty; Thurlow, Chancellor; and Wedderburne as Chief Justice—I will not object to see that great man when Lord Shelburne, Dunning, and Barré are placed already in office; but I solemnly declare that nothing shall bring me to treat personally with Lord Chatham. If I saw Lord C——, he would insist on as total a change as Lord Shelburne yesterday threw out."

Lord North seems to have hesitated, which drew from the King the following declaration :—

" Same day.

" I am fully convinced that you are actuated alone from a wish not to conceal the most private corners of your breast in writing the letter you have just sent unto me; but, my dear lord, it is not private pique, but an opinion formed on an experience of now *seventeen* years, that makes me resolve to run any personal risk rather than to submit to Opposition, which every plan deviating from strengthening the present Administration is more or less tending to. I am certain, while I can have no one object in view but to be of use to the country, it is impossible I can be deserted, and the road opened to a set of men who certainly would make me a slave for the remainder of my days; and, whatever they may pretend, would go to the most unjustifiable lengths of cruelty and destruction of those who have stood forth in public offices, of which you would be the first victim."

Again the King writes :—

" March 17th, 1778.

" I am grieved at your continually recurring to a subject on which we can never agree. Your letter is certainly personally affectionate to me, and shows no sign of personal fear; but, my dear lord, no consideration in life shall make me stoop to Opposition. I am still ready to accept any part of them that will come to the assistance of my present efficient Ministers; but whilst any ten men in the kingdom will stand by me, I will not give myself up to bondage. My dear lord, I will rather risk my crown than do what I think personally disgraceful. It is impossible this nation should not stand by me. If they will not, they shall have another King, for I never will put my hand to what will make me miserable to the last hour of my life; therefore, let Thurlow instantly know that I will appoint him Chancellor; and the Solicitor-General that, if he does not choose to be Attorney-General, we will treat with the Chief Justice of the Common Pleas to resign."

" March 18th, 1778.

" I am highly incensed at the language held by Lord Shelburne last night to Eden, and approve of that of the latter. I am fairly worn down; but all proposals and answers must in future go through you, for I will not change the Administration, but if I can with honour, let you make the acquisitions."

" March 18th, 1778.

" Convey to Thurlow and Wedderburne my intentions. Then, and not till then, I am open to the plan of Ministry proposed by you on Sunday. I never will accept the service of any part of Opposition, but to strengthen *you*. To give *you ease*, I consent to what gives me infinite pain; but any further, even that consideration would not make me go.

Rather than be shackled by these desperate men (if the nation will not stand by me), I will rather see any form of government introduced into this island, and lose my crown, rather than wear it as a disgrace."

Lord Mahon finds an excuse for the King's violence against Lord Chatham, in the conduct which Lord Chatham had pursued since his last resignation of office. But Lord Chatham had done no more than maintain, after leaving office, the same principles and opinions which he had avowed before accepting office, and which he had never abandoned. His inconsistency amounted only to his retaining the nominal leadership in the Ministry after his counsels had been set aside, and the taxation of America resumed. But his state of health fully accounted for this conduct. No man, however, could less tolerate an honest difference of opinion than George III. When Lord Chatham ceased to be an instrument of the Court, he became in the King's eyes a "trumpet of sedition." It is curious to see that Lord Chatham could not yet make up his mind to see Lord Rockingham in an efficient and ostensible office, and treated him with affected contempt. It was obvious that the Duke of Richmond, Mr. Burke, and Mr. Fox would have felt themselves bound in honour to support Lord Rockingham against the extravagant pretension of Lord Chatham to govern alone without a party, and without three men of ability as his colleagues.

Yet, although the King felt such strong objections to Opposition on personal grounds, he was not quite unprepared for the policy which both Lord Chatham and Lord Rockingham would have recommended. Writing on the 31st of January, on the probability of a war with France, he says: " Should that happen, it might be wise to withdraw the troops from the revolted provinces, and having strengthened Canada, &c., to make war on the French and Spanish islands. Success in that object will repay our exertions; and this country having had its attention directed to a fresh object, would be in a better temper to subscribe to such terms as Administration might offer to America."

Had Lord North persisted in his wish to retire, it has been asked, what success would Lord Chatham have had as Prime Minister in preventing the separation of America? Some have thought he would have succeeded, others that Heaven spared him the anxiety of the attempt, and the mortification of a failure. Reasoning from the complexion of the times, and the former conduct of Lord Chatham, we may perhaps form a conclusion tolerably sound. It seems hardly possible that Lord Chatham should have been able to persuade the Americans to relinquish their half-won independence; and, even had he induced them to treat, there is an obstacle which has always been fatal to similar negotiations. Monarchy and freedom can only exist together on the condition that the monarch act in good faith, and is believed to do so by his subjects. The powers of the Executive are naturally so extensive, that, if ill-directed, they are sufficient to overthrow the best-balanced constitution. Hence, when the people have no confidence in their sovereign, they ask for a limitation of the prerogative inconsistent with monarchy, and the King on his side refuses to part with the means which he deems necessary for the maintenance of his authority. This mutual distrust prevented the restoration of peace between Charles I. and his insurgent subjects; it would equally have prevented the re-establishment of the authority of George III. in America.

Indeed, the slight overtures which had taken place between Lord Chatham and Dr. Franklin three years before showed the nature of the breach. Dr. Franklin fairly asked that the King's troops should not be quartered in America without the consent of the separate legislatures; Lord Chatham as fairly declined to accede to a condition which, in his own phrase, would have plucked " the master feather from the eagle's wing." We may embrace as undeniable the axiom, that the first condition of free representative monarchy is good faith on the part of the monarch, and confidence on the part of his people.

We may therefore conclude that a Ministry formed at this time by Lord Chatham, although it might have wrung triumphs from France, would have failed in persuading the Americans to forego their independence. Lord Chatham, sinking into the grave, would have been unable to offer securities acceptable to Congress. His death or resignation could not be distant, and where was then to be the guarantee for the terms of union? Some flashes of glory might indeed have lighted up the darkness of the last months of the war; and the Americans, if not induced to renew the tie which had been broken, might have parted from Great Britain on more amicable terms, had the voice of Chatham pronounced the sentence of divorce. But a mightier hand was about to cut the thread of all such anticipations. The Duke of Richmond, who had assured Lord Mahon that if Lord Chatham, as Minister, tried to reconcile the colonies, he would support the attempt as long as any hope of success remained, now gave notice, that on the 7th of April he would move an address to the King, entreating him to withdraw his fleets and armies from America, and make peace with the revolted colonies. Lord

Chatham was at this time at Hayes, slowly recovering from a fit of the gout; but the moment he heard of the intended address he resolved to attend the House of Lords, and neither his family nor his friends could induce him to desist from his purpose.

On the 7th of April, accordingly, he came into the House with feeble steps, leaning with one arm on his son, William Pitt, and with the other on his son-in-law, Lord Mahon. After the Duke of Richmond had spoken, Lord Chatham rose. "The Earl spoke," writes Lord Camden to the Duke of Grafton, "but was not like himself; his speech faltered, his sentences broken, and his mind not master of itself. His words were shreds of unconnected eloquence, and flashes of the same fire which he, Prometheus-like, had stolen from Heaven, and were then returning to the place from whence they were taken. Your Grace sees even I, who am a mere prose man, am tempted to be poetical while I am discoursing of this extraordinary man's genius."

Lord Chatham spoke with natural indignation of the lowered position of this great country, whose fabric of empire he had himself raised and consolidated. "My lords, his Majesty succeeded to an empire as great in extent as its reputation was unsullied. Shall we tarnish the lustre of that empire by an ignominious surrender of its rights? Shall we now fall prostrate before the House of Bourbon? Surely, my lords, this nation is no longer what it was; shall a people that seventeen years ago was the terror of the world, now stoop so low as to tell its ancient inveterate enemy, 'Take all we have, only give us peace.' I wage war with no man or set of men. I wish for none of their employments, nor would I co-operate with men who still persist in unretracted error; but, in God's name, if it be absolutely necessary to declare either for peace or war, and peace cannot be preserved with honour, why is not war commenced without hesitation? I am not, I confess, well informed of the resources of this kingdom, but I trust it has still sufficient, though I know them not, to maintain its just rights. Let us at least make one effort, and if we must fall, let us fall like men!"

In speaking of foreign invasion he said: " Of a Spanish invasion, of a French invasion, of a Dutch invasion, many noble lords may have read in history, and some lords," looking keenly at Lord Mansfield, "may perhaps remember a Scotch invasion."

The Duke of Richmond answered Lord Chatham. Lord Camden allows his "candour, courtesy, and liberal treatment of his illustrious adversary." He observed that when Lord Chatham conducted our victorious arms it was Great Britain and America against France and Spain; "it will now be France, Spain, and America against Great Britain."

Lord Chatham rose to reply, but nature was exhausted, "he fell back," says Lord Camden, "upon his seat, and was to all appearance in the agonies of death. This threw the whole House into confusion; every person was upon his legs in a moment, hurrying from one place to another, some sending for assistance, others producing salts and others reviving spirits. Many crowding about the earl, to observe his countenance; all affected; most part really concerned; and even those who might have felt a real pleasure at the accident, yet put on the appearance of distress, except only the Earl of M——, who sat still, almost as much unmoved as the senseless body itself."

The Earl of M—— was Lord Mansfield. The Scotch invasion had not been forgotten. Lord Chatham was carried into the Prince's chamber, and laid upon the table, supported by pillows. After a few days, he recovered sufficiently to be removed to Hayes. But the attack was fatal. He expired at Hayes on the 11th of May following. I shall not dwell on the general lamentation that ensued, nor on the votes of Parliament, nor on the splendid monument erected in Westminster Abbey to his memory. Some remarks on the feeling evinced by the King, and on the public character of Lord Chatham, may, however, not be out of place. George III. gave to the last proofs of the narrowness of his mind and the vindictiveness of his temper. In 1775, upon some proposition for inserting the name of Lord Chatham's second son in the grant of pensions, he had said: " As to any gratitude to be expected from him or his family, the whole tenor of their lives has shown them void of that honourable sentiment. *But when decrepitude or death puts an end to him as a trumpet of sedition, I shall make no difficulty in placing the second son's name instead of the father's, and making up the pension 3000l.*"

In the same spirit he wrote on the day after Lord Chatham's death : " I am rather surprised at the vote of a public funeral and monument for Lord Chatham; but I trust it is worded as a testimony of gratitude for his rousing the nation at the beginning of the last war, and his conduct as Secretary of State, *or this compliment, if paid to his general conduct, is rather an offensive measure to me personally.* As to adding a life to the pension, I have no objection."*

In estimating the general conduct of a great man, the failings of the age must be allowed to palliate those of the individual. In this manner Tacitus vindicates the cha-

* "Letters of George III." Lord Brougham. " Corr. of Mr. Fox."

racter of Agricola; in this manner the admirer of Chatham must be allowed to plead the factiousness of many, the feebleness of most, the corruption of nearly all of his contemporaries. It cannot be denied that, in opposition to Sir Robert Walpole, he recklessly urged on the Spanish war, and cast undue odium on the Hanover connexion. The Spanish war is now generally admitted to have been forced on by this great orator against just views of policy; the Hanover connexion became to Lord Chatham himself, when Minister, a source of national strength. The great period of Lord Chatham's glory occurred in the four years between 1757 and 1761, when he wielded the thunderbolt and fulmined over Europe and America. A greater war Minister has never been seen; his spirit animated the nation, his sagacity descried the merits of Wolfe, and his firmness sustained the genius of Frederick of Prussia. In the American struggle, his wisdom was no less conspicuous; but his overbearing pride threw away the instruments by which his policy might have been assured, to adopt tools he thought more pliant, but which were sure to break in his hands.

Lord Chatham's eloquence appears to me to be marked by feeling and imagination beyond that of any orator, ancient or modern. In the regular sustained march of dignified language and close argument he was inferior to many: the fire of some orators is more skilfully prepared, their flame burns longer and more steadily, but Lord Chatham's flashes are from Heaven.

The meeting of the Rhône and the Saône, the immunity of an Englishman's home, where the wind might blow through every cranny, but the King's writ could not enter,

the statutes turned down in dogsears, the master feather in
the eagle's wing, and several more images of great beauty,
will occur to every one. They have no parallel in the speeches
of his son, of Fox, or of Sheridan—Burke alone, in a different style, and more sustained flight, can bear comparison
with the Great Commoner.

CHAPTER XI.

ATTEMPTS TO FORM A NEW MINISTRY—EVENTS IN AMERICA—FAILURE OF THE BRITISH COMMISSIONERS—VIOLATION OF THE CONVENTION OF SARATOGA.

1778.

In the summer, Lord Chatham being no longer an object of dread and antipathy, the King yielded so far to the importunities of Lord North as to permit a message to be sent through Mr. Fox to the Rockingham party. The substance of the message is thus stated by the Duke of Richmond :—

" The proposal was that Lord Weymouth should have the Treasury and Mr. Thurlow be Chancellor; that arrangements should be made to take into office the principal men in Opposition; and that Lords North, Germaine, Suffolk, Sandwich, Dartmouth, and perhaps some more, might quit their employments to facilitate these arrangements; that Lord Weymouth would be most glad to have Lord John Cavendish for Chancellor of the Exchequer, but would take any other we should agree upon; that Lord Rockingham and his friends might by themselves fill up the vacant offices, or take in the Duke of Grafton, Lords Camden and Shelburne." That none of the retiring Ministers were to be attacked, and that the King intended to bestow on them the three blue ribbons then vacant. " As to measures, none were proposed, except to withdraw the troops in general from North America, as from necessity or prudence, and to carry on a vigorous war against France, which was stated as unavoidable."

Mr. Fox was in favour of accepting these terms. In writing to Lord Rockingham in the beginning of the following year, he says: "You know how widely we differed upon that matter. . . . What you considered as a step of the most dangerous tendency to the Whig party, I looked upon as a most favourable opportunity for restoring it to that power and influence which I wish it to have as earnestly as you can do. The very circumstances which you thought likely to render the proposed arrangement weak, I considered as means of strength and stability, because it has always been, and I believe always will be, my opinion that power (whether over a people or a king) obtained by gentle means, by the good-will of the person to be governed, and above all, by degrees, rather than by a sudden exertion of strength, is in its nature more durable and firm than any advantage that can be gained by contrary means."* The Duke of Richmond, on the other hand, argued with great force and ability that the means of carrying into effect a Whig policy must consist either in men or in measures. That as the first place in the Ministry was reserved for Lord Weymouth, the first of these securities was wanting; and as no measure except the withdrawal of the troops from North America was specified, the second was likewise deficient. He added a hint to Mr. Fox himself, who had asked whether he might not honourably accept office, if the offer was again renewed and declined. "I can only offer you my opinions, taken not from prejudice, I trust, but from a real anxiety for your welfare, that such a step will be far from being for your interest. I am sure you will pardon

* "Correspondence of Charles James Fox," vol. i. p. 207.

the sincerity of so near a relation. You have many of those social virtues which command the love of friends, you have abilities in abundance, and your conduct of late years has done much to regain that public confidence which is so necessary to a public man. By a steady perseverance you may accomplish so essential an object. Once more pardon the effusion of a sincere heart, and believe me," &c.

In spite of the logical force of the Duke of Richmond's arguments, it may be doubted whether on this occasion Mr. Fox was not in the right. Lord Weymouth was a personal friend of Mr. Fox, and was extremely acceptable to the King. He was a man of good sense, and by no means wedded to the war. It was agreed that the troops should be withdrawn from North America; and as they could not have been sent there again, the American war must of necessity have ceased; for it was obvious that no Minister could have advised the recommencement of such a contest. As to men, the retirement of Lords North, G. Germaine, Suffolk, Sandwich, and Dartmouth, "and perhaps some more," leaving only Weymouth and Thurlow, would have put the Cabinet entirely in the hands of the Whigs. But perhaps the Duke of Richmond was suspicious of Fox himself. He may have feared the influence which Weymouth might gain over Fox, and the influence of the Court over both. In this way it is possible to account for the rejection of an offer which would have put an end to the American War in 1778, four years before its actual termination, and procured for the country a fair prospect of domestic reforms. It is curious to reflect that five years after this time the Duke of Richmond was for governing the King by "gentle means," while Fox endeavoured to establish his power by "a sudden exertion of strength." But to return. The present overture being rejected, the King continued to govern through Lord North, the war in America was prolonged, and Mr. Fox, rising with the occasion, became the leader of the Whig party in the House of Commons.

Let us now turn to the progress of the war in America. The great event of Saratoga, although it had been prepared by the skill and foresight of Washington, yet being decided at a distance from his head-quarters, went near to overthrow his authority. The envy of General Gates, the vanity and presumption of General Conway, and the cabals of a number of inferior persons whose machinations Washington too scornfully despised, were all set in motion to misrepresent his character, and to depreciate his wise and successful caution. The difficult circumstances of his position furnished his adversaries with abundant means of attack : if he supplied his army by forced requisitions, the names of liberty and property resounded in the ears of a jealous people ; if he desisted from these measures, the wants of his soldiers excited discontent in his camp. Yet, being at last roused to defend himself, his honest, straightforward explanations, the support of his friends, and a sense of returning justice, restored him to the good opinion of his deluded countrymen. His popularity was rather increased than diminished by the base attacks which had been made upon him. The conclusion of the Treaty of Alliance with France appeared to open brilliant prospects. Washington was eager to take advantage of this propitious circumstance to strike a final blow. Lord George Germaine, after indulging in a visionary plan of campaign, took fright at the dangers of a French war, and ordered General Howe to evacuate Philadelphia. On the 17th of June that city was evacuated by 10,000 British troops; on the 28th they were attacked at Monmouth by Washington, and suffered considerably, but repulsed the American troops, and inflicted upon them an equal loss. The British army then retired to New York, and Washington took up his position on White Plains. He remarked with some exultation that, after two years of marches and counter-marches, he had returned to his old position, and that his enemy was busy on works of defence with the spade and the pickaxe. On the 11th of July the Count d'Estaing appeared in the neighbourhood of New York with a French fleet of twelve sail of the line. On their arrival Washington was eager to make a combined attack on the British position, and thus, if possible, end the war. This plan, however, was rendered impracticable by the size of the French ships, which could not pass the bar of New York. It was then proposed to attack Rhode Island, where 6000 English were posted. The approach of a British fleet, however, made, d'Estaing fearful of being blockaded or attacked in a confined space, and he preferred going out to sea, with a view to bring the British to a general action. But a hurricane separated the two fleets; d'Estaing went to Boston to refit, and afterwards sailed for the West Indies. Thus the only immediate effect of the French alliance in America was the evacuation of Philadelphia. The alliance itself was not a natural nor a cordial one; and the conduct of d'Estaing in retiring from the scene of action produced an explosion of invective and rage among American patriots. Washington appeased this storm; but when the French proposed to redeem their fame by the conquest of Canada, Washington himself was the first to advise the Congress not to trust too much to the good faith of France. The words of a treaty would not, he thought, be proof against the temptation of regaining for France that valuable colony. It is curious to observe traces of the old partiality for Great Britain and the old jealousy of France still bearing their impression on the mind of so true a patriot as Washington.

Some curiosity may be felt as to the fate of Lord North's last conciliatory propositions. The Commissioners, on arriving at New York, sent Dr. Adam Ferguson to ask from Washington a safe conduct to the seat of Congress; but this Washington refused. The Commissioners then sent their proposals to treat and their full powers to the President of the Congress. But the Congress at once resolved that they would only treat on the basis of the withdrawal of the British troops from America, or on the basis of the acknowledgment of the independence of the thirteen States. The Commissioners endeavoured in vain to persuade the Congress to depart from this ground; and, finding their mission fruitless, returned in the month of November to England. This result justified the sagacious advice which George III. had given to Lord North. He had pointed out that the moment when the Americans had gained the alliance of France was not a favourable period for treating; that if the troops and ships were withdrawn from the American coast, and a heavy blow inflicted on the power of France, Great Britain might be in a better position to make concessions, and America in a better disposition to receive them. But, unhappily, the only wise suggestion made by the King during this contest was set aside by the folly of his Minister. Lord North humbled Great Britain by surrendering all the original grounds of quarrel; held out his imploring hand to the Congress, whose existence he had two years before refused to acknowledge; and, as a reward for his submission, was spurned by the body which he had tried to subdue by threats, and to win by cajolery. If, however, the British Commissioners had no right to expect a satisfactory answer to their overtures unless the basis of the independence of America were explicitly admitted, their representations on another subject were founded in justice. They claimed the performance of the convention of Saratoga, by which General Burgoyne's army was to be transported to Great Britain, on condition of not serving against America during the war.

Unhappily, every kind of flimsy excuse and paltry evasion was resorted to by the Congress in order to elude the performance of this engagement; and at last, taking advantage of an incautious expression in a letter of Sir Henry Clinton, they closed the correspondence, shamefully violated their promises, and retained the British troops prisoners during the remainder of the war. At the end of December a small force, under Colonel Campbell, was despatched to Georgia, and, owing to the skill and bravery of the commander and his troops, totally defeated an American body of regulars and militia, penetrated into Savannah, the capital of Georgia, and made themselves masters of the town with a great amount of military stores and provisions. The whole of the province soon submitted to the British commander.

CHAPTER XII.

THE session of Parliament commenced on the 26th of
November, 1778.　Mr. Thomas Townshend moved an
amendment to the address in reply to the King's speech,
distinctly separating the war with France from the contest
in America.　"We are ready," the amendment stated, "to
give the most ample support to such measures as may
be thought necessary for the defence of these kingdoms, or
for frustrating the design of that restless power which has
so often disturbed the peace of Europe; but we think it
one of our most important duties, in the present melancholy posture of affairs, to inquire by what fatal counsels,
or unhappy systems of policy, this country has been reduced from that splendid situation which, in the early part
of his Majesty's reign, made her the envy of all Europe,
to such a dangerous state as that which has of late called
forth our utmost exertions without any adequate benefit."

Mr. Fox seconded this amendment.　In speaking of the
offers of the Commissioners, he said there seemed to be a
censure passed on them for not executing "the conciliatory
measures planned by the wisdom and temper of Parlia-

ment." " What," Mr. Fox pursued, "were those plans of Parliament? for I never heard of them before. That the Commissioners should be sent out in the dark as to everything intended—was that the plan of Parliament? That General Clinton should leave Philadelphia without giving the Commissioners two hours' warning, and that distrust should be saddled on them the moment of their arrival—was that the plan of Parliament? That they should offer terms of reconciliation equally degrading to this country and unlikely to be listened to by Congress—was that the plan of Parliament? I never heard of these plans before, and I now disclaim all share in them. Parliament formed no plans, but the Ministry did, and we now see what they were; the speech is a libel upon Parliament when it attributes to us such pitiful plans; the speech is slanderous and libellous in calling them plans of Parliament." He went on to criticise both the naval preparations and the overtures made to America, and finally summed up the main circumstances of the war in the following masterly manner: " You have now two wars before you, of which you must choose one, for both you cannot support. The war against America has been hitherto carried on against her alone, unassisted by any ally. Notwithstanding she stood alone, you have been obliged uniformly to increase your exertions, and to push your efforts to the extent of your power, without being able to bring it to any favourable issue; you have exerted all your strength hitherto without effect, and you cannot now divide a force found already inadequate to its object. My opinion is for withdrawing your forces from America entirely, for a defensive war you never can think of: a defensive war would ruin this nation at any time and in any circumstances; an offensive war is pointed out as proper for this country; our situation points it out, and the spirit of the nation impels us to attack rather than defence.   Attack France, then, for she is your object—the nature of the war with her is quite different; the war against America is against your own countrymen—that against France is against your inveterate enemy and rival. Every blow you strike in America is against yourselves, even though you should be able, which you never will be, to force them to submit: every stroke against France is of advantage to you; the more you lower her scale the more your own rises, and the more the Americans will be de-tached from her as useless to them. Even your victories over America are favourable to France, from what they must cost you in men and money: your victories over France will be felt by her ally. America must be con-quered in France: France never can be conquered in America.

"The war of the Americans is a war of passion; it is of such a nature as to be supported by the most powerful virtues—love of liberty and of country—and at the same time by those passions in the human heart which give courage, strength, and perseverance to man; the spirit of revenge for the injuries you have done them, of retaliation for the hardships inflicted on them, and of opposition to the unjust powers you would have exercised over them; everything combines to animate them to this war, and such a war is without end; for, whatever obstinacy enthu-siasm ever inspired man with, you will now have to con-tend with in America. No matter what gives birth to that enthusiasm, whether the name of religion or of liberty, the effects are the same—it inspires a spirit that is unconquer-able, and solicitous to undergo difficulties and dangers;

and as long as there is a man in America, so long will you
have him against you in the field.

"The war of France is of another sort — the war of
France is a war of interest; it was interest that first induced her to engage in it, and it is by that same interest that
she will measure its continuance. Turn your face at once
against her; attack her wherever she is exposed; crush
her commerce wherever you can; make her feel heavy and
immediate distress throughout the nation, and the people
will soon cry out to their government. Whilst the advantages she promises herself are remote and uncertain, inflict
present evils and distresses upon her subjects; the people
will become discontented and clamorous; she will find the
having entered into this business a bad bargain, and you
will force her to desert an ally that brings so much trouble
and distress, and the advantages of whose alliance may
never take effect.

"What, sir, is become of the ancient spirit of this
nation? Where is that national spirit that ever did
honour to this country? Have the present Ministers exhausted that, too, with almost the last shilling of your
money? Are they not ashamed of the temporizing conduct they have used towards France? Her correspondence
with America has been 'clandestine;' compare that with
their conduct towards Holland some time ago; but it is
the characteristic of little minds to exact in little things,
while they shrink from their rights in great ones. The
conduct of France is called clandestine; look back but a
year ago to the letter of one of your Secretaries of State
to Holland, 'it is with surprise and indignation your
conduct is seen'—in something done by a petty governor
of an island—while they affect to call the measures of

France clandestine. This is the way the Ministers support the character of the nation, and the national honour and glory! But look, again, how that same Holland is spoken of to-day; even in your correspondence with her your littleness appears—

> 'Pauper et exul uterque,
> Pròjicit ampullas, et sesquipedalia verba.'

From this you may judge of your situation, from this you may know what a state you are reduced to. How will the French party in Holland exult over you, and grow strong! She will never continue your ally while you meanly crouch to France, and dare not stir in your own defence; nor is it extraordinary that she should not, while the present Ministers remain in place. No power in Europe is so blind, none stupid enough to ally itself with weakness, to become partner in bankruptcy, to unite with obstinacy, absurdity, and imbecility."

The division was—for the amendment, 107; against, 226.

When Parliament met after Christmas, Mr. Fox turned the whole force of his eloquence against the Admiralty. For some years Lord Sandwich, who had called the Americans cowards, had boasted of the efficiency of the navy. He had stated that, besides thirty-five sail of the line, we had seven other large ships in preparation, and that our naval forces would more than match those of the whole House of Bourbon. The time had come to put these loud professions to the test. Admiral Keppel, who, like some other officers, had declined to serve against the Americans, was now called into active service, and placed in command of the Channel fleet, with twenty sail of the line. In the month of June he was able to enter the

Channel; but, having taken two French ships, the *Pallas* and *Licorne*, it appeared from their papers that twenty-seven ships of the line were lying in Brest harbour, and five more were in great forwardness. In point of fact, thirty-two sail of the line, with fifteen frigates, were at sea early in the month of July.

Upon this alleged state of affairs Mr. Fox grounded a motion of censure against the Admiralty. Before stating his case, he laid down, in the following terms, the constitutional functions and duties of the House of Commons: "The general opinion which prevailed was, that in governments merely arbitrary, or where the direction of the power, force, and resources of the commonwealth were vested in a single person, or in a few, all the functions of government were performed with greater facility and dispatch, particularly in times of war. Secresy, which was the life of counsel, was secured; dispatch and vigour were only bounded by the abilities of the State. The blow was struck, or the necessary precautions were taken, as it were, before the cause was known, and the people acquiesced in the power and wisdom of their rulers. On the other hand, in governments where the political machine consisted of different movements, where its parts were more complex, and the motion of the whole depended upon a combination of various movements, its motions were slower; they were regular, but less vigorous; they were liable to be defeated, because their stated progress was made public before the proposed effect could take place.

"This was a speculative proposition, the truth of which no man could deny. It was an abstract proposition, equally clear, that those advantages arising in arbitrary governments were balanced by others enjoyed in free governments.

" The latter were better calculated for times of peace ; men were more effectually protected in their persons and properties ; free governments gave encouragement to the exertions of private individuals. They called forth talents out of obscurity into the service of the State ; they were favourable to mercantile adventure, to the extension of trade and commerce ; they inspired a love of country, and a spirit of honest independency ; in short, free governments, while they put every man upon a level, and rendered him independent of everything but the law, combined every member of the society in one common interest, and created a personal, as well as public pride, which, when properly directed and judiciously restrained, was the strongest excitement to great and glorious actions.

" Such were, on one hand, the advantages that in theory were supposed to be annexed to governments where the whole power of the community was vested in, and exercised by, a single person ; and such, on the other, were the distinguishing characteristics of governments constituted upon the broad basis of public freedom. But, although in theory each proposition seemed equally evident, experience held a different language. The truth was that the arts of peace had not at all times been more successfully cultivated in States republican and free, nor yet those of war in countries purely arbitrary and despotic. No nations had been more successful in war than those in which the body of the people had a share in the public counsels ; none had oftener failed than those which excluded them entirely from interfering in the administration of public affairs.

" The ancient republics of Greece and Rome exhibited the strongest proofs of the former. This country would remain a monument to the end of time of the fortunate and almost irresistible exertions of a mixed government. Holland and Switzerland further confirmed the truth of this proposition, that no form of government is so well calculated for the happiness of its subjects, for internal prosperity, and external strength, as that in which the power is delegated by the people, and exercised by the executive power under their control. The reason which struck him was this: the legislative and executive powers of the State, being separate and distinct, the Crown and its ministers are conditionally vested with as much power as is necessary for the discharge of the trust committed to their care. The executive power may make peace and war, may enter into alliances, may incur expenses, may, in short, adopt every measure which the terms of such a trust can be supposed to be supply, in as full and ample a manner as they think proper, followed only with this single condition, that they are responsible to Parliament for their conduct. If they act negligently, corruptly, or traitorously, they do it at their peril—at the hazard of their lives, honours, and fortunes; whereas, in arbitrary governments, where men are subject to the same failings and vices, being not subject to a like control, or to be called to any account, their conduct being directed by the only person in whose power it is to disgrace or punish them, so long as they preserve the confidence of the sovereign they have nothing to fear, or to deter them from giving the most pernicious counsels their ambition or personal interests may prompt them to. They have no after-reckonings to settle with the public, whom they have oppressed or betrayed; if they have been able to flatter a weak prince into a favourable opinion of their services, or to persuade a wicked one that their incapacity was the effect of a zeal for his person, and an implicit obedience to his commands, they are sure to be honoured and caressed at Court, while, perhaps, they are execrated and detested throughout the nation.

"How far the doctrine of a free government, retaining a final control over the executive power, was applicable to the constitution of this country, was a subject worthy of the particular attention of the House, because it was a matter most intimately connected with the subject of debate of the present day. The control he alluded to was the inquisitorial power vested in that House—a control which he presumed no gentleman present would deny had been beneficially exercised upon many former occasions. It amounted fairly to this: we have confided in Administration for the effecting such and such purposes, which can be better brought about by the few than the many; the trust is conditional; we, who have delegated the power, reserve a right to withdraw our confidence when we discover that it has been improperly bestowed or abused; a want of ability or integrity equally disqualifies the persons entrusted, and subjects them to punishment or dismissal.

"Parliament might forbear the exercise of this right of punishment and inquiry, but they could not divest themselves of it, it being of the very essence of the Constitution. They had a right to exercise it in two ways: the one by way of prevention, the other judicially. It was the duty of Parliament to remove upon good grounds, in order to put a stop to further evils. Wicked and weak counsellors were proper objects of removal, in the first instance; of condign punishment upon a constitutional investigation and legal proceedings in the second. Parliament stood between the people and the executive power, and it was only through that medium the people could constitutionally seek, or legally obtain, redress."

Mr. Fox then proceeded to state his facts, and point to his conclusions. He maintained that his motion would lead to removal, not to punishment. After a good deal of confusion, caused by an attempt to take evidence, the Ministers, in their defence, stated that the French information was erroneous, and that in July we had forty-eight or forty-nine sail of the line ready for sea. Still they only defeated the motion by 204 to 170 ; an unusual strength on the part of Opposition. Lord North declared that the motion, if carried, would force him to retire, and his scanty majority gave a correct measure of the confidence he still retained.

On the 8th of March Mr. Fox moved : "That the state of the navy at the beginning of the war was unequal to what the House and the nation were led to expect, and inadequate to the various services for which it was the duty of his Majesty's Ministers to provide." This motion was negatived by 246 to 174. When he further moved, on the 19th of April, an address to the Crown, to remove from his presence and councils John Earl of Sandwich, as First Commissioner of the Admiralty, he was defeated by 221 to 118. It was thus made clear that the House of Commons, although dissatisfied with the conduct of the war, were not prepared entirely to refuse their confidence to Lord North, or to censure directly one of his colleagues.

There were some parts of Mr. Fox's speeches, however, on various occasions, which were calculated to make a deep impression on the House and in the country. Thus, on moving a censure on Ministers for not sending reinforcements to Lord Howe at New York, he dealt with a favourite.

argument of Lord North, which had made much impression on independent members, that whether the American War were wise or unwise, it was a war of the House of Commons, and that Government had done no more than carry into effect the measures prescribed by Parliament. Mr. Fox thus represented the defence of the followers of Government: "Said they, 'We have brought Ministers into a dirty lane, we have encouraged them to prosecute the American War, let us bring them through, and not basely desert them in the moment of distress, occasioned by measures of which we have been the authors.'"

Mr. Fox answered the argument in this way: "This mode of reasoning was apparently mistaken, and the motives misconceived: they had not brought Ministers into the American War, but Ministers had led them into it by misrepresentations of all kinds, by promises broken as often as they were made, by false hopes, false fears, and by every species of political delusion. He then made a particular application of the whole of the measures respecting the American War; the promise of a revenue, of obtaining unconditional submission, and finally, giving up every object contended for at the outset, and promised in the subsequent progress of the war. He charged the noble lord in the blue ribbon with an act of public perfidy, with a breach of a solemn specific promise. He reminded the House, that in February, 1775, the noble lord moved his conciliatory proposition, and pledged his honour to the House and nation that he would never agree to any measure which should go to enlarge the offers therein made; yet, at the end of three years, after sacrificing 30,000,000 of money, and 30,000 lives, the noble lord, in the same assembly, not only solemnly renounced all claim to superiority, revenue, and internal legislation, but consented, by the mouth of his commissioners, to the giving up the monopoly of the American trade, the appointment of governors and all subordinate officers, and the royal prerogative of keeping up or sending an army to any part of the empire his Majesty might think proper. From this state of facts he drew this conclusion: that Ministers had led the Parliament into the war, and had broken the promises which induced Parliament to adopt the measure; that the motion, as stated by him, involved a dilemma which incontrovertibly proved the charge of misconduct and neglect; and, of course, that those gentlemen who voted upon independent principles were neither bound by previous engagements, subsequent measures, nor any obligation of honour, to vote against their conscience and conviction."

A bill for doubling the militia having been introduced by Ministers, was supported by Mr. Fox and the Opposition. Lord Nugent congratulated the House on the unanimity displayed, and proceeded imprudently to say that we were allied among ourselves. Mr. Fox took up this expression with great warmth. "The noble lord," he said, "after owning that we had no foreign alliances, had triumphantly spoken of unanimity, and congratulated gentlemen on that side of the House upon having allied themselves with those who sat on the other. This was an assertion for which there was not the smallest foundation, and it was impossible for him to state, in any phrase that language would admit of, the shock he felt when the noble lord ventured to suggest what was most exceedingly grating to his ears, and he doubted not to those of every gentleman who sat near him. What! enter into an alliance with those very Ministers who had betrayed their country, who had been prodigal of the public strength, who had been prodigal of the public wealth, who had been prodigal of what was still more valuable—the glory of the nation! The idea was too monstrous to be admitted for a moment. Gentlemen must have foregone their principles and have given up their honour before they could have approached the threshold of an alliance so abominable, so scandalous, and so disgraceful! Did the noble lord think it possible that he could ally himself with those Ministers who had led us on from one degree of wretchedness to another, till at length they had brought us to the extreme moment of peril, the extreme verge of destruction? ally himself with those Ministers who had lost America, ruined Ireland, thrown Scotland into tumult, and put the very existence of Great Britain to the hazard? ally himself with those Ministers who had, as they now confessed, foreseen the Spanish war, the fatal mischief which goaded us to destruction, and yet had from time to time told Parliament that a Spanish war was not to be feared? ally himself with those Ministers who, knowing of the prospect of a Spanish war, had taken no sort of pains to prepare for it? ally himself with those Ministers who had, when they knew of a Spanish war, declared in Parliament no longer ago than last Tuesday, that it was right for Parliament to be prorogued, for that no Spanish war was to be dreaded, and yet had come down two days afterwards with the Spanish rescript? ally himself with those Ministers who, knowing of a Spanish war, and knowing that they had not more than thirty sail of the line ready to send out with Sir Charles Hardy, had sent out Admiral Arbuthnot to America with seven sail of the line and a large body of troops on board! ally himself with those Ministers who, knowing of a Spanish war, had suffered seven ships of the line lately to sail to the East

Indies, though two or three ships were all that were wanted for that service, and the rest might have stayed at home to reinforce the great fleet of England! ally himself with those Ministers who, knowing of a Spanish war, and knowing that the united fleets of the House of Bourbon consisted of at least forty, perhaps fifty, and possibly sixty sail of the line, had suffered Sir Charles Hardy to sail on Wednesday last, the day before the Spanish rescript was, as they knew, to be delivered, with not thirty sail of the line, although, if he had stayed a week longer, he might have been reinforced with five or six, or, as Ministry themselves said, seven or eight more capital ships! To ally himself with men capable of such conduct would be to ally himself to disgrace and ruin. He begged, therefore, for himself and for his friends to disclaim any such alliance, and he declared he was the rather inclined to disavow such a connexion, because from the past conduct of Ministers he was warranted to declare and to maintain that such an alliance would be something worse than an alliance with France and Spain—it would be an alliance with those who pretended to be the friends of Great Britain, but who were in fact and in truth her worst enemies."

He concluded with repeating that he had not the least confidence in the present Ministers, and that so far from being ready to enter into an alliance with them, he thought they merited punishment; and although there were among them individuals for whom he had the highest personal respect, yet he thought their official conduct collectively so infamous and so prejudicial to the interests of their country, that, were the times ripe for bringing them to punishment, he would join most heartily in supporting such a measure.

The fate of the Militia Bill was curious. In the House of Lords, the clause which enabled the King to double the militia was rejected by a large majority. Among those who voted against the compulsory part of the bill was Earl Gower, President of the Council. When the bill was returned to the Commons, Mr. Fox commented with severity on this circumstance.

The session, one of unusual length, was closed by the King on the 3rd of July, 1779. In America the alliance of France and Spain had a different effect from that which might have been anticipated. The Congress, instead of calling out all their resources to free their soil from British troops, became inactive, many of the principal leaders ceased to attend, and plans of rigid economy, combined with an issue of depreciated paper money, showed that the Americans wished to finish the war, not as speedily, but as cheaply as possible. Washington, burning to strike a decisive blow, had only under his command 15,000 troops engaged to serve till the end of the war, and 12,000 others whose service was for various limited periods. When one reflects that 3,000,000 of men had pledged their lives and fortunes to the attainment of independence, it seems extraordinary that their efforts should have been thus languid and remiss.

In Europe the alliance of two great powers at the head of regular forces forced Great Britain to reserve her armaments for her own defence. A combined fleet of France and Spain, amounting to sixty sail of the line, scoured the Channel. Fifty thousand men were assembled in Normandy to be ready for an invasion of England or Ireland. Paul Jones insulted the coast of Scotland. The Irish people, being left without protection, armed for their own defence, and Lord North, terrified at their formidable zeal, was almost as much afraid of the champions as of the enemies of his country.

In October Lord Gower resigned his office. " I feel," he said, " the greatest gratitude for the many marks of royal goodness which I have received, but I cannot think it the duty of a faithful servant to endeavour to preserve a system which must end in ruin to his Majesty and to the country." Still the mind of the King was .unsubdued. It is true that, in a letter dated the 3rd of December, he professed his readiness " to blot from his remembrance any events that may have displeased him, and to admit into his confidence and service any men of public spirit and talents who will join with part of the present Ministry in forming one on a more enlarged scale, provided it be understood that every means are to be employed to keep the empire entire, to prosecute the present just and unprovoked war, in all its brauches, with the utmost vigour, and that his Majesty's past measures be treated with proper respect." But it is obvious that the Opposition could not have acceded to these terms, and Lord Thurlow, who was entrusted with the negotiation, wisely avoided the use of the King's name, in the distant overtures he made to Lord Camden, Lord Shelburne, and others.

Thus these symptoms of a relenting purpose came to nothing.

Upon the failure of these overtures, Lord Bathurst, lately Chancellor, was made President of the Council; Lord Hillsborough, Secretary of State for the Southern Department, in the place of Lord Weymouth, who resigned with Lord Gower; Lord Stormont was appointed to the Northern

Department; and the office of First Commissioner of Trade was revived in favour of Lord Carlisle. These changes gave no strength in Council, and rather weakened the Ministry in Parliament. In the persons of Lord Gower and Lord Weymouth, two of the chiefs of the Bedford party retired from office; Lord Sandwich and Mr. Rigby still remained.

CHAPTER XIII.

RISING SPIRIT OF OPPOSITION TO LORD NORTH—PETITIONS FOR REFORM—
MR. BURKE'S SPEECH ON ECONOMICAL REFORM—MR. DUNNING'S RESOLU-
TIONS—RE-ACTION IN THE HOUSE OF COMMONS—CAMPAIGN IN AMERICA.

1779 — 1780.

AT length the misconduct of Lord North's Administration produced its natural fruits. When the French and Spanish fleets had insulted the coasts of England—when the people of America, alienated and offended, had made good their independence—when sixty or seventy millions of money had been spent, and many thousands of lives had been sacrificed for an unattainable object,—the people of these islands began to utter curses, loud as well as deep, against the authors of their misfortunes. In England great public meetings called for punishment of the Ministry, reform of corrupt expenditure, and a more equal system of representation. In Ireland 40,000 volunteers assembled in arms to assert their rights. The Irish House of Commons addressed the throne for removal of restrictions upon trade, and the repeal of the degrading laws which subjected the Parliament of Ireland to that of England. The Duke of Leinster, in the uniform of the Dublin Volunteers, escorted the Speaker to Dublin Castle; the streets were lined by the volunteers, and the acclamations of the people welcomed the birth of national freedom. But, however agreeable to the sense of justice and the love of liberty these cries might be, it was impossible for prudent and calm men to contemplate without alarm the excesses which might arise from the use of instruments so liable to perversion. Large assemblages, distrusting the House of Commons, which legally represented them, and an armed deliberative body overawing the Executive they professed to support, were ominous symptoms of the disorder of the State.

The Parliament of Great Britain met on the 25th of November, 1779. The King in his opening speech did not disguise the peril of the country, "contending with one of the most dangerous confederacies that ever was formed against the Crown and people of Great Britain." He complimented his brave people, and appealed to that national spirit " which had so often checked and defeated the projects of ambition and injustice, and enabled the British fleets and armies to protect their own country, to vindicate their own rights, and at the same time to uphold and preserve the liberties of Europe from the restless and encroaching power of the House of Bourbon."

Language of this kind could hardly deceive any one. It did not for a moment dazzle the clear sight, or abate the high courage of Mr. Fox. After going over in succession the misfortunes of the campaign, Mr. Fox alluded to the unconstitutional doctrine that the King was his own Minister. But while, he protested against the doctrine, he took occasion to observe that, when the evils of a reign reached a certain height, Ministers were forgotten. Thus Charles and his son James had both confided in wicked Ministers, to whom, no doubt, the errors of their reigns ought chiefly to be ascribed; yet one was punished with the loss of his life, the other of his crown. Then, again, there was no reign that so much resembled the present as that of Henry VI. Like the present King, Henry owed his crown to a revolution; like the present King, he was an amiable and pious prince; like his present Majesty, he had inherited from his predecessors great conquests and brilliant renown. Henry lost all his father's conquests, and all his hereditary provinces in France; George had lost the conquests of his grandfather in the West Indies, and had seen his hereditary provinces in America created into independent States. In the commencement of his speech Mr. Fox had made a vehement attack on Mr. Adam, who had changed from the Opposition to the Ministerial side, and had given as a reason for his change, that, although the Ministers were not very competent, no persons more competent were to be found among their opponents. Mr. Fox, confounding mental power with moral rectitude, described the Minister as turning round on his new defender and saying to him, "Begone! begone, wretch! who delightest in libelling mankind, confounding virtue and vice, and insulting the man whom thou pretendest to defend, by saying to his face that he certainly is infamous, but that there are others still more so."

Mr. Adam having in vain endeavoured to obtain an explanation of this speech from Mr. Fox, to be inserted in the newspapers, sent Major Humberston to arrange the particulars of a hostile meeting. The meeting accordingly took place in Hyde Park, at eight o'clock in the morning of the 29th of November. After the ground had been measured, Mr. Adam desired Mr. Fox to fire, to which Mr. Fox replied: "Sir, I have no quarrel with you, do you fire." Mr. Adam fired; Mr. Fox then fired without effect. Upon this the seconds, Colonel Fitz-Patrick and Major Humberston, interfered, asking Mr. Adam if he was satisfied. Mr. Adam replied: "Will Mr. Fox declare he meant no personal attack upon my character?" Upon which Mr. Fox said: "This was no place for apologies," and desired Mr. Adam to go on. Mr. Adam fired his second pistol without effect. Mr. Fox fired his remaining pistol in the air, and said that, as the affair was ended, he had no difficulty in declaring he meant no more personal affront to Mr. Adam than he did to either of the other gentlemen present. Mr. Adam replied: "Sir, you have behaved like a man of honour." Mr. Fox then mentioned that he believed himself wounded. On opening his waistcoat, it was found that Mr. Adam's first ball had taken effect, but that the wound was very slight. The wits of Opposition said that Mr. Adam had used Government powder, notorious for being deficient in strength. No men were better friends in after life than Mr. Fox and Mr. Adam. Mr. Adam had that openness of temper and cordiality of disposition which peculiarly suited Mr. Fox. Indeed, of all Lord North's adherents, he and Lord North's son were singular in remaining faithful to Mr. Fox during the French war.

In the debate which took place in the House of Lords Lord Shelburne followed the example of Mr. Fox in his personal attack upon the King. Yet, as these invectives were not likely to intimidate George III., and as they in some measure caused a diversion in favour of his Ministers, the policy of making them was very questionable. A long discussion on the affairs of Ireland was the next debate of importance before the Christmas recess. In his speech on this occasion Mr. Fox traced the difficulty of Ireland, like every other, to the American War. The noble lord at the head of the Treasury could not surely be in earnest when he declared that the American War had nothing to do with the affairs of Ireland. Did not that ill-fated project appear most conspicuous in every circumstance of the present condition of the kingdom? What stripped Ireland of her troops?—Was it not the American War? What brought on the hostilities of France and put Ireland in fear of an invasion?—Was it not the American War? What gave Ireland the opportunity of establishing a powerful and illegal army?—Certainly the American War. When he called the associated forces an illegal army, he did not mean to cast any odium on the associations. He was equally ready to acknowledge the necessity and the merit of the plan; but it was the accursed American war that made that measure necessary, and rendered its illegality meritorious.

The increasing dangers of the country had at this time roused a spirit, to which I have already alluded, adverse to the existing system of administration, and indeed to the acknowledged practice of the Constitution. But on contemplating the position and the convictions of those who were the organs of this discontent, we shall find the security of our form of government placed close by the side of its danger. The men who led this movement, both in England and Ireland, were eminent for their attachment to the Constitution, their moderation of temper, and generally for their connexion with the landed property of the country. The Marquis of Rockingham himself, the leader of the Whig party, was a man no less virtuous in his aims than temperate in his disposition. Indeed, the prudence of his conduct, during a period of great public danger, had laid him open to a charge of indifference and want of courage. Sir George Savile, a man of great fortune, much followed and much respected in the House of Commons, had kept aloof from efforts which he thought would not be sanctioned by the public opinion of the time. Mr. Burke was imbued with a reverence almost superstitious for parliamentary precedents, and with an attachment almost feudal to the great branches of the aristocracy known by the name of Revolution families. Mr. Fox, at this time leader of the Opposition in the House of Commons, had a deep and affectionate attachment to the Constitution. At a later period of his life he said: "That if by a peculiar interposition of Divine power, all the wisest men of every age and every country could be collected into one assembly, he did not believe that their united wisdom would be capable of forming a tolerable constitution." In the same spirit he said of the Constitution, that his object was " not to pull down, but to work upon it, to examine it with care and reverence, to repair it when decayed, to amend it where defective, to prop it where it wanted support, and to adapt it to the purposes of the present time, as our ancestors had done from generation to generation, always transmitting it not only unimpaired, but improved, to their posterity."*

Led by men thus temperate in their views, the freeholders of the great county of York met on the 30th of December, 1779. Never were there before seen at any county meeting so many persons of property and station, never was more public spirit displayed by the great mass of the inhabitants of Yorkshire. The petition agreed upon recited the alarming circumstances of the time: an expensive and unfortunate war ; the declared, though not acknowledged

* Fox's " Speeches," vol. v. p. 109.

independence of the North American colonies; the alliance
of France and Spain with the insurgents; the large addition
to the national debt; the heavy accumulation of taxes; the
rapid decline of the trade, manufactures, and land-rents of
the kingdom. After complaining of sinecure places and
other grievances, the petition ended with a most earnest
request, "That before any new burthens are laid upon this
people, effectual measures may be taken by your honourable
House to inquire into and correct the gross abuses in the
expenditure of public money; to reduce all exorbitant
emoluments; to rescind and abolish all sinecure places and
unmerited pensions, and to appropriate the produce to the
necessities of the State, in such manner as to the wisdom
of Parliament shall seem meet."*

On the 2nd of February, 1780, there was a great meeting
in Westminster Hall. It was headed by the Duke of
Portland, the Cavendishes, Lord Temple, and the Grenvilles,
Burke, Fox, Wilkes, Sawbridge, &c. Mr. Fox was placed
in the chair, and made a warm speech against Lord North.
The petition was in the same terms as that from the county
of York. Dr. Jebb proposed Mr. Fox as the future
candidate for Westminster; a proposal which was received
with the greatest applause. This was perhaps the moment
of his greatest popularity.

Mr. Burke had now given notice of his plan of Economical Reform. His speech on this subject was made on
the 11th of February. It is one of the greatest achieve-
ments of his eloquence. But, in the opinion of many good
judges, the eloquence and the ornament of the speech are
out of proportion to the solidity of the plan. Some useful
reforms are suggested, but the revering mind of the wor-

* "Parliamentary History."

shipper stayed the hand of the reformer. Even sinecures, which, from being peculiarly liable to abuse, had been denounced at all public meetings, were sacred in the eyes of Burke, as they might be the reward of a Walpole or a Pelham. Many of the reforms proposed struck rather at apparent blemishes than real abuses. For instance, the passage of the speech relating to the Duchies of Cornwall and Lancaster points rather to a harmless anomaly than to a practical abuse.

In the course of the discussion on Mr. Burke's bill Mr. Rigby questioned the competency of the House to disturb an existing arrangement between the Crown and Parliament. Mr. Fox thanked him for his straightforward conduct, but denounced the doctrine he professed in the strongest terms. He said, if such a doctrine should prevail, there was an end of the British Constitution, and that for his own part he should never set his foot in the House of Commons again. This violence savoured rather of declamation than of reason ; but there was one argument of Mr. Fox which appears to me decisive of the question. He referred to the applications which had been made to the House of Commons from time to time to pay the debts of the civil list; he mentioned a report that at that very time the salaries and bills were three quarters in arrear, and he justly inferred that, if the Crown could not adhere to its own contract, it was high time for Parliament to revise the system and examine into the causes of so much irregularity. In ordinary times, when the civil list was found sufficient, and no excessive burthens weighed on the people, the contract made with the Crown at the beginning of the reign might fairly be respected ; but when the privations and distress of the people were accompanied by fresh demands of money by the Court, it was preposterous to set up a barrier against inquiry and impose a veto upon reform.

Lord North, more cautious than Mr. Rigby, took care not to be the champion of his unpopular doctrine, but endeavoured to defeat in detail that which he had admitted in the gross. One of the first clauses of Mr. Burke's bill provided for the abolition of the third Secretary of State. After a long debate, this clause was rejected by a majority of 7.

On the 6th of April, however, the Opposition had a great triumph. On that day Mr. Dunning moved a resolution, "That the influence of the Crown had increased, was increasing, and ought to be diminished." Mr. Dundas moved, as an amendment to insert before the resolution, the words, "That it is now necessary to declare," &c.

Lord North had on several occasions defeated the Opposition by amending the words of their motions; but on this occasion Mr. Fox dexterously accepted Mr. Dundas's words, and the resolution, instead of being weakened, was strengthened by the amendment. On the whole resolution the House divided.

$$\text{For} \quad \ldots \ldots \ldots \ldots \quad 233$$
$$\text{Against} \ldots \ldots \ldots \ldots \quad 215$$
$$\text{Majority} \ldots \ldots \ldots \quad 18$$

The Opposition then moved and carried two other resolutions to the following effect :—

"2. That it is competent to this House to examine into and to correct abuses in the expenditure of the civil list revenues, as well as in every other branch of the public revenue, whenever it shall appear expedient to the wisdom of this House so to do."

" 3. That it is the duty of this House to provide as far as may be an immediate and effectual redress of the abuses complained of in the petitions presented to this House from the different counties, cities, and towns of this kingdom."

Mr. Fox moved, notwithstanding the lateness of the hour, to report the motions immediately to the House, and although Lord North exclaimed loudly against such proceedings, as violent, arbitrary, and unusual, the motion was carried. A day of reaction, however, was approaching; a dissolution of Parliament was impending, and the Ministers, having secured their supplies and ways and means, might defeat their adversaries by delay. In order to prevent such a discomfiture, Mr. Dunning, on the 24th of April, moved an address to the Crown not to prorogue or dissolve Parliament " until proper measures had been taken to diminish the influence and correct the abuses complained of in the petitions of the people." But this was too direct an interference with the prerogative to please the Tories, and the motion was rejected by 254 to 203. Lord North was again in the ascendant.

After the division Mr. Fox rose and uttered, with great vehemence and in his loudest tones, a powerful invective against those who had deserted him on this occasion. Referring to the third resolution of the 6th of April, he said, with some justice: " We are on the eve of a general election; the gentlemen alluded to would soon go down to their constituents. The first and most natural question would be, ' What have you done in consequence of our petitions? Is the influence of the Crown diminished? What redress have you procured for us? Has a more economical expenditure of the public money been determined upon and adopted? Have our burdens been lightened? Are all useless and sinecure places abolished? And have you established a reform in the expenses of the King's household?' "

The truth is that changes are effected in England more slowly than was suitable to the warm temper of Mr. Fox. The independent country gentlemen were willing to adopt the principles stated in the resolutions of the 6th of April; but they were not ready to take the initiative out of the hands of the Executive Government, far less to prolong their own existence in defiance of the acknowledged prerogative of the Crown. Nevertheless, the cause made progress; the King's household was revised, and by Mr. Burke's subsequent Act of 1782 many useful reforms were made. Nor was this all. A new spirit was infused into the Government by the popular movement of 1780. It is impossible to deny that for nearly a century after the Revolution the conduct of the House of Commons was far from pure. Walpole did not disdain to employ corruption, though with more moderation than his predecessors, to procure a majority; Pelham, Newcastle, and North made their patronage their means of government. Chatham, personally free from any stain of this kind, never presided at the Treasury.

It was reserved for the reformers of 1780 to purify the channel of Government, and raise the moral character of the House of Commons. There have since been instances of individual peculation; and some occurrences during Mr. Pitt's administration showed how ill his followers imitated the unspotted conduct of their chief. But, generally speaking, the Government of Great Britain has been, since the overthrow of Lord North, the most pure of the leading governments of Europe and America. I do not, of course, mean to compare it with a small canton of Switzerland, or a little republican city in Germany; but, both absolutely and relatively, the Ministers, the subordinate officers, and the Parliament have been for the last seventy years free from pecuniary corruption. Such is the happiness and the virtue of our form of government that, from the disasters, the misrule, and the profligate expenditure of the American War there arose a systematic order, and a sense of personal integrity, which had not previously been known.

I have observed that our progress is slow. A more equal system of representation was the second request of the petitioners of 1780; but, although brought forward by Mr. Pitt, and supported by Mr. Fox, the cause did not prosper, and when Mr. Pitt became Prime Minister, pined and perished. It was reserved for Lord Grey to propose and carry, after a lapse of fifty years, the measure which fulfilled the objects of the Yorkshire and Westminster petitions.

In June, 1780, occurred the disgraceful riots of Lord George Gordon. The King showed more spirit and presence of mind than any one on this occasion. But what is curious is, that the temporary success of the rioters, which was such damning evidence of the incapacity of Lord North and his cabinet, tended rather to strengthen the Government than to weaken it. Men clung to authority even in feeble hands, and sought shelter under a rotten shed rather than face the storm.

The object of the Protestant petitioners was the repeal of an act passed in the former session of Parliament, on the motion of Sir George Savile, to relieve the Roman Catholic subjects of the King from the penalties and disabilities imposed upon them by an act of the 11th and 12th of William III. The House of Commons, having resolved itself into a committee of the whole House, to consider of the petitions, Lord Beauchamp moved several resolutions affirming that the act had been misrepresented, and that it did not by any means invalidate the statutes made to prohibit the exercise of the Popish religion, passed previous to the 11th and 12th of William III.

On this occasion Mr. Burke and Mr. Fox each spoke three hours in defence of toleration and against persecution. Mr. Fox said that he could not think the Popish religion incompatible with government or civil liberty; because, in looking round the world, he saw that in Switzerland, where democracy reigned universally in the fullest manner, it flourished most in cantons professing that religion. He declared himself a friend to universal toleration, and an enemy to that narrow way of thinking that made men come to Parliament, not for the removal of grievances which they themselves felt, but to desire Parliament to shackle and fetter their fellow subjects.

Complimenting Lord North on the speech he had made in defence of toleration, he observed how the true talents and natural disposition of a man broke forth when relieved from the official trammels that fettered and controlled his mind. He then quoted, with great effect, the lines from *Paradise Lost :—*

> " As one who long in populous city pent,
> Where houses thick, and sewers annoy the air,
> Forth issuing on a summer's morn to breathe
> Among the pleasant villages and farms
> Adjoin'd, from each thing met conceives delight;
> The smell of corn, of tedded grass, of kine,
> Or dairy; each rural sight, each rural sound."

Thus early in his career was Mr. Fox the fearless champion of religious liberty.

The campaign of 1780 in America was not marked by any decisive event. Sir Henry Clinton, who had succeeded General Howe, finding the North intractable, had determined to throw himself upon the aid of the loyalists of the South. He invaded the Carolinas and was successful. General Lincoln, at the head of 5000 men in Charlestown, was forced to surrender. But this advantage was no equi-valent for Saratoga. In July, General Rochambeau, at the head of 5000 French troops, arrived in Rhode Island. Washington's army, it is true, was still weak and ill-disciplined, but he saw a glorious prospect before him; and by exhortations to Congress, letters to his friends, and friendly concert with his allies, he prepared for a struggle, the final issue of which should secure the independence of America.

While Washington was concerting with the French general the movements for a decisive campaign, he discovered, to his surprise, that Arnold, to whom he had confided the command of West Point Fort, the very key of his position, had deserted to the enemy, and was already beyond pursuit. But, unfortunately; the agent of Sir Henry Clinton, a young British officer named Major André, was discovered attempting to pass the American lines in disguise. He had ascended the river Hudson on board a British ship, in uniform; but the wind proving contrary, he had been persuaded by Arnold to attempt another mode of return. According to the laws of war he was liable to be hanged as a spy, just as General Lee, and many other British officers in the American service were liable, when taken, to be hanged as traitors. But the British Government had perceived the difference between a deserter to a foreign enemy and a volunteer who joins in an insurrection. Unhappily, Washington, while he acknowledged the merit and the courage of André, and was very reluctant to sanction his being put to death, could yet perceive no difference between his case and that of an ordinary spy. On the 2nd of October André was hanged in the camp. His execution leaves a blot on the fair fame of Washington never to be effaced.

CHAPTER XIV.

DISSOLUTION OF 1780—SESSION OF 1780–81.

THE dissolution of the Parliament which had been elected in 1774, took place on the 1st of September, 1780. It was on this dissolution that Mr. Burke lost his seat for Bristol, and that he made the famous speech, on giving up the contest, which is to be found in his works. It was at this election also that Mr. Fox was returned for the first time for Westminster, having defeated his competitor, Lord Lincoln, by a large majority. In a letter written during his canvass, he says: "Everything depends upon the choice of this Parliament, for, notwithstanding the boast of Ministers, it is quite clear that we shall rather gain than lose, which will make the thing very near."*

The general election, however, did not make any great alteration in the numbers of the respective parties. Many seats were in those days in the hands of the Treasury; a number of others, making, together with the Treasury boroughs, a majority of the whole House, were in the absolute possession of individuals whose interest led them to the support of the Minister. Thus the sound of the national voice was often lost amid the corners and crannies of the House of Commons. But, in truth, the nation had not

* "Correspondence," vol. i.

yet made up its mind to renounce the hope of subduing America, and the successes of Lord Cornwallis enabled Ministers to open the session, which began on the 1st of November, with a boastful and confident speech :—

"By the force which the last Parliament put into my hands," the King was made to say, "and by the blessing of Divine Providence on the bravery of my fleets and armies, I have been enabled to withstand the formidable attempts of my enemies, and to frustrate the great expectations they -had formed; and the signal successes which have attended the progress of my arms in the provinces of Georgia and Carolina, gained with so much honour to the conduct and courage of my officers, and to the valour and intrepidity of my troops, which have equalled their highest characters in any age, will, I trust, have important consequences in bringing the war to a happy conclusion."

An amendment to the address having been moved by Mr. Grenville, Mr. Fox spoke with his usual talent in its support. Ridiculing the profuse eulogies which Mr. de Grey, the mover of the address, had pronounced upon a long list of officers, he exclaimed—

"Quem virum aut heroa lyrâ vel acri
Tibiâ sumes celebrare, Clio?"

The division was 212 for the address and 130 for the amendment.

Mr. Fox's speech gave great satisfaction to the electors of Westminster; they not only in their committee of association highly applauded the firmness with which " he exposed the pernicious principles and destructive measures of an abandoned Administration," but, alluding to the duel of the past year, they resolved, " That this committee, being sensible that the firm, constant, and intrepid performance of his duty will probably render him, in common with other distinguished friends of liberty, the object of such attacks as he has already experienced, and to which every unprincipled partisan of power is invited by the certainty of a reward, most earnestly exhort the inhabitants of Westminster to do their utmost, by every legal measure, to preserve to the great body of citizens by whom he has been elected, and to his country,. the benefit of his services, and the inviolable security of his person."

Mr. Adam made a complaint of this resolution as a personal threat to himself. After a good deal of discussion, the House passed to the orders of the day.

On the 26th of February Mr. Burke's renewed bill for the reduction of the civil list was rejected by 233 to 190. On this occasion Mr. Sheridan and Mr. John Townshend made their first speeches. But, above all, Mr. William Pitt spoke with a fluency, a precision, a dignity, and a method which are usually the acquirements of many years of practice. Lord North declared it was the best *first* speech he had ever heard.* The effect appears to have been prodigious. By no one was Mr. Pitt's success more warmly greeted than by Mr. Fox. Lord Holland has related an anecdote, which illustrates the presence of mind of the young orator: "As Mr. Fox hurried up to Mr. Pitt to compliment him on his speech, an old member, said to be General Grant, passed by and said: 'Aye, Mr. Fox, you are praising young Pitt for his speech. You may well do so; for, excepting yourself, there's no man in the House can make such another; and, old as I am, I expect and hope to hear you both battling it within these walls as I have done your fathers before.' Mr. Fox, disconcerted at

* Horace Walpole.

the awkward turn of the compliment, was silent, and looked foolish; but young Pitt, with great delicacy, readiness, and felicity of expression, answered: 'I have no doubt, general, you would like to attain the age of Methuselah.' " Before long Mr. Fox had an opportunity of testifying in public the admiration he had avowed in private; and early in the following year, in praising a speech of Mr. Pitt, he said "he could no longer lament the loss of Lord Chatham, for he was again living in his son, with all his virtues and all his talents."*

One of the most prominent subjects of debate in the session of 1781 was the loan. Upon this topic Mr. Fox's abilities shone no less than upon every other.

In order to explain this matter it is necessary to recur to general principles in regard to a national debt. When a country engaged in war finds a difficulty in raising by taxes the sums necessary for its yearly expenditure, and has recourse to a loan, it is obvious that this expedient charges upon a succeeding generation the burthen of the actual expenditure. For this reason the resource of borrowing should be employed with great reserve. For if a nation can be buoyed up by the excitement of war, the hopes of conquest, and the gambling chances of victory, without any corresponding increase of taxes, the game would be played with eager readiness; the motives for hostilities would be lightly examined, and the distant bloodshed of a battle would cause only a transient sorrow. It is desirable, therefore, that the expenses of a war should, as far as possible, be defrayed by the generation which encounters its hazards; and that no more burthen should be placed on posterity than is absolutely required by the weight of the existing

* "Romilly's Correspondence," vol. i. p. 192.

taxes, and the inability of the nation to bear further demands. It should be another element of loans that the interest really required at the time should be openly and ostensibly paid. In time of war the interest of money sometimes rises to six or seven per cent.; in time of peace it often sinks to three per cent., or even lower. If the State pay in time of war for every hundred pounds borrowed the interest of the time, it may in time of peace discharge its debt by the offer of the principal, unless the creditor consents to reduce the interest in conformity with the current rate. Such was actually the case during the war of the Spanish Succession, and the subsequent peace. The money required was borrowed at five, six, and seven per cent.; and when peace was restored, Sir R. Walpole reduced to five and to four, and Mr. Pelham to three per cent., the interest of the existing debt. Thus the stock for 100*l.* issued in 1710 at six per cent. was charged only three per cent. in 1752, and the nation gained the difference.

Lord North sought rather to raise money on the easiest terms for the moment than to make a good bargain for the country. He thus, in 1781, gave for every 100*l.* subscribed 150*l.* three per cent. stock, reckoned at a price of 58 per 100*l.*, 25 four per cent. stock reckoned at 70, and 1*l.* lottery ticket. He, therefore, in the first place, gave 105*l.* 10*s.* for every 100*l.** He next gave an interest exceeding 5*l.* in perpetuity to every creditor. This interest would remain in perpetuity, however the interest of money might fall in time of peace. It is true the money to be subscribed at the rate of four per cent. might be reduced one-quarter per cent. when money should sink to three per cent; but, on the other side, the lottery ticket must be added. It is

* 58*l.* + 29*l.* + 17*l.* 10*s.* + 1*l.* = 105*l.* 10*s.*

therefore obvious that this bargain gave upwards of five pounds interest for all succeeding time for the benefit of the creditor and against the country.

But this was not all. By allowing a discount for prompt payment, and by making the loan bear interest from the 1st of January, although it was only contracted for in March, he raised the scrip or omnium to eleven per cent. premium; thus throwing away a million of money for the benefit of the contractor. To complete the iniquity of the transaction, a large portion of the loan was distributed among the political supporters of the Ministers.

The subject is one of so much importance, that I shall make large extracts from Mr. Fox's speeches on this matter. On the 7th of March he proposed, upon Lord North's opening the budget, that the clause respecting the lottery should be omitted. In the course of his speech "he showed, in a chain of arithmetical reasoning, what we might expect to be the price at which it would be in our power to buy in the debt; and by this means deduced the fair conclusion, that it was much more for the interest of the country to borrow money by annuities than by adding to the capital of our debt; and if we must borrow on the latter plan, it was a much more beneficial bargain to borrow money at four per cent. than at three, and at five per cent. than at four. It was more in our favour in the result, because it was probable that it might be bought in at a cheaper rate. If we looked at the state of the funds, we should always perceive that the three per cents. stood higher in proportion than the four; because, from the probable profit being greater, they were more an object of estimation and pursuit.

"Independent of the strong objections he felt to the

loan, as a question of finance and a matter of economy, he felt it to be still more important when considered in a political view. The profit on the loan now proposed, in every way he had been able to take it, and subject to every probable contingency, was 900,000*l.*; and this large sum was in the hands of the Minister to be granted in douceurs to the members of that House as compensation for the expenses of an election, or for any other purpose of corrupt influence which might suit his views. An honourable friend of his [Mr. Burke] had brought in a bill to lessen the influence of the Crown by controlling the expenditure of the civil list. The design was wise and proper; but, like every other design of that description, it had failed by means of that very influence which it was calculated to prevent. But the objection to which he now wished to call the attention of the House was of much greater magnitude; it was not the excesses in the expenditure of the civil list, which amounted in the whole to 900,000*l.*, including the support of his Majesty and many great, important, and national services; but it was an entire sum of 900,000*l.* and upwards, to be given away in the douceurs of a loan, not merely from the effect of an idle and wanton extravagance, but from much worse causes: it was given as a means of procuring and continuing a majority in the House of Commons upon every occasion, and to give strength and support to a bad administration. The noble lord had attempted to flatter the House that, upon a number of supposed contingencies, many events highly favourable, and a train of economy so extremely rigid, pure, and incorrupt, that in stating it the noble lord did not appear to flatter himself it could ever be practised; but if practised, and if everything was to happen just as we could hope and wish, why then, at the end of fourteen or fifteen years, thirty millions would be paid off—that is, we should then be twenty millions more in debt than when we began the fatal American War; and we are now to look with an anxiety almost beyond the reach of hope for a state of things which would have been considered ruinous at the time the noble lord began his administration. The terms of the loan, such as they were, the noble lord had informed the House would have been much worse had it not been for some good news—and good news indeed it appeared to be if it really afforded any prospect of a peace. It was singular, however, if the bargain for a loan was to be influenced by such a prospect, that it was not more influenced by it; and that terms so extremely disadvantageous should be offered to the House, when the prospect of peace was avowed. Upon that prospect he wished to speak out; he wished to declare that he felt himself ready to support almost any terms that could be offered whilst the affairs of the nation were in the present hands. He thought no peace could be a bad one—that is, a general peace; for any partial or patched-up peace which would leave us involved in all the necessities of a war establishment, he thought would rather be injurious than useful, and might only tend to draw us on farther in a ruinous system, and plunge us deeper into difficulties and disgrace."

He now took a general review of his objections to the terms of the loan; urging, as the result of the whole, that the lottery was an unnecessary part of the *douceur*, and ought to be omitted from every principle of policy and of regard for the morals of the people. It had been said by a learned gentleman, speaking on the subject of riots a few evenings ago, that if anything could excuse an illegal and violent mode of redressing grievances, it would be the pulling down gaming-houses. This he considered as the most pernicious and destructive of all species of gaming, as immediately affecting the morals, habits, and circumstances of the lower orders of the people, and which, upon every principle of policy, should be carefully avoided.

Mr. Fox's motion was supported by Lord Mahon, but was lost on a division by 169 to 111. Yet the speech he had made excited so much attention, that on the 26th Sir George Savile moved the appointment of a committee "To examine the circumstances of the late loan, to form estimates of the value thereof, and to report the same to the House." Mr. Fox's speech on this occasion was very masterly. He first mentioned a position laid down by Mr. Dundas, that the Minister was responsible.

"But for what purpose had the learned gentleman said this? Why had he so warmly trumpeted the responsibility of Ministers, and particularly of the noble lord in the blue ribbon? For what, but in the same breath to defeat the use and the end of that responsibility, and to convince the House that they ought not to exercise their right and power; to show that the noble lord was, in fact, not responsible in this instance; that, if there was any blame, or any corruption, or any sinister purposes in view, by the late bargain, it was not the noble lord who was the criminal, for the noble lord was honest, and everybody acknowledged that he had clean hands; his secretary, his friend Mr. Atkinson, or any other man, might be guilty, except the noble lord. If the House complain of the conduct of the Minister, the accused immediately answers, 'Oh! he is responsible.' If they call for an inquiry into that conduct, and think it necessary to exercise their powers of calling him to an account, 'Oh! he is irresponsible in that case, for, being honest and disinterested, he could not be guilty.' Thus his responsibility in one instance is to silence complaint, his irresponsibility in another is to stifle inquiry."

On the 8th of May Sir George Savile moved to refer to a committee of the whole House a petition from certain freeholders, praying for an abolition of sinecure and unnecessary places, and a reformation of pensions unmerited by public services. Only seventeen persons signed the petition. These seventeen had exposed themselves very unwisely to the jealousy of the House of Commons, by assuming the character of delegates, thus apparently usurping the rights of the legal representatives of the people.

Mr. Fox, according to Horace Walpole, "shone transcendently;" and his speech, as reported, is a very able one. Yet an anecdote he told contains a just remark on his own conduct. "When he was about to sign the petition, he said a friend told him, 'If you should sign it as a delegate, by Heaven, you will be hanged; if as a petitioner, by Heaven, you will be laughed at.'" In the course of his speech he took occasion to pay high compliments to Lord Thurlow and Mr. Burke. Of Lord Thurlow he said, "He was able, he was honest, he possessed a noble and independent mind. He was the only person who formed a part of the present Administration entitled to the character." Of Mr. Burke he spoke thus: "Men of talents and sincerity had nothing to interrupt their view of distant objects, nor were liable to have it distorted or misrepresented through a false medium. This was the case of his honourable friend near him, which appellation he deemed one of the greatest honours that fortune could bestow on him; a man who, with the virtue of one of the best citizens in the most virtuous and unsullied times, united the abilities of the first-rate orator, the mind and extensive knowledge of a philosopher, the learning of a real scholar, the manner of a gentleman, the humanity of a moralist, the charity of a Christian."

He then alluded to Mr. Burke's loss of his seat for Bristol, in consequence of his maintaining that the people of Ireland were entitled to the rights of commerce. " Ministers were deaf, this nation was infatuated; it was blinded by prejudice and a narrow policy. What was the consequence? That justice which could not be procured, even by his eloquence, was sought and procured too in another manner. In what manner? By the point of the bayonet." Such has been always the course of our conduct towards Ireland. In 1780, in 1793, and in 1829, that which had been denied to reason was granted to force. Ireland triumphed, not because the justice of her claims was apparent, but because the threat of insurrection overcame prejudice, made fear superior to bigotry, and concession triumph over persecution.

Two more motions were made this session, with a view to put an end to the American War. Mr. Hartley on the 30th of May moved for leave to bring in a bill " to invest the Crown with sufficient powers to treat, consult, and finally to agree upon the means of restoring peace with the provinces of North America." In answer to this motion, Lord North stated that the Crown was already in possession of all the powers necessary for concluding a peace with America, with the exception of some reserved points afterwards to be settled by Parliament. Mr. Fox denied the position of Lord North. His arguments are thus reported :—

" He begged leave to contradict the noble lord. The Crown had not the power of making peace with America, as with France, and Spain, and Holland. What, were we then at war with America? Is America, then, recognised as an independent state? No, you are at war not with America, but with your revolted colonies in America. It is not a war with an independent enemy in which you are engaged, but an attempt to quash a rebellion, to subdue an insurrection. By an act of Parliament no Massachusetts trader dare come into any of your harbours. Can peace be restored without repealing that act, and can that act be repealed without the authority of Parliament? The present hostilities commenced in consequence of the Prohibitory Act, as it was called. It was that act that made the war with America. We were therefore very differently situated with America than we were with France and Spain. The Crown had never made war with her, but the war was brought on by an act of Parliament, which act of Parliament must necessarily be repealed. The present motion was therefore a necessary preliminary to the opening a door for a reconciliation. I maintain," continued Mr. Fox, " that there is not one point in dispute between Great Britain and America that can be settled by the Crown without the consent of Parliament— not one point; so that the noble lord's reserved points comprehend all the points in question. The rebels in America were declared so by an act of Parliament, and through the whole course of the contest this position had been held, that against the authority of the British Legislature they were contending. Surely, then, it was not competent in the Crown to decide on the privileges of Parliament.

" With regard to the opinion the Ministry entertained of the present situation of affairs in America, whatever they might think some few years ago, sure he was they did not in their own minds believe there was the least prospect of their now mending in our favour. The noble lord in the blue ribbon, who talked so very fluently, and affected so much candour, would be put in a very awkward situation were he to be asked the question, for in answering it he would be obliged to contradict facts which he had again and again asserted. As to the noble lord, he was a man of experience; he was a man, too, naturally inclined to moderation and mildness. Whence, then, was he induced to be so strenuous a supporter of the American War? whence was his inclination to that war deducible? He might put an answer in the noble lord's mouth from an Italian poet: 'My will to execute this deed is derived from Him who has both the will and the power to execute it. Ask no further questions.'*

"He placed the noble lord in all the situations in which he had stood within the last seven years in that House, and said that his versatility arose from motives highly unbecoming. The Ministers found it necessary to protract the war, to avoid every tendency to pacification, because they knew that the American War was necessary to their continuance in power and place. They sacrificed honour and duty, they sacrificed the interests, and perhaps the existence, of their country to the temporary gratification of their avarice and their ambition, in the enjoyment of the places and honours which they now held, and which were so connected and interwoven with the American War as to depend upon its existence. The Minister, then, knowing this fact, knowing that he lived and must die with the American War, had encountered shame, and embraced it, in order to its continuance. He had been forced into all those vile

---

* "Vuolsi cosí colà dove si puòte
  Ciò che si vuole."
          DANTE, *Inferno*, c. 3, 5.

measures of contradiction and absurdity which had brought infamy on the present age, and would bring ruin on posterity. There was no accounting for the credulity, the servility, and the meanness of Parliament, in either believing or submitting to receive all the monstrous and incredible stories which they had been told by the Minister, in any other way than by referring to the means which influence possessed, the emoluments of contracts, and the profits of a loan. It had, no doubt, been the study of the Minister to tell his friends that their payment, like his own bread, depended on the American War. The American War begot extraordinaries; extraordinaries begot loans; loans begot douceurs; and douceurs begot members of Parliament; and members of Parliament, again, begot all these things. There was a mutual dependence among them absolutely inseparable. Thus the power and the security of Ministers were generated by that war which was the ruin of the country."

Again, reverting with great force to the corruption of Parliament and the consequences of the war, he " personated the Minister conversing with some dependent member of Parliament, at his levee, on the subject of continuing the war; supposing that any remonstrance should be made on that score, what would the noble lord say? ' Why, you know that this war is a matter of necessity, and not of choice; you see the difficulties to which I am driven, and to which I have reduced my country; and you know also that in my own private character I am a lover of peace. For what reason, then, do I persist, in spite of conviction? For your benefit alone! For you I have violated the most sacred engagements; for you rejected the suggestion of conscience and reason; for you a thousand times forfeited my honour and veracity in this business; and for you I must still persist! Without the American War I shall have no places, no emoluments, to bestow; not a single loan to negotiate; nor shall I even be able to retain this poor situation of mine that I have thus long held most disinterestedly. You see me now in the most elevated situation, with the disposal of places and pensions, and with the whole power of the nation in my hands; but make peace with America to-day, and to-morrow I shall be reduced to the level of private life. If you do not vote with me,' continues the noble lord, 'against a peace with America, how am I to give you anything? It is true that my situation as Minister is a respectable and elevated situation, but it is the American War that enables me to give you douceurs, and to put into your pockets eight or nine hundred thousand pounds by a loan. Put an end to that, and you undo all. My power will be miserably lessened, and your pay as miserably reduced. As to myself, why, I am perfectly indifferent about that; I get a little, and it is my happiness that a little, thank Heaven, contents me. I therefore cannot be supposed to care if a peace takes place with America to-morrow, as far as I am personally concerned; but for your own sakes do not let such a thing come to pass. Nay, were I to go out of office—a situation I never courted, always disliked, and heartily wish to be rid of—still I hope the American War would be continued.' Such pathetic reasoning could not fail having its effect. Thus it was the noble lord induced members of the House to sacrifice the interests of their constituents, by proving that their own interests were essentially connected with the prosecution of the war. Was it possible, therefore, that peace with America could ever be obtained but by a renunciation of that system which the present Ministry had with so much obstinacy adhered to? And here was another obstacle arising from the noble lord's feelings. 'O spare my beautiful system!' he would cry; 'what! shall I part with that! with that which has been the glory of the present reign, which has extended the dominions, raised the reputation, and replenished the finances of my country! No; for God's sake, let this be adhered to, and do with all the rest what you please; deprive me, if you please, of this poor situation; take all my power, all my honour and consequence, but spare my beautiful system, O spare my system!'"

The motion was supported by 72 against 106; a thin House for so great a question. But when accounts came of the battle of Guildford and its consequences, Mr. Fox seems to have hoped that debate, backed by disaster, might influence some votes in the House of Commons. He accordingly, on the 12th of June, moved, at the close of a powerful speech, "That this House will resolve itself into a committee of the whole House to take into consideration the present state of the American War," intimating that, in case of success, he should move in committee "That his Majesty's Ministers ought immediately to take every possible measure for concluding peace with our American colonies." In his reply Mr. Fox alluded to Dr. Franklin :—

"The noble lord who spoke second had called the American War a holy war. The application of the word holy to the present war may have appeared new to every gentleman present but myself. It is not new to me, and I will tell the House why it is not. I was over in Paris just at the eve of this very war, and Dr. Franklin honoured me with his intimacy. I remember one day conversing with him on the subject, and predicting the fatal consequences; he compared the principle of the war, and its probable effects, to the ancient Crusades. He foretold that our best blood and our treasure would be squandered and thrown away to no manner of purpose; that, like the Holy War, while we carried ruin and destruction into America, we should impoverish and depopulate Britain; and while we went thither, under the pretence of conferring temporal, not ghostly benefits upon the vanquished, our concealed purpose was to destroy, enslave, or oppress, as it promised best to answer our ends; while, like the pretended martyrs or zealots in ancient times, we concealed, under this fair semblance, every vice and passion which constituted human depravity and human turpitude: avarice, revenge, ambition, and base as well as impotent resentment."

The division was, for Mr. Fox, 99, against, 172.

Before the end of the session Mr. Fox brought in a bill to repeal the Marriage Act. On the second reading of this bill, on the 15th of June, he made a speech against the Marriage Act which surpassed all the efforts of his father on the same subject. The argument would be injured by any attempt to abridge it; yet the picture he presented of a couple lawfully married, and a similar couple living in illicit intercourse, which the reporter declares he is " not able to imitate or to report," is worth reading, even in an imperfect transcript:—

"In that generous season, which this Marriage Act labours and intends to blast, a young man, a farmer or an artisan, becomes enamoured of a female possessing, like himself, all the honest and warm affections of the heart. They have youth, they have virtue, they have tenderness, they have love, but they have not fortune. Prudence, with her cold train of associates, points out a variety of obstacles to their union, but passion surmounts them all, and the couple are wedded. What are the consequences? happy to themselves and favourable to their country. Their love is the sweetener of domestic life. Their prospect of rising becomes an incentive to industry. Their natural cares and their toils are softened by the ecstacy of affording protection and nourishment to their children. The husband feels the enticement to so powerful a degree, that he sees and knows the benefit of his application. Every hour that he works brings new accommodations to his young family. By labouring this day he supplies one want; by labouring another, he imparts one convenience or one comfort; and thus, from day to day, and week to week he is roused into activity by the most endearing of all human motives. The wife, again, instigated by the same desires, makes his house comfortable, and his hours of repose happy. She employs what he earns with economy; and while he is providing food and raiment for his children, she is busied in the maternal cultivation of their minds, or the laudable exertion of their young hands in useful labour. Thus, while they secure to themselves the most sober and tranquil felicity, they become, by their marriage, amiable, active, and virtuous members of society.

"View the same couple in another light. Bound together in heart by the most ardent desires, and incited by their passion to marry without having any great prospect before them, their parents intervene. They are not arrived at the age of twenty-one: under the authority of the Marriage Act their parents prevent their marriage. They restrain them from committing, agreeably to this law, the crime of matrimony without their consent—

'Sed metuere patres quod non potuisse vetari.'

They may restrain them from marriage, but they have it
not in their power to prevent their intercourse. The couple,
restrained in their desire of marriage, with a transition, as
natural as it is easy, give way to their inclinations, and a
connexion ensues in which there is more of indiscretion
than of guilt. What are the consequences? Enjoyment
satiates the man and ruins the woman; she becomes preg-
nant; he, prosecuted by the parish for the maintenance of
the child, is initiated in a course of unsettled pursuits and
of licentious gratifications. Having no incitement to industry, he loses the disposition, and he either flies the place
of his residence, to avoid the expense of the child, or he
remains the corrupter and disgrace of his neighbourhood.
The unhappy female, after suffering all the contemptuous
reproach of relations and all the exulting censure of female
acquaintances, is turned out of doors, and doomed to
struggle with all the ills and difficulties of a strange and a
severe world. The miserable wanderer comes to London,
and here, after waiting, perhaps in vain, to procure some
hospitable service, in which she might be able to retrieve or
conceal her misfortune, she is forced, much oftener by
necessity than inclination, to join that unfortunate description of women who seek a precarious subsistence in the
gratification of loose desire. Good God! what are the
miseries that she is not to undergo! what are the evils that
do not result to society! but, above all, what must be the consolation of that Legislature who, from pride and avarice, are
mean enough to inflict such misfortunes on their country!"

While debates on the subject of America were passing in
England the sword of Washington cut the knot of parliamentary deliberation.

In the autumn of 1780 he had prevailed upon his countrymen to make at length adequate preparations for the war. His task, in this respect, had been a painful and laborious one. Congress had no authority to hire a soldier or impose a tax. Each state, anxious to preserve its own influence, and jealous for the purity of its new liberty, desired to have just as much military force as would defend the country against the power of Great Britain, but not enough to endanger the freedom of America. Convinced at length of the justice of Washington's representations, satisfied of the honesty of his intentions, and wearied with the prolongation of the war, the Congress agreed to measures by which the army might be rendered efficient. Accordingly, the engagements of the soldiers were made to last during the duration of the war; the officers were promised half-pay; the discipline of the troops was established by impartial, though severe regulations. Washington now felt that he was in command of a regular army, and that army amounted to between thirty and forty thousand men. The French Government had also the sense and temper to place under his command their own auxiliary force. Rochambeau, who had learnt tactics in the Seven Years' War, and had a high reputation as an accomplished, though pedantic officer, placed himself under the orders of the militia colonel of America. Washington knew how to command without giving offence : Rochambeau knew how to obey without sacrificing the military pride of his country. Thus the two nations acted in perfect harmony, and their emulation was the parent of success.

The early part of the campaign of 1781 was not, however, productive of much apparent result. Washington, decciving his own officers as well as his enemy, appeared to give all his attention to the siege of New York. But his eagle eye swept the whole continent of North America, and fixed with fatal precision on a distant and unsuspecting prey. In pursuit of the plan of Sir Henry Clinton, Lord Cornwallis and General Arnold led their forces into the Southern States. Arnold, with the violence of an apostate, laid waste and pillaged the province of Virginia. After numerous combats, in which the English had the advantage, General Greene succeeded in covering South Carolina. Lord Cornwallis, leaving him undisturbed, marched at once into Virginia. Reinforced by Arnold, and by troops from New York, the British army occupied that important province; and Lord Cornwallis, in command of upwards of 16,000 men, took post at York Town, where he began to entrench himself.

In the month of August, 1781, Washington received intelligence at the same time that Cornwallis was fortifying York Town, and that the Comte de Grasse was preparing to sail with twenty-eight ships and 3000 men from Domingo to the Chesapeake. Instantly forming his plan, he gave orders that, with the exception of a single division, the army should embark, abandoning the siege works on which they had been employed. The Marquis of Lafayette, who was then in command in Virginia, and the Comte de Grasse were prepared for this movement, and everything was so well combined that, on the 30th of September York Town was invested by 9000 American, and 7000 French troops. The force under Cornwallis had by this time been reduced by fighting and sickness to 8000 effective men, and their position was not regularly fortified. On the 10th of October the trenches were opened, and a heavy fire brought to bear on the place. Two redoubts protected the British position; an American and a French column were ordered to attack them, and so well was the duty performed in the sight of the two armies, such was the emulation of the American and French soldiers, that both redoubts were carried by assault, and the British forces who defended them partly surrendered, and partly retired into the body of the place. But that place was no longer tenable, and on the 17th, three days after the assault, Lord Cornwallis capitulated and surrendered his whole force as prisoners of war.

This was the last humiliation to which the King and Lord North exposed their country. The independence of America had been won; France triumphed; the fruit of the victories of Lord Chatham had been lost by the glaring folly of his successors.

In considering the contest carried on in America from first to last, nothing is more extraordinary than the inadequacy of the efforts made by Great Britain when compared to the magnitude of the task she had undertaken. Some thirty to thirty-five thousand troops, of whom twelve thousand were Germans, seem to have been thought sufficient to subdue a whole continent and keep in subjection three millions of exasperated insurgents. It is difficult to account for such negligence, except by supposing that the Ministers really believed that the Americans were cowards, and that the flame of loyalty only required a match to be applied to burst forth into a blaze. But this is only to excuse one kind of incompetency by alleging another. Either the Ministers grossly deceived themselves, or their measures were disgracefully inadequate. One or the other of these conclusions is unavoidable. It must be admitted also, that while the British soldiers displayed their accustomed valour, the American

War did not produce any military talent on the part of the British generals. Sir William Howe, General Burgoyne, and their subordinates, contributed, by their over-caution, or their over-confidence, to the defeat of the Ministry which employed them.

The sagacity, the temper, the choice of ground, the mixture of boldness and prudence displayed by Washington were admirable. Perhaps indeed against a more skilful foe he might have appeared a still greater general; for his intellectual, like his moral qualities were never brought out to display his own talent or enhance his own glory. They were forthcoming as occasion required, or the voice of the country called for them : largeness of combination, quickness of decision, fortitude in adversity, sympathy with his officers, the burst of impetuous courage, were the natural emanations of this great and magnanimous soul.

CHAPTER XV.

DEFEAT AND RESIGNATION OF LORD NORTH.

1781 — 1782.

On the 27th of November, 1781, began that memorable session of Parliament which was destined to put an end to the fruitless and bloody war in which the country was engaged. The King's speech, while admitting the loss of the Southern army, was as strong as ever on the subject of continuing the contest. "I should not answer," he declared, "the trust committed to the sovereign of a free people, nor make a suitable return to my subjects for their constant, zealous, and affectionate attachment to my person, family, and government, if I consented to sacrifice, either to my own desire of peace or to their temporary ease and relief, those essential rights and permanent interests, upon the maintenance and preservation of which the future strength and security of this country must ever principally depend."

Mr. Fox never spoke with more force than he did on this occasion. When the address had been moved by Mr. Perceval, afterwards Lord Arden, and seconded by Mr. T. Ord, he rose to move an amendment. After some observations very personal to the King, he said: "There was one thing which he must take notice of—the honourable gentleman who had made the motion had been unadvised. He had lavished in an attack part of that oratory which was all necessary to defence. He advised him to husband his abilities and reserve them all for the defence of the Ministry below him, rather than waste them in attacking the Opposition. He had charged them with expressing joy at the triumphs of America. It would have been becoming in him to have had one quality of youth—namely, candour—on the occasion, and to have stated fairly what he chose to represent. It was true he had said, in a former session, that it was his sincere opinion that, if the Ministry had succeeded in their first scheme on the liberties of America, the liberties of this country would have been at an end; and thinking this (as he did), in the sincerity of an honest heart, he was pleased with the resistance which Ministers had met. If the honourable gentleman had thought the same thing, if he had joined him in the opinion that Ministry, had they succeeded in their first attack upon America, would afterwards have succeeded in an attack upon Britain, he no doubt would have wished success to American resistance; at least, if he had been an honest man, he would. This was his opinion: it had always been so. He might be wrong, but he from his heart believed it; and he called upon the honourable gentleman, when he next mentioned the assertion, to take notice also (as in candour he ought) of the opinion that accompanied it. That great and glorious statesman, whose memory every gentleman would revere—the late Earl of Chatham— entertained this opinion in the very commencement of the dispute; and feeling for the liberties of his native country, thanked God that America had resisted the claims of this country. But 'all the calamities were to be ascribed to the wishes, and the joy, and the speeches of Opposition.' Oh, miserable and unfortunate Ministry! oh, blind and incapable men! whose measures are framed with so little foresight, and executed with so little firmness, that they not only crumble to pieces, but bring on the ruin of their country, merely because one rash, weak, or wicked man in the House of Commons makes a speech against them! Oh, what miserable statesmen must these be who frame their measures in so weak and wretched a manner as to make no provision for the contingencies of fortune nor for the rash passions—say, if it pleases the House, the wicked passions —of men? Could they expect that there would be no rash, no weak, no wicked men in this kingdom, or were they so rash, so weak, and so wicked as to contrive measures of such a texture that the intervention of any unforeseen circumstance broke them to pieces, and with their failure destroyed the empire of which they had the government? It was said against administration, that they had no responsibility. People desired to know who was the Minister, and who was answerable for the iniquitous measures of Government. The Ministry felt the difficulty of the question, and hesitated a long time in the answer; but at last, having found out an expedient, they exclaimed in triumph, ' Oh, yes, responsibility! to be sure there must be responsibility! there are persons accountable to the people for the measures of Government.' Who are they? 'The persons,' reply the Ministry, ' are responsible who have always opposed our measures.' This was the strange and the ridiculous manner in which they argued and endeavoured to shuffle themselves out of that responsibility which they knew to be so dangerous. If they had succeeded, they would have taken all the credit and all the praise to themselves; but because they have failed, they throw the blame upon those men who endeavoured to prevent the calamities by hindering the cause of those calamities; they throw it upon the men who saw them in their career to a dreadful precipice, determined to throw themselves from the immeasurable height, careless of the death that must ensue from dashing on the rocks and plunging in the sea below, and who endeavoured in vain to stop them in this mad intent. 'They seized us upon the brink,' say Ministry, 'and by their efforts to stop us prevented us from taking the glorious leap which we had intended; if they had suffered us to dash into the abyss without molestation, then we should have been happy.' When this sort of language was held, he had always treated it with silent ridicule, and if he had now given it any serious reception, he begged the House to pardon him. It was unintentionally if he had, for it merited nothing but ridicule and contempt.

"The honourable gentleman who had seconded the motion said that 'the House had impatiently heard narratives of the American War, and of the measures that had led to it, and he trusted that there would be no more retrospective censure at the present moment.' Impatiently! Had the House heard them impatiently? Ministers must bear to hear them again, and on that day they must hear them; that was the day when the representatives of the people must recall to the ears of his Majesty's Ministers the disgraceful and ruinous measures that had brought us to this state. They must hear of them not only here, but he trusted that, by the aroused indignation and vengeance of an injured and undone people, they must hear of them at the tribunal of justice, and expiate them on the public scaffold. He saw a learned gentleman smile at the word scaffold [Mr. Dundas, the Lord Advocate of Scotland]. What! did not the learned gentleman think that it was yet time for punishment? Had they not, in his imagination, done enough, or had they more calamities to inflict, more negligence to exemplify, or rather more treachery to complete? What was the learned gentleman's opinion? When did he think the fit moment would arrive when suffering would be supineness, and retribution be just? It was his opinion that the day was now approaching; that it was at hand when the public would no longer submit, nor the Ministry escape. Their conduct was unprecedented in any age or in any history; it beggared the records of nations; for, in all the annals of kingdoms ruined by weakness or by treachery, there was not an instance so glaring as the present of a country ruined by a set of men without the confidence, the love, or the opinion of the people, and who yet remained secure amidst the storms of public disaster. The honourable gentleman who had seconded the motion had called for unanimity. He demanded to know if they meant to insult that side of the House when they asked for unanimity, and designed to continue the American War? They had opposed it from its commencement; they had opposed it in all its progress; they had warned, supplicated, and threatened; they had predicted every event, and in no one instance had they failed in predicting the fatal consequences that had ensued from the obstinacy or from the treason of the Ministry. If in a moment like the present—a moment of impending ruin— men who loved their country could have any comfort, he confessed he must feel it as a comfort and consolation that, when the history of this dreadful period should come to be written by a candid and impartial hand, he must proclaim to posterity that the friends with whom he had the honour to act were not to be charged with the calamities of the system. In justice to them he must declare that they did all that men could do to avert the evils, to direct them to a more safe and honourable track; but they had failed in their anxious endeavours to save their country. Thus much at least the historian would say, and thus would they be exempted from sharing the condemnation, though they now suffered the calamity in common with the rest of their unhappy fellow-subjects.

"The honourable gentleman had told us that we must not despond; and at the same time he had given us a picture of our situation, which he confessed to be more serious than pleasing. He talked hope to the ears, but he had spoken despondency to the heart. This was his serious picture, and a most serious one it was. 'You are now suffering these things from measures the most wise, the most prudent, the most necessary, executed with firmness and with foresight, and in a cause the most just and upright.' Was it so? Then how much farther distant from despondency was the picture which he would give than this serious, but not desponding, picture of the honourable gentleman? I cannot express my sentiments of the situation of this country better than by applying to it the address of the celebrated orator Demosthenes to the Athenians: 'I should,' says he, 'be dejected and despairing, I should consider your situation as desolate and irreparable, if I did not reflect that you have been brought to this state by weak and improvident measures, and by weak and treacherous men. If your affairs had been managed wisely, if your operations had been firm and steady, and, after all, you had been reduced to this situation, I should have indeed despaired of deliverance; but, as you have been reduced by weak and by bad men, I trust you may be recovered by wise and by upright governors. Change your system, and you may yet flourish; persevere, and you must be ruined.'

" This was exactly his opinion of the present situation of this country. If their cause had been just and virtuous, if their measures had been wise and vigorous, if their Ministers had been capable and zealous, and, after all, we had been brought to our present situation, he should have despaired of deliverance; but as it was, there were yet hopes, by substituting a just and a virtuous system in lieu of the present oppressive and disgraceful one, by substituting wise and vigorous measures in room of the present ridiculous and impotent schemes; by substituting activity and zeal in the place of indolence and treachery; and by changing, in short, the whole plan and conduct of Government. His motive for this advice was not that he wished to succeed to those places of trust; he sincerely wished their present possessors joy of them. They had rendered the offices of trust and power most unenviable to men who loved their honour, and whose only object in accepting them would be to promote the splendour, the security, and the happiness of this country. Let them, in the name of Heaven, enjoy the emoluments for which they have lavished so much; and if our ruin must be accomplished, let it be completed by the same baneful hands !"

Mr. Fox went on to exhibit two pictures of this country, the one representing her at the end of the last glorious war, the other at the present moment : " At the end of the last war this country was raised to a most dazzling height of splendour and respect. The French marine was in a manner annihilated, the Spanish rendered contemptible; the French were driven from America; new sources of commerce were opened, the old enlarged, our influence extended to a predominance in Europe, our empire of the ocean established and acknowledged, and our trade filling the ports and harbours of the wondering and admiring world. Now mark the degradation and the change. We have lost thirteen provinces of America; we have lost several of our islands, and the rest are in danger; we have lost the empire of the sea; we have lost our respect abroad and our unanimity at home; the nations have forsaken us; they see us distracted and obstinate, and they leave us to our fate. 'This *was* your husband; this *is* your husband.' This *was* your situation when you were governed by Whig Ministers and by Whig measures; when you were warmed and instigated by a just and a laudable cause; when you were united and impelled by the confidence which you had in your Ministers; and when they, again, were strengthened and emboldened by your ardour and enthusiasm. This *is* your situation, when you are under the conduct of Tory Ministers and a Tory system; when you are disunited, disheartened, and have neither confidence in your Ministers nor union among yourselves; when your cause is unjust, and your conductors are either impotent or treacherous.' . . . There was one circumstance in the conduct and language both of the Minister and of men of all parties which he could not help taking notice of; it was, that, amidst all their sorrow for the loss of Earl Cornwallis and his brave army, there was one great consolation—it was, that our fleet had not ventured to fight the enemy. Hear it, Mr. Speaker! it is a source of joy new in the history of Great Britain that we rejoice in the occasion of one of our fleets not venturing to meet and fight the enemy! To this even were we reduced, and our joy on the circumstance was well founded! The honourable gentleman who seconded the motion had given great praise to Earl Cornwallis, and justly so; but, in his opinion, the most brilliant part of the noble earl's conduct was that, even in the midst of his embarrassment, in the very moment of peril, when he expected every hour to be assaulted, and himself with the whole army to be put to the sword, he retained and expressed the purest patriotism and love for his country in the anxiety which he showed for the safety of the fleet! 'Do not venture to relieve me—my fate is determined; do not decide the fate of our country by including yourselves in the disaster.' But, indeed, the whole conduct of Lord Cornwallis was great and distinguished. Where enterprise, activity, and expedition were wanted, no man had more of these qualities. At last, when prudence became necessary, he took a station which, in any former period of our history, would have been a perfect asylum. He planted himself in York and Gloucester, and preserved a communication with that which used to be the country and the dominion of Great Britain—a communication with the sea. It used to be the country of an English commander, to which he could retire with safety, if not with fame. It used to be the country in which he was invincible, whatever might be his strength on shore. Here it was that Earl Cornwallis was stationed, on the borders of Great Britain, and by which he preserved a communication with New York—nay, with the city and the port of London. But even this was denied him; for the ocean was no more the country of an Englishman, and the noble lord was blocked up, though planted on the borders of the sea; nay, was reduced even to thank God that a British fleet did not attempt his rescue!

"He said he was far from meaning to insinuate that Admiral Graves was in fault; the ablest commander in the universe would have acted as he did. Even Lord Hawke, the great and the gallant Lord Hawke, whose memory would ever be held dear, as the father of the British navy, would have acted in the same manner. He who lived during the splendour of the British navy, and who, perhaps, was happy to retire that he might not live in its decline—even he would have acted in the same manner. He had taken a good deal of pains to inquire; he had conversed with the ablest officers on the subject; and he had it in his power to do so, for all the ablest officers were on shore; and they declared unanimously, that it would have been madness in Admiral Graves to have ventured to attack the French fleet in the Chesapeake; that it could not have been done without the utmost risk of losing the whole fleet, as well as the army that was on board. How different was this from what it used to be in the English navy! In former wars, to meet an enemy and to fight, to command a squadron and to vanquish, was the same thing. A British admiral knew not what it was to retreat from a French squadron, or be apprehensive of engaging them. But this, among other things, the Earl of Sandwich had introduced into the service of Great Britain. He had made it an essential part of the duty of an English admiral to run away from an enemy. He, that First Lord of the Admiralty who had declared, in his place in the House of Peers, that he deserved to lose his head if he ever failed to have a fleet equal to the combined naval power of France and Spain. He had forfeited the penalty of his bond—the Earl of Sandwich had forfeited his head, for the Earl of Sandwich had not a fleet in any quarter of the world equal to that of the House of Bourbon! In America, the British squadron, under Admiral Graves, amounted to twenty-five sail of the line; the French squadron, under De Grasse, to thirty-five sail; in America, then, we were unequal. In the West Indies a decided superiority against us had been manifested by the occurrences of the campaign. We had lost the island of Tobago; a large Spanish squadron was now triumphant in those seas, unopposed by any British force whatever, capable and ready to do what they pleased. . . . In the West Indies, then, we were inferior; and so inferior, that there was not a man of any experience who did not tremble for the safety of our dearest possessions in those seas. Unequal in those two places, it might be thought that our great superiority was employed in some exploit in another part of the world. Where? How? Was it in Europe? In Europe the Channel fleet did not at any time consist of more than twenty-seven ships of the line, and the combined fleets amounted to forty-seven sail, blocked up the mouth of the English Channel, claimed the proud dominion of the seas on our coasts, and took within our view a valuable and numerous fleet of traders. In the English Channel, then we were inferior. But, perhaps, in the northern seas there was a great commanding squadron to overcome, or to destroy the Dutch marine. Was there so? Admiral Parker met and fought the enemy with an inferior force; and there was a circumstance occurred in this part of our naval management which gave a most striking picture of the Admiralty system. After Admiral Parker had written home to inform the Board of Admiralty that the Dutch squadron was much larger than they had given him to understand or expect, they despatched a cutter to him with the intimation that there were two ships lying at Harwich, fully equipped and ready for sea at an hour's notice, which he might have if he desired them. Instead of sending these ships, in consequence of the information which the admiral had given them, they sent a cutter, and lost the opportunity. Admiral Parker met the Dutch fleet in the meantime, and fought without the addition of these ships; by which, perhaps, and indeed in all probability, he would have procured a decisive victory, and have destroyed or maimed the Dutch force for the rest of the war. But by this ignorant, treasonable conduct, instead of a victory, there was only a drawn battle. But, perhaps, we had been superior in the Mediterranean and in the Baltic? No; in the Mediterranean we durst not even attempt to relieve an invested island—the island of Minorca; nor relieve a blockaded garrison—the garrison of Gibraltar; two places that were always hitherto considered to be of the last importance. In the Baltic we had given up the right of fighting, even when attacked—we must not dare to fire a gun in the Baltic. In the European seas, then, we had been unequal to the enemy in all the operations of the campaign. In the East Indies we were not superior to the enemy. He had heard in the King's speech of the prosperous state of affairs in the East, but he professed he knew of no prosperity in that quarter. Was there any news of conquest, or of advantage, or even of escape, come from the East? It was a hidden secret to everybody with whom he conversed; and he believed was to be found nowhere but in the King's speech. In every corner of the world, then, were we inferior to the enemy; and yet, with a fleet diminished and inferior, rendered still more weak by the infamous manner in which it was directed—after the present disaster to our arms in Virginia, with the same men to conduct, and what was worse, with the same system,— were we, the representatives of the people of Great Britain, called upon to address the Crown, and promise to support his Majesty in the same pursuit that had brought us to this state.

" In giving this detail of our situation he had avoided entering into the minute and subordinate measures of Government. He had confined himself merely to the leading features of their management, and of our situation; and though he had not enumerated our domestic grievances, he by no means forgot or despised them. There was one grand domestic evil, from which all our other evils, foreign and domestic, had sprung—the influence of the Crown. To the influence of the Crown we must attribute the loss of the army in Virginia; to the influence of the Crown we must attribute the loss of the thirteen provinces of America; for it was the influence of the Crown in the two Houses of Parliament that enabled his Majesty's Ministers to persevere against the voice of reason, the voice of truth, the voice of the people. This was the grand parent spring from which all our misfortunes flowed. . . . Change the system *in toto*, and remove the men in power, and you would purify the fountain-head by which all the flood was contaminated.

" He called upon the House to know whether they were still ready to go on with this cursed and abominable war. He called upon them as the representatives of the people, and not as the creatures of the Minister, to do their duty, to execute the trust reposed in them, and to act up to the sentiments that they really felt. Did they really believe that we could ever conquer America? He desired them to lay their hands upon their hearts, and proclaim in the presence of God and men, whether they thought that all the power of Great Britain, strained and exerted, was equal to the task. He would leave the question to this conscientious test, and he would venture to say, that if no man but he who thought the contrary of this would presume that night to vote for the address, the Minister would be left in the smallest minority that was ever known in that House; nay, he believed in his soul that the Minister himself would vote against the war. Were they determined rashly and vehemently to go on? Had they not done enough for the Minister, and was it not now time to do something for their constituents? . . . .

"He concluded with moving to leave out from the words 'and we,' in the third paragraph, to the end of the paragraph, in order to insert these words: 'will, without delay, apply ourselves with united hearts to prepare and digest such counsels as may in this crisis excite the efforts, point the arms, and, by a total change of system, command the confidence of all his Majesty's subjects,' instead thereof."

The amendment was supported by Admiral Keppel, Mr. Burke, Colonel Barré, and Mr. Sheridan; but was rejected in a division by 218 to 129.

Thus it would seem that little progress had been made in changing the opinion of the House of Commons. But the news of the surrender of Cornwallis had still to produce its full effect. The progress of decline became more and more rapid, and Lord North fell with accelerated force. In December Sir James Lowther made a motion against any further attempts in America, which was rejected by a majority of forty-one. Admiral Kempenfeldt had been sent out with twelve sail of the line to prevent the French from despatching a squadron to the West Indies. Admiral Keppel had said publicly that Lord Sandwich was mistaken, and that Kempenfeldt would find nineteen or twenty sail of the line at Brest. This turned out to be true; the French sent six or seven ships to see their squadron safe out of the Channel; and Kempenfeldt, finding their force too superior, retired, and left them to pursue their voyage unmolested. This intelligence produced an impression so unfavourable to Ministers, that Lord North consented to an inquiry after the recess. Accordingly when, on the 24th of January, Mr. Fox moved " That it be referred to a committee to inquire into the causes of the want of success of his Majesty's naval forces during the war, and more particularly in the year 1781," it was agreed to without a division. The committee was ordered to be a committee of the whole House. On the 7th of February Mr. Fox moved " That it appears to this committee that there has been gross mismanagement in the conduct of his Majesty's naval affairs in the year 1781." This motion was defeated by 205 to 183; majority 22.

On the 20th Mr. Fox renewed his charge. A resolution nearly in terms identical with that moved in committee was now moved in the whole House. It was ably supported by Mr. Pitt. The division was 217 to 236; majority for Ministers 19.

It now became evident that a Ministry so nearly outvoted on vital questions must soon be driven from office; yet the King held out to the last. At the end of the year he consented to the resignation of Lord George Germaine; but only on condition that he should be created a peer. " No one can then say that he is disgraced; and when the appointment of Sir Guy Carleton (an enemy of Lord George) accompanies his retreat, it will be ascribed to its true cause, and not to any change in my sentiments on the essential point, namely, the getting a peace at the expense of a separation from America, *which no difficulties can get me to consent to."**

On the 22nd of February General Conway moved that an address be presented to the King, "That he will be graciously pleased to listen to the humble prayer and advice of his faithful Commons that the war on the continent of North America may no longer be pursued for the impracticable purpose of reducing the inhabitants of that country to obedience by force." The address went on to promise the assistance of the Commons to effect a reconciliation with the revolted colonies. The name of General Conway, his position as an officer, his freedom from party ties, his mild and persuasive eloquence, all contributed to incline the Commons to listen favourably to a proposal which was in fact a condemnation of the policy of the last fifteen years.

The substitution of Mr. Welbore Ellis for Lord George Germaine had not strengthened the Ministry, and his speech on this occasion showed, as Mr. Burke said, "that the person was changed, not the system."

Mr. Fox alluded, in very intelligible terms, to the influence which had prevailed : adverting to Mr. Jenkinson, he called him " the mouth of the oracle," and said he was glad he had discovered " the evil spirit" (Walpole says, " the infernal spirit") " that really ruled, and had nearly ruined the country. It was a person higher than the noble lord, for the noble lord was only his puppet, and acted as he was told."

On a division, the numbers were—

> For General Conway 193
> Against 194
> ———
> Majority 1

Mr. Fox immediately gave notice that the same question in another shape would be revived in a few days. Colonel Barré attacked Lord North violently, calling him the scourge of the country. Upon this Lord North, for almost the only time in his life, lost his temper, and said, "he had been used, from that quarter, to language so uncivil, so brutal, so insolent——" At these words the House got into an uproar, and Mr. T. Townshend called upon Lord North to apologize. Lord North said he was ready to ask pardon of the House, but not of Barré. At the end of a tumult of three hours he consented to ask pardon even of Barré.

After this division Lord North must have despaired. Mr. Fox, writing to Lord Ossory, says: "Wednesday is fixed for renewing the American question. I think it seems to be the general opinion that the thing is over, and that they must go; but it is not mine." The general opinion, however, was justified by the event.

On the 27th of February General Conway moved, "That it is the opinion of this House that the farther prosecution of offensive war on the continent of North America, for the purpose of reducing the revolted colonies to obedience by force, will be the means of weakening the efforts of this country against her European enemies; tends, under the present circumstances, dangerously to increase the mutual enmity, so fatal to the interests both of Great Britain and America; and, by preventing a happy reconciliation with that country, to frustrate the earnest desire graciously expressed by his Majesty to restore the blessings of public tranquillity."

Lord North objected to this motion on the ground that it entirely took away from the Executive Government the use of its discretion; and he said, truly enough, that if the House suspected the sincerity of the servants of the Crown—if they had any doubts of their ability or integrity, —they ought to address the Crown for their removal. But, in fact, this was a motion for the removal of the Ministers, based on the overthrow of their policy. Lord North, however, did not meet the question with a manly negative. His Attorney-General, Mr. Wallace, said there were obstacles of which the House did not seem to be aware—acts of Parliament which were an insuperable bar to peace with America. In order to afford time to prepare a bill to remove these obstacles, he proposed to adjourn the debate for a fortnight. This, from a Ministry which had the year before opposed the bringing in a bill by Mr. Hartley for these very purposes, was somewhat too shameful, and the shallow device was torn to shreds by Mr. Pitt. Speaking of the Ministers, he said : " Was there a promise which they had not falsified? Was there a plan in which they agreed? Did any two of them accord in any specific policy?"

Every effort had been made by the two parties to swell the numbers of the division. But, while the Ministry had already produced nearly their whole strength, the Opposition were able to bring up many whom indolence, despair, or an unwillingness to desert their former standard had hitherto kept away. The confidence of a rising power cheered the hopes of the Opposition ; the despondency of a declining cause blighted the prospects of the Government. Thus, while the Opposition added forty-one to their numbers, the Ministry could only collect a reinforcement of twenty-one. The final numbers were—

<pre>
        For General Conway 234
        For adjournment 215
                                         ———
        Majority   19
</pre>

The resolutions, and an address founded upon them, were then agreed to without a division. The address was ordered to be carried up by the whole House.

The King was not yet prepared to give up his title to the allegiance of America. The vote of the House of Commons appeared to him a weak abandonment of national rights and interests to obstinate rebellion and a foreign enemy. For the present he told the House of Commons that, "in pursuance of their advice, he would take such measures as should appear to him most conducive to the restoration of harmony between Great Britain and the re-volted colonies, so essential to the prosperity of both; and that his efforts shall be directed in the most effectual manner against our European enemies, until such a peace can be obtained as shall consist with the interest and per-manent welfare of his kingdom." There was something very ambiguous in this answer. The words, "in pursuance of their advice," looked like a compliance, but there was no direct promise; and the words, "so essential to the pro-sperity of both," were words hitherto used to imply the connexion of the two countries.

The Opposition were not to be thus foiled. It is said that Mr. Fox wished to complain of the King's answer, but that he was overruled by General Conway, Thomas Pitt, and others. Thanks were voted to the King for his gracious answer. A resolution was, however, immediately passed, declaring any persons who should advise the further prosecution of offensive war in North America enemies to the King and country.

Mr. Fox stated in his speech that he was not in the House when the address of thanks for the King's answer was voted; but if he had been, he should have agreed in the vote. He stated also that news had that day been received of the loss of Minorca, with a garrison of 1500 men. These repeated losses abroad, and defeats at home, had weakened the Government to such a degree, that Lord John Cavendish, on the 8th of March, was induced to move four resolutions, reciting that the country had expended 100,000,000*l.* in a fruitless war; that we had lost thirteen colonies, Florida, and many of our West India Islands; and that we were then engaged in an expensive war with America, France, Spain, and Holland, without a single ally. These facts were undeniable. But the opinion stated in the fourth resolution, "That the chief cause of all these misfortunes has been the want of foresight and ability in his Majesty's Ministers," was a stumbling-block to many who had supported the Ministers even up to the period of the address in the preceding November. Nevertheless this direct and severe vote of censure only failed by a majority of 10—the numbers being 216 and 226.

On the 15th of March Sir John Rous, who had been a follower of Lord North, who had loved the amiable virtues of his private character, and was a Tory in principle, made a new motion against the Ministry. His premises did not differ from those of Lord John Cavendish, but his conclusions were so far milder, that, instead of blaming the Ministry for want of foresight and ability, he contented himself with moving that the House " can have no further confidence in the Ministers who have the direction of public affairs." Lord North seems to have thought that this motion opened a door for his escape from office : he said he did not object to it so much as that of the preceding week ; it was divested of anger, its terms moderate, and its objects clear and defined. The motion was rejected by 9 only—236 to 227.

On the 20th of March Lord Surrey was to renew the motion in a different shape. When the day arrived the House was remarkably crowded, and curiosity was on tip-toe to learn the event. Before Lord Surrey commenced, Lord North rose, and said he had some information to give to the House, which might make any further proceeding in the motion unnecessary, and might require an adjournment. Upon these words there was great confusion, many members calling out " No adjournment!" some " Lord Surrey ! Lord Surrey !" and some " Lord North ! Lord North !" Upon this Mr. Fox rose and moved: " That Lord Surrey be now heard;" upon which Lord North, with great quickness, said : " And I rise to speak to that motion !" Lord North then said he could assure the House, with authority, that the present Administration was no more, and that his Majesty had come to the full determination of changing his Ministers. He then took leave of the House as Minister, thanking them for the honourable support they had given him during so long a course of years, and in so many trying situations.

" A successor of greater abilities was easy to be found ; a successor more zealously attached to the interests of his country, more anxious to promote them, more loyal to his Sovereign, and more desirous of preserving the Constitution whole and entire, he might be allowed to say, could not easily be found. He ended with declaring that he did not shrink from trial, and should always be prepared to meet it ; nay, he demanded it from his adversaries."

Thus ended the Administration of Lord North, and with

it the American War. For it was equally impossible that he should terminate it, and that his successors should continue it. On reviewing his Ministry, some allowance must be made for the circumstances in which he first entered the Cabinet: difficulties with America were already pressing; a great flood was coming down, and a stronger arm than his might have been unable to stem the torrent. But when this allowance has been made, justice requires that it should be added, that all difficulties were aggravated, and all perils heightened, by his weak conduct as a Minister. Ignorance of the extent of the danger, want of preparation for a struggle, want of discrimination in choosing a time for concession, mismanagement of the war, inopportune overtures, perseverance in wrong, vacillation, surrender of his own opinion to please the King, corruption in the government of the House of Commons, extravagant expenditure—in short, every fault, except personal dishonesty—may be justly imputed to Lord North. His good humour, his ability in debate, the amiability of his character, so fitted to attach friends and appease enemies, are qualities which no one will refuse him. But still less can it be denied that no other Minister of Great Britain since the Revolution so lowered her dignity, and quelled her pride.

The country had emerged out of the Seven Years' War with a consciousness of strength and of triumph: her navy had defeated those of France and Spain; her army had been victorious under Prince Ferdinand in Germany, and under Wolfe in Canada; the conquest of Havannah had been the crowning victory of the united naval and military service. In the American War the British army could scarcely ever drive from the field the raw levies of

Washington; while two divisions, under Burgoyne and Cornwallis, were forced to lay down their arms. The fleet under Keppel at one time, and Kempenfeldt at another, had retired before a superior force; for two years together a combined French and Spanish fleet had swept the Channel, while the British squadron ran to harbour, or hugged the shore. Thirteen colonies were lost for ever. Florida and St. Lucia were captured by the enemy; Minorca fell unrelieved; the finances were drooping; trade was depressed; the national heart laboured with grief. The siege of Gibraltar and Rodney's victory furnish the only lights in this dark picture.

Lord North had borne his elevation with modesty; he showed equanimity in his fall. A trifling circumstance evinced his good humour. On the evening when he announced his resignation to the House of Commons, snow was falling, and the weather was bitterly cold. Lord North kept his carriage. As he was passing through the great-coat room of the House of Commons, many members (chiefly his opponents) crowded the passage. When his carriage was announced, he put one or two of his friends into it, and then making a bow to his opponents, said, "Good night, gentlemen; it is the first time I have known the advantage of being in the secret."

Mr. Adam, from whom I heard this anecdote, says, in his memoranda: "No man ever showed more calmness, cheerfulness, and serenity. The temper of his whole family was the same. I dined with him that day, and was witness to it."

A more amiable man never lived; a worse Minister never since the Revolution governed this country. Even the King, who prompted his measures, despised his weakness of character.

CHAPTER XVI.

1782.

WITH Lord North a whole system passed away. George III., the inventor of that system, remained with all the power of a Constitutional King, but was no longer to be his own sole Minister. The scheme of governing by the will of the Monarch, and ruling the House of Commons by Court favour and thinly disguised corruption—that scheme, in short, which Mr. Burke denounced in his "Thoughts on the Causes of the Present Discontents," was no longer practicable. Mr. Fox and Lord Rockingham were men too considerable to act the humble part which Lord North had reluctantly performed. The position of the King was for the moment humiliating in the extreme. He had tried to destroy party—the Rockingham party had grown strong under his displeasure; he had tried to subdue America—America had conquered her independence; he had tried to preserve Lord North as his Minister—that Ministry was for ever at an end. Nor did the anger of the King arise merely from the defeat of his plans and the curb placed on his ambition—he was himself the first Tory gentleman in his dominions, and he felt deeply the separation of America as a diminution of the British empire and a loss of reputation to the British name. A great portion of his Parliament and many of his subjects had a similar feeling, and it would be unjust to attribute to a harsh or sanguinary nature that feeling of national pride which was somewhat akin to a regard for the national honour. In this situation it is no wonder if George III. brooded over a desperate resolution. It was said that for a fortnight together the Royal yacht was preparing to convey the King to Hanover. So late as the 17th of March the King wrote to Lord North : " I am resolved not to throw myself into the hands of Opposition at all events, and shall certainly, if things go as they seem to tend, know what my conscience as well as honour dictates, as the only way left for me."

These impulses of despair, however, always gave way to reflection. George III. never yielded till he knew it was inevitable; he always yielded fully when it was so.* In 1804 he would not admit Mr. Fox to the closet; in 1806 he made not the slightest objection to him. Had he lived and reigned till 1829, he probably would have conceded the Catholic Question with far more readiness than his son displayed on that occasion. At least, in the present instance, his concessions were ample.

On the day following the letter I have quoted, the King wrote to Lord North, and, after repeating that his sentiments of honour would not permit him to send for any of the leaders of the Opposition and personally treat with them, said, with

---

* In reference to the affairs of the Duke of York, Lord Grenville writes to his brother, Lord Buckingham, on March 16th, 1809 : " The King's mind is, I believe, more difficult to satisfy. He holds out, as he has always done, just as long as he thinks his perseverance is likely to be of any use in carrying his point; and when he sees there is no longer any hope of that, he will give way, as he has always done in such cases."—" Court and Cabinets of George III." vol. iv. p. 333.

an evident change of purpose, "If you resign *before I have decided what to do*, you will certainly for ever forfeit my regard." At this time the Chancellor (Lord Thurlow) was employed in sounding Lord Rockingham. Lord Rockingham answered that the terms upon which he would propose to form an Administration were as follows: "A power to accede to the independence of America; a reduction of the influence of the Crown by an abolition of offices; and bills to deprive contractors of their seats in the House of Commons, and revenue officers of their votes at elections. With respect to any reform in the representation, or limiting the duration of Parliaments, he declined laying himself under any restrictions."

Lord Thurlow was surly and morose upon the subject of the three bills. He said "he would have no further communication with a man who thought the exclusion of a contractor from Parliament and the disfranchisement of an exciseman of more importance than the salvation of the country in its present situation."* Yet, if these were small things for Lord Rockingham to require, they were small things for the Crown to yield. But, in fact, Lord Rockingham knew that his character and that of his party were involved in the reduction of the influence of the Crown, and it was more important to preserve that character than to respect the prejudices of the Chancellor, or even of the Sovereign.

The King next tried Lord Gower; but Lord Gower had too much sagacity to embark alone on so stormy a sea. Lord Gower, if he represented anything, represented the Bedford party; but Lord Sandwich, who was also of that party, was one of the most obnoxious of Lord North's

* Walpole.

colleagues. The King, who had no real attachment to Lord North, had now kept him in office long enough for his purpose, and seems to have paid no further regard to him. Without informing him, he sent to Lord Shelburne, and gave him an audience at Buckingham Palace on Thursday, the 21st of March, and proposed to him to form a government. The King's motive for sending for Lord Shelburne was, no doubt, that he was not the head of a party; but this very reason made Lord Shelburne decline the King's offer. He did not, however, relate to Lord Rockingham what had passed; and, although he spent the evening at Devonshire House, he avoided conversation, and, sitting down to Faro, did not tell any one that he had been that morning with the King. Friday and Saturday passed without any further overture to Opposition. On Sunday morning Lord Shelburne was again sent for, and after his interview with the King came to Lord Rockingham with an offer of the Treasury, himself to be one of the Secretaries of State. He told Lord Rockingham he had declined to form a government, saying : " You could go on without me, but I could not go on without you." Lord Rockingham's first impulse was to decline the offer, saying, if he was to be the head of the Treasury, the King could have no objection to see him on the subject. Mr. Fox and the Duke of Richmond persuaded him to waive this objection. The decision was unfortunate, for from this moment Lord Shelburne became the chosen organ of the King, and a barrier against Whig influence in the Cabinet. Mr. Fox perceived this when it was too late. Lord Rockingham, however, accompanied his acceptance with a list of those whom he expected to see in the Cabinet, leaving a blank for Lord Shelburne to fill the office of Chancellor, as he might be

supposed to know Mr. Dunning's inclinations upon that
subject. The list was as follows :—

Lord Rockingham .	First Lord of the Treasury.
Lord John Cavendish	Chancellor of the Exchequer.
Admiral Keppel . .	First Lord of the Admiralty.
Duke of Richmond .	Master General of the Ordnance.
Mr. Charles Fox Lord Shelburne } .	Secretaries of State.
Lord Camden . . .	President of the Council.
Duke of Grafton . .	Lord Privy Seal.
General Conway . .	Commander-in-Chief.

A large meeting of members of the House of Commons
was held in the evening at the house of Mr. Thomas
Townshend, to whom this list was communicated. According to the general conduct and principles of the persons
composing it, Lord Rockingham and Mr. Fox seemed to
have the preponderating scale in this arrangement; the
list was approved of; Lord Shelburne expressed his perfect
approbation of it, and transmitted it to the King.

On Monday, the 25th, Lord Shelburne was to see the
King to receive his answer. He wished, if the arrangement was agreed to, to adjourn the House of Commons over
Easter; but to this Mr. Fox would not consent. Lord
Shelburne, after staying with the King from eleven till two
o'clock, came to Mr. Fox, and said the proposals were substantially agreed to, and that Mr. Dunning would move an
adjournment of one day only to complete the arrangements.
The choice of Mr. Dunning for this duty was an ostensible
proof of Lord Shelburne's share in the formation of the
Ministry. Besides this, Lord Shelburne had agreed that
Lord Thurlow should continue Chancellor, and had proposed
to the King that Mr. Dunning should have a seat in the

Cabinet as Chancellor of the Duchy of Lancaster, with a peerage.

Mr. Fox at once saw the drift of these arrangements. He told Lord Shelburne that he perceived this Administration was to consist of two parts, one belonging to the King, the other to the public. Yet he accepted office, and had soon to rue the fulfilment of his own prophecy. It was obvious that the addition of Dunning, as well as Thurlow, to Lord Rockingham's list, made a complete alteration in the character of the Ministry. Lord Shelburne could count upon the voice of Lord Thurlow, the Duke of Grafton, Lord Camden, Lord Ashburton (Mr. Dunning). Against these five were ranged Lord Rockingham, the Duke of Richmond, Mr. Fox, Lord John Cavendish, and Admiral Keppel. General Conway had never belonged to any party. "That *innocent* man, General Conway," said Lord Shelburne to Fox afterwards, " never found out that he had a casting vote in the Cabinet." General Conway, pure and virtuous as he was, had such a fund of moderation in his character, that he was easily swept into currents which carried him in a directly opposite direction from that in which he wished to move. He was for ever in a maze, without any clue from his own sagacity, or any aid except that which he derived from the caprice and malevolence of Walpole.

In addition to this obvious insecurity, there was a danger no less patent, namely, the infirm and precarious state of Lord Rockingham's health. Yet a measure might at this time have been taken which would at once have been justice to a man of genius, a tribute to economical reform, and a security for the Whig party in the House of Commons. This was to give Mr. Burke a seat in the Cabinet. Instead of this real guarantee for themselves, the Whig Ministers asked for a peerage for Sir Fletcher Norton, a man whose character no one trusted, and upon whose friendship no one could depend. Such was the first great fault of the Rockingham Whigs upon entering office. It may be said, indeed, with regard to Mr. Burke, that his violence and indiscretion often exceeded all bounds. But he was steady in his attachments, and, with Mr. Fox as his leader, might soon have learnt the necessary caution of office. Another omission, owing to the same cause, was the entire neglect of any guarantee for those conditions respecting the influence of the Crown, upon which Lord Rockingham had insisted in his interview with Lord Thurlow. Thus, Lord Shelburne and Lord Thurlow were left at liberty to thwart all those measures to which Mr. Fox, Mr. Burke, and the Duke of Richmond were so deeply pledged.

Other circumstances displayed the Shelburne influence. Lord Ashburton obtained a grant of a pension of 4000*l.* a year for life; Colonel Barré the post of Treasurer of the Navy, with a life pension of 2000*l.* a year. Lord Barrington was removed from the Post Office with 2000*l.* a year for life, to make room for Lord Tankerville, a friend of Lord Shelburne. These pensions, granted to please Lord Shelburne, created much public disgust, and indisposed many reformers to Lord Rockingham's Ministry.

Thus the King, after a short interval, obtained the object for which he had struggled, and on account of which he had retarded the resignation of Lord North. Two parties were made in the Ministry, one of which looked to the favour of the Court, not to the support of the country. The tares were sown, and could hardly fail to grow up and choke the healthy plants of reform and economy. After the thorough failure of the American war, and amid the popular cry against abuses, it must be owned that the composition of the Rockingham Ministry was a masterpiece of royal skill.

Let us now turn to the position of the new Ministry. The difficulties which pressed upon the country at the time when the Rockingham Administration was formed, were not of a single kind or of an ordinary complexity.

In Ireland an armed body of volunteers overawed the Government and pretended to impose its own terms upon the Legislature. At home the mismanagement of the finances, and the prevalence of gross abuses had caused general distrust and discontent.

In America the gallant conduct of our troops had only served to develope the desperate nature of the conflict; and the military disaster of Lord Cornwallis had extinguished the flame of loyalty in many of those bosoms in which it had hitherto been kept alive. In Europe, France, Spain, and Holland were openly at war with us; and the two former powers, by combining their fleets, had obtained the command of the British Channel. At Gibraltar, a brilliant defence maintained by General Elliot could only be prolonged by the arrival of naval succours. The Empress of Russia, who might have been expected to watch with jealousy the onward progress of France and Spain, was intent on overthrowing the rules by which since 1756 our naval warfare had been regulated. She had proclaimed in a famous declaration that the goods of an enemy may be covered by a neutral flag; that a blockade, to be valid, must be effective; and that no articles are contraband of war except those which have been specified in a treaty between the respective powers.

The attention of Mr. Fox was turned to all these subjects.

The first difficulty with which the Ministry had to struggle was the state of Ireland. The demand for legislative independence was loudly echoed by forty thousand men in arms. The American War, amongst its other evils, had drained Ireland of regular troops. The Irish, by a spontaneous movement of patriotism, had raised volunteers to supply the place of the force of which they had been deprived. They were at the same time contending against the Court for legislative independence; and the patriotic sympathies of all parties in Ireland were engaged in this contest. By an easy and natural transition the volunteers turned the arms which had been assumed to meet a foreign foe against a domestic enemy. Deliberation took place, not in county and parochial meetings, but in brigades and battalions. The combination of parliamentary parties and organized regiments might have been formidable, had not the movement been led by two men of extraordinary virtue and paramount authority. These two men were the Earl of Charlemont and Mr. Grattan. Lord Charlemont, with a well-tempered mind and highly-cultivated understanding, governed the multitude by his authority, and awed the Senate by his virtues. Henry Grattan, endowed with a singular eloquence, used epigram and antithesis as the vehicles of deep feeling; and roused enthusiastic patriotism in language so balanced and metaphor so fanciful, that in any other man they would have appeared like affectation. Both were honest, sincere, and devoted to the welfare of Ireland.

However well inclined Lord Charlemont and Mr. Grattan might be to confide in Lord Rockingham and Mr. Fox, they felt they could not keep in suspense the nation which looked to them for relief from those shackles against which there was an unanimous protest. Another and unexpected circumstance forced on an early decision. Lord Carlisle, the Lord Lieutenant of Lord North, had sent over his Secretary, Mr. Eden, to explain to the new Government the state of Ireland. Mr. Eden, finding that the Ministry intended to give their instructions to a Lord Lieutenant of their own choice, and that Lord Carmarthen was to be restored to the Lord Lieutenancy of the East Riding of the county of York, which had been given to Lord Carlisle, refused, upon these vain pretexts, to give any information to the Government, and hurried down to the House of Commons to lay before that assembly the state of Ireland. After drawing a most alarming picture of the numbers, influence, and power of the volunteers, he concluded with moving a repeal of so much of the Act of 6 George I. as asserted a right in the King and Parliament of Great Britain to make laws to bind the kingdom of Ireland. Mr. Fox, who rose for the first time in the character of a Minister of the Crown, had no difficulty in meeting this intemperate motion. He pointed out the indecency of forcing a Ministry just formed to pronounce an off-hand opinion upon arduous and complicated affairs. He declared that the conduct of Mr. Eden was of a piece with the whole policy of the late Ministry. They had refused the most reasonable requests of an unarmed people; they were willing to yield British supremacy without conditions to an armed and menacing confederacy. He spoke with great respect of the Irish patriots, and only asked for a reasonable time to enable the Ministry to arrange a satisfactory settlement of questions of such vast importance. He called upon Mr.

Eden to withdraw his motion, and said that, unless he did so, he (Mr. Fox) should move the order of the day. This proposal was too reasonable not to meet the immediate assent of the House. The following account of this debate is given by Horace Walpole. It is lively, and apparently accurate :—

"The new Ministers being re-chosen, the House of Commons met again, when, instead of any crimination produced by them against any of their predecessors, an attempt was made to embarrass the Ministers by a deed that, though aimed at them, might have produced the most mischievous consequences and confusions to the nation. Eden, Lord Carlisle's secretary, had posted over with the earl's resignation. So exasperated was he, that, not only keeping himself private, he had secret intercourse with, and private incitement from, Lord Loughborough; but he positively *refused* to communicate a syllable of the state of Ireland to Lord Shelburne, the Secretary of State. On the contrary, Colonel Luttrell, an ominous name, instigated probably by Loughborough and Eden, rose, as soon as the House met, and called on the Ministers to declare what measures they meant to pursue for pacifying the disquiets and alarms of Ireland, not yet satisfied that what had been done for her was either substantial or irrevocable. On this hostile ground mounted Eden, and in a passionate speech, ill-covered over with pretended zeal, called for a repeal of the Act of George I., which was the most grievous link of their chain of subjection. Unfortunately for this incendiary, a spear, like that of Milton's angel, that, touching Satan, made him start up in his proper shape, was in the hand of Charles Fox. His vehement eloquence that had so often borne down Lord North, Sandwich, and the late junto, was now displayed in detecting and exposing the mischievous conduct of Eden, while with the utmost address and discretion he steered clear of any offence to Ireland. He overwhelmed Eden with shame — not with remorse; for, though universal indignation burst on the head of Eden, his obstinate pride would not recant; nor would he withdraw his motion until General Conway, as powerful in indignant virtue as Fox in the thunder of abilities, threatened him with a vote of censure, which was re-echoed by a hundred voices; when, more terrified than abashed, he submitted to waive his purpose."*

On the following day Mr. Fox brought down a message from the Crown to the following purport: " GEORGE R. His Majesty being concerned to find that discontents and jealousies are prevailing among his loyal subjects in Ireland upon matters of great weight and importance, earnestly recommends to this House to take the same into their most serious consideration, in order to such a final adjustment as may give a mutual satisfaction to both kingdoms."

Mr. Fox declared that it was owing more to accident than design that the message had not been brought down on the previous day. He said that, as a new Lord Lieutenant was about to set out for Dublin, it was desirable that he should be able to carry with him a proof of the sincerity of the Ministers and of the friendly inclinations of the Crown and the Parliament towards the people of Ireland. The Ministers wished to interpose a short delay, in order that, instead of applying a temporary remedy to a temporary evil, they might act in such a manner as to give permanent peace to both countries.

The Duke of Portland, the new Lord Lieutenant, and

* " Memorials and Correspondence of Fox."

Colonel Fitzpatrick, his secretary, repaired at once to Dublin. Mr. Grattan had given notice of resolutions for the 16th of April, asserting the legislative and judicial independence of Ireland. Mr. Fitzpatrick, in conformity with the wishes of Lord Shelburne and the Duke of Portland, endeavoured to obtain a postponement; but Lord Charlemont and Mr. Grattan would not, and could not, consent to any delay. Mr. Grattan, however, agreed to change his resolutions into an address, which he thought more respectful and more open to negotiation. The Duke of Portland would not on his part sanction Mr. Grattan's motion; but an address to the new Lord Lieutenant having been moved in the ordinary form, Mr. Grattan rose, and in a speech of wonderful eloquence proposed his address as an amendment. It was carried unanimously, and with great applause.

There were three points upon which the Irish patriots principally insisted: 1. The repeal of the 6th of Geo. I., declaring the legislative dependence of Ireland upon England. 2. The renunciation of the power of appeal to the English House of Lords from the Irish courts. 3. The conversion of the perpetual Mutiny Bill into an annual bill. These three proposals were all so reasonable, that it was impossible for a Whig Ministry to refuse them. The power of altering and defeating bills passed by the Irish Parliament had been exercised by the Privy Council in Ireland and by the Attorney-General in England, and by both so vexatiously, that the practical grievance was considerable. The case is thus stated in a letter of Mr. Grattan to Mr. Fox :—

" The power of suppressing in the Irish, and of altering in the English council, never has been useful to England; on the contrary, frequently the cause of embarrassment to the British Government. I have known Privy Councillors agree to bills in Parliament, and in council alter them materially by some strong clause inserted to show their zeal to the King at the expense of the popularity of Government. In England, an Attorney-General or his clerk, from ignorance, or corruption, or contempt, may, and often has, inserted clauses in Irish bills which have involved Irish governments in lasting consequences with the people; for you must see that a servant of Government in Great Britain, uninformed of the passions of Ireland, may, in the *full exercise* of legislative power, do irreparable mischief to his King and country, without being responsible to either. . . . The negativing our bills is a right never disputed, the poisoning them is a practice we do most ardently deprecate, from sound reason and sad experience. I brought to Parliament a list of the alterations made for the last ten years in Irish bills by the Privy Council or Attorney-General, and there was not a single alteration made upon a sound legislative motive. Sometimes an alteration to vex the Presbyterians, made by the bishops; sometimes an alteration made by an over-zealous courtier, to make Government obnoxious and to render himself at the same time peculiarly acceptable to the King; sometimes an alteration from ignorance, and not seldom for money."*

The power of deciding appeals in the English House of Lords was useless to Great Britain, and was so considered by Mr. Fox. A perpetual Mutiny Bill was totally contrary to all constitutional notions. The question of concession was well put by Mr. Grattan: "Can England cede with dignity? I submit she can; for, if she has consented to enable his Majesty to repeal all the laws respecting

* "Memorials and Correspondence," vol. i. p. 404.

America, among which the Declaratory Act is one, she can with more majesty repeal the Declaratory Act against Ireland, who has declared her resolution to stand and fall with the British nation, and has stated her own rights by appealing not to your fears but your magnanimity. You will please to observe in our address a veneration for the pride as well as a love for the liberty of England. You will see in our manner of transmitting the address, we have not gone to the Castle with volunteers, as in 1779. It was expedient to resort to such a measure with your predecessors in office. In short, sir, you will see in our requisition nothing but what is essential to the liberty and composure of one country, and consistent with the dignity and interest of the other."*

Equally conciliatory and friendly was the language of Lord Charlemont. In writing to Mr. Fox, he says : " I have seen Grattan, and have communicated the kind paragraph in your letter respecting him. He desires his most sincere thanks for your goodness and friendly opinion of him. We are both of us precisely of the same mind. We respect and honour the present Administration. We adore the principle on which it is founded. We look up to its members with the utmost confidence for their assistance in the great work of general freedom, and should be happy in our turn to have it in our power to support them in Ireland in the manner which may be most beneficial to them, and most honourable to us; consulted but not considered. The people at large must indeed entertain a partiality for the present Ministers. True Whigs must rejoice at the prevalence of Whiggish principles. The nation wishes to support the favourers of American freedom, the

* " Memorials and Correspondence," vol. i. p. 405.

men who opposed the detested, the execrated American War. Let our rights be acknowledged and secured to us—those rights which no man can controvert, but which to a true Whig are self-evident—and that nation, those lives and fortunes which are now universally pledged for the emancipation of our country, will be as cheerfully, as universally, pledged for the defence of our sister kingdom, and for the support of an Administration which will justly claim the gratitude of a spirited and grateful people, by having contributed to the completion of all their wishes."

The ground being thus laid by the address of the Irish Parliament, and the restoration of confidence in the King's Government being both publicly and privately expressed, Mr. Fox, on the 17th of May, moved to refer to a committee of the whole House the King's message of the 9th of April, and the address of the Irish Parliament. In opening the subject in committee, Mr. Fox stated, that the points to which the claims of the Irish Parliament were directed appeared to be the repeal of the 6th of George I., the restoration of the appellant jurisdiction, the modification of Poyning's law, and the repeal of the perpetuating clause in the Mutiny Bill. He laid down as a principle that, when local legislatures were established in different parts of the empire, it was clearly for this purpose, that they might answer all municipal ends; and the great superintending power of the State ought not to be called into action but in aid of the local legislature, and for the good of the empire at large. Proceeding upon this principle, he showed that the late Ministry had in Ireland, as in America, used the power of external legislation as an instrument of oppression, had employed it to establish an impolitic monopoly in trade, and to enrich one country at the expense of the other.

When the Irish complained of this monopoly, their requests, which were no less modest than just, were disregarded. But when the Irish armed, and their Parliament spoke out aloud, the same Minister who had before put a negative on all their expectations, came down to the House, and, making the *amende honorable* for his past conduct, gave to the demands of an armed people infinitely more than he had refused to the applications of an unarmed, humble nation. The lesson which the Irish had been taught was this: "If you want anything, seek not for it unarmed and humbly, but take up arms, speak manfully and boldly to the British Ministry, and you will obtain more than you at first might have ventured to expect."

Mr. Fox proceeded to say that, if he should be obliged to make any proposition that might appear hurtful to the pride of Englishmen, the fault was not his, it was the fault of those who had left it in the power of the volunteers to make the demands contained in the addresses on the table; who had left it in their power, not by leaving arms in their hands, but by leaving them injuries and oppressions. "For his part, he would rather see Ireland totally separated from the Crown of England than kept in obedience only by force. Unwilling subjects were little better than enemies; it would be better not to have subjects at all, than to have such as would be continually on the watch to seize on an opportunity to make themselves free. If this country should succeed in the attempt to coerce Ireland, the consequence would be that, at the breaking out of every war with a foreign power, the first step must be to send troops over to secure Ireland, instead of calling upon her to give a willing support to the common cause."

Acting on these generous and large views, Mr. Fox proposed : 1st. To repeal the act of George I. by which Great Britain assumed the right to legislate for Ireland. 2nd. To give up the appellate jurisdiction of the British House of Lords. 3rd. To modify Poyning's law in such a manner as no longer to authorize the interposition of the English or Irish Privy Council. He ended with a motion to repeal the act of the 6th of George I. This being agreed to without a division, he moved an address to the Crown, founded on a previous resolution : " That an humble address be presented to his Majesty that he will be graciously pleased to take such measures as his Majesty in his royal wisdom shall think most conducive to the establishing, by mutual consent, the connexion between this kingdom and the kingdom of Ireland, upon a solid and permanent basis."*

We must now refer to those measures for correcting abuses, and diminishing the influence of the Crown upon which, and upon the abandonment of the war in America, the Rockingham Administration was founded. I have already stated that the Earl of Shelburne came into office, not so much the colleague as the rival of Lord Rockingham, the chosen Minister of the Court, and the head of a separate party in the Cabinet. The evils which were sure to flow from such a division were aggravated by the peculiar character of Lord Shelburne.

William Earl of Shelburne, after receiving an irregular education, came early into the House of Lords. His talents soon made him remarked, and he was placed at the head of the Board of Trade. In the course of the revolutions of party which occurred in the subsequent years, he attached himself to the Earl of Chatham ; and that great man paid

* " Parliamentary History." Fox's " Speeches."

him the compliment of saying that, if they were in different parts of the globe, he was sure they should think alike. His mind, if not disciplined by regular study, was enlarged by the knowledge of the writings of Scotch and French economists; and he far excelled most of his cotemporaries in the liberality of his opinions on commerce. His power of speaking was considerable. The shrewdness of his observations and the force of his sarcasm made him feared as well as admired. But his want of knowledge of men led him into gross blunders, which he mistook for refined contrivances. To Lord Thurlow he spoke of his admiration of the genius of the King; Lord Thurlow, instead of reporting his adulation in the closet, as Lord Shelburne expected, repeated it everywhere else as a proof of Lord Shelburne's flattery. To Lord Cholmondeley, who came to him for a place, he recommended a "high independent line;" to Lord Carlisle, who founded much of his pretensions on the seats he held and the members he influenced in Parliament, he gave the unwelcome advice "not to have anything to do with such dirty work." Such modes of dealing with men, and the mistake of confounding flattery with courtesy, made his sincerity questioned, and obtained for him the nickname of "Malagrida." Hence, Goldsmith's equivocal remark, "I wonder they should call you 'Malagrida,' for 'Malagrida' was a very honest man." Hence, too, George III. wrote of him as "the Jesuit." Lord Holland says: "He was capable of strong attachments, but he was too suspicious to feel, and too restless in his dealings with public men to inspire, implicit confidence."

Such was the man who considered himself as destined to be a Sully, and whom George III. was willing to employ, as he had employed Lord North, and would fain have employed Lord Chatham, as a tool. Lord Shelburne had no respect for the mental powers, and no belief in the physical health of Lord Rockingham. He looked to the Court for favour, and to the day when he should have neither superior nor rival. Instead of seeking support in the artless, open, and candid nature of Mr. Fox, he endeavoured to thwart him in the Cabinet, was jealous of his private correspondence with Lord Charlemont and Mr. Grattan, and attempted to supplant him in his own proper business, the negotiation for peace. Mr. Fox soon perceived this malignant influence. So early as the 12th of April he writes to Fitzpatrick: "We had a Cabinet this morning, in which, in my opinion, there were more symptoms of what we had always apprehended than had ever hitherto appeared. The subject was Burke's bill, or rather the message introductory to it. Nothing was concluded; but in Lord Chancellor there was so marked an opposition, and in your brother-in-law (Lord Shelburne) so much inclination to help the Chancellor, that we got into something very like a warm debate. I told them I was determined to bring the matter to a crisis, as I am; and I think a few days will convince them that they must yield entirely. If they do not, we must go to war again, that is all; I am sure I am ready."

On the 15th he writes again: "We have had another very teasing and wrangling Cabinet, but I rather think everything is or will be settled right. I am to carry a message to-day to the House of Commons, which looks and points to Burke's bill. The King is, in the first instance, to abolish of his own accord the offices, but that abolition is in every instance to have the sanction of an act of Parliament for the appropriation of the money, the preventing their revival, &c. Lord Chancellor, as you may imagine, dislikes it. Lord Shelburne seems more *bothered* about it than anything else—does not understand it; but, in conjunction with Lord Ashburton, rather throws difficulties in its way. General Conway quite with us in the general view, but unfortunately *doubts* in almost every particular instance. Lord Camden, evidently with us in his mind, yet is so terribly afraid of dissensions that he does not do us all the good he might. The Duke of Grafton rather hostile, though professing *right principles* in the strongest terms, but full of little projects of his own, and troublesome in the extreme. The remaining five* just as you would expect and wish. This is a tolerably accurate sketch of our councils; but I have no doubt but things will jumble themselves into something more to our mind, or come to a crisis the other way. Indeed, if they do not, it will be very uneasy to me, and to everybody. We met yesterday at eleven, and did not get to the drawing-room till four, when it was over. All this time the King seems in perfect good humour, and does not seem to make any of those difficulties which others make for him."

There can be little doubt that the King heard from his Chancellor all that passed, and was quite willing to wait patiently for the explosion of the train which he had laid. At this time Dundas was so well informed as to advise Lord North not to let his friends attack Lord Shelburne, "for he is quite with us." But Lord North had been too much offended with Lord Shelburne's scorn and sarcasm in the House of Lords to be inclined to an alliance in that quarter.

---

* The "remaining five" were, Lord Rockingham, the Duke of Richmond, Lord John Cavendish, Admiral Keppel, and Mr. Fox himself.

The popular feeling, both in the House of Commons and in the country, was too strong to allow of Lord Shelburne's breaking with Fox on the subject of abuses in Administration. Burke's bill for reduction of offices and regulation of pensions was accordingly carried. The negotiations for peace, however, afforded a more favourable opportunity for dissension. Before we give any account of these transactions, it will be useful to cast our eyes on the state of our relations with the neutral powers.

Mr. Fox contemplated with much uneasiness the position of Great Britain. While France, Spain, Holland, and America were against us, the Northern Powers were anything but friendly. The Empress Catherine of Russia was bent on attaining the objects of the armed neutrality; the King of Prussia, old and infirm, was not inclined to risk, for the sake of Great Britain, the enmity of France on the one side and of Russia on the other.

Mr. Fox was desirous of raising in the North of Europe some counterpoise to the power of France. But he saw that, unless he could make some concession to the Northern Powers on the subject of neutral rights, it would be vain to hope to engage Catherine of Russia and Frederick of Prussia on the side of Great Britain.

The questions in dispute were: 1. Whether free bottoms make free goods? 2. Whether contraband of war should in all cases be excepted from the benefit of this principle? 3. Whether ships under convoy should ever be searched? Subordinate to these questions were the arguments relating to blockade, and to the coasting and colonial trade of belligerents. It appeared to Mr. Fox that on these questions great concessions might be made.

In a letter to Lord Grey, written in 1800, he says:

"The first act of the Rockingham Ministry, before I had had the seals twenty-four hours, was to make an offer to Holland upon the principles of the armed neutrality; and this more with a view to satisfy the Empress, than with much hope of procuring peace with the United Provinces. This measure was one of the few upon which that Cabinet was unanimous."*

In writing to Lord Holland, on the 24th of January, 1801, he says: "As to the Northern business, I have forgot a good deal what passed twenty years ago; but I remember I was a friend then to the Russian system, and *that* to a degree that, in the Rockingham Administration I was upon one question alone, or had only Lord John Cavendish with me, but what that question was, is quite out of my head."†

With regard to the general merits of the questions at issue, it appears to me impossible that Mr. Fox's views can be better stated than they are stated by Mr. Fox himself in a speech on the state of the nation on the 25th of March, 1801. But of that speech I shall only here extract a passage which relates to the facts:—

"I certainly did, in my capacity of Secretary of State, offer, by his Majesty's command, to the Empress of Russia, in the year 1782, the recognition of the principle in question, for the purpose of inducing that princess to enter into a closer alliance with this country. In rejecting the insinuation of this proposal being my sole act, let me not be understood to shrink from that measure as 'rash and inconsiderate;' on the contrary, I affirm that it was most wise, timely, and judicious; but, for the sake of truth, let it be remembered that the measure, which it fell officially

* "Correspondence," vol. iii. p. 300.   † Ibid. vol. iii. p. 185.

to my lot to propose to the court of Russia at the time alluded to, was of course the measure of the King's whole Council, which Council consisted of some of the greatest names of the country, such as the Marquis of Rockingham, Lord John Cavendish, the Duke of Richmond, the Marquis of Lansdowne, Lord Keppel, &c. It was, in a word, the act of an Administration which has been the least censured and the most praised of any that have existed during the King's reign.

"The right honourable gentleman challenges any person to discuss the question with the neutral powers as 'a statesman or a lawyer.' Now, though I can venture to touch the matter only in the first of these characters, I can assure the House that the concession, whatever it was, of the Ministry, which I offered as our joint act to the Empress of Russia in the year 1782, had the concurrence of as great lawyers as ever distinguished this country at any one period; for, whatever may have been the other defects of that short Administration, in it there certainly was no want of eminent lawyers. No less than three of the luminaries of that profession—namely, Lords Ashburton, Camden, and Thurlow—were members of that Cabinet; and far enough from thinking that the offer then made to the Russian court, 'laid at the feet of that government all the sources of the naval greatness of this country,' to repeat the rant of the right honourable gentleman, these learned and noble persons, together with the whole body of that Administration, were profoundly convinced, not that what we offered was slight and trifling, but that, important as it was, it would have been highly to the advantage of this country that our proposal had been adopted by the Government of Russia.

"In making this offer, I was so far from being mysterious—so little apprehension did we feel that our proposition to Russia would involve our country in any of the perils from other powers which the fatuity of the right honourable gentleman's Ministry has brought upon it, that, instead of sending through the more usual channel of our ambassador at that court, who, if I mistake not, was Lord Malmesbury, I applied here directly to M. Simolin, the Russian Minister at this court, and with him endeavoured to accomplish the negotiation. To him I offered a *quid pro quo;* and meant to give nothing without getting a full equivalent. I wished to separate Russia entirely from any connexions injurious to Great Britain, and to attach that power solidly and permanently to this country. The right honourable gentleman has dwelt with some satisfaction upon the expressions of my letter to M. Simolin. He has the advantage over me of having lately read that letter in the office, and seems, strangely enough, to think that he derives some pretext for his own policy in my description of the magnitude of our proposed concessions in 1782. Why, what would the right honourable gentleman, or any other man, think of me if I wrote otherwise than he states me to have written on that occasion? If he were negotiating with France about the surrender of Belgium, the retention of which he has so lately made a *sine quá non,* would he begin by understating the extent, fertility, and population of those provinces? I, of course, did not begin by depreciating to the Government of Russia the very boon I was tendering as an inducement to a great and beneficial alliance."

The full statement on the merits of the question may be reserved till the period when the debate of 1801 took place.

The negotiations for peace with the belligerents belonged properly to Mr. Fox. Independently of all other considerations, a new but natural arrangement had been made of the office of Secretary of State on the accession of the Rockingham Ministry. Instead of the Northern and Southern Departments, the office had been properly divided into Foreign and Home. The office of third Secretary of State had been abolished, and the colonies were comprehended in the Home Department. But Lord Shelburne was not disposed to leave his colleague in the foreign office unembarrassed. At the moment when Lord North's Ministry was falling, and on the day after Lord North had announced his resignation to the House of Commons, Dr. Franklin wrote a private letter to Lord Shelburne, containing expressions of his desire to co-operate in the re-establishment of a general peace. Lord Shelburne in return despatched Mr. Oswald to Paris as " a pacifical man, and conversant in those negotiations which are most beneficial to mankind."

What this meant, and how far Mr. Oswald's mission was communicated by Lord Shelburne to his colleagues, does not appear. Mr. Oswald, however, having made a favourable impression upon Dr. Franklin, his mission was adopted by the Ministry, and a minute of the Cabinet, apparently drawn up by Lord Shelburne, contains their advice that Mr. Oswald, who had now come back to London, should return to Paris with authority to settle with Dr. Franklin the most convenient time for setting on foot a negotiation for a general peace, to take place at Paris upon the basis of " the allowance of independence to America, upon Great Britain's being restored to the situation she was placed in by the treaty of 1763." Mr. Fox was to name a proper person to make a similar communication to M. de Vergennes.

Mr. Fox gives the following account of this mission, in a letter to Fitzpatrick: "Shelburne has had an answer from Dr. Franklin, who seems much disposed to peace, if general. Mons. de Vergennes has, it seems, expressed the same sentiments, and wishes to have some opening from hence: in consequence of this, Shelburne's man is to go back this day to Paris, and, upon pretence of the business having begun with the American Ministers, he had a great mind, if I would have consented, to have kept even this negotiation in his own hands; but this I would not submit to; and so Grenville is to set out to Paris to-morrow or next day, in order to state our ideas of peace to Mons. de Vergennes. Whether anything will come of this one cannot tell. I think it will all depend upon this point, whether the French like peace enough to make them influence the Spaniards to be reasonable; for, with respect to France, I still think there cannot be many difficulties."

In consenting to open the negotiation through Mr. Oswald, Mr. Fox made a great mistake. In point of form, so soon as the independence of America was in question, and not her relations as a dependency, America became, not a colony, but a foreign country—"a friend in peace, an enemy in war," as the Congress of 1776 had expressed it. In point of substance, the independence of America was the grand subject of difference between Great Britain and France; and Mr. Fox, in allowing Mr. Oswald to precede his negotiator, did effectually allow the negotiation to be taken out of his hands. This result soon appeared, and to a greater extent than any one could have anticipated.

Mr. Oswald reached Paris on the 4th of May; Mr.

Grenville on the 8th. On the 10th Mr. Grenville wrote to Mr. Fox that if the overtures he was to make were not to go beyond his present instructions, they would not probably even set the business agoing. In fact, the peace of 1763 having been made at the termination of a most glorious war, it was not reasonable to expect that, after a most unfortunate one, Great Britain should obtain the same conditions. In answer to Mr. Grenville's request for instructions, Mr. Fox was empowered by the Cabinet to propose to France, as a basis of negotiation, the independence of America and the peace of 1763; and in the case of this basis not being accepted, M. de Vergennes was to be called upon to make some proposition on his part. M. de Vergennes now objected to the powers given to Mr. Grenville. Those powers only enabled Mr. Grenville to treat with the French Ministers, whereas France had declared that she would only treat in conjunction with her allies—Spain, Holland, and America.

On the 14th of May Mr. Oswald returned to London. On the 23rd the Cabinet agreed, on the proposition of Mr. Fox, to advise the King to direct Mr. Grenville " to propose the independency of America in the first instance, instead of making it a condition of a general treaty."* Matters were in this situation, without much prospect of a favourable issue, when a letter from Mr. Grenville revealed to Mr. Fox the cause of the unwillingness of Dr. Franklin and M. de Vergennes to listen to his overtures. This letter and the answer to it are of so much importance that I shall insert them entire.

* " Correspondence," vol. i. p. 359.

MR. GRENVILLE TO MR. FOX.

" Paris, June 4th, 1782.

" The *public* letter which I send to you by Lauzun is, as you will see, of no other use than that of accounting for his journey, and enabling him to carry to you this *private* one, of which I had once almost determined to be myself the bearer. An apprehension, however, that so sudden an arrival might be embarrassing to you, has decided me not to take that step till I had explained to you my reasons for wishing to do so, though I should not care to write them, except in the full confidence that they will be seen by no person whatever but yourself. Recollect always that this letter is written in that confidence, and I am sure I never can repent of having sent it. You will easily see from the tenor of the correspondence we have hitherto had, that what little use I could be of to you here, appeared to me to be in the communication that I had with Franklin. I considered the rest of the negotiation as dependent upon that, and the only possible immediate advantages which were to be expected seemed to me to rest in the jealousy which the French Court would entertain of not being thoroughly supported in everything by America. The degree of confidence which Franklin seemed inclined to place in me, and which he expressed to me more than once in the strongest terms, very much favoured this idea, and encouraged me in wishing to learn from him what might be, in future, ground for a partial connexion between England and America. I say in future, because I have never hitherto much believed in any treaty of the year 1782, and my expectation, even from the strongest of Franklin's expressions, was not of an immediate turn in our favour, or any positive advantage from the Commissioners in Europe, till the people of America should cry out to them, from seeing that England was meeting their wishes. It was in this light, too, that I saw room to hope for some good effects from a voluntary offer of unconditional independence to America—a chance which looked the more tempting, as I own I considered the sacrifice as but a small one, and such as, had I been an American, I had thought myself little obliged to Great Britain in this moment for granting, except from an idea that, if it was an article of treaty, it would have been as much given by France as by England.

"I repeat this only to remind you that, from these considerations, the whole of my attention has been given to Franklin, and that I should have considered myself as losing my time here, if it had not been directed to that subject. I believe I told you in my last that I had very sanguine expectations of Franklin's being inclined to speak out when I should see him next—indeed, he expressly told me that he would think over all the points likely to establish a solid reconciliation between England and America, and that he would write his mind upon them, in order that we might examine them together more in order, confiding, as he said, in me, that I would not state them as propositions from him, but as being my own ideas of what would be useful to both countries. (I interrupt myself here to remind you of the obligation I must put you under not to mention this.) For this very interesting communication, which I had long laboured to get, he fixed the fourth day, which was last Saturday; but on Friday morning Mr. Oswald came, and having given me your letters, he went immediately to Franklin, to carry some to him. I kept my appointment at Passy the next morning, and in order to give Franklin the greatest confidence, at the same time, too, not knowing how much Mr. Oswald might have told him, I began with saying that, though under the difficulty which M. de Vergennes and he himself had made to my full power, it was not the moment as a politician, perhaps, to make further explanations till that difficulty should be relieved; yet, to show him the confidence I put in him, I would begin by telling him that I was authorized to offer the independence in the first instance, instead of making it an article of general treaty. He expressed great satisfaction at this, especially, he said, because by having done otherwise we should have seemed to consider America as in the same degree of connexion with France which she had been under with us, whereas America wished to be considered as a power free and clear to all the world; but when I came to lead the discourse to the subject which he had promised four days before, I was a good deal mortified to find him put it off altogether till he should be more ready; and, notwithstanding my reminding him of his promise, he only answered that it should be in some days. What passed between Mr. Oswald and me will explain to you the reason of this disappointment. Mr. Oswald told me that Lord Shelburne had proposed to him, when last in England, to take a commission to treat with the American Ministers; that upon his mentioning it to Franklin now, it seemed perfectly agreeable to him, and even to be what he had very much wished, Mr. Oswald adding that he wished only to assist the business, and had no other view; he mixed with this a few regrets that there should be any difference between the two offices, and when I asked upon what subject, he said owing to the Rockingham party being too ready to give up everything. You will observe, though—for it is on that account that I give you this narrative—that this intended appointment has effectually stopped Franklin's mouth to me, and that when he is told that Mr. Oswald is to be the commissioner to treat with him, it is but natural that he should reserve his confidence for the quarter so pointed out to him; nor does this secret seem only known to Franklin, as Lafayette said laughingly yesterday, that he had *just left Lord Shelburne's ambassador at Passy.* Indeed, this is not the first moment of a separate negotiation, for Mr. Oswald, suspecting by something that I dropped that Franklin had talked to me about Canada (though, by the bye, he never had), told me this circumstance as follows: When he went to England the last time but one, he carried with him a paper entrusted to him by Franklin, under condition that it should be shown only to Lord Shelburne and returned into his own hands at Passy. This paper, under the title of ' Notes of a Conversation,' contained an idea of Canada being spontaneously ceded by England to the thirteen provinces, in order that Congress might sell the unappropriated lands and make a fund thereby, in order to compensate the damages done by the English army, and even those, too, sustained by the Royalists. This paper, given with many precautions, for fear of its being known to the French Court, to whom it was supposed not to be agreeable, Mr. Oswald showed to Lord Shelburne, who, after keeping it a day, as Mr. Oswald supposes, to show to the King, returned it to him, and it was by him brought back to Franklin. I say nothing to the proposition itself, to the impolicy of bringing a *strange* neighbourhood to the Newfoundland fishery, or to the little reason that England would naturally see, in having lost thirteen provinces, to give away a fourteenth; but I mention it to show you an early trace of separate negotiation which perhaps you did not before know.

" Under these circumstances, I felt very much tempted to
go over and explain them to you *vivâ voce*, rather than by
letter; and I must say, with the further intention of sug-
gesting to you the only idea that seems likely to answer
your purpose, and it is this: the Spanish Ambassador will,
in a day or two, have the powers from his Court; the
Americans are here, so are the French; why should you not,
then, consider this as a Congress in full form, and send
here a person of rank, such as Lord Fitzwilliam (if he would
come), so as to have the whole negotiation in the hands of
one person? You would, by that means, recover within
your compass the essential part, which is now out of it;
nor do I see how Lord Shelburne could object to such an
appointment, which would, in every respect, much facilitate
the business. Let me press this a little strongly to you,
for another reason. You may depend upon it, people here
have already got an idea of a difference between the two
offices; and consider how much that idea will 'be assisted
by the embarrassments arising from two people negotiating
to the same purpose, but under different and differing
authorities, concealing and disguising from each other what,
with the best intentions, they could hardly make known,
and common enough to each. I am almost afraid of pressing this as strongly as I should, for fear you should think
me writing peevishly; but if I did not state the thing to you
in the situation in which I see it, I should think I was betraying your interests instead of giving attention to them.
I must entreat you very earnestly to consider this, to see
the impossibility of my assisting you under this con-
trariety, to see how much the business itself will suffer,
if carried on with the jealousy of these clashing interests,
and to see whether it may not all be prevented by some

single appointment in high rank, as that I mentioned. *Au reste*, I cannot but say that I feel much easier, with the hope of making over what remains of this business; I begin to feel it weighty, and you know how much I dislike the *publicity* you packed off to me in that confounded silver box. I could not bring myself to say anything civil about it in my last letter, and you ought to give me credit for great self-denial in not taking this opportunity of telling you my own story at the secretary's office, as nothing but the embarrassment it might give you upon the sudden prevented me. Once more I tell you, I cannot fight a daily battle with Mr. Oswald and *his* secretary; it would be neither for the advantage of the business, for your interest or your credit, or mine; and even if it was, I should not do it.

" Concluding, then, the American business as out of the question, which personally I cannot be sorry for, you surely have but one of two things to do; either to adopt the proposition of a new *dignified* Peer's appointment, which being single, may bring back the business to you by comprehending it all in one; or Lord Shelburne must have his minister here, and Mr. Fox his; by doing which, Mr. Fox will be pretty near as much out of the secret—at least, of what is most essential—as if he had nobody here, and the only real gainers by it will be the other Ministers, who cannot fail to profit of such a jumble; besides which, upon this latter part of the subject, I must very seriously entreat you, with regard to myself, not to ask me to keep a situation here, in no circumstances pleasant, and in none less so than those I have described. The grievance is a very essential one; the remedy is Lord Fitzwilliam. Adieu. I recommend to Lauzun to make all the haste he can, as I shall not stir a step till you answer this letter, and my step then will, I hope, be towards you.

"Sheridan's letter of suspicion was written, as you see, in the spirit of prophecy. I owe him an answer, which by word of mouth, or word of letter, he shall have very soon.*

"The news of the day is, that the Cadiz fleet, twenty-six sail of the line and five French, are sailed for Brest; but I rather imagine they have no authentic account of it yet.

"Adieu. Let Lord Fitzwilliam answer my letter."

MR. FOX TO MR. GRENVILLE.

"St. James's, June 10th, 1782.

"I received late the night before last your interesting letter of the 4th, and you may easily conceive am not a little embarrassed by its contents. In the first place, it was not possible to comply with your injunction of perfect secresy in a case where steps of such importance are necessary to be taken, and therefore I have taken upon me (for which I must trust to your friendship to excuse me) to show your letter to Lord Rockingham, the Duke of Richmond, and Lord John, who are all as full of indignation at its contents as one might reasonably expect honest men to be. We are now perfectly resolved to come to an explanation upon the business, if it is possible so to do without betraying any confidence reposed in me by you or in you by others. The two principal points which occur are the paper relative to Canada, of which I had never heard till I

* There is a letter of Sheridan's to Mr. Grenville, dated May 26, 1782, in "Court and Cabinets of George III.," vol. i. p. 30. It is a very judicious letter.

received your letter, and the intended investment of Mr. Oswald with full powers, which was certainly meant for the purpose of diverting Franklin's confidence from you into another channel. With these two points we wish to charge Shelburne directly; but pressing as the thing is, and interesting as it is both to our situations and to the affairs of the public, which I fear are irretrievably injured by this intrigue, and which must be ruined if it is suffered to go on, we are resolved not to stir a step till we hear again from you, and know precisely how far we are at liberty to make use of what you have discovered. If this matter should produce a rupture, and consequently become more or less the subject of public discussion, I am sensible the Canada paper cannot be mentioned by name; but might it not be said that we had discovered that Shelburne had withheld from our knowledge matters of importance to the negotiation? And, with respect to the other point, might it not be said, without betraying anybody, that while the King had one avowed and authorized Minister at Paris, measures were taken for lessening his credit, and for obstructing his inquiries, by announcing a new intended commission of which the Cabinet here had never been apprised? Do, pray, my dear Grenville, consider the in-credible importance of this business in every view, and write me word precisely how far you can authorize us to make use of your intelligence. It is more than possible that before this reaches you, many other circumstances may have occurred which may afford further proofs of this duplicity of conduct; and if they have, I am sure they will not have escaped your observation. If this should be the case, you will see the necessity of acquainting me with them as soon as possible. You see what is our object, and you can easily judge what sort of evidence will be most useful to us. When the object is attained—that is, when the duplicity is proved—to what consequences we ought to drive, whether to an absolute rupture, or merely to the recal of Oswald and the simplification of this negotiation, is a point that may be afterwards considered. I own I incline to the more decisive measure, and so I think do those with whom I must act in concert. I am very happy indeed that you did not come yourself; the mischiefs that would have happened from it to our affairs are incredible, and I must beg of you—nay, entreat and conjure you—not to think of taking any precipitate step of this nature. As to the idea of replacing you with Lord Fitzwilliam, not only it would be very objectionable on account of the mistaken notion it would convey of things being much riper than they are; but it would, as I conceive, be no remedy to the evil. Whether the King's Minister at Paris be an Ambassador Extraordinary or a Minister Plenipotentiary can make no difference as to the question. The clandestine manner of carrying on a separate negotiation, which we complain of, would be equally practicable and equally blameable if Lord Fitzwilliam was Ambassador, as it is now that Mr. Grenville is Plenipotentiary. I must, therefore, again entreat you, as a matter of personal kindness to me, to remain a little longer at Paris; if you were to leave it, all sorts of suspicion would be raised. It is of infinite consequence that we should have it to say that we have done all in our power to make peace; not only with regard to what may be expected from America, but from Europe. The King of Prussia is certainly inclined to be our friend, but he urges and presses to make peace, if possible; if we could once bring the treaty to such a point as the stating the demands on each side to him, and we could have his approbation for breaking it off, I think it not impossible but the best consequences might follow; and, with regard to North America, it is surely clear to demonstration that it is of infinite consequence that it should be publicly understood who is to blame if the war continues. I do hope, therefore, that you will at all events stay long enough to make your propositions, and to call upon them to make others in return. I know your situation cannot be pleasant; but as you first undertook it in a great measure from friendship to me, so let me hope that the same motive will induce you to continue in it, at least for some time. What will be the end of this, God knows; but I am sure you will agree with me that we cannot suffer a system to go on which is not only dishonourable to us, but evidently ruinous to the affairs of the country. In this instance the mischief done by intercepting, as it were, the very useful information we expected through you from Franklin is, I fear, in a great degree irremediable; but it is our business, and indeed our duty, to prevent such things for the future. Everything in Ireland goes on well, and I really think there is good reason to entertain hopes from Russia and Prussia, if your negotiation either goes on or goes off as it ought to do."

It appears to me that Mr. Fox was wrong in not taking Mr. Grenville's advice. The appointment of a new person of rank and consequence sufficient to justify the change, with a positive engagement in the Cabinet that no negotiation should take place except through him, must have brought these affairs to a creditable issue. Dr. Franklin could not then have said, "I should be loth to lose Mr. Oswald. He seems to have nothing at heart but the good of mankind and the putting a stop to mischief; the other (Mr. Grenville), a young statesman who may be supposed to have naturally a little ambition of recommending himself as an able negotiator."* Nor could Lafayette have laughingly related that "he had just left Lord Shelburne's ambassador at Passy."

It was clear that without some decisive step Mr. Fox was outwitted, and the negotiation for peace would be taken out of the hands of the Foreign Secretary to be placed in those of the Home Secretary of State. Mr. Fox was greatly embarrassed by this state of things. On the one hand he could not bear to weaken the country, and shake public confidence by openly charging Lord Shelburne with supplanting him in his office. On the other hand, he seems to have determined to bring before the Cabinet some decisive question which should determine, not so much the course of negotiation as who should be the negotiator. In a speech in the following session upon the peace he made this statement: "As to the provisional articles of peace with America, it was impossible for him at this moment to approve or condemn them, because he was utterly unacquainted with them; but he would take it for granted that the independence, the unconditional independence of America, was recognised by the first article. The great difference between him and the present Minister on that head was, that the latter wished that the independence should be the price of peace; while, on his part, he was of opinion that no barter should be made, but that Great Britain should, in a manly manner, recognise at once that independence which it was not in her power to check or overturn. For this he had two reasons; one was, that it would

* Franklin's "Works," by Sparks, vol. ix. p. 314–317.

appear magnanimous on the part of England, and inspire
America with confidence to treat with us when we should
set out by irrevocably granting her independence, a confidence which she could not feel if this independence was to
depend on other measures which were not yet agreed to.
His other reason was, that by a provisional treaty (to take
place when France and Great Britain should have settled
terms of peace with each other), the very preliminary
article of which was an acknowledgment of American independence, England and America would have so completely
determined all their differences, that nothing more would
remain to contend for between them, the two countries
might then be said to be virtually at peace; or if America
should continue the war as the ally of France, it would be
a war so very like a peace, that France, deriving little or
no advantage from it, would be the more easily induced to
think of peace, and be the less forward to propose harsh or
dishonourable terms to this country. These were the
reasons by which he was influenced to advise the recognition of unconditional independence; and he was the more
surprised to find that Ministers had been so tardy in making
peace with America by a provisional treaty, when the same
happy effect might have been produced months ago, if unconditional independence had been earlier offered. For his
part, he was unable to account for the delay; when his
Majesty had given him orders to write to Mr. Grenville,
at Paris, to authorize him to offer independence unconditionally to America, he obeyed the orders with a degree of
pleasure which could be equalled only by that which he
felt when he read the letter of Lord Shelburne to Sir Guy
Carleton, in which the words of the letter to Mr. Grenville
were recited; when he read that letter, he carried it with

pleasure to the late Marquis of Rockingham, and, with joy, told him that all their distrusts and suspicions of the noble lord's intentions were groundless. But his pleasure on that occasion was not of long duration; for even before death had removed the noble marquis from the Treasury, the Earl of Shelburne began to speak of the dreadful consequences that must ensue to this country if America should be separated from it; and gave a decisive opinion that the letter to Mr. Grenville, and the recital of the same to Sir Guy Carleton, were not an unconditional recognition of American independence, but a conditional offer to be recalled in certain circumstances." "This gave me suspicion," said Mr. Fox, "which I could not conceal; for in writing the letter to Mr. Grenville I had chosen the most forcible words that the English language could supply to express my meaning. As far as I can recollect they were these, or exactly to this meaning: 'To recognise the independence of America, in the first instance, and not to reserve it as a condition of peace.' When I saw the recital of these words in the letter of the Earl of Shelburne to Sir Guy Carleton, all my doubts vanished, and I was completely relieved. What, then, must be my astonishment and torture, when, in the illness and apprehended decease of the·noble marquis, another language was heard in the Cabinet, and some even of his own friends began to consider these letters only as offers of a conditional nature—to be recalled if they did not purchase peace? I considered myself as ensnared and betrayed; I therefore determined to take the measure by which alone I could act with consistency and honour—I called for precise declarations—I demanded explicit language; and when I saw that the persons in whom I had originally no great confidence were so eager to elude, and so determined to

change the ground on which they had set out, I relinquished my seat in the Cabinet, with the heartfelt satisfaction of having maintained my principles unstained, and
with the prospect of being able to do, by leaving it, what I
could not accomplish by remaining there."

These differences in the Cabinet respecting America were
brought to a crisis by the death of Lord Rockingham. He
died on the 1st of July. Few men have ever ruled a party
more absolutely. The fervour and fancy of Burke were
controlled; the extreme doctrines of the Duke of Richmond
moderated; the sluggish patriotism of the landed aristocracy
warmed and quickened by the sober and judicious and intelligent love of freedom which guided Lord Rockingham's
political course. Writers who care nothing for principle
cannot imagine how honest purpose and calm reason could
have had so much influence. They cannot understand
Mr. Burke's panegyric on his monument, that " his virtues
were his arts." Still such was the fact; and much as the
Duke of Newcastle had lowered the character of the Whigs,
so much and more did Lord Rockingham exalt it. The
" Annual Register" and the " Parliamentary History"
contain many reports of his speeches. They are marked by
enlightened principles, just reasoning, and an accurate
knowledge of details, but are without brilliancy or fire.

The King and Lord Shelburne were equally prepared for
this event. The King sent at once for Lord Shelburne,
and offered him the Treasury, and Lord Shelburne at once
accepted it.

The position of Mr. Fox now became one of extreme
difficulty. He had proposed to a Cabinet assembled at
Lord Camden's, that the independence of America should
be acknowledged unconditionally. It would seem that this

point had been already decided in the Cabinet of the 23rd of May. But Lord Shelburne had understood that minute in a sense different from that put upon it by Mr. Fox. The decision was against Mr. Fox, who then told General Conway he should resign; but before taking this step he summoned another Cabinet to meet at his house on Sunday, the 30th of June. The decision was again unfavourable. We may easily conjecture the division :—

For Mr. Fox's Proposal.	*Against.*
Duke of Richmond.	Lord Shelburne.
Lord John Cavendish.	Lord Chancellor.
Admiral Lord Keppel.	Lord Camden.
Mr. Fox.	Duke of Grafton.
	Lord Ashburton.
	General Conway.

Mr. Fox, the Foreign Secretary, being thus outvoted on a question of foreign policy, determined to resign. But he refrained from disturbing the dying hours of Lord Rockingham by carrying his intention into effect. Lord Rockingham's death on the following day changed the complexion of affairs. In contemplation of this contingency, or upon its occurrence, Mr. Fox took the advice of Mr. Burke. That eminent man, Mr. Fox's pastor and master in political affairs, advised that Mr. Fox should endeavour to bring the followers of Lord Rockingham to support either the Duke of Portland, or Mr. Fox himself, as First Minister of the Crown; and in case of the refusal of any of his colleagues to make this a vital question, that he should then openly avow that on the meeting of Parliament he would try the issue with Lord Shelburne.

Mr. Burke's paper begins as follows: "The more I think of the matter of our conversation this day, and the more I tumble it over in discourse with others, the more fully I am convinced of the utter impossibility of your acting for any length of time as a clerk in Lord Shelburne's Administration."

The paper concludes in these words: "But if you do neither the one or the other of these things, then you are fairly bullied, and may be obliged to act a truckling and subservient part to those whom you neither love nor respect." The second mode of proceeding was that already mentioned, of "telling the King that you are not willing to throw his affairs into disorder, that you cannot confide in Shelburne, and that you remit the matter to the sense of Parliament, which in some way you are resolved to take as soon as it meets."

This was evidently an impossible course. Besides the obvious objection of unfairness to Lord Shelburne, it was clear that no surer way of throwing the King's affairs into disorder could have been devised than that of a Secretary of State appealing to Parliament against the First Lord of the Treasury. Mr. Fox was disposed to bring the matter to an instant decision. Lord John Cavendish was still less inclined than Mr. Fox to listen to any compromise. Lord Shelburne indeed proposed, that Lord John should be Secretary of State; and should the arrangement be accepted, he expressed himself ready to give way on the point of American independence.* This plan would have given Mr. Fox a brother Secretary on whom he could depend; but, as Mr. Pitt would probably have been appointed Chancellor of the Exchequer, Mr. Fox would have been weaker than before in the Cabinet, and would have had all his measures thwarted by Lord Shelburne's insidious oppo-

* Fox to Fitzpatrick: "Correspondence," vol. i.

sition. Yet, although this was evident, the colleagues upon whom he had a right to count as the friends of Lord Rockingham were much divided. The Duke of Richmond, who had been warm in favour of resistance to Lord Shelburne, expected himself to be acknowledged as the successor of Lord Rockingham in the lead of the party. On finding from Mr. Fox that this was not intended, and that the Duke of Portland was to be proposed as the head of Administration, he not only resolved to remain with Lord Shelburne, but used all his influence to induce others to do the same. Keppel considered himself bound to watch over the success of his naval administration till the end of the campaign ; General Conway, averse to party, resolved to stay.

It must be owned that the choice of a leader to succeed Lord Rockingham was not a happy one. The Duke of Portland was indeed connected with the Cavendishes, and had been lately entrusted with the government of Ireland. But he had not, like the Duke of Richmond and Lord Shelburne, taken a leading part in opposition to the American War. There seemed no propriety or fitness in putting forward a man so unknown as the proposed head of the Administration. In the words of Walpole: " He had never attempted to show any parliamentary abilities, nor had the credit of possessing any. Nor did it redound to the honour of his faction, that in such momentous times they could furnish their country with nothing but a succession of mutes." Such was the man who, in 1782, became the leader of the Whig party; who in 1783 was the Whig Prime Minister, and who, after serving in high office under Mr. Pitt and Mr. Addington, became, in 1807, again Prime Minister, as the leader of the Tories.

On the Wednesday after Lord Rockingham's death, Mr. Fox told the King that he considered it his duty to inform him that in his opinion the only means of securing the support of those whom he believed to be the firmest friends to the Government was to appoint some person to succeed Lord Rockingham in whom that description of persons could place their confidence. The King answered, that upon the change of Ministry he had intended to give the Treasury to Lord Shelburne, who had declined it in favour of Lord Rockingham; it seemed now therefore naturally to devolve upon him. Fox replied, that he did not consider Lord Shelburne as a person who would answer the description he had before given. Accordingly, Mr. Fox on Thursday resigned the seals into the King's hands, saying that the appointment of Lord Shelburne was a departure from the principles upon which they had come into office, and that it would create distrust among that description of men whom he believed to be the best friends of his Majesty's family, and of the interests of the public. The King expressed some surprise, and wished him to take time to consider.

We have the authority of Fitzpatrick for saying that Mr. Fox would have consented to remain if Lord John Cavendish had agreed to become Secretary of State. But it is evident Mr. Fox himself preferred resignation. With Mr. Fox and Lord John Cavendish, Mr. Burke, Lord Althorp, Mr. Sheridan, Lord Duncannon, Mr. Townshend, and Mr. Lee the Solicitor-General, resigned.

The question came to be debated in Parliament on the 9th of July. Mr. Fox regretted the necessity he had been under of resigning; and declared that the system of Lord Rockingham having been abandoned, he, who was responsible to the House of Commons for the continuance of that system, could no longer remain.

General Conway, in reply, deeply lamented the death of Lord Rockingham, and regretted the loss of Mr. Fox's splendid abilities at a time when their value and consequence were beginning to be felt. He denied that there was such disagreement in the Cabinet as to justify Mr. Fox in withdrawing from it. He also denied that any change of principles had taken place.

In order to show this he stated, apparently from a paper in his hand, the principles on which they set out. These were :—

" 1st. That they should offer to America unlimited, unconditional independence, as the basis of a negotiation for peace.

" 2nd. That they should establish a system of economy in every department of Government, and that they should adopt the spirit and carry into execution the provisions of the Bill of Reform introduced into that House by Mr. Burke, and which was now ready for the Crown to pass.

" 3rd. That they would annihilate every kind of influence over any part of the Legislature.

" 4th. That they should continue to the kingdom of Ireland, and secure to it the freedom now settled by Parliament, and to do this in the most unequivocal and decisive way."

With regard to all these principles there was, General Conway stated, no deviation, and no cause either for apprehension or jealousy, and he was himself determined to continue in office only so long as these were adhered to ; with respect to three of them, the House would judge ; and with regard to the independence of America, time would show that the Cabinet was as firm in adhering to it as to the others.

The terms of the political creed thus stated to the House with much solemnity, backed by the high character of General Conway, were calculated to throw upon Mr. Fox the odium of making a division in the King's councils at a very critical and alarming moment. Mr. Fox spoke twice in explanation; he reproached General Conway with too generous a confidence, and reminded him of his conduct in consenting to tax America in 1767, after declaring against such a measure in 1766. He declared he could not rely on the promises and professions of the present Ministers.

In thus stating the difference between himself and Lord Shelburne without going further into detail, Mr. Fox must have been aware that he did himself great wrong. If the Cabinet were agreed upon the acknowledgment of the independence of America, General Conway was right in saying that a difference about the means by which the object was to be accomplished was "a difference very immaterial." It was because Mr. Fox could not trust Lord Shelburne that he left office. This distrust was founded upon Lord Shelburne's constant intrigues to play the part of the King's friend in the Cabinet; upon his resistance to reforms in the Civil List; and, above all, upon the separate negotiation with America through Oswald. All this Mr. Fox withheld. His duty as a councillor of the King did not allow him to make the best defence for his conduct. It was shortly this: There can be under our present Constitution only two modes of forming a Government. The one consists in placing at its head a member of the House of Commons having the full confidence of the Crown : this was the mode of Sir Robert Walpole, of Lord North, and of Mr. Pitt. The other places at the head of the Ministry a peer, represented in the House of Commons by a Minister who shares the power and enjoys the entire confidence of the First Minister. Lord Shelburne was not ready to share his power, or to impart his confidence. Mr. Pitt, when he afterwards filled the situation of First Lord of the Treasury, is said to have declared, in private, that whatever sins he might commit as a Minister, he had atoned for them beforehand, by serving for nearly a year under Lord Shelburne.*

Lord John Cavendish added little to what had been said by Mr. Fox. Mr. Burke was more personal to Lord Shelburne. He said if he was not a Cataline or a Borgia in morals, it must not be ascribed to anything but his understanding. Mr. Lee, the late Solicitor-General, said that the Minister of this country should join to a sound head purity of mind, steadiness of principle, and unsuspected integrity. Were these the reputed characteristics of Lord Shelburne? All these personal reflections, however, and the dislike of the Whig party to the new Minister availed but little while the Duke of Richmond, Lord Keppel, and General Conway remained in office as his colleagues.

The following letters from Mr. Fox to Mr. Thomas Grenville pourtray his own feelings on this rupture :—

MR. FOX TO MR. THOMAS GRENVILLE.

"St. James's, July 5th, 1782.

" DEAR GRENVILLE,—You will not wonder at my being hurried too much at this moment to write you a detail of

* Lord Holland.

what has happened. I do assure you that the thing that
has given me most concern is the sort of scrape I have
drawn you into; but I think I may depend upon your way
of thinking for forgiving me; though to say one can depend upon any man is a bold word, after what has passed
within these few days. I am sure, on the one hand, that
you may depend upon my eternal gratitude to you for what
you have undergone on my account, and that you always
must have the greatest share in my friendship and affection. I do not think you will think these [less] valuable
than you used to do. I have done right, I am sure I have.
The Duke of Richmond thinks very much otherwise, and
will do wrong; I cannot help it. I am sure my staying
would have been a means of deceiving the public and betraying my party; and these are things not to be done for
the sake of any supposed temporary good. I feel that my
situation in the country, my power, my popularity, my
consequence, nay, my character, are all risked; but I have
done right, and therefore in the end it must turn out to
have been wise. If this fail me, ' the pillared firmament is
rottenness, and earth's base built on stubble.'

"Adieu. Your brother disapproves too.

"Yours most affectionately,

"C. J. Fox."*

MR. FOX TO MR. THOMAS GRENVILLE.

"Grafton-street, July 13th, 1782.

"DEAR GRENVILLE,—I am exceedingly obliged to you
for your kind letter; and, indeed, if political transactions
put one out of humour with *many*, they make one love the

---

* "Court and Cabinets of George III." The brother alluded to is Lord
Temple.

few who do act and think right so much better, that it is some compensation. I understand a messenger is just going, by whom I send this letter; he will bring you others, from whence you will learn that your brother is going Lord-Lieutenant to Ireland. If you go with him as secretary, I hope you will be so good as to endeavour to serve my friend Dickson, who by this change has for the third time missed a bishopric.

"I called upon your brother yesterday, and left with him the letters that passed between you and me, explaining that it was at your desire that I did so. I was very glad to have your authority for this step, for, to tell you the truth, I was very much inclined to take it even of my own when it was supposed he was to be my successor; now that he knows the whole of the narration, if he still chooses (as I fear he will) to go into this den of thieves, neither you nor I have anything to answer for. If this transaction had been withheld from him, he might have had reason to complain of me, but much more of you. I have not heard from him since he has been *au fait*. His expressions, both to me personally and to the party, were so kind that I am far from considering him as lost; but whether he is or not, and whatever part your situation may make it right for you to take in politics, I shall always depend upon your friendship and kindness to me as perfectly unalterable; and I do assure you that this consideration is one of the things that most contributes to keep up my spirits in this very trying situation.

"Yours affectionately,

"C. J. Fox."

The opinions of politicians upon this rupture may be

gathered from the following extract of a letter of Colonel Fitzpatrick to his brother Lord Ossory, dated the 5th of July :—

"I agree with you perfectly that honesty is the worst policy, and always was of that opinion. It is that, however, which Charles has had the magnanimity to adopt, and that in a manner which all men of real sense and spirit admire, though, perhaps, few will dare to imitate. The opinions of the public stand thus upon the question. All persons who have any understanding and no office are of opinion that Charles has done right. All persons who have little understanding are frightened; and all persons who have offices, with some very few brilliant exceptions, think he has been hasty."

It must be owned that Mr. Fox's position was a very difficult one. It was his misfortune that he did not carry the whole Rockingham party with him out of office; it was his fault that, instead of taking the lead himself, or offering it to the Duke of Richmond, he made an idol of wood, and asked the nation to bow down to it. The whole proceeding thus appeared to the public intemperate and unintelligible. It may be observed, in closing these comments, that Mr. Fox's conduct would finally be judged by his course when out of office. If he could keep strictly in view the principles he had always professed, and preserve his independence, he would clear his character of all imputation, and probably triumph over all his adversaries. But if he should give rise to any suspicions in this respect, and especially if he should join any of the old Ministry, he would rivet the opinion which Mr. Pitt dextrously insinuated, and impress the world with a conviction that his resignation had arisen only from his being worsted in a struggle for power. Some observations on Mr. Fox's conduct and policy when in office for the first time may conclude this chapter.

His personal behaviour to the King, to his colleagues, and in his office, were above all exception. His respectful bearing to the King was that of a gentleman, not a courtier. To his colleagues he was always frank and open; in his office punctual and exact in business, without being troublesome or harsh to those under him, or busy and meddling in little matters. Horace Walpole, no very favourable judge, thus writes to Sir Horace Mann, on the 5th of May :—

" Mr. Fox already shines as greatly in place as he did in Opposition, though infinitely more difficult a task. He is now as indefatigable as he was idle. He has perfect temper, and not only good humour, but good nature ; and, which is the first quality in a Prime Minister in a free country, has more common sense than any man, with amazing parts that are neither ostentatious nor affected." In his Journal he says : " The material features [of the Administration] were the masterly abilities of Charles Fox and the intrigues of Lord Shelburne : the former displayed such facility in comprehending and executing all business as charmed all who approached him. No formal affectation delayed any service or screened ignorance. He seized at once the important points of every affair, and every affair was thence reduced within a small compass, not to save himself trouble, for he at once gave himself up to the duties of his office. His good humour, frankness, and sincerity pleased, and yet inspired a respect which he took no other pains to attract. The foreign Ministers were in admiration of him : they had found few who understood foreign affairs, or who attended to them, and no man who understood French so well, or could explain himself in so few words."

His policy was based on his endeavour—1. To propitiate America by an unconditional offer of independence; 2. To hold out for favourable terms from France; 3. To rouse the Empress of Russia and the King of Prussia to jealousy of French ambition.

In the first of these objects he was thwarted by Lord Shelburne; yet he must finally have succeeded, as his reasons were irresistible. Indeed, we have seen that Lord Shelburne, before the final rupture, expressed himself ready to yield upon this point. In respect to the third, his overtures to Catherine and Frederick, although unsuccessful at first, would probably have led to such intimations from Russia and Prussia as would have induced France to consent to better terms than Lord Shelburne was able to procure. But had not M. de Vergennes consented to Mr. Fox's terms, the vigour of Lord Keppel, the recall of the troops from America, their application to aggressive purposes against France, and an acknowledgment of the principles of the armed neutrality would probably have given an entirely new complexion to the war.

On the affairs of Ireland Mr. Fox showed great wisdom, and a generous spirit. In conceding he took care to show that he did not yield from fear, but in a spirit of justice, and for national interests. Upon economical reform his earnestness and sincerity swayed the Cabinet in favour of Burke's bill. Upon parliamentary reform he was steady, and at the same time moderate. "It had been said," he remarked in a speech upon this subject, "that to add members to the counties would be increasing the aristocratic influence: he owned it would, and in some measure he confessed himself a friend to that doctrine; but he would wish to be understood, at the same time, not to mean the influence of peers, but to consider the monied interest as part of the aristocracy. It had been suggested to him that the army and navy ought to be excluded that House: he was of quite a different opinion, for he could wish, in order to make that House perfect, that it should contain the landed, the navy, the army, the monied, and in short every interest; but it did not at present, and the city for which he had the honour to sit was so little represented, that the county in which it stood, although it contained one-eighth part of the whole number of electors of Great Britain, although it paid one-sixth part of the land-tax, and a full third of all other taxes, yet it had not more than a fifty-fifth part of the representation."

Even from this imperfect account of his speech, it appears that Mr. Fox was aware of the great changes that had taken place, and that he wished property to be represented as well as numbers. He was greatly disappointed at the result of the division; he writes to Fitzpatrick: " Our having been beat upon Pitt's motion will, in my opinion, produce many more bad consequences than many people seem to suppose; among which the kind of spirit and confidence which it has given to the old Ministerialists is perhaps not the least."

In all Mr. Fox's speeches and letters he spoke strongly against the old Ministry; and his first disagreement with Mr. Pitt arose from the softened tone of the latter towards the men who had lost America. The two following letters are especially worthy of attention. The first is from Mr. Fox to Mr. Fitzpatrick, written on the 11th of May; the second is from Mr. Hare to Fitzpatrick, written about the same time. Both show the divided state of Lord Rockingham's ministry.

"Carlisle received the staff* on Sunday, and is, I believe, in perfect good humour. The history of that transaction is a most curious one. Lord Rockingham offered, Lord Carlisle, after some time to consider, accepts; and then Lord S—— says, he had thought of it for the Duke of Marlborough, and that something at least must be done for Lord Charles Spencer before this matter is settled. I talked to him very roundly upon this affair, and of course he and his friend gave way, and the thing was done, only less graciously than it ought. In short, everything that we apprehended upon this subject is true even beyond our apprehensions: it must be our business to preserve our credit and character, which I think we cannot lose but by our own faults, and which is *most clearly indeed* all that we have to stand upon. He thinks, I know he does, that he has other ground. How it will bear him, *il faut voir*. That he will not delay long trying it, I very much believe, especially if we should be fortunate enough to make a peace, which I do not wish for less ardently than I did, although I am convinced that in signing it I shall sign the end of this ministry. *Faisons notre devoir arrive qui pourra* is the maxim which prudence as well as honesty must dictate to us.

"You recommended me to keep up my attention to two great political persons, and I have, I do assure you, spared no pains to follow your advice. With respect to the first in rank of the two,† I have succeeded to my utmost hopes; so much so, that, if we fail in his object, I am sure he will be rather displeased at others than at us. I like him better every day: he is natural, open, and remarkably free, at least as far as I can judge, from those

* Of Lord Steward. † Probably the Prince of Wales.

meannesses which from his blood and his situation might be expected. I wish I could say I was quite as well satisfied in regard to the other person, who is perhaps the most material of the two.*   He is very civil and obliging, profuse of compliments in public; but he has more than once taken a line that has alarmed me, especially when he dissuaded against going into any inquiries that might produce heats and differences. This seemed so unlike his general mode of thinking, and so like that of another, that I confess I disliked it to the greatest degree. I am satisfied he will be the man that the old system, revived in the person of Lord S——, will attempt to bring forward for its support. I am satisfied that he is incapable of going into this with his eyes open; but how he may be led into it, step by step, is more than I can answer for. I feel myself, I own, rather inclined to rely upon his under-standing and integrity for resisting all the temptations of ambition, and especially of *being first*, which I know will be industriously thrown in his way, and contrasted with that secondary and subordinate situation to which they will insinuate he must be confined while he continues to act in the general system."

Let us now listen to Mr. Hare :—

" The Advocate† has, on so many occasions, shown such hostility, mixed with a great degree of arrogance, if not impertinence, towards Charles, that Charles, with all his goodnature and forbearance, has been rather exasperated against him. I thought it proceeded from the Advocate's being out of humour at the late reverse in his fortunes, and apt to take offence when none was meant; but Charles suspected it was a concerted scheme between the Advocate

* Mr. Pitt.   † Mr. Dundas.

and a friend of yours, whom I need not name. Charles
sent a civil message to the Advocate by the Duke of
Buccleugh, and he returned a very general, vague answer,
which convinced Charles that his suspicion was founded.
I literally have not spoken to Charles for some days, and
do not know whether anything more has passed; but
when I last talked with Charles, he was determined that
if the Advocate persisted in this improper behaviour, he
should be turned out, or that he, Charles, would go out.
What made this conduct in the Advocate more alarming
was, that William Pitt, one day after Charles had declared
the state of the nation to be in all respects more distressful
than he had imagined, and the conduct of the late
ministers more culpable in rejecting all offers of mediation,
or neglecting all overtures of peace, and after he had
declared that these things must be inquired into, William
Pitt agreed with the Advocate, who had objected to any
inquiry, on the pretence that it would cause altercation,
revive animosity, and take up too much of the time of
Ministers; and he totally differed from Charles in everything he had said on the subject. This circumstance very
much increased our suspicion that the Advocate's hostility
was systematical, and concocted not a hundred miles from
Berkeley-square."

Thus the Ministry, sapped in its foundations, was not
destined to endure. But it must be said, to the credit of
this second short Administration of Lord Rockingham,
that it broke the continuity of Tory power, gave legislative
sanction to Mr. Burke's economical reforms, laid the ground-
work of a reconciliation with America, and put an end, for
a time at least, to the King's personal government.

CHAPTER XVII.

THE SHELBURNE ADMINISTRATION—PEACE OF 1783.

THERE can be little doubt that personal antipathy to Mr. Fox was from this time rooted in the royal bosom. Before Mr. Fox's entrance into office, George III. looked upon him as a dissolute and unprincipled man in whom he could place no confidence, and from whom he could expect no support. But a stronger feeling than distrust and dislike now sprung up. The Prince of Wales, as soon as he was old enough to appear in public, took a course very distasteful to his father. Coming from a strict and religious home, he surprised and shocked society by his very lax morals, while he gained the goodwill of many by his agreeable manners and convivial disposition.* He offended the King by inattention, and by evincing openly his want of respect for his royal parent. One day when the Prince of Wales, with his uncle the Duke of Cumberland, attended the King's hunt, the Prince and the Duke, at the end of the day's sport, got into the only hack-chaise that could be procured, and went off to London, leaving the King to shift as he could. Another offence was the Prince's habit of frequent visits to Mr. Fox's house, where, though not in his presence, language

* Walpole's " George III."

little decorous to the Sovereign was frequently heard. On the day Mr. Fox resigned the seals of office the Prince dined with him, and, expressing much kindness towards him, assured him that he should ever consider Lord Rockingham's friends as the persons the most to be depended upon and as the best friends of the country.* Thus the King was shocked by the morals, thwarted by the politics, and deeply irritated by the personal connexions of his son. While he was painfully struggling against party, he saw a new banner of Opposition unfurled by the heir to the throne, and attributed to his late Minister the alienation of one from whom he had expected submission and obedience.

Charles Fox, now released from the forced industry of office, fell back into licentious habits and idle dissipation. Mr. Hare, one of his best friends, said he saw him seldom except at supper at Brooks's, with Lord John Townshend.

Lord John Townshend, then Mr. John Townshend, was the son of the Marquis Townshend. He was a young man of very lively parts, and by his talents and devotion seems to have gained at this time an influence with Mr. Fox, the results of which were of great importance.

Lord Shelburne used the time of the prorogation of Parliament to hasten the negotiations for peace. On the 23rd of November these negotiations were so far advanced that the Secretary of State wrote to the Lord Mayor of London to acquaint him that the negotiations carrying on at Paris were brought so far to a point as to promise a decisive conclusion, either for peace or war, before the meeting of Parliament, which on that account was to be prorogued to the 5th of December. On that day, expectations having been raised to the highest pitch, the King

* Fitzpatrick's "Journal." Corr.

addressed his Parliament on the subject of peace in the following terms :—

" Since the close of the last session I have employed my whole time in that care and attention which the important and critical conjuncture of public affairs required of me.   I lost no time in giving the necessary orders to prohibit the further prosecution of offensive war upon the continent of North America.   Adopting, as my inclination will always lead me to do, with decision and effect, whatever I collect to be the sense of my Parliament and my people, I have pointed all my views and measures, as well in Europe as in North America, to an entire and cordial reconciliation with those colonies.   Finding it indispensable to the attainment of this object, I did not hesitate to go the full length of the powers vested in me, and offered to declare them free and independent States by an article to be inserted in the treaty of peace.   Provisional articles are agreed upon, to take effect whenever terms of peace shall be finally settled with the Court of France.   In thus admitting their separation from the Crown of these kingdoms, I have sacrificed every consideration of my own to the wishes and opinion of my people.   I make it my humble and earnest prayer to Almighty God that Great Britain may not feel the evils which might result from so great a dismemberment of the empire, and that America may be free from those calamities which have formerly proved in the mother country how essential monarchy is to the enjoyment of constitutional liberty.   Religion, language, interest, affections, may, and I hope will, yet prove a bond of permanent union between the two countries; to this end, neither attention nor disposition on my part shall be wanting.   While I have carefully abstained from all offensive operations against America, I have directed my whole force by land and sea against the other powers at war, with as much vigour as the situation of that force at the commencement of the campaign would permit. I trust that you feel the advantages resulting from the safety of the great branches of our trade. You must have seen with pride and satisfaction the gallant defence of the governor and the garrison of Gibraltar; and my fleet, after having effected the object of their destination, offering battle to the combined force of France and Spain on their own coasts, those of my kingdoms have remained at the same time perfectly secure, and your domestic tranquillity uninterrupted. This respectable state, under the blessing of God, I attribute to the entire confidence which subsists between me and my people, and to the readiness which has been shown by my subjects in my City of London, and in other parts of my kingdoms, to stand forth in the general defence. Some proofs have lately been given of public spirit in private men which would do honour to any age and any country. Having manifested to the whole world, by the most lasting examples, the signal spirit and bravery of my people, I conceived it a moment not unbecoming my dignity, and thought it a regard due to the lives and fortunes of such brave and gallant subjects, to show myself ready, on my part, to embrace fair and honourable terms of accommodation with all the powers at war. I have the satisfaction to acquaint you that negotiations to this effect are considerably advanced, the result of which, as soon as they are brought to a conclusion, shall be immediately communicated to you. I have every reason to hope and believe that I shall have it in my power, in a very short time, to acquaint you that they have ended in terms of pacification, which I trust you will see just cause to approve. I rely, however, with perfect confidence on the wisdom of my Parliament and the spirit of my people that, if any unforeseen change in the dispositions of the belligerent powers should frustrate my confident expectations, they will approve of the preparations I have thought it advisable to make, and be ready to second the most vigorous efforts in the further prosecution of the war."

The speech, which was unusually long, proceeded to inform Parliament that the King had carried into effect the reductions in the Civil List directed by an act of the last session; that he had abolished many sinecure places in other departments; that he had made many beneficial regulations which, besides expediting business, would produce a considerable saving; that he had directed an inquiry into the management of the landed revenue of the Crown and of the Woods and Forests—into the department of the Mint—into the state of receipt and expenditure— and, above all, into the state of the public debt. " It is my desire that you should be apprised of every expense before it is incurred, as far as the nature of each service can possibly admit. Matters of account can never be made too public."

The high price of corn, the rights and commerce of Ireland, and the regulation of the vast territory acquired in Asia, were the remaining topics of the speech.

Mr. Fox's remarks on the speech were chiefly directed to the point of the acknowledgment of American independence. After the explanation of his own conduct, of which we have already spoken, he said that his hopes and expectations were fulfilled, just as he had foreseen and stated to that House: he had been able to persuade his

Majesty's Ministers to the discharge of their duty more effectually in that House than he was able to do in a private room. Thank Heaven the measure was now taken, the deed was done, and done, he hoped, in the most effectual way; and he agreed with the honourable seconder of the address, that in doing this we gave away nothing.

After some personal remarks he proceeded :—

"There were some expressions in the speech with which, though he did not intend to find fault, he would have been as well pleased had they been left out; and these were the expressions of the concern felt by his Majesty at the idea of renouncing the claims of this country over America: it would have been surely much better had his Majesty been advised boldly and manfully at once to give way to necessity, and not to express so much dejection at parting with a sovereignty which it was no longer in his power to assert and maintain; but much as he disliked these expressions, he was as much pleased with those in which his Majesty indulges the philosophic speculation of prospects of future connexion with America, from similarity of language, manners, religion, and laws. For his own part, he did not doubt but the day would come when, by a firm alliance between Great Britain and America, the Courts of France and Spain would awake from their idle and illusory dreams of advantage which they think will follow to them by the separation of America from the mother country; through that alliance the sun of Britain might rise again and shine forth with dazzling lustre. But to induce America to confide in us, we should convince her, by the most open and unreserved conduct, that we mean fairly, honestly, and sincerely by her. He was always of opinion that it was not right, in our present circumstances, to think of treating with America by way of bargain for her independence. He conceived that the only method of acting which was at once political and wise, was to behave with manliness and generosity, and to show them that there was still a disposition in the Government of this country to treat them with the nobleness of Englishmen."

With respect to an acknowledgment of the independence of America before the conclusion of a general peace, Mr. Fox himself had, in the year 1781, while in Opposition, made some remarks which are well worthy of attention. Answering Mr. Rigby, he had said :—

"The right honourable gentleman, and several others who have spoken since, particularly the learned Lord Advocate of Scotland, have made, what they seem to think, a most important discovery—that I have declined to move a vote, declaring the American colonies in resistance independent; though, say they, my motion goes precisely to the same point. If this is meant to hold out to the House, that while I profess one thing I mean another, nothing, I do assure you, sir, can be more unfounded; for, to be very plain, had not I other reasons but such as might militate against the mere naked question of declaring America independent, I should not hesitate a single moment upon what was proper to be done; for, thinking as I do, that America is lost, irrevocably lost to this country, we could lose nothing by a vote declaring America independent. But I had more than one reason for hesitation : the first and most pressing motive on my mind was, that I did not choose to go the full length of what I feared we must, what I know we must, without reserve consent to—to declare America independent; because such a declaration on our part, being an ultimatum, might beget still higher pretensions in the minds of the people of America on their own account. The other, that although we should hold out an offer of independence, we are not so fully and perfectly acquainted with the connexion between France and America as to say whether, the point of independence being once gained, France would not improve that circumstance to her own partial advantage, and on that ground urge further claims, to comply with which both the interest and honour of this country must be sacrificed."

As these observations appear to be in themselves sound and just, the question of Mr. Fox's resignation again resolves itself into one of confidence in Lord Shelburne. His alleged insincerity, coupled with his very obvious desire to thwart and mortify Mr. Fox, remain the only defensible grounds for Mr. Fox's resignation.

The preliminary articles of peace between Great Britain and France, and between Great Britain and Spain, were signed at Versailles on the 20th of January, 1783. The substance of these treaties, coupled with the provisional treaty with the United States of America, may be thus stated :—

1. The United States of America were acknowledged as free and independent States.

2. East Florida was ceded to Spain, and she was allowed to retain West Florida. The French obtained St. Pierre and Miquelon, and the Americans were allowed to fish on the British part of the Bank of Newfoundland.

3. In the West Indies we restored the Island of St. Lucia, besides ceding Tobago. On the other hand, Nevis and Montserrat were restored to us.

4. In Africa we ceded to France the river Senegal and all its dependencies, and engaged to restore the island of

Goree. In return, the French guaranteed to us Fort James and the river Gambia, but without mentioning the dependencies.

5. In Asia we engaged to restore to France all the establishments which belonged to them at the beginning of the war on the coast of Orissa and in Bengal.

6. In Europe we ceded to Spain the island of Minorca, and consented to the suppression and abrogation of all articles relative to Dunkirk, from the treaty of Utrecht to that of 1763.

It must be owned that these were immense concessions. But they all sank into insignificance in comparison with that article which was the basis of the whole, that upon which the House of Commons had insisted—that upon which Mr. Fox, Mr. Burke, Lord Shelburne, General Conway, and Mr. Pitt were agreed—namely, the independence of the thirteen colonies of North America. To have acknowledged that independence, and to have continued the war with France and Spain, seems to have been the favourite idea of Mr. Fox. Had he remained in power, it is probable that the war with France would have been for some time continued, while the independence of America would have been fully acknowledged. But although America might not have been hearty in the war, when her own interests were no longer concerned, she would still have been bound by treaty to France; and those feelings of alienation from the parent country which it was Lord North's high crime to have kindled and fanned into a flame, might have obtained a complete mastery by the continuance of a war in which she would have fought as the ally of France and Spain against Great Britain. There was probably much carelessness on the part of Lord Shelburne in drawing up the articles of treaty, and some of the cessions might have been avoided by holding out and arguing the disputable points. Upon the whole, however, it seems to me, that with the independence of America as a starting point, with the want of allies still unsupplied, with our debt still increasing, and our trade greatly depressed and embarrassed, Great Britain was more likely to rise buoyant from an inglorious peace, than from the continuance of a war hitherto disastrous and sure to be costly.

The opinion of Mr. Fox was different; and his dislike of the terms of peace led him to a junction with a statesman whose errors he had often chastised, and whose want of foresight and firmness he had been ever ready to censure.

The authors of the coalition between Mr. Fox and Lord North appear to have been Mr. Eden (afterwards Lord Auckland), Mr. Adam, and George North (Lord North's son), on the part of Lord North; and Lord John Townshend on the part of Mr. Fox. Lord John Townshend, in a letter to Lord Holland, of June 15th, 1830, says: " I should certainly say that George North, myself, and Adam were the most active and instrumental negotiators in the business of the coalition. George North and I had laid our heads together long before the first overtures were begun, in order to plan the best means of effecting this object," &c.*

Lord Shelburne was quite aware of the insecurity of his situation. Lord North had preserved the attachment of the old Tories, and of many personal friends. Mr. Fox and Mr. Burke had the entire confidence of the Rockingham Whigs. The Ministry were breaking up. Lord Keppel, who had only remained in office to put the navy

* "Correspondence," vol. ii. p. 22.

in a respectable condition, resigned on the 24th of January. On the 5th of February he was followed by Lord Carlisle. The office of Lord Steward was given to the Duke of Rutland, with a seat in the Cabinet. This proceeding disgusted the Duke of Grafton. In this emergency Lord Shelburne endeavoured separately to gain Lord North and Mr. Fox. Lord North was asked to support the peace with a view to bring his friends into office, but with a marked exclusion of Lord North himself. Lord North said that if the Ministers did not ask for approbation, he would be no party to a censure; "but if they insist on approbation," added Lord North, "they make us the judges." On the other hand, Mr. Pitt, authorized by Lord Shelburne, saw Mr. Fox. Mr. Fox at once proposed that the Duke of Portland should be First Lord of the Treasury. Mr. Pitt drew himself up, and would go no further. Lord Shelburne, who, as Horace Walpole says, did not mean to sacrifice himself in order to serve himself, said the King insisted on his keeping the Treasury. Matters were hastening to a crisis. The treaties had been laid on the table of the two Houses at the end of January, and Monday, the 17th of February, was appointed for taking them into consideration.

In this state of affairs a desperate move of Mr. Dundas brought on the coalition he most deprecated. He endeavoured to alarm Lord North by a report that Lord Shelburne could not stand; that Fox and Pitt would unite; the Parliament be dissolved, and the North party scattered to the winds. For this purpose he sought Mr. Adam, and said to him in confidence, with strong injunctions of secresy: "It appears to me that the Government with Lord Shelburne at the head of it is at an end. I had not seen him from the time the message had gone by Pitt to Fox till this morning. He sent for me early. He asked me when I came into the room whether I had ever heard the story of the Duke of Perth. I answered, ' No.' He then said, ' The Duke of Perth had a country neighbour and friend, who came to him one morning with a white cockade in his hat. " What is the meaning of this?" said the duke. "I wish to show your Grace," replied his country friend, " that I am resolved to follow your fortunes." The duke snatched the hat from his head, took the cockade out of it, and threw it into the fire, saying, " My situation and duty compel me to take this line, but *that* is no reason why you should ruin yourself and your family." I find,' continued Lord Shelburne, ' that it will now be necessary for me to quit the Government; and as you are beloved by all parties, I wished you to have early notice of it, that you might be prepared for what must happen. Fox and the Duke of Portland will make up a Government with Pitt, for I cannot hear of Pitt's high notions of not taking part in any Government where I am not one. He shall not think of resigning with me. Lady Shelburne is so distressed that I cannot think of remaining longer in this situation; and, having worked the great work of peace, I am not desirous to remain.' Lord Shelburne," said Mr. Dundas, " spoke with so much calmness, that I believe him sincere, and that it will end in the resignation of Lord Shelburne, and in the union of Pitt and Fox, which will be followed by a dissolution of Parliament and extinction of the party of Lord North."—" Can nothing," says Adam, " be done with Lord North to prevent that calamity?"—" I see nothing," replied Dundas, " but Lord North's support of the peace; in which case his friends will be gradually preferred, and at the end of the session Shelburne and I must prevail over the prejudices of Pitt and of the other Ministers; but at present I see no prospect of a coalition with him." At parting Dundas said to Adam: "You will not mention Lord Shelburne's intended resignation; but you may say in general terms to Lord North himself, and to Charles Townshend and his other friends, that it is my conjecture there will be a Government of Fox and Pitt, with the Rockinghams and all Lord Shelburne's friends but himself; that they will dissolve Parliament, and there will be an end of Lord North; that I see no means of preventing this but a support of the address; in which case the difficulties will be got over, but at present no coalition can be made."

These peremptory terms seem to have driven Lord North towards Mr. Fox. Mr. Fox had already sent him a civil message, informing him of what had passed with Mr. Pitt. When Mr. Adam, on the 13th, told Lord North, George North, and Charles Townshend what he had been desired to communicate, it appeared to them all that the only means of preventing the ruin of their party was to make an immediate overture to Mr. Fox. George North went that evening to Mr. Fox, who agreed to an interview with Lord North for the next day.

On Friday, the 14th of February, at two o'clock, Mr. Fox and Lord North met at the house of Lord North's son, George North. Mr. Fox was willing to lay aside all animosity, and hoped their future administration would be founded on mutual goodwill and confidence. They agreed that economical reform had been carried far enough, and that on parliamentary reform every man should follow his own opinion. Mr. Fox urged that the King should not be

suffered to be his own Minister. Lord North, after some
reference to government by departments, said : " The
King ought to be treated with all sorts of respect and
attention ; but the appearance of power is all that a King
of this country can have." There was some little conversation about men and offices. They agreed to oppose the
Address, and Lord North drew up a draft of an amendment.

An account of this meeting spread rapidly. Robinson,
an adherent of Lord North, told the news to Jenkinson,
who admitted that Lord North had been shamefully used,
and attributed to Dundas's message the issue he deplored.
Adam suggested that all parties might unite, with the exception of Lord Shelburne, who was so obnoxious to the
Rockingham party that they would have nothing to do
with him. Dundas replied : " It was strange the impression entertained of Lord Shelburne's character, but it was
so."*

Thus easily and smoothly was made that coalition which
in the first place overthrew Lord Shelburne's Administration ; next destroyed that large and extensive popularity
which Mr. Fox at that time enjoyed ; and finally ruined the
Whig party. Nor was it without reason that popular
opinion condemned the coalition now made by Mr. Fox.
He joined the Minister whom for many years he had condemned as a statesman without foresight, treacherous,
vacillating, and incapable. If these invectives had been
just, Mr. Fox never should have joined the object of them ;
if they had been unjust, Mr. Fox should have found some
less suspicious mode of retracting exaggerated censure.

* " Correspondence," vol. ii. p. 40.

Neither was it true that the termination of the American War brought with it a close of all political differences.

Lord North was honourably and consistently a Tory—a protector of the influence of the Crown, a patron of ancient abuses, and the leader of those who had always defended corruption against reform. Nor was it to be forgotten that, with the exception of Lord Keppel and Lord John Cavendish, a majority of the persons whom Lord Rockingham had put into the Cabinet—the Duke of Grafton, Lord Camden, General Conway, and even the Duke of Richmond —were opposed to this junction.

. Mr. Fox stood high when he declared that distrust of Lord Shelburne, and not a desire to struggle for power, had forced him to resign office. He abandoned this ground when he joined with Lord North for the undisguised purpose of regaining power.

Let it be remembered, however, that there was nothing in the character of Lord North and Mr. Fox which, had circumstances favoured it, would have prevented their union either in office or in opposition. Lord North was a man of honour and integrity, kind and liberal in his temper, without religious bigotry or personal rancour. Mr. Fox was made to lead a party; Lord North to manage a department. "I may assert," says Mr. Gibbon, "with some degree of assurance, that in their political conflict, those great antagonists had never felt any personal animosity to each other; that their reconciliation was easy and sincere; that their friendship has never been clouded by the shadow of suspicion or jealousy."* But the American War from which Lord North had just emerged left him too deeply stained by the foul stream to allow any statesman to join

* Gibbon, " Miscellaneous Works," vol. i. p. 246.

him without suffering from the contamination. In his previous sway of official rule it might be said of Mr. Fox—

"Intaminatis fulget honoribus."

But public confidence was shaken, and alarm succeeded to applause when he appeared in the House of Commons in the colours of his new alliance.

On Monday, the 17th of February, the concourse of members was large, and curiosity was on tiptoe. After a number of papers had been read, Mr. Thomas Pitt, seconded by Mr. Wilberforce, moved an address of thanks to the Crown. The terms were modest, but sufficient for the purpose of the Administration. The King was thanked for "his wise and paternal care for the welfare and happiness of his subjects, in relieving them from a long and burthensome war, and restoring the blessings and advantages of peace by the preliminary articles agreed upon with the Courts of France and Spain."

Lord John Cavendish moved an amendment to the effect that the House would examine the treaties with serious and full attention, and that, whatever might be the result, "they assured his Majesty of their firm and unalterable resolution to adhere inviolably to the several articles for which the public faith is pledged, and to maintain the blessings of peace."

This amendment was supported by Mr. Fox, Mr. Burke, and Mr. Sheridan among the Whigs, and by Lord North, Lord Mulgrave, and Mr. Adam among the members and adherents of the old Ministry. The coalition was patent. Mr. Fox spoke with even more than his usual force. He began by a reference to his former exhortations in favour of peace :—

" Allusions were made to former opinions which he had

given, and assertions he had made in circumstances different from the present, and to which, indeed, they bore not the smallest affinity. It was proclaimed, as an unanswerable argument against everything he could say: 'Did you not, some months ago, declare that almost any peace would be good, would be desirable, and that we must have peace on any terms?'

"If," said Mr. Fox, "I could suffer myself for a moment to be so far led away by conceit, and fancy myself a man of so much importance as to excite the jealousy of the Minister, I might give ear to the reports of the day that every measure which the Minister adopted — every plan which he formed—every opinion which he framed—and, indeed, every act of his administration, was calculated and designed to embarrass me. How well might I ascribe the present peace to this motive! You call for peace, says the noble person, you urge the necessity of peace, you insist on peace; then peace you shall have, but such a peace that you shall sicken at its very name. You call for peace, and I will give you a peace that shall make you repent the longest day you live that ever you breathed a wish for peace. I will give you a peace which shall make you and all men wish that the war had been continued—a peace more calamitous, more dreadful, more ruinous than war could possibly be; and the effects of which neither the strength, the credit, nor the commerce of the nation shall be able to support! If this was the intention of the noble person, he had succeeded to a miracle. His work had completely answered its purpose; for never did I more sincerely feel, nor more sincerely lament, any advice I ever gave in my life, than the advice of getting rid of the disastrous war in which the nation was involved."

In defence of his junction with Lord North, he said:—

"I now come to take notice of the most heinous charge of all. I am accused of having formed a junction with a noble person whose principles I have been in the habit of opposing for the last seven years of my life. I do not think it at all incumbent upon me to make any answer to this charge: first, because I do not think that the persons who have asked the question, have any right to make the inquiry; and secondly, because if any such junction were formed, I see no ground for arraignment in the matter. That any such alliance has taken place I can by no means aver. That I shall have the honour of concurring with the noble lord in the blue ribbon on the present question is very certain; and if men of honour can meet on points of general national concern, I see no reason for calling such a meeting an unnatural junction. It is neither wise nor noble to keep up animosities for ever. It is neither just nor candid to keep up animosity when the cause of it is no more. It is not in my nature to bear malice or live in ill-will. My friendships are perpetual, my enmities are not so. '*Amicitiæ sempiternæ, inimicitiæ placabiles.*' I disdain to keep alive in my bosom the enmities which I may bear to men when the cause of those enmities is no more. When a man ceases to be what he was, when the opinions which made him obnoxious are changed, he then is no more my enemy but my friend. The American War was the cause of the enmity between the noble lord and myself. The American War and the American question are at an end. The noble lord has profited from fatal experience. While that system was maintained, nothing could be more asunder than the noble lord and myself. But it is now no more; and it is, therefore, wise and candid to put an end also to the ill-will, the animosity, the rancour, and the feuds which it occasioned. I am free to acknowledge, that when I was the friend of the noble lord in the blue ribbon, I found him open and sincere; when the enemy, honourable and manly. I never had reason to say of the noble lord in the blue ribbon that he practised any of those little subterfuges, tricks, and stratagems which I found in others—any of those behind-hand and paltry manœuvres which destroy confidence between human beings, and degrade the character of the statesman and the man."

The impression made upon many of the Whigs who had followed Mr. Fox is thus fairly described by Mr. Fitzpatrick in a letter to his brother, Lord Ossory, of the 18th :—

" I am not very sorry that your indolence prevailed upon you to stay in the country, as I should have feared that your *pacific* disposition and that general partiality to peace, that strengthened the Administration in yesterday's question, might have inclined you to follow the example of some of your brother country gentlemen (I mean of those who know black from white), and to have voted in favour of a Ministry you wished to destroy. But what hurt us infinitely more than the general propensity to peace was the apparent junction with Lord North. Powys took an early part in the debate in support of Administration, and many of the independent supporters of the Whigs followed his example. Lord North's phalanx, as you may suppose, were less capricious, and by the division we carried our amendment by 16. The amendment, as you will perceive, was very *soft,* suited to the *modesty* of their address, and calculated for the squeamish stomachs of scrupulous friends, which were not, however, strong enough to digest it. Lord

.North, according to his character, was, in concerting the question, amazingly indecisive; he would agree to no censure, though the amendment we carried must necessarily be followed by one, which, however, must of course be gentle, as from his official situation Shelburne cannot be the object of it, and nobody wishes to bear hard upon either Lord Grantham or Poor Tommy.* What will be the change of Administration it is difficult to foresee; the *coup de pied* is given to Lord Shelburne. Who will succeed him is a matter for speculation. I think North will hardly undertake it alone, and I think those who undertake it with him will risk their credit with the public upon very unsafe ground."

Such was the opinion of Fitzpatrick of the probable success of the coalition. On the 21st Lord John Cavendish moved resolutions of censure on the peace. He proposed four resolutions : the two first pledged the House to maintain and confirm the preliminary treaty, and to improve the blessings of peace. The third declared that his Majesty, in acknowledging the United States of America, by virtue of the powers vested in him by an act of the previous session, had acted as circumstances indispensably required, and in conformity to the sense of Parliament. The fourth resolution was as follows : "That the concessions made to the adversaries of Great Britain by the said provisional treaty and preliminary articles are greater than they were entitled to, either from the actual situation of their respective possessions, or from their comparative strength."

Mr. Fox, in his speech on this occasion, thus defended

---

* Mr. Thomas Townshend, afterwards Lord Sydney. Lord Grantham and Mr. Thomas Townshend were Secretaries of State.

his own conduct: "And now I must beg leave to say a few words on what I feel of the most serious nature, as far as it relates to the complacency of my own feelings. The sentiments which have fallen from gentlemen of whom I had flattered myself to have possessed the friendship and good opinion have occasioned in me a retrospect of my past conduct. I have reviewed my conduct with a severity of retrospect that I should scarcely have endured, had it not been from a conviction that I really committed a fault which merited the most painful of all feelings, that of losing the support and approbation of men whose virtues I reverence, and whose good opinions it is my greatest pride and happiness to cultivate.* But however painful this severity of retrospect may have proved, I find it amply compensated in the pleasure every honest mind feels when it can bear testimony to the purity and consistency of its intentions. As no inquisition can be so formidable to sensibility as that which our own reflection holds on our actions, the result of my inquiry is attended with an increase of satisfaction proportionate to the pain I felt for its necessity, and fear lest I should find myself deserving of what I have this night so painfully experienced: I mean the forfeiture of friendship, support, and confidence where I have always sought its enjoyment. It is only from such characters as have my esteem that I have sought support and connexion. However, I find myself this evening deserted by those whom I thought never to have given a pretence for losing their estimation; and the regret I experience on the occasion would be insupportable indeed, were it not from a consciousness of its being undeserved.

---

* This is obviously an incorrect report—perhaps, "had it not been from," should be read, "had it resulted in."

And this conviction is in a great measure confirmed by what I have seen since I receded from that Administration, in which there was no principle of stability and connexion to support it with honour to itself and welfare to the people. That we were justified in our receding from such an Administration has been daily evinced by those who have since followed our example. Have not those who were deluded by pretence, not confirmed by principle, to take share with a man whom they now see the absolute necessity of deserting, proved the necessity of our conduct? It must be no small satisfaction to me to see those follow my conduct whom indeed I could rather have chosen to follow. Can there be a greater demonstration of the propriety of our conduct than seeing others receding one by one from a connexion which has betrayed every principle on which their confidence was founded? But while I produce these as indisputable arguments in favour of the propriety of our resignation, and opposing the measures which have been since pursued to the disgrace and injury of the country, I shall not disavow my having an ambition to hold such a situation in office as may enable me to promote the interest of my country. I will confess that I am desirous of enjoying an eminence which must flatter my ambition, promote my convenience, and enable me to exert myself in my country's service; and in confessing this desire, I trust that it cannot be termed presumption. I flatter myself that I am not inadequate to the importance of such a situation; nor do I think that I gave, during the short time I held a respectable place in Administration, any reason why I should not offer myself a candidate for a share in that new arrangement which the late neglectful, not to give a worse epithet, conduct of the First Lord of the Treasury has rendered indispensable. But this is a subject which I think more prudent to waive, than to enforce by adducing arguments, or referring to instances."

The division took place at half-past three in the morning, and was decisive of the fate of Lord Shelburne's Ministry :—

For the Resolutions 207
Against 190
____
Majority 17

On the 22nd Fitzpatrick writes to his brother: "Last night we had a second victory in the House of Commons upon a stronger question, and with the additional majority of one: to the Administration it is *cita mors*, but not *victoria læta* to us. The apparent juncture* with Lord North is universally cried out against, though, at the same time, all moderate and reasonable men approve of it as the only means of establishing any Government in the country. Charles made a most admirable speech; but as the chief merit was the *policy* of it, probably it would not be so well understood out of doors, as Pitt's, which was upon the highest stilts that even his father was mounted. Pitt was understood to announce the resignation of Ministers if the question went against them; yet the report of the day is that Shelburne holds a contrary language. The King is gone to Windsor, and I believe feels this is a more decisive defeat than the former. I dare not venture to Shelburne House to tell our *beau frère* that, if he is mad enough (which, however, I do not believe) to allow the House of Commons to meet in the present state of things, he must be removed by an address of the House. I find that most

* Union, amity.—JOHNSON.

of the country gentlemen who have voted against us in these questions are ready for such a measure. The formation of the new Ministry is the great point at present; and the difficulty (independent of public appearances) is to secure Lord North, whose weakness of character and indecision has been even more conspicuous than ever since this *unnatural alliance.* Unless a *real good Government* is the consequence of this juncture, nothing can justify it to the public."

It is clear from this letter that Fitzpatrick, who had more weight with Mr. Fox than any one else, was in his heart opposed to the coalition. It was, as he justly said, "an unnatural alliance." Mr. Fox in vain declared that he was ready to join with the party opposed to him, and out of the three parties to form a Government. Mr. Pitt already saw his advantage. He had at one time thought it impossible any Government could stand if opposed by a man of Mr. Fox's abilities. But his opinion was now changed. Mr. Dundas said:—

" Pitt is impracticable on the subject of union : he proscribes Lord North, and does not even express himself clearly disposed to unite with Fox. He has a high opinion of Fox's abilities, and had always wished to have him in the Government, because he thought it impossible to conduct great and difficult affairs with such abilities to criticise them. But now he seems much estranged from him."[*]

Pitt was, in fact, much pleased with the coalition, which opened to him a prospect of reaping all the success of Mr. Fox's efforts for the last nine years. Mr. Fox ought to have felt that his true place was side by side with the Duke of Richmond, General Conway, and the whole body of men

* " Correspondence," vol. ii. p. 41.

who had opposed Lord North on the war, supported Mr. Burke on economy, and called for parliamentary reform. By his union with Lord North he committed the one great political error of his life; he falsified his previous declarations, he divided the public mind, and lost in a party contest the palm he had won in a national cause.

In relating these disputes, however, we must not lose sight of the great change, the record of which was signed and sealed by Lord Shelburne.

The United States of America were acknowledged by England as an independent State, and admitted as such into the family of civilized nations. There are many important considerations connected with this event.

The first and most obvious is that the old parent in Europe, and the young offspring in America, parted in enmity.

In 1760 the inhabitants of the thirteen colonies felt a wound inflicted on England as a wound inflicted on themselves; they were proud of her greatness, and rejoiced in the extension of her dominion. In 1780 they looked on the King and Parliament of England as oppressors who had tried to rob them of their liberties—as enemies who had employed German mercenaries to ravage their fields and pillage their houses—as tyrants who had been worsted in an attempt to reduce them by force of arms to a state of slavery. Such was the change which George III. and Lord North had made—such was the historical lesson which Americans for eighty years have had preached from their pulpits, proclaimed from their platforms, and taught in their schools. As Great Britain abjured the Stuarts, so the Americans abjured George III. and his descendants.

Every subsequent diplomatic discussion, every national

dispute, every untoward accident, has down to this very day been embittered by the recollection of the American War.

On looking, on the other hand, at the results of the struggle to France and Spain, we shall find that the hope and expectation which had induced those powers to interpose in the quarrel between Great Britain and her colonies were signally disappointed. By husbanding her resources, cultivating her commerce, and maintaining her free Constitution, Great Britain upheld her character, improved her wealth, and extended her dominions. France saw with exultation her great rival stripped of her magnificent colonies, but while the British monarchy remained entire, the democracy in behalf of which she had fought returned upon herself. On the morning of the 5th of October, 1790, a popular tumult disturbed the slumbers of Versailles; and the sword which Lafayette had drawn against George in the camp of Washington, was worn by the same chief before the palace of Louis. Thus was Great Britain revenged upon the faithless sovereign who had taken advantage of her distress to dismember her dominions. Spain was as little a gainer by the struggle. The Florida she obtained dropt from her palsied hand into the lap of the new State she had so improvidently helped to create. Nor was the lesson of American independence lost upon the benighted and enslaved inhabitants of the Spanish colonies. Forty years after the Spanish declaration of war, Mr. Canning informed the Minister of his Catholic Majesty in London, that his Master had acknowledged the independence of the South American States.

The greatest question, but that which is only partly solved, remains. What was the nature of the new power? what the influence of such an addition to the European system upon the welfare of mankind? what the permanent institutions of the new Power?

The creation of the United States of America was an event entirely new in the history of Europe, nay, in the history of the world. The rise of the Swiss and Dutch Republics, both limited in space, and both surrounded by powerful monarchies, could bear no comparison with the birth of this western giant. With a continent stretching from Maine to Florida, and from New York to the Pacific, such a Republic might easily, in the course of a century, contain fifty millions of free citizens, of a race famous for its energy and enterprise. But the dangers to be feared from a State so vast would be greatly abated by the distance of its seat of Government from Europe. Its position would make it secure from the military ambition of France, Austria, or Russia; its interests could hardly require any active participation in the wars of Europe. The sage advice of Washington to beware of entangling alliances was likely to govern its policy for at least a century to come.

The future influence of the new State upon the fortunes of mankind is a matter of interesting but doubtful specu-lation.

The internal institutions of America were partly formed by circumstances, and partly framed by policy. The cha-racter of the original emigrants, the nature of the local governments, and the popular spirit which had been roused in the contest for independence, all pointed to a Republic as the form of government to be adopted. Nor were there wanting in the laws and customs of England sufficient means to enable a people to administer justice, to preserve order, and to collect the public will. Accordingly, as Mr. Burke observed, it was wonderful how little anarchy followed the subversion of the Royal authority which had hitherto been the keystone of the arch. But, when looking beyond trial by jury, municipal authority, and local assemblies, the problem occurred how to form a central government for millions of people spread over thousands of square miles, the task was one of no ordinary difficulty. The separate colonies, now separate states, were unwilling to part with their independent action. The balances which had kept in due and regular movement the spring of democracy in the mother country were wanting. Monarchy, aristocracy, church establishments, were not to be thought of. In these circumstances the sense and foresight of the American statesmen were conspicuous. Their provisions for the safety and regularity of the working of the constitution were chiefly of three kinds: 1. They controlled the immediate organs of the people by a Senate, chosen, not directly by universal suffrage, but indirectly, by the State Legislatures, and for a longer term than the House of Representatives. 2. They framed a Supreme Court of Justice, chosen from the most distinguished judges of the Republic, to decide on certain fixed principles which not even the whole Legislature could set aside. Questions of international law were likewise referred to this tribunal. 3. Throughout the New England States a system of national education was established, which, under the name of the common schools, is considered by her best citizens as the strongest bulwark of the Republic.

On the other hand there were, and are, some extraordinary defects in the Constitution :—

1. The President of the Republic was to be elected for no more than four years. Hence the whole mind of the people is kept in a continual state of agitation. Hence also,

with the jealous instinct of a democracy, men of superior virtue and superior talent are set aside in favour of candidates from whose character and eloquence no predominant influence is to be feared. Aristides and Alcibiades are removed to make way for Cleon and Nicias.

2. With this defect is combined another, which causes some surprise, especially in men who shook off the curb of the British monarchy, and ran their free career through the wilderness of political speculation. They took no security that the President should shape his policy by the prevailing opinion of the people's representatives. We have seen that when the House of Commons resolved that war should no longer be carried on upon the continent of North America, the Ministry was changed, and the resolution was at once carried into effect. It could not be otherwise. But if the House of Representatives in Congress were to come to a similar vote, the President need not change his Ministers or alter his policy. Thus the safety-valve of the British monarchy is wanting in the American democracy.

3. Another difficulty is inherent in the composition of the Congress. The bodies are both elective; equally independent; equally free from the control of the Executive. What if they should differ on a vital question? A similar difficulty in Great Britain could only be temporary; either the people would support the House of Lords as in 1784, or the Lords would yield to the popular voice as in 1832. In America it is not easy to say in what manner the American Constitution could recover the shock.

4. One spot remains which oceans cannot wash out. The slavery of the African race, which the North Americans had inherited from the ancient monarchy, was adopted and fondly cherished by the new Republic. Washington, from

the impulse of his warm heart, set free by his will his own slaves; Jefferson, from the calculations of his cool head, deduced the conclusion that the black race ought to be sent back to Africa. The logic of the Constitution declared that all men were free; the pride and avarice of the slave-owners, disowning the image of the Creator and the brotherhood of nature, degraded men of a dark colour, and even all the descendants of their sons and daughters, to a level with oxen and horses. But as oxen and horses never combine, and have no sense of wronged independence, oxen and horses are better treated than the men and women of African blood. All the cruelties which fear and jealousy induced the despotic tyrants of the Roman Empire to commit, are consecrated by law and permitted by custom in the free States of the New World. Neither the civilization of commerce, nor the diffusion of letters, nor the refinement of manners could eradicate the vices or prevent the crimes which God has affixed as a befitting curse to the institution of slavery. Constitutional statesmen argued that if the black race were acknowledged as men, they must rule in States where they had the majority: learned judges and able lawyers showed that slaves were property, and entitled their owners to its inviolable rights. But neither the philosophical dogma of the authors of the Constitution, nor the strict pedantry of law, can stifle the cry of outraged humanity, nor still the current of human sympathy, nor arrest for ever the decrees of Eternal Justice.

Before taking leave of the American War, a few words may be allowed on a topic where there can be little difference of opinion. George Washington, without the genius of Julius Cæsar or Napoleon Bonaparte, has a far purer fame, as his ambition was of a higher and holier nature. Instead of seeking to raise his own name, or seize supreme power, he devoted his whole talents, military and civil, to the establishment of the independence, and the perpetuity of the liberties of his own country. In modern history no man has done such great things without the soil of selfishness or the stain of a grovelling ambition. Cæsar, Cromwell, Napoleon, attained a higher elevation, but the love of dominion was the spur that drove them on. John Hampden, William Russell, Algernon Sydney, may have had motives as pure, and an ambition as unstained; but they fell. To George Washington nearly alone in modern times has it been given to accomplish a wonderful revolution, and yet to remain to all future times the theme of a people's gratitude, and an example of virtuous and beneficent power.

END OF THE FIRST VOLUME.